Turning WHEELS

SATAN'S DEVILS #1

MANDA MELLETT

Disclaimer

This is a work of fiction. Names, characters, businesses, places, events
and incidents are either the products of the author's imagination or
used in a fictitious manner. Any resemblance to actual persons, living
or dead, or actual events is purely coincidental.

Warning

This book is dark in places and contains content of a sexual nature. It
is not suitable for persons under the age of 18.

ISBN: 978-0-9954976-5-8

AUTHOR'S NOTE

It might seem strange that an English author is writing a book based in the U.S. and about an American outlaw motorcycle club, but sometimes there's no telling what characters are going to get up to. *Turning Wheels* evolved after *Second Chances* as Sophie cried out for her own story to be told. She needed a place of safety and as her new friend, Horse, was affiliated to an MC in Arizona it seemed the logical step to take her there.

I have a love of MC (Motorcycle Club) books (if you want to read some really great ones check out AJ Downey!) my husband owns a Harley and I also have a licence to ride a bike although I haven't actually ridden for a while now. So I do have some qualifications for writing about motorbikes even if nowadays I prefer the security of a cage around me.

If you're reading this book as part of the Blood Brothers Series and haven't read any other MC books you may find there are terms that you haven't heard before, so I've included a glossary to help along the way. I hope you get drawn into this mysterious and dark world in the same way I have done—there will be further books in the Satan's Devils series which I hope you'll want to follow.

If you've picked this book up because, like me, you read anything MC, I hope you'll enjoy it for what it is, a fictional insight into the underground culture of alpha men and their bikes.

GLOSSARY

Motorcycle Club – An official motorcycle club in the U.S. is one which is sanctioned by the American Motorcyclist Association (AMA). The AMA has a set of rules its members must abide by. It is said that ninety-nine percent of motorcyclists in America belong to the AMA

Outlaw Motorcycle Club (MC) – The remaining one percent of motorcycling clubs are historically considered outlaws as they do not wish to be constrained by the rules of the AMA and have their own bylaws. There is no one formula followed by such clubs, but some not only reject the rulings of the AMA, but also that of society, forming tightly knit groups who fiercely protect their chosen ways of life. Outlaw MCs have a reputation for having a criminal element and supporting themselves by less than legal activities, dealing in drugs, gun running or prostitution. The one-percenter clubs are usually run under a strict hierarchy.

Brother – Typically members of the MC refer to themselves as brothers and regard the closely knit MC as their family.

Cage – The name bikers give to cars as they prefer riding their bikes.

Chapter – Some MCs have only one club based in one location. Other MCs have a number of clubs who follow the same bylaws and wear the same patch. Each club is known as a chapter and will normally carry the name of the area where they are based on their patch.

Church – Traditionally the name of the meeting where club business is discussed, either with all members present or with just those holding officer status.

Colours – When a member is wearing (or flying) his colours he will be wearing his cut proudly displaying his patch showing which club he is affiliated with.

Cut – The name given to the jacket or vest which has patches denoting the club that member belongs to.

Enforcer – The member who enforces the rules of the club.

Hang-around – This can apply to men wishing to join the club and who hang-around hoping to be become prospects. It is also used to women who are attracted by bikers and who are happy to make themselves available for sex at biker parties.

Mother Chapter – The founding chapter when a club has more than one chapter.

Patch – The patch or patches on a cut will show the club that member belongs to and other information such as the particular chapter and any role that may be held in the club. There can be a number of other patches with various meanings, including a one-percenter patch. Prospects will not be allowed to wear the club patch until they have been patched-in, instead they will have patches which denote their probationary status.

Patched-in/Patching-in – The term used when a prospect

completes his probationary status and becomes a full club member.

President (Prez) – The officer in charge of that particular club or chapter.

Prospect – Anyone wishing to join a club must serve time as a probationer. During this period they have to prove their loyalty to the club. A probationary period can last a year or more. At the end of this period, if they've proved themselves a prospect will be patched-in.

Old Lady – The term given to a woman who enters into a permanent relationship with a biker.

RICO – The Racketeer Influenced and Corrupt Organisations Act primarily deals with organised crime. Under this Act the officers of a club could be held responsible for activities they order members to do and a conviction carries a potential jail service of twenty years as well as a large fine and the seizure of assets.

Road Captain – The road captain is responsible for the safety of the club on a run. He will organise routes and normally ride at the end of the column.

Secretary – MCs are run like businesses and this officer will perform the secretarial duties such as recording decisions at meetings.

Sergeant-at-Arms – The sergeant-at-arms is responsible for the safety of the club as a whole and for keeping order.

Sweet Butt – A woman who makes her sexual services available to any member at any time. She may well live on the club premises and be fully supported by the club.

Treasurer – The officer responsible for keeping an eye on the club's money.

Vice President (VP) – The vice president will support the president, stepping into his role in his absence. He may be responsible for making sure the club runs smoothly, overseeing prospects etc.

Brothers protecting their own

CONTENTS

PROLOGUE

Eighteen months ago

Walking into the typical English pub in Guildford, I spy my friend hovering by the entrance and have my greeting ready as I approach her. "Hey, girlfriend!" At my voice, Zoe turns around and pulls me in for a hug and a kiss.

I lean over at the same time as she turns her head, and accidentally end up giving her a smacker on the lips. Of course I make the most of it. "Mmmm mm! Hi yourself, babes!"

My face splits into a wide grin as she slaps me lightly on my arm. "Carry on like that and they're going to think we're a couple of lezzies," she warns me.

I make a show of pulling away, and as I do, glance around to see if there are any likely looking males in the vicinity that could have been turned off—or alternatively on—at our little show. Zoe barks a laugh at me, then together we go to the bar and order a round of drinks. While waiting to be served, I started regaling her with all I've been up to. The only time I pause is to nod briefly at the bartender and give my choice of vodka and Coke. By the time we are sitting at a table in the corner where we can gossip to our hearts' delight, her mouth had already fallen open.

"Both of them? Together?"

I smirk at her. *Well a girl's got to live life to the full, hasn't she?* While she's rendered speechless, the smile slowly fades from my face. Not even my best friend Zoe knows there's a reason why it seems my goal in life is to collect as many varied sexual experiences as I'm able to. Forcing painful memories to their rightful place at the very back of my mind, I give her a light rap on the hand to get her attention. "So what's up with you, bitch? 'Bout time you got laid, isn't it? How long's it been now?"

Zoe and I have a long friendship going back to our uni days when we shared a flat together. Living a fair distance apart, our contact nowadays is limited to these girls' nights out on every other Friday, which tended to follow the same pattern. Each time we met, I would entertain her with my long list of conquests while she sits back and listens. She encourages me, seeming to enjoy living my exploits vicariously. As far as I know, it's been an awfully long time since her last sexual encounter with anything that wasn't battery operated, and even that, like the others before it, hadn't been anything to write home about.

Tonight starts off following the same pattern but, for once, she has something to say. She surprises me when she drops it in there, her voice animated. "Guess who I'm working for?" I shrug, as obviously it was impossible for me to answer without her explaining, and she continues excitedly, "Ethan bloody St John-Davies!"

"What?" I know of the name—well, who doesn't? "He's like one of the richest men in the country, Zoe!" Quickly I flash my eyes towards her, showing her she's caught my interest, and grab my phone out of my bag. "Go on, tell me more," I encourage while gazing intently at the screen, fingers of one hand flying over the keys, but waving the other to show I'm still listening.

"I'm working on a project to renovate a sixteenth-century walled garden on a massive estate; his estate." Zoe gestures towards the picture of the handsome looking man who's appeared on my phone.

I stare at the image of a handsome-enough-looking man. Enough to spark my interest. "I could so do that! Wow! Just look at him! And look at that house behind him. It's a fucking mansion! Is that where you're working? Do you need an assistant?" When she tells me she'd been introduced to him my mouth drops open. "You actually bloody met him? What's he like?"

"Gorgeous!" She taps her finger on my phone. "In his case, the camera doesn't lie. And it certainly doesn't show you his rather tight backside. Soph, his glutes are something else!"

Now my mouth hangs open. "I'm surprised you noticed, Zoe! Go you!"

I zone out when she goes into detail, and my eyes narrow as she deviates from what interests me most. "Hey, babe! Get back to the good stuff!"

"Okay, so he introduces me..."

"I got that bit, babe. Now get to the fucking part."

Her drink almost shoots out of her mouth as she splutters, "What the heck?" She gives me a long stare, and I return a rueful smile. "So," she ignores my interruption, "he introduces himself in this really upper-class, cultured voice, you know, pronouncing his name as Ethan 'sinjun' Davies."

I tilt my head to one side. "So what happened next?"

"Nothing, Soph. He went his way, I went mine," she tells me, honestly. "To tell the truth, we've been working on the site for a month now and that's the first and only time I've seen him. I doubt I'll see him again." She points to my empty glass. "Another?"

Seventeen months ago

When our next girls' night out comes around, Zoe is so eager to see me that she's arrived early. I immediately see she had something to tell me, as she's almost bouncing in her seat with excitement, impatient to share. She's terrible at keeping secrets, so when I slide up the bench next to her in our regular booth, I throw her a sharp look. "Well! You've either got fucked or fucked up!" I announce as I take a sip of the vodka and Coke she'd already bought for me, ginning widely. "Spill!"

Snorting, she almost spits out her mouthful of wine, and a short laugh bursts out of her at my crudeness. Taking a tissue out of her bag, she blots it over her lips to dry them.

"Come on! Which is it?" I look at her carefully. "Or have you just been playing too hard with your BOB?"

"Sophie!" Admonishing me, she quickly glances around to make sure no one heard my reference to her vibrator, then puts me out of my misery. "Ethan St John-Davies has asked me out on a date!"

My gasp is loud. "He fucking what?"

"Shush!" she chides me again, noticing heads turn at my exclamation. "Calm down a bit, and I'll tell you what happened."

"Well fucking come on then, don't leave me hanging!" My eyes were wide open; I didn't see that coming.

Grinning, happy and pleased with herself, she tells me about her meeting with the millionaire.

I laugh my head off as I picture it. "You fell at his fucking feet? Way to go, Zoe! What happened next?"

"He helped me up." And then, in a round-a-bout way, she tells me how he came to ask her to have dinner with him.

My mouth drops open. I'm both impressed and pleased for her. "Fucking hell, Zoe. When you get back on that horse you do it properly, don't you? You've landed yourself a fucking thoroughbred stallion!"

Fifteen months ago

Tonight I beat Zoe to the pub and lined us up with a couple of shots. It seems ages since I'd seen her. As soon as she was within hearing distance I yell out, "How's it going with lover boy?"

She comes over, laughing. "Oh, Sophie, he's gorgeous. He's so gentle and kind! I've moved in with him. I live in a fucking mansion now. Servants and everything! I don't have to clean, cook, or even do my own laundry!"

It isn't often she's able to shock me. "Blimey, that was quick! So, what's the fucking catch?"

"No catch!" She giggles. "He's amazing. So generous. So attentive and caring. He does everything he can to make me happy."

"What?" My face creases. I'm incredulous, but over the moon for my friend that she's at last found a good man for herself. "Shit! You've hit the bloody jackpot babes." Then I think about it, and my eyes narrow suspiciously. "It's moving a bit fast, isn't it? You're actually living with him? Have you given up your place?"

She nods her head and grins. "Yes, I've terminated the lease. Let's face it, it was a crap place in anyone's eyes, and Ethan persuaded me to let it go. It feels right, Sophie-girl. He spoils me something rotten, and I want for nothing."

Hmm. "So what's he like to fuck? Must be good if you moved straight in. Tell me you did the deed before you committed? You can't live with someone without putting him through his paces first. What's his dick like? Large, medium? Does he know what to do with it? Ah, wait a fucking minute! Don't tell me it's tiny? You're living the life of Riley, but there has to be a snag somewhere. Still, I suppose if he's got the money, the size of his prick probably isn't so important, as long as he can use his hands and mouth. Does his tongue compensate?"

"Sophie!" She covers her mouth to stop her shocked giggles escaping. "Why is it all you can think about is sex?"

"Hey, Zoe, bless you, you're beautiful, but sex is what makes the world go round. But if you're telling me he's got a big dick, then go you! You've won the fucking lottery!"

5

"I am not discussing the size of his appendage with you," she tells me primly.

I try to hurry her up. "Come on, spill the fucking beans!"

I should have been glad that my friend had fallen on her feet, but the things she tells me make warning bells ring in my mind. *What have you got yourself into, Zoe?* But there'll be no telling her, so I don't even try. And in truth, maybe my worries are all in my mind and say more about me than her. I won't ever be committing myself to one man. Why should I when there's a whole world full of them to explore?

Fourteen months ago

Something was up with Zoe tonight—she keeps shifting awkwardly in her seat and comes up with some lame excuses about why she keeps missing our Friday nights together, and evades the question when I ask whether I can visit her in that fucking mansion which is now her home.

Her eyes keep flicking shiftily away and eventually she changes the subject, turning it back to me by asking, "How's you?"

"Same old fucking same old." I grin. "Hey, you ought to have seen the fella I met last week. He was an electrician doing some wiring at work. Well, we got chatting and one thing led to another. Let's just say I'll never look at the broom cupboard in the same way again."

"Soph, you didn't! Not even you would do that!" She covers her mouth, but is unable to suppress her snort of laughter.

"I fucking did! I couldn't walk straight the rest of the day." My grin widens. "Another thing crossed off my bucket list. Now, what's going on with you and Ethan? I'm not joking about that visit; I'd love to see how the other half live."

"Didn't anyone see you?"

"No. And don't change the subject. How's that man of yours treating my bestie?"

Unusually for us, the conversation lags, and it deepens my suspicions that she's not living the perfect life she's describing. For once the atmosphere is awkward between us, but if I try to get her to talk, she just turns the topic back to me. Oh, I'm happy enough to tell her about the guy from the solicitors I bagged when I'd dropped some documents off at his office, but could I get information about her? No way.

Six months ago

Zoe had cut off all contact with me and I hadn't a clue why. I'd tried phoning her, but it seemed she'd changed her number. I even tried calling Ethan's mansion, but was told Zoe didn't want to talk to me and was told in no uncertain terms that I shouldn't try to get in touch again. At first I was hurt, then puzzled and worried about my friend. Finally, I shrugged it off. She knew where I was if she needed me.

Then out of the blue, there was a knock at my door.

"Zoe!" My pleasure at seeing my friend was quickly chased away by my concern when I saw the bruises on her face and the hunched way she was walking. It wasn't hard to see she was in a lot of pain. "Oh my God, Zoe! What the fuck?"

She put her hand on the door frame, leaning on it for support. "I've left Ethan, Soph. I'm going to my mother's in France, but I don't have any money…"

"Hey, come in. I've got some I'll give you." I ushered her inside and sat her down. "Do you want a coffee or anything?" I was over the moon she'd come to her senses about Ethan—I'd always suspected there was something off about the man. *And he'd been hurting her? The bastard!*

Declining my offer, she shook her head. "No, I just want to get away."

It seemed like every word was an effort for her, the stress of leaving the man who'd been her world for almost a year had got to her. I didn't press for details; that first look at her face told me all I had to know, and there was no thought in my mind but that I had to help her.

Not too far from my house was a garage with a convenient ATM, so with no hesitation I grabbed my keys and jumped in my car to go and get all my available money out. Returning as fast as I could, I gave her everything I had, enough for her journey and a little on top to keep her going. She burst into tears as she thanked me, and we clung together like the best friends we'd always been. She gave me her new number and promised to let me know when she was safe with her mum. Then, after an emotional goodbye, she was gone. I watched as she drove down the road until the car disappeared into the distance.

I'd never see her again. She'd never called me. But I knew she didn't make it to France.

And the very next day my life was shattered.

CHAPTER 1

Sophie

Oh for crying out loud! Who's ringing my flipping doorbell now? Well, whoever it is can just go away and leave me to my pity party. I'm not expecting a delivery and am definitely not in the mood to be disturbed.

I stare down at my phone, having just ended the call, a conversation I'd rather not have had. My boss wants me back at work. Oh, he was really nice about it, telling me about the adaptations that have been made following the access audit the health professionals had required the company to carry out. They've bought me a new fucking desk for God's sake—one that can accommodate a wheelchair. At that point he'd paused, as though he expected me to make some comment showing I was over the moon about that information. Then, when I'd only grunted, he'd helpfully added that the building had been confirmed as fully Disability Discrimination Act compliant, so I'll have no problems getting in and out and, of course, there were accessible toilets on every floor. He'd made changes to my job description too; I'd be working from head office now, and not expected to be out and about. Shit, why not admit I'm only a pathetic excuse for a human being now, one they're only keeping on because they have to? Oh, and to make their stats look good on government returns when they can add my name to the number of disabled people they employ.

Disability Discrimination Act or not, and however much people say it will do me good to return to my job and normality, they're missing the fucking point. I'll never be normal again. Never! Every fucking minute of every fucking day I have to live with the body I'm left with, having to endure the pitying looks and false sympathy from people I once called my friends, and who have forsaken me now. No one wants to be bothered with the ex-party girl who can't even fucking walk!

The knocker rat a tat tats now. Christ! Go away and leave me alone! I'm in no mood for company.

Another long ring and then a loud banging. Who the heck is it? Why haven't they got the message by now? Who the hell is trying to knock my door down?

More knocking. Oh for goodness sake! It doesn't sound like they're going to give up. Fuck it!

Eyeing my wheelchair across the room, and the crutches, slightly closer, leaning against the side of the sofa, I wonder which is easiest to get to and use. Knowing my physiotherapist would tell me I need to try to use my legs—well, what's left of them—I bend down as another knock comes, followed by three urgent presses on the bell, indicating the person seems determined to make me go out of my way to answer.

"Alright, alright I'm coming!" I yell as loudly as I can while pulling the crutches towards me. "Give me a fucking minute, will you?" Whoever is so desperate to see me will have to curb their patience a bit longer, as getting to my feet isn't easy. Mind you, just about anything is difficult these days. Placing my hands on the handles, I push down on them until I'm sufficiently up-right to get the supports under my armpits, and then, very care-fully, making sure all my weight is on my hands, I pull myself to my feet. I'm unbalanced and wobbling, as usual. Shit, I know I ought to have kept up with my physio appointments. But when you don't have much desire to go on living, pushing yourself to try to learn to walk again when no one seems prepared to give any guarantees that that will be a possible result, comes in right around the bottom of the damn list of things I want to do.

Eyeing my wheelchair again, I wonder whether I should just give up and go plonk myself in that. Or do I try to make it to the door under my own steam? Oh fuck, I'll go for it.

There's silence now from the front door. Hopefully they heard me and are giving me the time I need or, even better, whoever it is has given up and gone away. I bloody well hope it's the latter. I'm categorically in no mood to be sociable. That call from my boss emphasised I'm no longer a fully functioning member of the human race, and I'd prefer to be left alone to wallow in my misery.

I'm out of my chair, balancing on my crutches and one good—hah! That's a joke!—leg, and start to get into the rhythm my physio taught me. By the time I get to the door of the lounge, I realise I shouldn't have even tried this. The muscles in my arms are trembling as the weakness and pain in my remaining wasted leg stops me from putting much weight on it. But the awareness I shouldn't have tried this comes far too late. One of my crutches catches on the threshold bar joining the carpets by the door and I can do nothing to stop myself from falling, crashing into the hall table and sending it and everything on it toppling to the floor. *FUCK!* Yes, I've hurt myself, but the scream I emit is as much frustration as from pain. *I can't even do something as simple as opening the bloody door!*

Within seconds there's a tremendous splintering sound, and my eyes widen in disbelief at the sight of my front door swinging from its hinges, and looming in the now open gap is one of the largest men I've ever seen in my life. Gazing up at his face, standing what must be at least six feet above me, I shake my head in disbelief. As well as his huge size, I can't help but notice a rugged but handsome-enough face surrounded by dark hair,

11

and in one ear glints a golden earring. I don't know him from the proverbial Adam.

Lying prone on the floor with no dignity-saving way of getting myself up, I feel a flicker of fear as I study him more carefully. *Who is he? And why is he here?*

Dressed in a black leather jacket, wearing dark denim jeans, he's holding a motorcycle helmet in one hand and is rapidly taking off his gloves as he walks towards me, his dark eyes narrowed as he takes in my plight, immediately crouching down in front of me, assessing. Though a scar across the lower part of his face suggests he's no stranger to violence, he looks concerned rather than threatening.

That he's worried is confirmed when he opens his mouth. "Are you alright? Where are you hurt?" No introductions, he just gets straight to the point, asking his short, urgent questions in a deep, gruff voice.

Deciding he's not asking for a catalogue of my injuries from my original accident, I don't answer for a moment, and instead test my arms and leg, and decide though I'll probably have a few bruises later, I haven't done any permanent harm. Well, nothing more than I've already got, and yet another dent to my self-respect, so I tell him, "I'll live." Then after a moment's thought, I swallow down my pride and add, "But I'd appreciate you giving me a hand up. Then you can explain what the fuck you're doing in my house!" He could be here to burgle or murder me for all I know, and here I am, relying on a stranger for assistance. Well, it's either that or perform a degrading crawl back to my chair.

To my surprise, he doesn't offer me his hand to help me to my one remaining foot, but simply gathers me into his strong muscular arms and picks me up as if I weigh nothing at all.

"Where to?" His voice is rough and gravelly, but not at all unpleasant.

Gobsmacked I'm being held by an unfamiliar man, I wave back into the room I've just struggled from, and when he steps over the threshold, I point to the couch. With a gentleness I don't expect, he sets me down, and once again crouches down in front of me.

"Are you sure you're okay? Do you need a doctor or anything?" he queries, his voice laced with worry.

"No, I'm sure." Yes, I hurt and I'm sure I'll be feeling it later, but it fades into insignificance with everything else I've been through, so it's nothing I can't handle. And to be honest, I'm sick to death of being prodded and poked by anyone from the medical profession.

"I didn't mean to make you hurry to the door." As the corners of his mouth turn down and his gaze drops briefly to the floor, he sounds rueful.

"Well, you shouldn't have kept bloody banging on it then!" I admonish him, probably snapping more than I should have, but fuck it, I don't know who the hell this is, or why he's here. "And what about my fucking door? You kicked it in!"

He has the grace to look sheepish but is unrepentant. "Yeah, but what was I supposed to do? Leave you lying on the floor? You could have hurt yourself badly for all I knew. I heard the crash and didn't know what the hell had happened." He pinches the bridge of his nose and his brow furrows, and he is silent for a moment before he decides on a course of action. "Don't worry, I've got a friend who can come fix it. I'll take care of that now."

Evidently, this man doesn't hang about once he's got a plan. While I sit with my mouth hanging open, he gets out his phone, dials a number, and is soon telling the person the other end of the line that there's a broken door that needs fixing. When he's clearly not asked for an explanation, I start to wonder whether he makes a habit of kicking doors in and calling on his friend to make good the damage. *Who the hell is he?*

When he ends the connection after chuckling at a joke I'm not privy to, he turns back to me. "Cut will be around in an hour."

Slowly I move my head from side to side, my eyes wide as I try to make sense of everything. Who exactly is Cut, and what kind of name is that? Presumably he knows what he's doing and will be able to fix my smashed-in front door. But, except for the workmen making necessary adaptations, how on earth have I gone from not having a male visitor in my house for six months, and now will be faced with two?

The stranger gives me an assessing look. "Here, do you need anything? Can I get you something? Make you a drink… Grab some painkillers for you?"

Suddenly I've had enough of this and sit up straight, my eyes blazing. "You can tell me who the fuck you are. And why you're here." My brain kicks into gear, and I need to know why a huge, scary biker is in my house in the first place. I've never seen him before, or anyone like him for that matter. Anger gives way as a shiver of fear runs down my spine, and I start to shake.

He stares at me for a moment, recognising beneath my bravado that I'm scared. He heaves a sigh and indicates the chair behind him, as though asking my permission to sit. My lips drawn tightly together and not completely certain I'm doing the right thing, I nod to give my consent, accepting I'm in no position to throw him out of my house. Hell, he's so big I wouldn't have a chance even if I had the use of my legs. At least he won't be looming once he's seated, and as I've found, it's easier talking to someone when you're on the same level.

My gaze glued to his, I wait for his explanation, but he seems in no hurry to enlighten me. I scowl as he removes his jacket and gets himself settled. But even though his presence is annoying, I can't prevent myself noticing underneath all that leather is a very large, muscular body—and now they're revealed, I can see full sleeve tattoos down each arm. He's got that bad boy image down pat, and a physique that would have attracted me in my previous life, but now has no effect on me at all. *Yeah, the old Sophie would have been all over that.*

My chair groans audibly under his weight, making me hold my breath, hoping it doesn't break. I'm convinced I see it sag, but it must be up to the job as he sits back into it, folding his arms and crossing his legs, resting one ankle on the opposite knee. After he's made himself comfortable, I cock my head to the side in encouragement.

At last, he takes the hint and introduces himself. "My name's Horse."

Yup, it would be. My eyebrows rise as I question his unusual moniker, and he smirks and glances down at himself, drawing my eyes to his crotch. I give an exasperated sigh. *Fucking men!*

"So?" Even if his package lives up to that of the animal that's his namesake it's of no interest to me. Not nowadays. "Okay, so you're hung," I say scathingly, deciding to be blunt. "That doesn't tell me anything about why you're here." Or at least, I hope it doesn't. No one has to spell out how vulnerable I am.

After a quickly snorted laugh at my crude comment, he sits forward, his expression quickly growing serious. "Sorry about the door, but I came over in a bit of a rush to make sure you were alright. I didn't mean to scare you, okay?" He pauses, and the corners of his mouth turn up in a weak smile, then, finally, he gives me the explanation I'm looking for. "Your friend Zoe Baker sent me."

Zoe? Zoe Baker? My friend from uni days and who I'd kept up my friendship with, meeting regularly until her bastard boyfriend put a stop to both our regular get-togethers as well as me ever walking again? Bloody hell. I hadn't heard from her for months, since the day before I had my accident! Pulling myself up straighter I put my hands on my knees. "Zoe? How the fuck is she? *Where* is she? Is she all right? How do you know her?"

For an answer, he shakes his head, and the sad look on his face gives me a bad feeling about what he's going to say next. "Tell me she's not still with him, is she?" I don't explain who 'he' is, but it seems Horse knows exactly who I mean.

"No," he's quick to reassure me, "she's left St John-Davies. She got away this morning." As he pauses I have time to thank God for that. He draws in a deep breath and continues, "He hurt her quite badly, Sophie, but she left under her own steam, and my partner, Josh, is helping her get away as we speak."

My hands go to my face, my palms cupping my cheeks. And though I'm pleased Zoe's escaped, I can't help but remember the last time she tried to get away from Ethan. I'd given her money to help her leave and paid a hefty price for it. I shudder, remembering just how much.

Horse studies me, then resumes, "Zoe's concerned about you. She thinks St John-Davies might come after you again."

Oh, fuck. No! I collapse back on the couch and put my head back, closing my eyes. I'd always known Ethan St John bloody Davies had been behind my accident, though officially there had never been anything to prove it or to link the hit and run driver back to him. It had been too much of a coincidence, coming a day after I'd helped Zoe escape his abusive clutches. And the conclusive evidence had come a few days later when a bouquet of flowers was delivered to my hospital bed, so beautiful all the nurses had been oohing and ahhing over them. And so did I, at first. Until I'd taken out the card that accompanied them and read, 'Never help my woman try to leave me again.'

As soon as I was able to I'd tried ringing Zoe, but she must have changed her phone yet again, and I couldn't get through. I'd tried the number for the mansion but had no joy there. Of course, I'd worried about her for months, but she hadn't made any move to contact me, and in my position, well, I couldn't think of anything else I could do.

And that's the point. I hadn't seen her in yonks and had nothing to do with her current escape, so I can't understand why Zoe would think I'm in any danger now. There must be something I'm missing. "Why would Ethan be a threat to me? I've not heard from Zoe in ages, and how could he possibly think I could help her like this?" I wave my hand down my body to emphasise the state I'm in.

His face softens. "Zoe cares about you, Sophie, and St John-Davies knows that. She's worried he might come after you out of spite, or use you as a way to force her to return to him."

With a quick shake of my head, I dismiss his concerns. "He can do what he likes to me. He can't do worse than what he's already done."

For some reason my comment makes his face grow red as he tells me angrily, "Don't underestimate him. He can make your life a living hell."

"It already is," I rasp out, my own temper flaring as I again point to my useless legs. "He's left me nothing worth living for. If he killed me, he'd be doing me a favour."

Horse inhales sharply, his eyes blaze. "Don't fucking say that! You're alive, and be thankful for it!"

Taken aback by the vehemence of his tone, I push myself back into the sofa as though seeking the safety of its comfort. His fierce expression shows me he's not a man I'd like to cross.

As quickly as his temper rose, it recedes just as fast. Horse's stare loses its intensity and he resumes his explanation in a much calmer tone. "Zoe's worried about you, and I promised I'd keep you safe and out of his clutches."

I'm incredulous. "Why the fuck would you do that? And just how do you know Zoe? I didn't know she had any friends, well, like you." A huge tattooed biker is what I mean, but don't say.

Suddenly I'm suspicious. Ethan successfully isolated her from all her friends as I well know, and it's inconceivable he'd let her consort with someone like him. I'm even more sceptical when he gives me an honest answer.

He shrugs. "I don't know her at all, I only met her today."

Then why is he here? It puts me on my guard. "And *I* certainly don't know *you* either. You've delivered your message. Now please get out of my house. Thank you for your warning, I'll be careful, and I won't open my door to anyone I don't know." I think for a second. "Well, when I have a door that is." Then I realise the flimsy barrier hadn't stopped him.

Another shrug. "Nope, sorry, no can do. I promised your friend." Suddenly he's back on his feet and pacing around the room. His hands brush his long hair back over his shoulders, and then he pauses, holding the back of his neck. "You might not care what St John-Davies does to you…" His head shakes in exasperation. For some reason, my lack of an instinct of self-preservation seems to annoy him. "If you won't think of yourself, think of your friend. Don't you want to give her a chance to make a clean getaway? He knows how much you mean to her. If he threatens you, she'll feel pressured to go back to him." He breaks off, and astonishingly bright blue eyes seem to stare right through me. "If you'd seen her today, Sophie… If you'd seen what that bastard did to her. If she returns, I don't fancy her chances."

Tears prick at my eyes at the thought of my friend in such pain, and realise I owe it to her to keep away from Ethan. But still, I'm cautious. "Look, you say you didn't meet either of us until today? I'm having a lot of difficulty understanding why you're so set on helping. Give me something more to help me figure out why you're even bothering."

"It's simple. You're alive and breathing, and I want to help keep it that way." He brings his hands down in front of him and

18

looks down at his fists, which I notice are clenched. "You were involved in a hit and run. You lost the use of your legs. But you're still alive, Sophie. You've still got the chance to have a life, unlike..."

As his voice breaks off, I see his hands clench and his face tightens. It seems there's something he's not telling me, and that something is painful for him. Closing my eyes for a moment, I try to comprehend what could be driving this rough biker to offer me his protection and all in order to let my friend—who by his own admission he'd only met briefly this morning—escape the clutches of the man who's basically held her prisoner for the last eighteen months.

Oh, at first Zoe thought she'd landed on her feet, and I was even envious for a while. Such a prestigious man, head of a huge electronics company, ElecComs, with more than enough money to do whatever he wanted, and power that's impossible even to imagine. But I didn't comprehend the extent of the hold he had over Zoe, or how difficult it was for her to walk away until she came to me that morning six months ago, the last day I'd had the use of my legs. I never saw her again, and could only surmise Ethan caught up with her. My assumption was confirmed four days later when I got those bloody flowers delivered to my hospital bed.

I realise I'd been lost in my thoughts when Horse asks gently, "What happened to you, babe?" He indicates my legs. "What did that fucker do to you?" His curiosity brings me back to the present, and I see he's staring at the bottom of my jeans, and knowing exactly what he's seeing, my spirits plunge. It's not pretty, the material ending, but there's no foot sticking out. In fact, all my leg from below my left knee is gone.

For a moment I say nothing. I don't want to go through it all again. Everyone always wants to know the gory stuff. Then I sigh loudly. *I can show him what he's up against.* Leaning slightly forwards so I can reach into my back pocket, I extract my phone, scroll to the correct item, and hand it to him. When his eyebrows go up in question, I point to it the screen. "Play the video. Some 'kind' person happened to be taking a selfie that day. Once they saw the action start, they began filming. They helpfully sent me the film in case it was useful for insurance purposes."

His eyes sharpened with interest, Horse peers down at the screen. I don't need to watch with him. As my screams start to fill the air, I know he's at the beginning when the speeding car has just hit me for the first time, and I'm lying, broken in the road just outside the offices where I worked. Then I hear his gasp of disbelief when the car stops, then reverses and purposefully runs over my legs for the second time. The shocked shouts of the onlookers drown out my cries of pain.

"What the fuck?" He's still staring at the screen, his eyebrows rising almost to his hairline. "That was a deliberate attempt to kill you." The hand not holding the phone strokes over the stubble on his chin as he throws me a glance. "Babe, I don't know what to say." And then he has to ask the obvious, "You give this to the police?"

What type of idiot does he think I am? "Of course I did," I snarl. "The car had no number plates and was found abandoned soon after. The sun was shining direct on the windscreen so no one could make out the driver."

"There were loads of witnesses…"

I wave at him to stop. "And they were all looking at me, not the driver. Oh, a few tried to give descriptions, but they all conflicted with one another. Nobody actually saw anything. With nothing to go on, when I couldn't come up with a feasible enemy, the case was dropped. Eventually deciding there wasn't anyone to investigate, they put it down as a random act of violence or mistaken identity. Oh, and that's the only evidence. The CCTV cameras in the area were mysteriously not working."

"Did you point them in St John-Davies' direction?"

Yes, I did. Much good that had done. "I told them he had a beef with me as I'd helped his girlfriend get away from him. It was then the investigation started to go very quiet." And when I got the card with the flowers suddenly they weren't interested at all.

"Fuck!"

Yup. That about sums it up.

A rapping at the broken door startles me. Motioning for me to stay where I am—not that I could move easily on any account—Horse gets up and goes to answer it. I hear another man's voice and make out from their conversation it's his friend who's come to fix the damage Horse had caused. Though I'm uncomfortable with yet another man in the house, I'm glad he was quick—the sooner it's sorted the faster this strange man will be gone.

I frown as the question only just occurs to me as to who's going to be picking up the tab? *I* wasn't the one who kicked my bloody door down. My pulse quickens and my cheeks grow red. After Horse's explanation as to why he was here, my fear of him had dissipated, and now my emotion swings back the other way as I start to get incensed all over again.

It's not long before Horse comes back into the room and stands, regarding me thoughtfully for a moment. At last he asks, a little cautiously having noted my change in mood, "Is it alright if I use your kitchen to make Cut a cuppa?"

Now there are a couple of things you find out quickly once you've lost the use of your legs. One is that you don't have much option to object when an able-bodied person's intent on doing something for you, and the other is it's a pain in the arse doing even simple things like making coffee for yourself. So, it's a simple answer. "There's coffee and tea bags on the side and milk in the fridge. And as long as you make one for me as well, knock yourself out."

As I hear the sounds of cupboards opening and closing, suggesting Horse is finding his way around my kitchen, I think about the things he's told me. Despite some days not having the will to get out of bed, let alone the desire to continue living, the thought that Ethan could be after me is a chilling one. The sounds of domesticity give me a strange comfort that the massive man is in my house. St John-Davies is a nasty piece of work, and now Zoe's left him again—could she be right to be worried he'd come after me? Suddenly I don't feel quite as anxious to send Horse on his way. Once more my emotion trips in another direction, to that of concern and worry. *What's going to happen now?*

"Sugar?"

I answer the shouted question, "No thanks, just milk please."

It's not long before Horse is back with my beverage and places it on a side table within my easy reach. "Cut won't be long; he reckons it will only take an hour or so. It's a standard size, so he's got a replacement in the back of his van. He's going to fit a better lock too." Horse plonks himself down in the armchair again, and I wince on behalf of that poor piece of furniture.

I don't have too much spare cash lying around. I haven't worked for months, my sick pay—which is fast running out—is now half my regular salary, and I've yet to receive any compensation as the driver of the car that hit me was never found, so money worries me. "How much is that going to cost?" I ask, wearily.

Again he pinches the bridge of his nose. "Don't worry about it. Cut owes me a favour. And it was me who broke down your door, anyway. Hey, you sure you're alright after that fall? You took a nasty fucking tumble. I straightened up your table, by the way, and put your things back on it."

"Thanks. It's par for the course. I usually use the wheelchair," I explain, "but stupidly tried to give it a go with the crutches." I won't be doing that again.

"Hmm." He nods and takes a mouthful of his drink—he must have a mouth made of iron, it's far too hot for me to even sip yet. After scrutinising me for a moment, he asks as I thought he would, "That video, fuck, I'm surprised you survived. How badly were you hurt?"

I shrug. I've had time to get used to answering the question, even if I'll never get used to what I lost. "I've lost my lower leg below my left knee, and my right was badly smashed up. They just about managed to save that leg, but it's weak as hell."

"Have you got an artificial limb?"

I have, and I hate the darn thing. I hate my stump and everything about it. With a shudder I reply, "A prosthesis, yes, but it's so darn uncomfortable."

"So you make do with your wheelchair?"

Another shrug. "It's easier."

His eyes glare into mine. "Fuck, that bastard."

He's summed it up, there's nothing else to say. We continue to sit in an awkward silence, then he goes and chats with his friend Cut for a while, leaving me to muse about the stranger who's come to my house. *Before* I would certainly have been interested. With that size of body and those hands the size of dinner plates, I've no doubts other parts of him would live up to his name. But along with my leg, my sex drive has completely disappeared, mainly, I admit, as a way of protecting myself. Who'd want me nowadays? A cripple in a wheelchair missing half of one leg and the other full of steel pins and covered in scars? No one in their right mind.

The thought of getting intimate with someone and seeing them turned off when they get sight of my stump kills any arousal within me stone-cold dead. So I just don't go there anymore. Leaning forwards, I put my head in my hands, rubbing at the growing pain in my temples. After all these months I'm still unable to come to terms with what happened to me, still find it impossible to move forward, always looking back and regretting ever stepping out into that road, and regretting I never did more to act on my uneasiness when Zoe first got involved with that fucking Ethan. Her rags to riches story always rang a little too good to be true; a stark lesson to lift the lid of the pot to see what's inside before diving in with your spoon.

Heavy footsteps announce Horse has returned. Once again he just stands in the doorway looking at me. For once I don't see pity on someone's face—his brow is creased, and as he runs his hands through his shaggy hair I realise he looks like he's trying to solve a problem. Then his back straightens and he walks across to me, crouching down on his haunches. "Babe, your door will be fixed in a few, but we've got to decide what to do about you."

"You don't need to do anything about me. I'm not your responsibility. You've warned me." It's hard to suppress a shiver at the thought that I've no idea what I'd do if Ethan came calling. But is there any real likelihood he'd turn up? I can't decide whether it's a real possibility or not. Surely he's got much bigger fish to fry?

His gaze drops to the floor, and when he looks back up at me his eyes have darkened and he gives a shake of his head. "Fuck, you don't get it, do you? I promised your friend I'd keep you safe, and that's what I'm going to do. You got a spare room I can doss down in?"

No. Just no. Despite my earlier thought that his presence was comforting, I don't want a stranger actually staying in my house.

24

Narrowing my eyes, I say waspishly, "You need a place to stay? Find somewhere else. I'm not running a bed and breakfast service here."

"What the fuck? That's what you picked up from today? That I'm taking advantage of you? Shit, I want to protect you!" He pulls away, his eyes flashing.

If I could have stamped my foot I probably would have done exactly that at this point. "I've told you! I haven't had contact with Zoe for months! There's no reason for St John-Davies to come here." Why would he bother about me? He's already left me in a living hell.

"And how many times do I have to tell you that he could use you as bait?" Horse stands up fast, his hands raking through his hair again as he looks back at me, clearly exasperated. But whatever he was going to say next is interrupted by shouting in the hallway.

"Hey, what do you think you're fucking doing?"

Christ! What is it about today? Another man I don't know pushes his way into my lounge. He's not quite as big as Horse, but at over six-foot tall and bulked out with muscles, not someone to be trifled with. His face is scarred and his nose crooked, the kind of injuries that might have come from a boxing career. He's intimidating in a way that Horse isn't, and the vibe he's emitting is evil. Automatically I realise this is not Horse's friend, Cut.

My thought confirmed when Horse immediately puts himself between the man and me. "Who the fuck are you?" he snarls.

Cut, who I'd heard but not seen before, rushes in apologising, "I'm sorry, I was getting a screwdriver from the van and he just walked straight past me." Cut is only slightly smaller than the man who's assigned himself my protector, and he comes to a halt just inside the doorway at the intruder's back.

If I'd been alone I'd have panicked, but with these two men apparently on my side, my lips purse in anger, not fear, and I want answers. "Good question, just who are you? And what gives you the right to barge straight into my home?"

The stranger draws himself up to his full height. "My name's Hargreaves." His voice is full of disdain, and though I already had the beginnings of it before, I start to get an ominous feeling about him now.

"Doesn't tell us much, man," Horse gets in before I do.

"I work for Mr St John-Davies," he continues. "And Mr St John-Davies would very much like to know where his girlfriend is." His eyes, which I notice are far too close together, seem to burn into me as he spits out the reason why he's here.

A feeling of dread settles in my stomach like a stone as Horse is proved to be right. And I'm relieved that Zoe had the forethought to send him. Any idea I might have of telling him to get lost disappears now, as I look at Ethan's man in front of me and realise how dangerous he could be. Tension is rolling off him in waves. Enraged, his hands are curled tight by his sides as though it's an effort to keep himself under control, his nostrils flaring in barely suppressed rage. The only thing that's comforting about the situation is there are two other irate men in the room giving off equally angry vibes. At least numbers are on my side.

I'm first to break the silence. "Mr Hargreaves, I have absolutely no idea where Mr St John-Davies' girlfriend is. I don't even know who that might be." As his face grows red and he takes in a deep breath, I continue before he has a chance to speak, "My friend, Zoe, *was* his girlfriend, but I've had no contact with her for months. If that's who you're talking about, I assure you I haven't a clue where she could be or, if she's left him, where she might go. And I'd be the last person she'd contact for the very reason you're standing here. She'd know better than to come to me or confide in me."

Hargreaves is making an effort to control himself. His eyes flick to Horse, and then he glances around him. Cut is leaning up against the doorjamb, his legs crossed at his ankles, looking deceptively relaxed. But the fierce expression in his eyes shows he's anything but. At the moment I couldn't be safer. *But what would have happened had I been alone?*

Hargreaves' Adam's apple bobs up and down as he swallows rapidly. When he speaks next, it's in an even tone that appears to be alien to him. "Mr St John-Davies would like to talk to you in person. He's anxious about Miss Baker. She's been depressed lately and he's concerned she might do herself an injury. I'd like you to accompany me so I can take you to see him. You might have some ideas of where she would go, so he can catch up with her before she does anything we'd all regret. Miss Weston, will you please come with me?" The way he almost stutters over the wording of his request suggests he doesn't need to plead very often.

"She's going fucking nowhere with you." Horse is adamant. He puts out his hand and rests it possessively on my shoulder.

"Horse is quite right, Mr Hargreaves. I have absolutely nothing to say that would be of help to your employer. Now could you please get out of my house?"

"I believe the lady asked you to leave." Cut adds his two pennies worth, and steps aside from the doorway, leaving room for Hargreaves to pass through.

It appears it's not often anyone refuses Ethan's henchman. Suddenly he drops the mask. "Lady? She's a fucking whore! That's probably what you two are here for anyway." He's spitting with rage as he addresses the two men, then he turns back to me. "You won't always have your punters here, and Christ, they must be scraping the bottom of the barrel to want anything from a cripple like you. Or are they just here for a pity fuck?"

My mouth drops open; tears come to my eyes. Trying to tell myself Hargreaves is a despicable man working for an even worse employer, I force myself to ignore the offensive words he's spouting, but they hit the mark, echoing my own thoughts about my desirability. I manage to speak, rasping out while trying not to let him see how much he's hurt me. "Just get out of my fucking house."

"Oh, I'll leave, but I'll be back when your clients have gone. Don't try to run, Miss Weston, you won't escape me." He breaks off and sneers. "Oh, hang on, you can't run, can you? You can't even bloody walk!"

With a roar, Horse launches himself at Hargreaves. Cut moves quickly for such a large man, and they both take hold of his arms and propel him out of the door. I hear the noise of scuffling outside, then a car door banging, an engine over-revving and roaring away, and then silence.

Angrily I brush the tears, which are now falling in earnest, away from my face. Even if I had the use of my legs I'd be feeling helpless after a visit from such a horrible man, but as immobile as I am, I'm completely vulnerable and defenceless. My hands cover my eyes. I'm shaking and can't stop.

"Shush, it's alright, he's gone."

Lifting my head, I see Horse once again hunkered down in front of me, his large hands coming out to cover mine. Cut hovers behind him, concern written all over his face.

"I'm not a whore!" Why I should feel it necessary to refute that accusation immediately, I'm not sure, but it's the first thing that comes into my head.

"Of course you're fucking not!" Horse's immediate forceful assertion comforts me. "But one thing's for certain, you can't stay here."

What? It's my house, my home, my refuge. I've barely stepped foot outside these four walls for months. It's adapted for me, I can't just leave and go somewhere else where I'll have to worry if my wheelchair would get through the doorways. "I can't go. You mentioned staying in my spare room?"

For the first time, Cut addresses me directly. "Even if Horse stays with you, now Hargreaves knows what he's dealing with, he could come back with more men. It sounds like this St John-Davies has got a fucking hard-on for you. I agree with Horse— you're not safe here and you need to go somewhere he can't find you."

Horse looks at me for a few seconds, his brow creased as though he's deliberating, then his features relax. He pulls his phone out of his pocket, nods at Cut, then walks out of the room.

I started today like any other I've lived through over the past few months, with nothing to think about other than how to get myself out of bed, then into my wheelchair, onto the sofa, then reverse the process again. With nothing for company other than my books and TV, the only things to concern me are the phantom pain from my non-existent leg and the very real pain from the other one. While I'm unsure whether I can cope with such a drastic change to my lonely existence, I know I wouldn't have had a chance against Hargreaves alone. *He'd have taken me with him. I couldn't have put up much of a struggle.* Eventually, I glance up to Cut. He's standing, leaning against the door-jamb, legs once again crossed at the ankles, giving me time to process what's gone on.

"I don't have much choice but to accept Horse's help, do I?" I admit in defeat, having failed to come up with any alternative. Folding my arms across my chest, I lean back on the sofa. If these two men hadn't been with me today, Hargreaves might already have delivered me to Ethan. And even if I don't much care what happens to me, I *have* to think of Zoe. If keeping my-self safe somehow allows her the freedom to get away, that's what I've got to do, however much I dislike being dependent on others—notably people I don't know.

Cut nods slowly and the corners of his mouth turn up as he smiles. "We've got your back, Sophie. Trust Horse to get you somewhere safe."

Somewhere safe? I've no idea where that could be. Oh, I've googled Ethan bloody St John-Davies, and I know the kind of resources he can bring into play if he truly wants to discover someone's whereabouts. Especially a person who sticks out like a sore thumb. "There's probably nowhere I can hide." My chin drops down to my chest in defeat. "If he wants me, nothing will stop him from finding me."

Horse has been gone quite a while, but he chooses this moment to return, his features relaxed and smiling. "I should have everything sorted, babe. Just have to wait until I get the nod, but I don't see it being a problem. Trust me, if it works out, I know exactly the right place. Not only won't he be able to find you there, he won't even think of looking."

CHAPTER 2
Wraith

Shutting off my engine, I remain sitting astride my bike for a moment, breathing in winter evening air. Up in the foothills above Tucson, Arizona, I prefer this season's milder temperatures to the scorching heat of the mid-summer months, and the more predictable weather. Riding can be a real bitch in July when the torrential rainstorms, often preceded by dust storms, can blow up out of nowhere, forcing any sane rider to pull over and stop. Arizona doesn't have a stupid motorist's law for nothing—if you're crazy enough to try to drive through the floods, you end up picking up the tab for any damage caused. Yup, winter's definitely my favourite season. Sure it still rains, but it's either a steady drizzle or occasional showers, and nothing like the summer monsoons.

Swinging my leg over the bike, I dismount and straighten my cut. I'm early for church, so there's no need to rush. I can take a moment to enjoy the fresh air—only slightly tainted by the smells of gasoline and hot oil—and the early evening light. Today has been warmer, signalling spring is on its way. *Almost time for the prospects to fill up the pool!* I grin. That's a job and a half to keep it clean over the summer months; you never know what might be found in it after a party. What with the other major task of keeping the brothers' bikes sparkling, and chains and belts free of the sand which otherwise can literally grind us to a halt, I'm so glad those days of being at everyone's beck and call have long been in my rear view. I've been a patched member for ten years and prospected for a year before that. And those arduous twelve months were quite enough for me, thank you very much!

Satan's Devils hit pay dirt when they found this location for their clubhouse shortly before my time. An ill wind decidedly didn't blow the previous owners of the Blazing Trails Resort any favours when a fire ripped through the complex, destroying well over half of the accommodations and public areas, leaving them financially ruined and unable to rebuild. And no one else was interested in acquiring the burned-out shell, being relatively isolated a few miles outside town—part of the reason why the fire was able to take such hold. No one that is, except for a club of bikers looking for a new home.

The fact we run a construction company, as well as a garage and the standard obligatory strip club together with a few other businesses—some not quite so legitimate as the rest—meant we could complete essential repairs at very little cost to the club. The result being that all patched members, the prospects, and the sweet butts all have comfortable accommodation on site for when they want to use it, living in the blocks which used to house the guest bedrooms, each complete with an en-suite. Luxury in the biker world. And the views from the compound are magnificent, looking out as we do over the city of Tucson sprawled out below, while above us the Coronado Forest reaches up to the mountain tops. The Sonora Desert, with its magnificent fauna, including the saguaro cactus—some growing strongly, some dead, surrounds us. Here in Arizona, even the felled cacti are protected by law. The scenery sometimes makes me feel like I've got the star role in a Western.

It's a peaceful spot and, to me, it's the only real home I've ever known.

The ticking of my cooling engine is the only sound I hear until a gust of wind gets up, and a small tinkling sound reaches my ears. Ha! It's the darn prospect's Gremlin Bell. Fuck knows why, but young Hank seems to believe in that shit. Even though I've suffered from the attention of the evil road spirits over the years, I don't put any stock on the ringing of the bell driving them crazy enough to drop off my bike, and you wouldn't catch me hanging one of these on my handlebars. *Uh uh.*

Shaking my head, I start to make my way towards the clubhouse.

"Hey, Wraith! What'cha doing out here? Stop playing with your dick and get your ass inside. Time for church!"

"Hey, Peg!" I stumble as he plants a hearty slap on my back on his way past. *Fuck, that man doesn't know his strength!* Falling into step beside him, I follow him through to what was originally a large reception-come-lounge area for residents, now our bar. "Get the deliveries done okay?"

"Fuck yeah, too fuckin' right. No problem. Get me a fuckin' beer, Marsh!" Peg thumps his meaty fist on the bar and shouts his order at another of our prospects.

Not being stupid, Marsh slides one over to me too. I take a long drink and turn to survey the room. The bar and the old dining area out through an archway make up our clubroom. Tables, chairs, and a few mismatched and well-used couches dotted here and there combine to form a decent area for the members to relax. A pool table and a couple of arcade machines—where, not surprisingly, Adam is currently hammering the hell out of one of them—complete our area for recreation. And tonight, after church, we'll be letting our hair down and having a fucking party. The sweet butts, who get food and lodging in exchange for their services, as well as city girls up from Tucson, will be put to good use, and the prospects will be kept busy at the bar. It's gonna be a gooooood time. My cock twitches in anticipation, but I shut that shit down fast. Not so good joining my brothers in church sporting a hard-on!

"Come on you jackasses! Church! Now!" The irritated voice of our prez, Drummer, gets our attention, and a load of leather-clad bikers stop what they're doing with a variety of grunts and stretches and get to their feet in no particular hurry. It's doubtful anything in particular has upset the prez—Drummer always sounds that way, and usually has an expression to match. Sometimes it's pretty damn difficult to work out whether you've upset or pleased him. Still, he's got a good head on his shoulders and has our backs, so he gets our respect.

Traipsing into the room, which has a large oval wooden table in the centre, we make our way to our allotted seats. Drummer takes the head, of course; Peg, as sergeant-at-arms, is to his right; me, as VP, on his left; Dollar, a man so talented with figures and exceptional at making money make more money that we had to make him our treasurer, sits next to me; and Blade, the enforcer, is to Peg's right. Next to him sits Heart, who we made our secretary by virtue of the fact he has a business degree. The other brothers sit in the same places as they always do. There's a gap down at the end, which Drummer isn't slow to miss.

"Buster?" he growls, the deep lines on his brow showing his annoyance.

"Doing what he does best, Prez. Bustin' balls I expect!" A roll of laughter runs around the table at Dart's flippant comment.

Viper pipes up, "Not back from his run to Phoenix yet."

"Anythin' I need to worry about?" Now Drum sounds concerned, as he'd be for any of us missing without reason.

"Nah, last thing I heard his contact was delayed," I reassure him. As VP it's my job to know exactly what anyone's doing at any time. "He should be here soon."

"Fuckin' better be! Right, Dollar, how's the fuckin' money looking?"

And so it starts. The club's run exactly like a business, and of course we all take an interest in how the bucks are coming in as our personal take depends on our rank in the club and how much we make. It's all fairly standard tonight, but the income from the strip club is down a bit, down to losing one of our star attractions who's moved out of state. The motion to try and attract in new pussy is agreed.

As Heart records the vote, a loud sniff has me glancing at Adam, and it doesn't surprise me to see him wiping the back of his hand under his nose, reminding me I need to get the prospects to stock up the room with boxes of man-sized tissues. Christ, do I have to think of everything? They'll be getting me to change the toilet rolls next!

Movement catches my attention as Dart flicks ash off the end of his cigarette, most of it landing on the table. My eyes are drawn to the sign some joker put on the wall, 'When the floor's full of cigarette butts, please use the ashtray'. The offending member throws me a grin when he sees where I'm looking, and pointedly takes more care to tap off his cancer stick in the correct depository.

"VP?" Drum prompts me to give my report, bringing my full attention back to the meeting. My brief summary is then followed by those from the other officers, and then by those of the other members.

It's been a quiet week, and there's not much going down that's giving us cause to worry, and one by one everyone gives updates on a similar line. Observing that everything's copacetic doesn't seem to ease Drummer's irritation any, but that's not surprising, nothing ever does. As we plough on through the business, I take a second to cast my eyes around my brothers around the table. For the main part they're a good bunch, and as always it gives me a warm feeling to have found my place in such a family. For the main part that is, the exception being Buster, our newest and missing member, having only recently patched over from another chapter. I've still got to take to the man. But for all that, he's my brother, and I'd give my life if necessary for his, just like I would any of the others. That I might not be quite so happy about having to do so is another matter.

Church is winding down and looks like it's coming to an end. The brothers are getting antsy to get out and start partying. A couple are even getting to their feet when Drummer shouts out, "Did I say church was fuckin' over?"

Casting quick glances at each other, those standing sit down again and pay attention. I cock my head in the prez's direction. He hadn't discussed any new business with me, which is unusual.

Drum nods at me, acknowledging he hadn't had a chance to fill me in, but then, I'd only just got back from a run so couldn't hold it against him. Still, showing proper respect for my rank, he's looking in my direction as he starts to speak. "Got a call from Horse yesterday. He's gonna be here a month early this year."

"Fuckin' sweet!" Slick's face widens into a grin. "I'll get him started on my new ride. Got some great fuckin' ideas for it. Fuckin' A."

While Drummer shoots him a glare, I feel like high-fiving someone myself. Horse is an amazing artist and does some great work for us. The delicacy of his airbrushing is beyond amazing. I'd been planning to treat myself to a brain bucket to match the detail he did on my bike last year. Of course, in Arizona, once you're over the age of eighteen there's no requirement to wear one, but I value my brain too much to ride without.

Horse isn't a patched member, but we treat him as an honorary one. Horse usually spends six months with us each year, accompanying us to Sturgis in August, where his skills are much in demand. Apart from being a fucking ace with an airbrush, Horse is a great dude, and we've long accepted him as one of our brothers. It's no trouble for us to let him make his base here, and it means we're first in line for his services.

Slick's comment sparks a round of conversation around the table. Drummer brings us back to order by banging the gavel loudly.

"Cool it!" He glares, waiting for everyone to quiet. "Horse wants a favour from us. He's bringin' a girl with him."

"Fuck yeah! The more the fuckin' merrier!" Tongue's famous organ comes out and waggles, the stud in it catching the light and glinting.

"Fresh meat!" Beef's heavily muscled arm thumps the table.

"Shut the fuck up and let me fuckin' finish!" The voice of our prez cuts through the shit being thrown around. "The woman is under his protection. It will be hands off for all you fuckers."

Now a collective groan.

Drummer is the only one who brings his phone into Church, the rest of us leave them in a basket outside, and now he pulls it out of his pocket. I watch, curious as he presses a few keys then passes it to me. I can see he's started a video playing. Dollar peers over my shoulder.

As the drama unfolds in front of my eyes, I find it hard to watch, but can't look away, like seeing a car crash happen. Which is exactly what I'm viewing. "Fuckin' motherfucker!" I shake my head, unable to believe what's on the video. Dollar snatches the phone out of my hand and presses play again. Seeing the expressions on our faces, the others start to leave their seats and gather around. The phone gets passed around; Peg growls loudly when it gets around to him. After we've all seen the bastard run over a defenceless woman, the phone, at last, is returned to Drummer.

Quickly putting two and two together, I ask, "That's the girl? She survived?" I shake my head in amazement, wondering what cold fuck could have done such a thing.

"Apparently, yeah." Drummer wipes his hand over his face. "She's already been through some shit, as you've all just seen. She's in a fuckin' wheelchair. The fucker who put her there is comin' after her again. Presumably to finish the job."

Fuck! That's serious shit. "She's not safe in England?"

"According to Horse, she's not. This motherfucker's got a long fuckin' reach. Mouse!" Drummer gets the attention of a man who looks absolutely nothing like his name would suggest, but who's our expert with computers and all that shit. As usual, he's got a laptop open in front of him. "Find out everythin' you can about an Ethan St John fuckin' Davies. See whether this is going to blow back on us if we take her in."

"One English motherfucker against us?" Viper sneers; he just turned forty and is one of our older members.

Drummer rubs his fingers through his long dark hair, already beginning to turn grey at his temples even though he's a couple of years younger than Viper. "We need to know what we're up against. Can't see there being much of a problem myself, as you say. One fuckin' Brit shouldn't be a problem."

Dart's nodding. "At least the club's set up for a wheelchair."

"Yeah, all the ramps are still in place, we didn't take those out."

"Damn useful for getting bikes in the clubroom!" Everyone laughs. Yup, that's been done. And into ground-floor bedrooms as well. While the original resort had to comply with disabled access, it made it fucking handy for us bikers too.

"Alright, alright. Come to fuckin' order!" Drummer glares around the table and we all simmer down. "Do we want to wait until Mouse has done his stuff before we take a vote? VP?"

Now we're not a club who deals in pussy—we don't go after women or children—that's in our by-laws. And from that short, disturbing video, the fucker he's talking about has already harmed this woman beyond what any of us would deem acceptable. Quickly I think it through and look around at my brothers sitting at the table. A number of us served in the military and are no strangers to violence or protecting our own. And if we offer protection to Horse's woman, she'll by extension become one of ours. As far as I'm concerned, it's an easy decision to make, but I don't want to rush into it. "Do we know how long she'll want to hide out here?"

Drum shakes his head. "I don't think Horse knows. It all happened in a rush, but she's already been paid a visit—luckily he was there at the time—and he thinks she's in real danger, so he's in a rush to get her away. His small crew ain't enough over there. This St John-Davies apparently has a lot of muscle he can call on."

Growls now replace the earlier light remarks, and I know my brothers are with me when I give him my answer. "Let her come.

How much trouble can one woman be, particularly with Horse vouchin' for her? It's on him, though; she's his responsibility."

Drum's eyes circle the table and he gives a sharp nod. Not one to make hasty decisions, I suspect he's already given some thought on this as he wastes no time giving his view. "Right. I happen to agree with the VP. As long as she knows we ain't putting on fuckin' airs and graces just because we've got an English bitch in the club-house! But we'll do this fuckin' right and vote on it."

There are no objections. It's all ayes as Drum gets votes from those seated around the table and the motion passes unanimously. It's settled, we're giving the woman our protection.

Drummer has the final word. "VP, you'll get the prospects sortin' out rooms for Horse and this woman?"

"On it, Prez."

"Mouse, I want that info immediately once you've got it."

"Yeah, man."

"Right, now get on out of here." With a bang of the gravel, church is officially and finally dismissed.

Various shouts of 'party', 'pussy', and 'fuck yeah' fill the air as one by one we all vacate the room. The main topic of conversation on most of our lips is predictably the mystery woman.

Beef, a solid tank of a man built like the ox that gives him his name, slaps me on the back in a way that makes me wish he hadn't. "You reckon her pussy still works?"

"Keep your hands to your fuckin' self!" I round on him, my eyes flaring even while I'm not entirely sure why I'm feeling defensive about a woman I've not even met, but put it down to following the instructions of my prez. "You saw what happened to her. She's been through enough without you plannin' how to get into her fuckin' panties!"

"You know me, up for a challenge and all that. You think Horse is already tappin' that?"

"Nah, man, Horse don't want no woman after his ol' lady died. Makes use of club pussy, but he don't want no bitch on the back of his bike again." Heart is the one who'd understand—he's so in love with his woman it makes me cringe when I see them canoodling, though admittedly they've made one cute as fuck kid together. First brother I've known not to run a mile when he saw two little blue lines.

"Never knew he had an ol' lady?" Beef asks. It's not unusual for him to be the last to know.

"Yeah," I bring him up to speed. "Nasty business, she was killed in a car accident. Hit and run on a pedestrian crossin'. She was DOA and never had a fuckin' chance." At least this woman's still breathing, even if she is broken.

That's enough for Beef. If it isn't attached to a pussy or bike he doesn't want to know. He gives me another hefty slap then walks smartly away, his attention and cock drawn to the city girls who've started to arrive. The conversation has me wondering whether Horse's desire to protect the girl has something to do with his dead wife; it wouldn't surprise me. Maybe he's making amends for the woman he couldn't save.

"You alright with this, VP?" Drummer's come up next to me, and putting his arm over my shoulder, leads me over to the bar. The prospects fall over themselves to get us our drinks before we can ask for them—as they should do. If they prove themselves to the club eventually they'll get patched in, and knowing which brother drinks what is part of their duties. Beer quickly put into my hand, I turn to him. "Do we know anythin' else about her, Prez?"

"Not a lot. Horse was damn worried though." And that concerns me. Now none of us is exactly fairy-like, but Horse gives Beef a run for his money. If a big man like him can't protect a woman, there might be more to the story than we know. While not exactly a chapter, Horse is a member of an associate club of ours in England, and if they're not confident they can handle the shit going down in their country, we shouldn't dismiss it lightly. My main unease is caused by the thought that in our hurry to give sanctuary to an un-known girl we'll be bringing a heap of shit down on ourselves. But then, as I give a quick look around at my brothers, all of which are now finding entertainment in various ways, I doubt it's anything we won't be able to handle. There's only one man in this club who I wouldn't trust with my life, and he's currently not in the room.

It's as if Drum has read my mind. Stroking his beard, now flecked with a little grey, he says thoughtfully, "Buster didn't turn up. You think he's got pussy somewhere?"

"Wouldn't put it past him." Turning back to face him, I give a shake of my head. Buster's being far too much of a pain in my ass lately.

"Well find out why he wasn't here and fine him if he ain't got good reason. All members attend church, even those heathens in Cali must know that."

Buster recently transferred in from our San Diego chapter, but as part of the same club, we all follow the same basic rules and regs. "I'll have a chat with him, Drum," I assure him while wishing Buster wasn't causing me so much trouble. As if in synchronised motion, we both drain our drinks at the same time, and turn together to look out into the club. I reckon Drummer's got the same idea in mind as me.

Heart and Bullet's old ladies aren't here, of course, party time after church is not for their eyes or ears. And I doubt Viper's old lady would take kindly to seeing her old man's cock disappearing down the throat of Pussy, one of our most popular, or at least well used, sweet butts. But she'll never find out; brothers know not to share that shit. Me, I'm not tied to anyone and have no desire to be.

After my long ride today, I cast my eyes around to see who's going to take my fancy tonight—one of the new girls or... Ah, there's Chrissy making a beeline towards me as usual. It crosses my mind that perhaps I shouldn't encourage her, else she might start getting ideas above her station, but fuck it, I might as well go for it tonight. She's not as tight as she could be, but damn it, she can suck like a vacuum, and has hair down to her ass. My fist tightens in anticipation of wrapping it around her long locks as she's on her knees in front of me, plump ass in the air as I pound into her wet cunt. Yeah, that'll do me. Thoughts of the Englishwoman forgotten, I nod at Drum, who's already got his eyes on Jill, currently sitting on Rock's lap, and I give him a knowing nudge. Jill's into twosomes, threesomes, you name it, and Rock doesn't mind sharing at all. Reckon our prez is fixed for the night as well. Devils know how to party.

Without ceremony or small talk, I snag another beer, push away from the bar, and grab Chrissy's hand. She's got a cocky smile on her face as I lead her away. While not adverse to performing in public, tonight I feel like playing in my room.

Chrissy's fingers entwine with mine as we go out into the night air and up to the block where my room's situated, her touch just a little too intimate for my liking. She's someone to scratch my itch, nothing more than that. Opening my door, I pull her inside and waste no time getting her over to the bed. Reaching up her hands, she tries to pull my head down to hers, her intention obviously to initiate a kiss. Well, I've got no time for that shit and just want to get down to business. The ride was long and hard today, and now I just want another of a different sort. Keeping my face well away from hers—for all I know she's just given one of the other brothers a blow job—I flip her onto her stomach, undo the zip on her tiny skirt and pull it down, taking her panties along with it.

"Up," I tell her shortly.

Knowing what I want, she pulls herself to her knees and takes off her top and bra. Reaching around her I palm her breasts, but my enjoyment is diminished knowing they're artificial and don't quite feel like the real thing. But her ass is pretty enough, and the fact there's a naked body in my bed is sufficient to make me hard enough to perform.

"You ready, darlin'?"

At her breathy confirmation, I wait no longer, opening the drawer to take out a condom and smoothing it on in one well-practiced move. Tapping her ass and putting my hand under her stomach, she takes the hint and pushes her face to the pillows, her back bowing as she offers herself to me.

Checking she's wet enough—she is—I push inside and start hammering away with only one intention, to get my release. As I thrust I'm not really aware who it is under me—it could be Jill, Allie, or Pussy here instead. All of them know the score. But as I feel my balls start to boil and that tingling sensation starting in my spine, I know I'm close, and not being a bastard, want to make sure the woman I'm with gets hers too.

She's moaning, pushing back into me, her muscles tightening.

"You close?" I ask.

"Yeah," comes her breathy confirmation.

Reaching my hand down I start to toy with her clit.

"That's it… Yeah… Oh, Wraith!"

As she comes with a little scream, I drive in hard a couple of times and then that blessed feeling as cum shoots up into the condom. Fuck, I needed that!

I roll off her, tying off the condom and dropping it by the side of the bed to dispose of later. Lying on my back, my arm up over my face, I wait for my breathing to slow and give her a moment to recover. Before too long I feel her hand on my now flaccid cock. I put mine on top of hers, stilling her wandering fingers.

"It's alright, darlin', I'm done."

Opening my eyes, I see her pouting. "But Wraith, how about I suck you off?"

"Not tonight, darlin'"

"But…"

I put my fingers over her mouth, not wanting to hear her whining. "I said no." I wait for her to move off the bed, get her clothes and go. She knows the score. But instead, she lies back down and snuggles beside me. I scoot away from her. "Chrissy, I said no. I've had a long day and I'm tired."

"Just let me stay with you then, Wraith."

What the fuck? Club whores know not to push when a brother's finished with them. The smell of sweat and sex mixed with the overpowering perfume she's wearing is getting to me, and not in a good way. I just want her out of here so I can have a shower and grab a beer out of the mini-fridge in the corner of my room. Sitting up, I gather her clothes, still scattered over the bed and floor where they'd landed, and chuck them at her.

"Just get dressed and go." I'm starting to sound fractious, but she's irritating me now.

"Wraith, I like you. A lot," she starts, her voice sounding breathy like a little girl's. Totally put on. "I was wonderin'…"

Whatever she's been thinking about, I don't want to hear it.

"Chrissy," I growl, and from the way she sits back I'm at last getting through to her. "You've been a sweet butt long enough to know how this goes. Now if you're not dressed in thirty seconds, I'm throwin' you out of here naked." I wouldn't be the first of my brothers to do that.

That gets her moving, but not before she exaggeratedly wipes fake tears from her eyes. As I watch her dress it dawns on me I might have been using her too often lately, and realise I haven't seen her with any other brother recently. Fuck, has she got designs on me? I make a mental note to avoid her, at least for the time being. Although it rarely, if ever happens, the dream of a sweet butt is to become a member's old lady, and if the brother is an officer, so much the better. I've got no desire to take anyone as an old lady anytime soon—if ever—and I'm certainly not going to be taking one who's serviced all my brothers. *Uh, uh.*

CHAPTER 3

Sophie

I haven't a bloody clue what's going on! When I asked Horse what the hell he meant by saying he was taking me somewhere out of Ethan's reach, he just grinned, then asked me if I had some lighter clothing for warmer weather. Open-mouthed, I pointed upstairs, to that domain of my house where I can no longer go. Now, overhead, I can hear banging and doors and drawers opening and shutting, so I presume he's rifling through my summer clothes. God, I should tell him to stop—what if he packs my old shorts and skirts? They'll be useless now! Surely he wouldn't be so crass?

Cut's stayed, presumably in case Hargreaves returns before we leave. They'd had one of those conversations in man language using grunts, nods, and the raising of eyebrows, so I suspect he knows full well where Horse intends to take me. But neither will let me in on the secret. The small smirk that Cut can't hide entirely suggests I might not jump at the idea.

As the noise from the upper floor continues, I think back to the day I last saw my friend, and remember the little Zoe had managed to tell me. But she hadn't had any need to use words, one look at her blackened eyes and the way she was holding herself showed me the pain she was in. Ethan is a bastard, and now his focus of attention is on me. A shiver runs down my spine as I acknowledge how helpless and useless I am, and my only option seems to be to rely on Horse to keep me out of his reach.

So wherever he's taking me, I'll go along. What choice do I have?

"Right." Horse comes back down the stairs and into the lounge—he's found my suitcase that was on the top of my wardrobe and it's already packed full of clothes. "I think I've got everything you need from upstairs. Toiletries and that shit?"

"In the bathroom." I point to the converted wet-room social services have made out of my downstairs toilet—it's not huge, but big enough for me to get in to do the necessary, even in my wheelchair. "Er, can I check what you've packed?"

Throwing me a curious look, he puts the suitcase down, unzips it, then picks out some clothing and shows it to me. I have to admit, he's done fairly well. He's packed T-shirts, light jumpers, a couple of pairs of smart trousers and leggings—nothing that would be too short and not cover my stump and prosthesis.

"What's that?" I wave at what he's not showing me. His mouth turns up with a beguiling smile, and he lifts out all the sexy underwear I possess—and it's quite a lot: lacy knickers, fancy thong and bra sets, and even a handful of teddies. Not that I have any use for them nowadays, but in my previous life it's all I'd think of wearing. You never know when you might meet an attractive electrician in a broom cupboard. "No," I protest, shaking my head violently. "You can put that lot back!" Those days are long gone now. "My everyday stuff is in the bedroom." No need to wear anything now that's not utilitarian and comfortable.

"Aw, shucks. You never know when it might come in handy." Ignoring me, he examines the contents of the suitcase again.

"What about shoes?" Cut cuts in. "You haven't got any, Horse."

"I couldn't find any." Horse frowns, seemingly not happy at the implied criticism.

"I can't wear them." At their twin flabbergasted expressions, I explain, "I only have one pair, the ones the prosthesis is for fitted for." As they exchange glances, I hate reading the sympathy there. And yes, another thing I regret with all my heart. I used to have a shoe fetish, buying new pairs to go with almost every new outfit, mostly high heels. One of my friends cleared the lot out for me very early on. They reminded me too much of what I had lost.

Getting off the topic of footwear, I point Horse in the direction of the kitchen. "I'll need my meds, Horse. Could you make sure you've got them? They're in a plastic container on the side."

Of course, when he comes back in he's taking the lid off and examining the contents. "Tramadol, babe? Are you in a lot of pain? And what the hell is this, anti-depressants?"

"Losing a fucking leg can bring you fucking down, you know?" I wish I could get up and stomp around the room, but I can't. I'm unable to make any show of temper other than raising my voice at his invasion of my privacy, and thumping my hands down on the seat cushions. And then the perfect solution hits me. "Look, this whole thing's stupid. Just leave me alone and I'll remove myself from the equation altogether. It's not like I've got anything to live for now." And what isn't a new idea seems the perfect solution all around. I wouldn't be a burden to anyone, and Ethan wouldn't be able to use me as a bargaining chip.

Horse moves so quickly, one moment he's standing by my suitcase, next he's leaning over me, a menacing look on his face. His hands are gripping my arms so tightly it almost hurts, and he shakes me. His face glows red—his lips have thinned as rage blasts off of him. I reel back as he shouts, "Killing yourself? Is that what you're talking about? You're fucking alive, and you want to throw that away?" I swear my teeth are rattling and that my arms will bruise as he holds me with such a firm grip. "You've got a chance to live; others aren't as lucky as you."

Well he doesn't have to tell me that! That's something I know only too well. I glare at him, feeling heat welling up inside me.

Suddenly he lets me go, but his intense eyes don't leave mine. "I never want to hear another sentence like that out of your fucking mouth again! You're coming with me, and I'm going to keep you safe. And I'm going to be taking charge of your medication."

"You can't do that." My eyes blaze at him, fire I thought long forgotten returns. It's my lifeline, my *choice* he is taking away. Why the fuck can't I have the chance to put an end to my suffering once and for all? Whether I take the easy route out or not is up to me, surely? I'm not sure I'd actually go that far, but I'd like the option to be there. *And maybe then I wouldn't be so alone.*

"Watch me!" Angry Horse, I decide, I definitely don't like.

"I wouldn't argue with him, sweetheart." There's something about the tone of Cut's voice that tells me it's best to beat a hasty metaphorical retreat.

Cut's intervention kicks my brain into gear. I realise something else is going on here. It can't be me he wants to protect so fiercely, but maybe it's something else? Someone he couldn't save, perhaps? Had someone close to him ended their own life? My features relax as sympathy takes over. Looking up at Horse I tell him quietly, "I'm sorry, Horse, but sometimes, it's just so hard, you know?"

He stares at me, the expression in his eyes shuttered and haunted, then gradually his hands loosen. "Some have it worse, babe."

I've been told that before, been told how lucky I was not to lose both legs or be completely paralysed. But somehow I don't think Horse means it the same way. I decide not to argue.

48

"You want me to take her and her stuff in my van?" Cut's practical suggestion breaks the tension in the room.

"Yeah, I'm on the bike." With one last lingering look at my face, Horse turns away and gives a chin lift to Cut, who starts busying himself folding my wheelchair.

"I'll need that…" I start to point out.

"I've got arms, haven't I?" Not wanting to get on the wrong side of Horse again, I don't argue his suggested mode of transport. Nor do I get into a debate when he goes into what was the dining room, but which has been converted into a downstairs bedroom, returning with some of the winter clothing I keep there. I watch as he empties armfuls of jeans and sweatshirts into the case, and note he's neglected to bring the plain white knickers and bras I wear nowadays. But I again, I keep my mouth shut as he zips up the now full suitcase which Cut, having returned, picks up easily in one hand. Taking my crutches under his other arm, he disappears outside again. Finally, I purse my lips and say nothing as Horse pockets my prescribed medication.

Then, with a gentler look, he comes over to me. "Anything else you want to take, babe?"

This is all happening so fast my brain can't keep up. I haven't got a clue. I try to think. "Er, my bag, phone, and iPad."

"Your iPad got a sim in it?"

I shake my head.

"Well, you can take that, but we'll have to get you a new phone. Don't want anyone to be able to trace you."

He slips the iPad into the pocket of my suitcase, passes me my handbag having taken out the phone, then moves closer, his features gentling, and a small smile appearing on his face. He reaches out his hand and softly caresses my cheek, his blue eyes gazing at me intently. He breathes in deeply then lets the air out as a sigh. "It's all a bit much for you, isn't it, babe? But don't worry, I'll take good care of you. You're going to be safe. Trust me."

I lean into his touch, welcoming the comfort. His kindness brings tears to my eyes. "Horse, I'm not normal, you've got to realise…"

"I'm not fucking blind, babe. Don't worry. You've got special needs, I can see that. I'll help you every step of the way." Then, without saying anything else, he picks me up in his strong arms and takes me out of my house and away to God knows where.

Goodness knows why I should trust a man I only met today. But he's saved me already when he chased Hargreaves out of my house, and unlike Ethan's henchman, I sense no threatening aura coming off him. And Zoe had sent him to me—she wouldn't put me in the hands of someone who'd do me wrong, would she? So without making any further protest, I let him carry me out of the home where at least everything had been adapted for me, and into an uncertain future, hoping to God I'm doing the right thing.

Cut drives me to Horse's home, a flat in a block on the outskirts of Guildford. Parking outside, he switches off the engine and warns me we'll have a bit of a wait.

"Where's Horse gone?" I ask Cut, not really caring, but wanting to break the silence.

Cut taps his fingers on the steering wheel as if he's impatient to get to something else he needs to be doing, which makes me think, while I don't like the way Horse is pushing me around, I should be grateful they dropped everything to help me today.

"He's gone to see his partner, Josh. He'll be dropping his bike off so Josh can put it in storage for him."

At that moment, a van pulls up behind us, emblazoned with the emblem of a local garage. I take a moment to admire the decal painted on the side—it's a beautifully painted picture of cars and bikes. Watching in the side mirror, I see Horse unfold himself from the passenger seat and go around to the driver's side.

His voice is loud and I can hear every word. "Thanks for this, mate. I'll let you know when I'm coming back."

I can't hear the response, but then Horse continues, "Yeah, it will probably be September as usual."

September? Doing the quick calculation in my head, I realise that's seven months away. Surely he isn't taking me somewhere for that long? I'll lose my job for sure—not that I want it. But, fuck it, months? I thought a few days and I'd been back home. Realising I need to know just what I might be letting myself in for, I resolve to start asking him some questions as soon as I can.

Then it's all down to business. Cut sorts out my stuff while Horse takes me in his arms again and carries me up to his second floor flat. While I worry about the weight strain I must be putting on his back, this is the easiest mode of transport since I came out of hospital. Not very independent, though. My physio wouldn't be pleased.

My earlier assumption that Cut's got something better to do is proved right as he hangs around only as long as it takes to say goodbye, and then the two men pull each other in for a one-armed man hug, accompanied by back slaps which would probably knock me over if they tried that on me. As Cut wishes him good luck and hopes that all goes well—well, that's what I interpreted from the man-speak—he comes over and takes my hand. Still bemused at everything that's happened to me, at last remembering my manners I thank him for his help, which he dismisses with a wink and a wave of his hand, then he leaves, and I'm alone with this mountain of a man.

Men have never intimidated me before. Shit, in my previous life I'd go after anything that attracted me, anytime, anyhow, and anywhere. I used to amuse Zoe with all my conquests—I loved sex. Why should I be ashamed about that? Never felt the need to tie myself to any one relationship; just enjoyed sampling as many of the various goods as I could. Now desire has completely left me, and instead of causing my lady parts to quicken, my breathing speeds up and my palms start sweating. I'm trapped in a wheelchair and unable to fight if any man wants to take advantage of me. *Was I stupid agreeing to come here?*

Horse looks down at me and I shift uncomfortably at his gaze —he's not said anything since Cut left. He seems to be waiting, but for what I don't know. I start feeling scared. As I'd been before, I wouldn't have said no to putting him through his paces in the sack, but now? Nope, not even a flicker of desire. If he makes any approach I'll have to make sure he knows that isn't on the agenda. Unless he uses force, of course, as I'm in no state to be able to press a refusal.

It's awkward, trapped in my wheelchair in the home of someone I don't know. Wanting to break the silence, I ask, "So, what happens now?" Twisting my hands in my lap, I hope he's not going to ask for more than I'm prepared to give.

He lifts his chin and narrows his eyes as if he can read my fears, then raising his head, his hands come up to massage his neck. "I'm pretty confident I've got everything squared away, but I'm waiting on a call to confirm it. Might take a couple of days so we'll hang out here until I get the okay. For now, I don't know about you, but I'm fucking hungry. Want some Chinese or something?"

I don't have much of an appetite nowadays—food is something I eat by rote, just enough to keep me alive. Even that holds no particular pleasure for me anymore. But he's a big man and probably needs feeding, so I shrug. "If you want."

Horse nods, asks whether I've any preference—I don't—and places the order. It's going to take about an hour to arrive. He puts on the TV, and I manoeuvre my chair until I'm in front of it, then settle in to watch programmes about motorcycles I've no interest in. I'm more concerned about what's going to happen to me, and whether Zoe got away safely.

The news comes on.

"Hey, Horse! Look!" My finger points to the screen and he comes to my side. Together we watch as the newscaster makes his announcement, letting the nation know that Zoe Baker has gone missing and that her partner, Ethan St John-Davies has put up a bloody quarter of a million pounds reward about information as to where she's gone. There's even a frigging picture of her! Minus bruises, of course. It must have been taken on a good day.

Oh my God! Two hundred and fifty thousand fucking pounds. That's hard for anyone to resist. What if Horse, Cut, or their mate Josh, who he'd told me helped Zoe escape, decide to drop her in it for that amount of money? My heart starts pounding as I glance warily at the huge man standing beside me.

"Fuck! Christ, I hope she got away safely." Horse smooths back the hair that's flopped down over his forehead. He's frowning and half mumbling to himself, "Her disguise was quite good—even Josh didn't recognise her at first. Hopefully it's enough to keep her out of his clutches."

The words I overhear cause tension to leave me in a rush, and I sigh with relief. If nothing else proved this man had good intentions, what he'd just said did, and it filled me with warmth. That amount is one heck of an incentive to turn Zoe in. I cross my fingers and, though not particularly religious, send up a quiet prayer. Anyone who watched that news item would be on the lookout for her now. I can only hope she's got a good enough plan to keep her safe.

We talk a little as we wait for the phone call he's expecting, but neither of us shares much. I've only just met the man, so I'm not going to tell him the story of my life, and he's obviously a private person and doesn't let on much about his. We spend the evening watching TV, then, when there's nothing on to interest us I try to read a novel on my iPad while Horse flips through car and motorcycle magazines, as well as some more artistic ones which make me ask him how he earns his living. When I find out this huge man built like a brick shithouse is an artist it surprises me. His hands look too big for finely detailed work. Seeing my interest, he gets out a portfolio of some of his work and I'm amazed. What a talent he has!

The one thing he still refuses to let on is where he intends to take me. The only answer I get is a sly smile and the response that he's waiting to check it's going to work out before he lets me in on the secret. I'm starting to feel wary and worried about what he's got planned. If it was, say, a cottage in the Outer Hebrides, why wouldn't he tell me? Sure, it might be a bit cold this time of year, but that I wouldn't much mind. It's not like I go out much, so wouldn't bother about being snowed in.

I go to bed in his spare room; my fears relieved when he showed me to the spare bed. But perversely, part of me is upset he's made no move on me, yet more confirmation any desirability I had as a woman has gone. Men don't see me any longer, they see the chair, and that's an immediate turn-off.

It's three in the morning when Horse gets the call. The walls are thin in this modern apartment and his voice is loud, so I can hear his side of the conversation easily, though it doesn't make much sense to me. I hear my name mentioned, then Horse replying, 'Yep' several times. The call seems to end abruptly, with none of the lingering goodbyes women tend to use.

The light goes on in the sitting room. After tossing and turning for a while and realising Horse is still apparently up, giving up on sleep for the night I decide to go and join him, suspecting the call might have been the one he was waiting for and he might have news for me.

He's sitting on the couch with a laptop open in front of him and looks up, one eyebrow raised in question as I wheel myself in. "You alright, babe?"

"I couldn't sleep. I heard you on the phone."

"Sorry." He grimaces. "These walls are like paper. Didn't mean to disturb you."

I shrug to show it doesn't matter.

"Well I might as well tell you now, everything's been sorted." As he glances towards me, his eyes are twinkling and one side of his mouth is turned up. "You're coming with me to Tucson as soon as I can get the flights. I'm booking them now."

Tucson? What? I open and shut my mouth a couple of times and swallow. The only Tucson I know is in the States. Surely he can't mean he's taking me there? My brow creases in consternation as I ask for clarification. "You're not talking about that place in, where is it now…" I break off, realising I have no fucking idea where exactly it is.

He looks up, a boyish grin on his face. "Arizona."

My frown deepens. "Ari-fucking-zona? Why the heck would I want to go there?" I'd have preferred the Outer Hebrides.

"To be safe." His reply is a simple one. "It's far out of St John-Davies' reach, and I've got friends there. I can promise you'll be well protected."

"But," I wave my hand at my chair, knowing I'm going to have to point out the obvious, "I can't go on a plane like this!"

"Of course you can!" Horse suddenly stands and comes over to me, his hands on the arms of my wheelchair. "What the fuck d'you mean you can't? Christ, woman, you can do anything you fucking want to!"

Of course I fucking can!

Which is why, somehow, just forty-eight hours later, I find myself being wheeled through London Heathrow Airport towards the departure gate for a direct flight to Phoenix, Arizona.

Horse has made me wear my prosthesis, and my crutches are attached to the back of the chair. He's organised and, despite my objections but to my relief considering my limited finances, paid for the tickets and everything, even arranging for his mate Cut to take us to the airport.

The crowded airport is just as overwhelming as I expected. Either people address Horse and expect him to speak for me as though I lost my mind as well as my leg, or they go to the opposite extreme, leaning over their desks and making sure they speak to me slowly and clearly as if I'm deaf. As we go through check-in and passport control, I start fuming. And getting through security? I had to take off my flipping leg as well as having the other one x-rayed due to the number of metal pins in it! At Horse's insistence, they took me to a private area to do it, but even so, unstrapping my leg in front of strangers and watching them examine it was an embarrassing start to the journey. Once they let me through, Horse was waiting with my bag and a sympathetic look on his face. For a moment his hand rests gently on my shoulder.

Although I know which city we're heading to, I still haven't been able to get Horse to tell me anything more than we'll be staying with some of his friends. His evasion suggests there's something about the situation that I might object to if he came clean. But however much I've pressed him, he won't tell me a darn thing he doesn't want to share. I suspect he doesn't want to get into an argument.

If I were a normal person I'd be excited to travel to the USA—it's something, when I had two working legs, I'd always wanted to do. But at the moment the very thought of the practicalities involved in a ten-hour flight worry me. Not being a normal person, I deliberately forewent my second cup of coffee this morning and haven't drunk anything since I arrived at the airport, despite Horse's encouragement. When making the booking, Horse informed the airline of my disability and confirmed that he'd be the companion the rules require, as I've got limited mobility. But I'm still worried. *What the fuck happens if I need to go to the loo?*

Toilets on planes are tiny at the best of times, how would I be able to manage? I can't balance on crutches sufficiently to be able to walk up the aisle—if there were the slightest bit of turbulence I'd fall over. Christ, my bladder feels full just with the worry of the realities that the majority of my fellow passengers would never consider. It's not the first time I've cursed my predicament. And Horse wonders why I've considered ending it all?

With the worry of how I'll keep comfortable on the plane in mind, I leave, making use of the full-sized disabled facilities at the airport to the very last moment, rushing in when the call for boarding is announced.

As it turns out, the flight isn't quite the nightmare I fear. Horse wheels me down the gangway to the plane's doorway. I'm then transferred into a smaller chair that they call an aisle seat, and the stewardess pushes me down the aircraft, and I'm able to shift myself over to where I'll be sitting on the outside of a central block, with Horse beside me. It means the other passengers can get out via the opposite aisle, without needing to clamber over me. I'm so thankful that I'm not sitting on the window side. When the dreaded time comes when I can't hold off any longer and have to answer the call of nature, I once again use the aisle chair, and Horse accompanies me, helping me get my balance in the slightly larger disabled cubicle before discreetly leaving me alone. It's awkward, but by using the handrails I'm able to sort myself out, make myself decent, and unlock the door. We then reverse the process to get me back into my seat.

All in all, relatively dignified, though I know I'm blushing red as I return to my allocated seat, keeping my eyes downcast to avoid the glances of able-bodied people who can barely hide their curiosity, probably wondering what was wrong with me and how I managed to do my business alone. *I hate this! I hate being different!*

Halfway through the flight, I'm suddenly gripped by pains in my lower left leg, which makes me gasp and lean forward to rub it. My hand hits the hard metal of the prosthesis. Tears come to my eyes in frustration at the phantom pain I can do nothing about, and once again reminding me of the loss of my limb. Horse knows I'm hurting, but he wouldn't understand, so I don't try to explain. But thank goodness he hands me some Tramadol, which has the side effect of making me sleepy. The next thing I know, we're coming into land at Phoenix and, at last, I'm arriving in the country which will be my new home. For how long, I have no idea.

It's new and different. It's exciting and bewildering. It's frightening. How the fuck has my life been turned upside-down again in only a few days?

Last off the plane, having to wait while they recover my wheelchair from the hold, I'm finally being taken through the unfamiliar but modern and accessible airport. Looking at my Apple Watch—the one luxury I'd treated myself to after my accident, I see the temperature outside will be warmer than it was when I left England. Here it's about twelve degrees Celsius. Or fifty-three Fahrenheit, I see flashing up on a large display. I suppose I've got to get used to the American way of doing things now.

Horse pushes me to baggage claim and collects our luggage. I wheel myself from there; he's got enough to carry with our bags. We go through customs without a problem, and then out into the arrivals area.

Suddenly a loud voice shouts 'Horse!' and a man, only an inch or so shorter than my companion and wearing black leather comes across to greet us, slapping Horse on the back and pulling him in for a manly hug. Another similarly clad man comes across and does the same. Loud voices exchange greetings, 'Good to see ya's' fly over my head and, as the men acknowledge each other, I take a moment to get my first good look at what are apparently Horse's friends, and with whom I'll be staying for the conceivable future.

I'm not naturally a shy or retiring person, but I'm only five-foot-two, and couple that with the fact I'm sitting down, I feel very small and shrink further back into my chair as if it could hide me. When I hear my name it takes me a moment to respond.

"Babe, Sophie, this is Dart and Slick. They're here to take us down to Tucson."

Swallowing a couple of times, I get up my nerve and look up to see two men beaming down at me, their eyes taking me in from head to toe.

"Hey, I'm Dart!" The man with long dark hair tied up in a bun reaches his hand down to me and gives me a wink. I lift my hand and shake it. I notice that with his aquiline features and dark brown eyes he's a very handsome man.

"Slick." The other, also a good-looking man with a shaved head, does similar. Both look curiously at me. I hate what they see—a disabled woman in a wheelchair. In the old days, I'd have been wondering how quickly I could get one or the other, or both, into bed. And what's with those strange names?

"Have a good flight?"

At least they're speaking directly to me; so many people wouldn't. I nod. "Yes, it was all right." For once I can't think of much else to say. I've met a lot of men in my life, but with the exception of Horse, never such tough and intimidating ones as these before. I find myself wary of saying the wrong thing. But I suppose if I need someone to protect me they certainly look up to the job.

"Let's get movin' then." Slick's eyes flick around as if he's worried about something, and as I see men in uniform eyeing them up, I start to suspect the amount of security around isn't making either of them feel comfortable.

Without further ado, Dart comes around and starts pushing my chair, and Slick takes one of the bags from Horse. We go outside, and a short distance away there's a black SUV and another leather-clad man waiting. At our approach, the new man opens one of the rear doors, reaches inside, and hands something to each of my companions.

Shit! Now, I've watched *Sons of Anarchy* like most people I know, I mean, who wouldn't lust after Jax? So I recognise the leather vest as the cut it's called here as soon as one turns his back. The wording across the top reads Satan's Devils, and across the bottom, Tucson Charter. *Horse's friends belong to a biker club?* My mouth goes dry. *What the fuck have I got myself into here?* I start to wonder whether, after all, it might have been safer to take my chances in England. The Outer Hebrides suddenly sound a decidedly attractive option.

But I have no opportunity to change my mind about going with them, as without ceremony Horse lifts me and plonks me into one of the seats, then folds up my chair and it disappears into the back. I just have time to notice the cut of the man who they didn't bother introducing to me and who's now in the driver's seat, says 'Prospect' on the back, before all three get in the car, and we're quickly on our way.

CHAPTER 4
Wraith

lancing at my phone, I notice it's almost ten o'clock. The clubhouse is relatively quiet as it's Tuesday. The weekends are our party nights, but there are still a few members around taking advantage of the sweet butts, and Adam's at his regular spot, monopolising one of the arcade machines and, of course, Hank's behind the bar. Spider will be out manning the gates, and Marsh, our other prospect, has gone down to Phoenix along with Dart and Slick to collect Horse and the mystery woman, Sophie, as I now know she's called.

Signalling Hank for another beer, I admit that I'm curious about the unknown female that we've offered our protection to. I'm also more than a little concerned about the information Mouse has managed to find out about the man who's apparently after her.

"Whaddaya reckon about the Brit?"

At the distinctive growling voice behind me, I turn to see Drum coming up behind me, not surprised he's on the same wavelength. We'd met earlier, an emergency church to go over what our internet expert, Mouse, had come up with. I shake my head. "St John-Davies sounds like a bad fuckin' enemy."

"You ain't fuckin' wrong there."

Drummer's on the whisky tonight, Hank gives him a glass clinking with ice cubes, and I wince. In my view, good scotch shouldn't be drowned, especially the top-end brand that the prez drinks while other members make do with that on the bottom shelf.

I take a gulp of my beer. "He got any pull over here?"

"Not that I'm aware of. His main base of operations is in the UK, but our military uses some of his software, so who knows? He's got good connections in the UK. There have been a few investigations into some of his activities, which all seem to have been dropped before they went too far. Nothin' sticks to St John-Davies it would seem." Drum taps his fingers on the bar, causing Hank to swing around in case his prez might need a refill. Seeing he's set for now, the prospect goes back to washing glasses.

"We gotta hope he hasn't got the same clout over here and gets the feds involved." As VP, I'm worried we might have bitten off more than we can chew.

"Yeah," Drummer's face tightens, "a fuckin' RICO investigation ain't somethin' we need."

That's my concern, and my face tightens. "You think he'd go that route?"

The president thinks for a moment. "He wants the girl, that's obvious. But whether he'd go so far as to get the authorities involved I couldn't say. I suspect it would be a last resort. Surely he wouldn't want it to be too obvious? Reckon if he finds out where she is he'll probably try to take her if he wants her as leverage like Horse suggests."

"We gonna let that happen?" I've never met the woman, and while I have sympathy for her—fuck, who wouldn't after watching that video—I certainly don't want to risk my club or my brothers to save someone I don't know.

"We'll give her protection as Horse wants, as long as it's at no cost to ourselves. I love Horse like a brother, man, as we all do. But he's not a full member—heck, he's not here most of the year."

As normal, Drum and I are thinking along the same lines, so I nod. Satan's Devils wouldn't want to put a woman in danger, but she's not club property or an old lady. Even though we've agreed to protect her, that was before we knew all the facts. If shit gets real, we might have to cut Horse loose to protect our own. "You got a bad fuckin' feelin' about this, Drum?"

He closes his eyes briefly, his hand idly pulling on his beard, a sure sign he's giving careful thought to the matter. And that's one thing our prez does, he thinks things through. "Not particularly. I think the Devils will prove a match for St John-Davies. Doubt he's come across folks like us before."

There is that.

Suddenly the front doors bang open. Swinging around, I realise the moment is here, as the mystery woman we've offered our protection to—or at least as long as it doesn't adversely affect the greater good—comes through, pushed by my old friend, Horse. Pulling up straighter to get a closer look, I suck in air as I get my first sight of the woman in the wheelchair, to find she's not what I expected at all. *Fuck, she's fuckin' beautiful!* For a moment I'm frozen to the spot as I examine her, noticing how much she looks out of place.

The Arizona sun makes it impossible for most residents to retain such pale, flawless skin, and there's a slight pinkish colour to her cheeks. Yellow-blond hair cut into a short bob shows off her slender neck and frames an oval face with symmetrical features. Her cornflower-blue eyes, currently flicking around the room with concern, are perfectly set, outlined by just a small amount of eyeliner and mounted under arched eyebrows which haven't been over-plucked. Her lips are made for kissing, full and a natural red. Having been used to the heavy makeup of the sweet butts for so long, she takes my breath away.

She's small, even taking into account she's sitting in that darn chair, and I don't need the club's instruction for my protective instinct to come to the fore. Unlike the other girls in the room, she's demurely dressed in simple jeans and a V-neck sweater, but the top outlines her breasts, which make me want to reach out and touch them. A pulsing in my jeans tells me I'm not unaffected, and a quick glance around the clubhouse shows me from the expressions on my brothers' faces that I'm not the only one. *Fuck, we're in trouble here.*

Viper pushes himself off the wall he'd been leaning against and moves toward her. "Hey, Wheels! Good to meet cha! I'm Viper." The way he's leering down at her suggests he's forgotten he's married—and that he's almost twice her age. Mind you, that's quite normal for him. Then I realise what he's said.

Wheels? Pushing back down the strange feeling of jealousy to where it belongs, hidden and buried, I huff a laugh and exchange amused looks with Drummer. One second into the club and she's already got a nickname. It suits her. But the way her eyes have narrowed, they suggest she's not happy about it at all.

It will stick though. And the more she protests about it, the more we'll all use it. We're cruel fuckers when we want to be. I know my brothers all too well.

The rest of the vultures start hovering, sensing fresh meat. Once again, Drummer meets my eyes. That I'm not the only one finding her attractive is blindingly obvious, and we can both sense trouble on the way unless we put a stop to that shit right now.

The prez steps forwards, taking charge. "Hey, you dogs. Give 'er some fuckin' space, eh?" He pushes through the men who've started introducing themselves, probably overwhelming her on what has to be her first foray into a one-percenter motorcycle club. "Hey, sweetheart." Having cleared an area around her, he leans down and offers his meaty hand. "Name's Drummer, I'm the president here, and any of these fuckers give you trouble you let me know."

She takes his hand; I notice hers looks tiny. She murmurs something I don't catch, but see she doesn't look at him for long. Again, her eyes scan the room as if she's looking for something, probably a way of escape.

"Horse—good to see ya!" The prez and Horse exchange man hugs. "You both want some refreshment?" Drum's eyes flick down to include Sophie in his invitation.

Her attention flits back to him. "Not for me, thank you. I'm pretty tired after the flight." It's the first time I've heard her speak. Her voice is so soft and sweet, and her quaint English accent pulls at something inside me.

I can't take my eyes off of her and am still staring when her mouth falls open. As I turn to see what she's looking at, I spot Allie giving head quite openly to Rock, who's about the only one taking no notice of the new arrival. Well, he's got other things on his mind, or rather his cock at the moment. Then as I look further around, I notice the other three resident sweet butts glaring at the new arrival with narrowed eyes, as though weighing up exactly what she's here for, and it's then I decide to get her some breathing space.

Pushing away from the bar, I go to stand beside Drum, nodding at Horse before shaking his hand. "I've got rooms organised for the two of you. I'll take you to them." Swinging around, I spot the prospect who'd driven them here. "Hey, Marsh, get their bags, will ya?"

"Do you mind?" I turn back to Sophie and put my hands on the back of her wheelchair. At the shake of her head, I start pushing; Horse walks alongside.

"Horse? Come back when you've got her sorted. There's a beer with your name on it here!"

"Sure thing, Drum!" Horse shouts back over his shoulder.

As clubhouses go, this one's not bad. There are still signs of fire damage and burned-out buildings we haven't yet bothered with, but we've done up a fair amount of the accommodation. Admittedly not to the previous five-star standard, but enough so it's comfortable and not too shabby. And, once having been a prestigious resort, there are ramps for disabled access everywhere, which we haven't bothered taking out. Comes in handy when a brother wants his bike in his room for some reason or other. And believe me, sometimes they do.

As I wheel her along, I make conversation with Horse, and after a while realise I'm not including her. I didn't exclude her on purpose, it's just that she's on another level. So I make an effort, bending over and waving my hand around. "I don't know what Horse has told you, but this used to be a vacation resort. Got burned out and the club bought it for peanuts. Disabled access everywhere so you shouldn't have any problems getting around."

"Horse hasn't told me anything." Now that she's away from the clubhouse I see some of her spirit coming through as she scowls at Horse.

He shrugs. "Didn't want to frighten you off."

"Hmm." I smile to myself, thinking he's probably going to hear more about that later. Then she looks up at me. "Thank you, er…?"

I realise I should have introduced myself. "The name's Wraith. I'm the VP. The vice president."

"Wraith?" She's intrigued by my name, not my position.

"He moves like a ghost," Horse explains for me.

She's scrutinising me as though trying to fit my solid, muscular six-foot-three frame with a mental image of an ethereal creature. Then she smiles, and it's like the sun coming out.

"I'm Sophie." As she introduces herself in that melodious voice, my cock twitches again. Something it shouldn't be doing. I might be VP, but I'm still bound by the promise we'd all be hands-off, and in my role I should be the one championing that instruction and making sure others toe the line. But I can't help wondering whether her woman bits still work. Then, to get my mind to matters higher than my crotch, I correct her.

"Wheels." I laugh. "You've got a club name now, and I reckon it's going to stick."

"That's sick," she spits out, and her smile fades. "I'm a person, not this bloody chair I'm stuck in."

I shake my head, knowing the boys too well. "Take it as a compliment, woman. A club name is a sign of acceptance in our world."

Her deep indrawn breath advises me she still doesn't like it. "Some fucking compliment," she adds, half under her breath so I only just catch it. The thought that there's still some spirit there in her broken body causes the corners of my mouth to turn up.

We arrive at the block I'd gotten prepared for them—they'll have it to themselves as it's used for officer accommodation when we have visiting chapters. Marsh rushes ahead, and dropping the bags for a moment extracts a key from his pocket and unlocks the main door. It's a two-room suite, both with adjacent bathrooms and a small living room in the middle. It would have been one of the most expensive in the old days, but now I reckon it will do for them both. The prospect brings the luggage in and then leaves.

"I've put you in together, but if you want to live separate, Horse, just let me know. I wasn't sure what you'd want." Suddenly I realise I don't like the fact he's going to be staying so close to her, and wonder what exactly the relationship between them.

"No, man, I'm happy with this for now. I'd like to keep Sophie company for the moment at least. That okay with you, Soph?" He would like the arrangement, wouldn't he? But then it comes back to me how he's lost his wife. Fuck, I should have more compassion. My face starts to relax as I remember Horse is probably the one man I could trust to keep his hands off of her. Probably. He's still human after all.

She's looking into the suite, noticing the two bedroom doors are open, and that there's the basic set up of a bed and cupboards and drawers for clothes and shit inside. I don't have to wait long for her reply. "Yeah, this will suit me fine. Thank you." Her voice sounds a little lost now, reminding me staying in a biker club is something she hadn't expected.

But I can't resist. "You're welcome, Wheels." I grin at the glare she tosses my way as she quickly turns her head around. Ignoring her, I continue, "There's food in the kitchen back at the clubhouse—just help yourselves. Sometimes the ol' ladies cook for everyone. If you're handy in the kitchen, you might want to help out, but there's no pressure there."

"Thanks, Wraith."

I nod at Horse. "Okay, I'll leave you to get settled. Don't forget that beer, Horse." I want to hang around, start to get to know her better, but try as I can, I can't think of any excuse to linger. I make a mental note to question Horse about her later when he comes down to the bar. So with nothing else for it, I leave them to get settled.

Striding back to the bar I shake my head, trying to rid it of inappropriate thoughts of the woman in the wheelchair, replacing them instead by deliberating how the fuck she's going to fit in with our lifestyle. Not for the first time I worry whether she'll be able to cope. The sweet butts will probably give her hell, and knowing my brothers, they'll be flirting with her even if they remember the boundaries Drummer has set. I curse Horse for not preparing her better; she doesn't have a clue what to expect.

Nearing the clubhouse and despite my best intentions, my thoughts sink lower once more. When I was pushing her wheelchair? Well, it gave me a glimpse of her cleavage, and the memory of the sight now has me sporting a hard-on. As I wonder whether her breasts were natural or enhanced, again I find myself considering just how much her disability affects her in that department.

After taking the necessary moment to adjust myself before going inside, I find Marsh is already back behind the bar, and as soon as he sees me has a beer ready and waiting. I sense he wants the patch as soon as possible, anxious as he is to please his VP or prez at every turn.

I take the beer, throw him a scowl as though he took too long to serve me, and turn to my brother, who's come up alongside. "Good one, Viper. Wheels! She hates it by the way."

As he laughs, I get a fist to my arm from another brother. "Got her settled?"

"Yeah, Peg. Well, I took them up there. Horse will see she's got what she needs. It's his responsibility, isn't it?"

"He tappin' that?"

I shake my head, hoping it's not just wishful thinking, but there was no sign of them being particularly intimate. "I doubt it. Just doing his good deed I reckon. Where's Drum?" I change the subject, not wanting to torture myself wondering just what the English couple might be getting up to in the suite.

Peg gives a hearty laugh. "Gone off with Pussy."

Well, that will be the last we'll see of him tonight, but if any brother walks past his room, doubtful the last they'll hear. Pussy's quite a screamer, and Drum certainly knows how to make her screech.

I shoot the shit for a while and can hardly suppress my sigh of relief when it's only a few minutes before Horse joins us. Hank and Marsh fall over themselves to get our visitor a drink, and it's not long before he's got a crowd around him, all pressing him for information about the woman he's brought to seek sanctuary in our clubhouse. It seems I'm not the only one to be intrigued by her.

"What's her story?" Peg doesn't give him much time even to sip his drink before he starts his interrogation, which isn't at all surprising if you think about it. "She ever gonna walk again? That wheelchair is a bit basic. It's not even motorised."

Horse swigs his beer—he looks like he needs it—then turns to Peg, but his voice is loud enough so we can all hear. "You see that video?" As the murmurs of confirmation come to him, he continues, "Well she's lost her left leg below the knee, and her right one is pretty busted up. She's got crutches, and I gather she's supposed to try to use them, but honestly? I think she's given up. That wheelchair is just a simple model as it's only meant to be temporary. She got minimal compensation as far as I can work out, as they didn't find the bastard who did that to her."

Peg's frowning. "She's got a prosthesis?"

"Yeah."

"She's got a snatch? That's all I care."

"Tongue!" I swing around snarling, curling my fingers into my palms to stop myself from hitting him. "She's off fuckin' limits. And that means to you and your namesake too! And that goes for the rest of you fuckers!" I'm incensed at the thought of any of my brothers touching her. Well, we're all under instructions from Drummer, aren't we? There's a general murmur of discontent, but they all knew the score. I have some sympathy—it had been easier to agree to be hands-off before we saw what we were dealing with.

"Hey, Horse! Been a long time, fucker!" The new voice puts a frown on my face, being one I'm not particularly pleased to hear. My fingers curl into my hands as I turn, then, before Buster can get into it with Horse, I grab hold of his arm and lead him outside.

My hands have formed fists again and I'm itching to use them. "You fuckin' missed church. Again!" I don't like this motherfucker and I'm done pretending.

"What the fuck? Church was Friday. It's Tuesday, you been samplin' the product or somethin'?" Buster sneers out, showing no respect for his VP.

This time I do let a punch fly. To accuse me of that when he knows my own sister died from an overdose is a step too far. As he stumbles backwards, I yell at him, "Check your phone, fucker. You've got no fuckin' excuse. You missed a text from Drummer. It was an emergency church today!"

Any other man might have pulled his phone out and checked. Buster doesn't, and the smirk he can't quite keep from his face shows me the message had been received, understood, and ignored. Christ, my dislike is turning to outright hatred, even though he's one of my brothers. Something about him just rubs me up the wrong way. Instead of making any apology he starts to draw back his arm. *Oh no, you're not going there, are you?* I flex my muscles. *Bring it on.* Before he can prepare himself I hit him hard in the stomach.

He goes to retaliate but he doesn't get a chance to let loose, as Peg, who's followed us out, grabs him from behind. "Drummer will want an explanation tomorrow as well," he snarls. "You've taken one from the VP, it might not be the last. Now suck it up like a man."

Buster's arm falls back to his side, but if looks carried any weight I'd be the one staggering back by now. I take it the feeling between us is pretty mutual, and I won't be losing any sleep over that.

With a careful eye on Buster, but confident Peg's watching my back, I turn towards the door, shouting a 'goodnight' over my shoulder. It's late, and I decide to call it a night. I can't be bothered with a club whore tonight—they're pretty much being used from what I saw earlier, and for some reason, even if there was one available I doubt she could interest me. Instead, I decide to go back to my room where I might take myself in hand in the shower, with thoughts of a cute blond-haired woman in my mind.

CHAPTER 5
Sophie

To say this place overwhelms me is an understatement. When Horse said he'd take me somewhere where I'd be safe and protected, I never thought I'd end up in a real-life biker club. Bloody hell! Waking next morning and remembering my introduction to their clubhouse, I'm not certain whether I'm dreaming or have been dumped into a nightmare. How the hell did I end up on the set of *Sons of Anarchy*?

All these men, most surprisingly good looking and built, though admittedly some a bit rougher around the edges than others—well, the old Sophie would have been in her element. But the new damaged version? She's justifiably scared. With restricted movement, I'm helpless, and the wheelchair I have to use makes me feel small and defenceless. What do I know of these people? Only that they're bikers living on the edge. What if any of them decided to take advantage of me?

Dragging myself out of bed, trying to shake off the jet lag from the seven-hour time difference between here and England, I shower and dress, the whole process necessarily made more lengthy by my disability. As I get ready for the day, I think more about the men I met briefly yesterday, still not able to believe the intention is they are going to be my companions for the foreseeable future.

And Wheels! Who would denigrate a disabled person by giving them such a despicable handle? Presumably, men who think it's funny. I certainly don't.

I pause in the middle of pulling on my jeans. The man who'd brought Horse and me to our suite, he's particularly good-looking and seemed pleasant enough—except even he insisted on calling me that godawful name. My eyebrows pull together as I try to bring his features back to mind. He has a beard, which I didn't think I'd like but which seems to suit him, shaggy dark blonde hair tied up in a man bun, and gold stud earrings in both ears. I'd noticed him standing at the bar, his face had been quick to darken in anger when he thought the others were crowding me, but seemed just as fast to beam with a welcoming smile which transformed him to beyond handsome. Even though I believed I'd become immune to such things, for the first time since my accident his proximity caused a flicker of excitement inside, the likes of which I never expected to flame again.

Resuming pulling the denim over my good leg, then feeding my stump through, the thought I wasn't completely immune from womanly feelings makes me want to cry. There's fuck all point in feeling any sort of attraction. Why would any man who wasn't desperate want to lumber himself with an inconvenience like me? And especially not now that I've seen what else is on offer—the other women in the club, they were stunning, if in a slutty kind of way. And most important of all, they each had two good legs that they could wrap tight around a man. Just like I used to do.

My hands ball in frustration, and then I hit the sides of my wheelchair with my palms. I hate the darn thing; hate everything that was taken away from me. Life's cruel to have brought me here. If it weren't for Zoe, perhaps I should have taken my chances or just let Ethan finish what he started.

Maybe it would be better to be dead than only half alive. What kind of life is this? It wasn't fair of Horse, plonking me down in the middle of a club filled with enough eye-catching men that I feel like a starving person wearing a gag at a banquet. Quickly cursing my hormones for causing physical reactions I've no chance of following up, I angrily wipe a stray tear from my eye.

A knock on the door startles me, dragging me out of my dark thoughts.

"Hey, Soph. You up yet?"

"Yeah, come on in, Horse. I'm decent." Decent. Yup. Jeans or jogging bottoms are all I wear now, hiding what I've lost from prying eyes. The short skirts and shorts the other girls were wearing last night are things of the past for me, mind you, even the old Sophie would never have gone to the extremes they had. Honest-to-goodness, their arses were hanging out under those skimpy skirts.

"You feeling alright?" His brow furrows as he picks up I might not have woken up in a particularly good mood.

I want to rail at him, berate him for bringing me here, but luckily my brain catches up, and I recognise he's done his best, getting me out of the country to a place that *he* thinks is safe, though I have my suspicions it's anything but.

Truthfully, Horse has been great. He makes no fuss about my disability, just gets on coping with it pragmatically in a way I can't seem to do. To give him his due, he's not once made me feel on edge or embarrassed around him, and has been quick to my defence when others do so, as demonstrated by his concern for my dignity at the airport.

So I decide to go easy on him. It's not his fault I feel so out of my depth, he's doing his best. "Okay, I guess."

I won't tell him the about the usual nightmare which had me waking, sweating, and panicking in the small hours. After the past months, I'm getting used to that. The sound of metal hitting flesh echoing through my head, lying helpless on the ground seeing the car stop and come back towards me again, hearing the shouts and screams of the onlookers; the dream that's hard to shake off even when I awake. It doesn't help give me a positive outlook when morning comes.

To get it out of my mind, I decide it's time to get some answers. "Horse, you've brought me to a fucking biker club for goodness sake! How the hell am I'm going to fit in here? How long will I be staying?" Part of me still hangs onto the hope this was just a stopover, and he's actually going to be taking me on somewhere else.

He heaves a sigh, then comes and sits down on my bed. I wheel over and position myself in front of him. Raising his eyes, he looks into mine and then takes my hands in his. "You're at the Satan's Devils clubhouse," he starts. "I usually spend six months of the year in the States. As you know, I'm an artist; my medium is airbrushing. Seems my skills are quite in demand. While I'm here, I use the clubhouse as my base and travel all over doing motorcycles, helmets, cars, you name it, and for the right price, I'll do it."

I nod, from what he's already told me of his occupation and the examples of his work I can see how his skills would be popular.

"Anyway," he continues, "I was due to come over next month. But having met that rather unpleasant gentleman, Hargreaves, I knew we had to get away fast. Just seemed to make sense if I could come a bit earlier this year, as it would be a good place for you to hide out for a bit. If Ethan's got the reach he's known for, then you couldn't be in a better place." He pauses and the creases on his forehead become more defined. After a moment, his lips curl up slightly. "I guess I didn't give much thought to how you'd fit here, just seemed a convenient place to bring you. I can see how it might seem a bit alarming to you at first, but know this, Soph — if you're good to the men they'll protect you with their lives."

Now I draw back, pulling my hands out of his. It seems my worst nightmare wasn't the one I had during the night. As a wave of panic floods through me, I repeat in a soft whisper, "If I'm good?" Then it hits me. "You expect me to act like one of those women last night?" Fuck, I saw one of them sucking a man off right there in the clubhouse. "What the hell have you got me into here, Horse?"

"No, no!" Horse stands and quickly waves his palms towards me in dismissal. "I didn't mean like that. You're not here as a club whore. Fuck no." He runs his hands over his head, and there's that familiar gesture again as he pinches his nose. "Hell, Sophie. All I meant was you shouldn't make waves, cause any trouble. And above all, keep your mouth shut about the club and anything that goes on here." He paces for a moment, then comes back, and putting his massive hands on the arms of my chair leans over. "I've taken responsibility for you, Soph. And these boys take that very seriously. If you said anything to the wrong person, then it would be on my back."

I gasp. He's taken responsibility for me? What exactly does that mean? And why and what has to be kept so secret? After staring up at his massive frame for a moment, it suddenly drops into place. My eyes narrow as it dawns on me. "I take it what they do isn't exactly legal?" They might be even closer to the Sons of Anarchy than I first thought.

Now his eyes fix on mine so forcefully I wish I could move away. "I'm telling you, anything you see, anything you hear, is none of your fucking business. Got it?"

His abruptness has shocked me, but has got the message through. I nod, my mouth gaping.

He stands, pulls down the cuffs of his shirt, an automatic action giving his hands something to do, and in a calmer voice he tries to explain, "Soph, I couldn't leave you in England, it wasn't safe. St John-Davies is a real threat. Christ, if you'd seen what he'd done to your friend when she turned up at Josh's garage… then you'd understand."

"Tell me, Horse." I obviously hadn't been told the full story before.

I can see he's reluctant to share the details, but then, as his shoulders slump he realises he has to. "Her wrist was broken—she'd bound it with vet wrap that you use for dogs for God's sake, and was too frightened to get medical attention. Her nose looked broken, and both her eyes were blackened, though she'd done well to disguise them. I don't know how old she was, but she walked like a fucking old woman, Soph. He'd given her a vicious beating."

My hand goes over my mouth. Oh Zoe, how could you let it get that far? I voice my thoughts out loud, "Why didn't she leave him before? I hadn't heard from her for months. I'd have helped her…"

"He's got a very long reach, Soph. Drummer's been digging and has found some stuff out about him. I think she waited until she had no other choice, when it was either make an attempt to escape or stay and quite possibly end up dead."

"But he couldn't get away with murder…"

"He got away with your accident." Horse's voice is rising again. "And he could likely get away with killing someone. He's well protected, Soph. Don't underestimate him."

If the purpose of Horse's little pep talk was to frighten me, that's precisely what he's achieved. While I might not be hugely enamoured of my temporary home, the picture he's painted makes the alternative decidedly unattractive.

He gives me a few moments to process what he's told me, then his tone lightens. "I don't know about you, but we didn't get much to eat yesterday; airline food sucks. Now, shall we go and see what passes for breakfast here? With luck one of the old ladies will be cooking."

Actually, I'd much rather stay here hidden in my room, but if I'm going to be stuck here for months, maybe I ought to make an effort and at least get out to take note of my surroundings. It was dark when we came to the suite. Then the strangeness of his words sink in. "Old ladies? Do they do the work around here?" I ask, raising my eyebrows. I'm surprised—doesn't seem the kind of place where old women would want to be employed. All at once I have a vision in my head of elderly grandmothers all standing around a stove with leather-clad bikers urging them on.

He barks a hearty laugh and my eyes crease as I can't see the joke. "No, love. An old lady is akin to a wife in the biker world. When a biker commits to a girl, they become known as his old lady, whatever their age."

Now I scrunch up my face in disgust. "What a horrible term." I'd hate to be called anyone's old lady.

"Babe, you've got a lot to learn." He shakes his head, still chortling. "To have one of these men give a girl that title, well, it's a real honour, and in the biker world, at least equivalent to, if not more of a commitment than marriage."

For a moment I wonder whether the scantily-dressed girls I saw last night are old ladies, and whether their biker men are happy with them having it all out on show. Then I shrug, that's none of my business.

"Are you a member of the club, Horse?" I realise I haven't seen him wearing a cut.

"Not really. They made me an honorary member out of respect for what I do for them, but I've not got the patch," he explains patiently. Though the way he's fidgeting on his feet suggests he probably wants to head out for some breakfast.

But while he's in a talkative mood I take advantage. "Have you got an old lady?"

His face tightens, and I realise I've touched a nerve. "No. Not anymore." And I know I won't be getting anything else out of him when he adds, "Breakfast. Now." Without waiting for my agreement, he moves behind me and starts pushing my chair. Now this is what I absolutely hate, people thinking they can literally push me around without me having any say in the matter.

"I've got this," I tell him firmly while putting my hands on the wheels and starting to propel myself.

It doesn't take long to get back to the clubhouse and, as there's a slight downhill to it, wheeling myself gives me no problem at all. The surface is good, so I'm able to glance around, interested to see the remains of the old resort the man called Wraith had described. The majority of the blocks have been repaired or rebuilt while others remain burnt-out shells. As the wheels turn smoothly over the ground, I'm glad to note I shouldn't have too much problem getting around by myself. One plus, I won't have to rely on other people.

Once I've taken in the view, I have another question for Horse. "I don't know what I'll be doing here, Horse, but I usually spend my time reading. Is there Wi-Fi here, do you think? I'd like to download some books and stuff." My life is so boring nowadays, I live vicariously through that of the characters in my books.

"You'll have to talk to Mouse, he's the computer guru here. He'll tell you what you can and can't do to avoid leaving a digital trail."

And now we're at the clubhouse, and even before we enter I catch the welcoming waft of bacon cooking in the air, and immediately my mouth starts to water. Horse was right, I hadn't eaten much the day before. Food always seems to taste better when someone else cooks it, so to my surprise, and for lately quite unusually, I start feeling hungry. Horse points the way to the kitchen, and I turn my wheelchair in that direction. Inside we find a pretty-looking girl, about my age, and a small child running around getting under her feet. She looks up tiredly as we enter, then her face widens into a broad smile.

"Hey," she greets us, "you must be Wheels. I've heard about you." She's tall, about five-foot-nine I'd guess. She's wearing a flowing cream blouse over leggings which have a seascape printed on them. Her auburn hair is tied up in a messy bun with strands escaping to frame a face reddened from the heat of the stove.

"Sophie," I correct her while wondering whether I should just give up and accept my acquired moniker.

After using a towel, she comes over and stretches a hand out to me. I reciprocate and raise mine to shake. "I'm Crystal," she introduces herself. "My man's Heart, and this is our daughter, Amy." She glances around and spots her child under the large table that is in the centre of the room. "Amy, come here and say hi to our guests."

A sweet-looking little girl who must be around two to three years old runs over and hugs her mother's legs, then peers out from behind. "Hi," comes out in a shy little voice.

I'm not particularly good with children, but I summon a smile and respond, "Hi, Amy."

A little hand comes out and a finger points at me. "Why you in a stroller? Mommy, isn't the lady too big for a stroller?"

"Hush, child, don't be rude." Crystal admonishes her.

The unexpected innocent question makes me laugh. "My legs don't work, Amy," I begin, making the explanation simple for her. "I'm in a buggy as I can't walk."

"Oh." She stares at me for a second as if she's having difficulty understanding that, and then quickly becoming bored, runs to the other side of the kitchen where she's got some kind of toy oven set up. Incongruously, there's a toy motorcycle poking out of a small saucepan.

Crystal looks at me and laughs. "Trust kids to be up front about things. Now, would you like some eggs and bacon? I've got waffles as well, and coffee."

"Coffee!" I giggle at the desperation in my voice, and taking pity on me, Crystal makes sure I soon have a mug of the life-giving nectar in my hand before going back to her tasks our entrance had interrupted.

Breakfast turns out to be delicious, and there's plenty of it. Necessary as while I start munching away various men wander in, some just filling plates and taking them off with them; others joining us and eating at the table. The banter around is light-hearted, and I sit, soaking it all up, wanting to know as much about this strange band of men as I can.

I recognise Dart as being one of the men who picked us up from the airport, and his friendly wink and easy grin encourage me to ask something I'm curious about. "What's with the strange names?"

The corners of his mouth turn up even more. "They're road names. When members get patched in the club gives them a name."

"So Dart's not your real name?"

He laughs and shakes his head.

I think for a moment, but I can't work out what it means. As my brow creases in confusion, my distinct lack of comprehension causes a ripple of laughter from those seated around the table. Then Dart stands, pulls out the tie holding his hair back, and dark wavy locks surround him, reaching well below his shoulders, making him look like an actor playing Charles the Second or similar. Then he waves his hand and makes a flourishing deep bow. "D'Artagnan at your service, ma'am."

It takes a second for the penny to drop, and then I realise he does look exactly his namesake in the old films I've seen. The old Sophie can't resist. "And how are your sword skills, then?"

"My sword is yours to command, and I assure you I'm excellent at usin' it." He adds a suggestive wink and clutches his crotch to leave me in absolutely no doubt as to his meaning.

Loud guffaws greet his display, and I'm bemused at such a blatant flirtation at the breakfast table. I've never met men so open about their sexuality before.

"I'm Tongue," another man introduces himself with a face-splitting grin. "Want to take a guess?"

"I'm afraid to ask." I'm already blushing.

Just as I suspected, he sticks out his tongue and waggles it. The metal stud piercing is clear to see. Hmm, I don't need him to draw a picture of what he uses that for!

I feel my cheeks growing red as I'm not too sure I want any further explanations. Crystal walks over and rests her hand on the shoulder of another man, who's made from the same mold as the others—tall, muscular, with a good-looking face. "Heart." She pats his shoulder as she introduces him, the love and affection apparent in both her expression and voice. "He's my husband, and he's got a huge, great fuckin' heart."

In a romance novel it would be an 'Awww' moment, but in real life, this admittedly handsome but fierce looking man doesn't look like he'd be giving his spare change to charity, but rather protecting his own with everything he's got. But I can see how aptly he's named when little Amy decides to come over at that moment, leaps on his lap, and tugs on his beard to get his attention. His face softens, and when one arm holds onto the child tight, and the other goes around his wife's waist, the love he has for them both comes shining through. Yup, Heart suits him.

"What about you, Horse?" Crystal throws out the question.

I cover my mouth with my hand, wondering how Horse will phrase his response.

He doesn't crack the smile I expected, just glances up and says matter-of-factly, "No mystery there, my surname's Horseman."

Oh! Shit! Now my head drops down into my hands, and as I feel my cheeks start to glow I peer at him over the top of my fingers. He barks a laugh towards me then pulls the plate of bacon towards him. I make a mental note never to make assumptions about names ever again.

Conversation falters as we get down to the business of eating all the sumptuous food Crystal had prepared, but when I've finished all I can stuff down without feeling uncomfortable, I look round the table again, remembering the name of their president. "How did Drummer get his name?"

There are grins all around, then almost as one, they all shout together, "Because he bangs everythin' in sight!" Then they simultaneously start slamming their meaty fists down on the table, making a thunderous sound. I look anxiously at Amy, still cuddled on her father's lap, but she's grinning and laughing and joining in, her little hand slapping the table as hard as she can. I'm hoping she doesn't get the joke.

It seems I'm not the only one to have completed their meal. As though it was a sign, the men stand, collect their plates, and take them over to the sink area where Crystal starts rinsing and stacking the dishes into the dishwasher. Breakfast is over. There's a kernel of disappointment inside that I haven't seen Wraith this morning. A small frown takes over from my smile as I wonder whether he's still tucked up in bed with one of the women I saw here last night.

"Earth to Sophie." As Horse looks at me with an expression of amusement on his face, I give a wry shrug and again smile. I'd been lost in my thoughts for a moment, thinking things I had no business thinking. Once he's got my attention he carries on,

"You mentioned the president. He's asked to see you this morning. Ready for it now?"

I didn't expect to get an invite to see the president. Was it just good manners to welcome me? I suck in my cheeks as Horse's words come back to me—no, it's probably a warning to keep my mouth shut about the club. To give Horse a response, I nod, though admit to feeling a touch of anxiety. The man in charge of these unruly men has to be a force to be reckoned with.

Having learned his lesson, Horse leads the way to the office used by Drummer, president of the Satan's Devils, leaving me to get there under my own steam. He knocks on the door, and a gruff voice invites us in. Horse steps back, letting me enter first.

Drummer is sitting behind an impressive-looking desk. On the wall at his back is a big flag with the logo of the club, three little devils all holding pitchforks. A dark figure hovering behind them is carrying a scythe. It's a gruesome image, bad enough on their cuts, but almost chilling in large scale and full technicolour.

Although I'd met him briefly the night before, power just oozes off this man now that I'm seeing him in his domain, and I sense an attack of nerves coming on like a naughty schoolgirl brought in front of the headteacher. My mouth goes dry, and I'm glad I've already eaten, as my appetite would have faded if I'd met him first.

It seems like hours that Drummer levels an assessing stare at me, and I start shrinking under the intense gaze of his steely grey eyes, which seem to see right into my soul. I bite my tongue to stop myself shouting out, 'it wasn't me!' but then his features relax, laughter lines—which on him are more likely to be called scowl lines—appear as his thin lips widen into a smile. "Mornin' Wheels. Your room alright for ya?" He adds a wink to the question.

Yup, the name's stuck, and this is the last person I'd have the guts to contradict, so I shrug off my annoyance and just reply, "Fine, thank you. I've got everything I need." Then, as my innate politeness rises to the fore I remember to add, "And thank you for having me here."

"Why, ain't you got pretty English manners there? And it's a pleasure, darlin'."

As he replies I study him. He appears to be in his late thirties or early forties. His dark hair is already greying at the temples, and he has a salt-and-pepper short but tidy beard. His nose is slightly crooked as though it was broken at some point, and his skin is brown and weathered, probably due to riding in the hot Arizona sun. There's a rugged beauty about him—when he smiles he's an attractive man. Though the way he holds himself, as though he's poised to jump into action, suggests he's not a man anyone would want to cross.

He continues to subject me to an examination of his own, but instead of asking anything personal, talks about the accommodation. "Yer room's probably not as fancy as you'd like, but hopefully clean. Otherwise, the fuckin' prospects are in deep shit."

I don't want anyone getting into trouble on my behalf, even though in all truth the sink could have been a bit cleaner. "It's fine, honestly." I note my vocabulary seems sadly lacking today.

"Good." He gives a slow nod then turns and indicates a man who I hadn't even noticed is in the room, such is the president's presence. "Let me introduce you. This is Mouse."

The computer guru. I'd wanted to meet him. But his name clearly comes from what he does. I'd been imagining a small, quiet man, and in the flesh, Mouse in no way resembles my mental image. His slightly darker skin and black hair suggests he's of some sort of mixed heritage. Like most of the other men here, he's big, almost as tall as Horse, but a bit slimmer. But like every other man I've seen so far, his build is all muscle, not fat. God these people must work out! Swallowing down saliva that's unexpectedly come into my mouth, I nod at the man I've just been introduced to.

"Mouse is our computer man." Becoming conscious Drummer's speaking again, I pull my attention back to him. "He's found out some stuff about this St John-Davies dude that I think you'd do well to hear."

Forgetting my nerves in the light of this revelation, I pull myself up straighter and lean forward, my eyes flicking between Mouse and Drummer. "What do you know?"

Mouse indicates the two chairs in front of the desk, and as Drummer nods both Horse and computer man sit down. I suddenly find the air less difficult to breathe when I no longer have two enormous men hovering over me.

Looking first at his president, and then at me, he throws a question out into the air. "Do you know what the dark web is?"

I shake my head. Drummer is looking smug, Horse is looking as mystified as I am.

"Okay, well, so there's the dark web, and the deep web," Mouse starts his explanation. "Now, IP addresses. The IP address is a string of numbers by which anythin' connected to the internet can be found. Your computer would have its own IP. If I had a website and you visited it, normally I'd be able to see which IP addresses, and thereby computers, had accessed my site, and likewise, you'd enter my website via its IP. Most IPs you'd come across are easy to find—you can search for them on Google or Bing or any of the other search engines." He pauses to check we're with him so far. "Now there's a huge fuckin' number of IPs you'd never come across. People using the dark or deep web hide their IP addresses so you can't look them up, and it's virtually impossible to find them. Unless you know what you're doin', that is." He pauses to smirk, which suggests he does. "Normally on the deep web this isn't for any nefarious purpose—banks use it to store your account details or companies for their intranets. But the dark web, well, that's where all the black deeds are done. Drugs, arms...and any types of services can be bought on the dark web, with only a few people bein' any the wiser."

"Mouse knows his way around the dark web," Drummer tosses in, sounding full of pride.

Useful, I would think, considering some of what I suspect the club is involved in.

Mouse throws a grateful nod at his president before resuming, "Yes, I do, and I check it regularly. What for is club business. But yesterday I picked up somethin' interestin'."

Club business? My suspicions about their illegal activities seem to be confirmed. Drugs and arms? I suppress a shudder, realising I don't want to know. It becomes clear these are the type of things Horse is warning me to keep my mouth shut about. I'm certainly not going to ask them to clarify. Deciding to stay away from dangerous topics and wanting to get things back on track, I prompt, "You've found something about Ethan?" I can think of no other reason why this discussion would involve me.

"About you, actually."

"Me?" My voice comes out as a squeak. What would anything on the dark web have to do with me?

The slow bobbing of his head accompanies his words. "Yes, I'm afraid so." He pauses to glance at Drummer, as if querying whether he should be the one to tell me what is looking like is going to be bad news. The president dips his chin towards Mouse, so it's the computer man who enlightens me. "There's a fuckin' contract out on you, Wheels."

"A contract to kill me?" I hold my breath and feel an icy shiver down my spine and goosebumps rising on my skin. God, Zoe, what kind of man did you get tangled up with?

Horse's hand reaches out to touch mine and gives it a squeeze.

My eyes are still fixed on Mouse, and I only exhale when he gives a quick shake of his head and hurries to reassure me. "Not at the moment. They want you located and presumably taken."

"Ethan St John-Davies, he's behind this?"

"That's the assumption we're makin'," Drummer butts in. "The identification of the person behind it is hidden, Wheels, but if there's anyone fuckin' else after you, we need to know."

I'm what I would have classed as an ordinary woman. I am, or was, a fashion buyer for God's sake, and a fairly lowly one at that, and probably now unemployed. I'm disabled in a wheelchair. I am not the type of person who'd have a contract put out on them! My mouth falls open, and although I'm ashamed to admit it, tears are pricking at the back of my eyes. *Why, why the fuck me?*

I come up with the only answer I can. "I've got to go to the police and tell them."

You'd have thought I'd used the dirtiest swear word possible from their reaction. All three men sit back and glare at me with a look of horror on their faces. "No fuckin' way are you bringin' the heat down on us," Drummer states firmly. "Your St John-Davies has the English police in his pocket. Horse tells us you found that out for yourself when they botched the investigation of the hit and run which injured you. Who knows how far his reach is here? And how are you gonna reveal how you know about the contract on you without givin' away Mouse and the rest of us? I won't fuckin' have us dragged into it. The police will not be involved, nor any other authority."

His obvious anger at the thought shows I don't have any choice in the matter. But I don't know what else I can do, so in a quiet voice overflowing with dejection I tell him so.

Drummer, for all his authority and daunting presence, changes expression. His features soften, and a look of understanding and compassion covers his face. "You're safe, Wheels, no one knows you're here."

"They can trace her to the airport." Horse speaks for the first time, frowning as he realises we must have left a trail.

"Easily, yes, she used her own passport." As I shudder and begin to doubt Drummer's soothing words, Mouse continues, "But Dart and Slick weren't wearin' their cuts in the airport."

"They could still recognise them." Horse remains concerned.

"They could," Mouse grins widely, "if the security cameras hadn't suffered a virus about the time you arrived. It took them half a day to get the bug out of their system."

At my look of incomprehension he continues, "Knowin' you wouldn't want your whereabouts broadcasted, Wheels, we took certain precautions when Horse said he was bringin' you here. It seemed a bit over the top and paranoid at the time, but I do like playin' with my toys. Worked to the good this time. No one knows you're here, and the last place anyone would search for a woman in a wheelchair is a biker compound."

My head slumps down into my hands. I can only hope he knows what he's talking about and that he's right.

CHAPTER 6
Wraith

Last night I jerked off to thoughts of the captivating woman in the wheelchair. This morning I wake up determined I'm not going to act on the strange attraction I feel towards her. Not only is she out of bounds to all us fuckers, but I'm a one and done type of guy, rarely, if ever, going back for seconds unless it's with the sweet butts who know the score, or who should. Briefly, I remember how Chrissy seems to think she's exclusive with me, and knowing that, I've got to shut that shit down fast. She's got nothing special over the other girls, and it certainly wasn't her I was thinking about in my shower. *Uh uh.* It will be no loss if I steer clear of her from now on. With the variety of pussy we get around the club, there's no need to tie myself to one person. And that's why I've got to put the Englishwoman well out of my mind. Someone like her, well, she wouldn't expect to be kicked out of my bed to be replaced with someone else the next night.

So while I didn't consciously avoid Wheels at breakfast—I'd been in a meeting with Drummer and Mouse at the time—it was a good opportunity to keep my distance. The less I'm around her, the less I'll be tempted.

I'm not going to be able to duck her for long though. She's going to be around the clubhouse for the next few months, so the sooner my cock gets the message she's off limits the fucking better. And there it goes. As soon as I fucking see her wheeling herself out of Drummer's office and back into the clubroom I feel myself swelling just at the sight of her. What the fuck is wrong with me?

While a particular part of me wants to get up close and personal, I force myself to stay leaning at the bar, observing instead of approaching. She's gone as white as a fucking sheet, paler even than I noticed last night, and it's not hard to fathom why. Prez had updated me earlier, and I didn't see the necessity to crowd the room by staying and hearing it all over again, nor risk in front of Drum getting the predictable hard-on being in her presence would cause; he'd give me fucking shit for that.

Putting my strange sexual attraction aside, this whole business is worrying. Mouse's ability to access the dark web is one of the reasons he's so important to us. Fuck, we make good use of it ourselves for club business, so I'm acutely aware of the dangers lurking beneath the surface of the internet and the bottom dwellers that skulk there—the type regular citizens like her would be in total ignorance of. She's staring vacantly ahead as she enters the main room; my features tighten and I feel anger growing on her behalf. Not only has she suffered such devastating injuries, but now she's being hunted by people who, without our protection, would quickly find and destroy her. And all because she did what any of us would do—she helped a friend.

But what's this going to do to the club? As VP, that should be my primary concern. At the moment there's only Drummer, Mouse, and myself who are aware of this latest development, but at the next church we'll bring all members up to speed. Knowing my brothers, the now real confirmed threat against her will only strengthen their resolve to offer her protection. But we have to consider the risk to ourselves. Fuck knows what shit this might bring down on our heads.

Horse has planted her by a table and is approaching the bar with the obvious intention of getting her a drink. My eyes move from her and track him, only out of idle interest, and I see him stop halfway and answer his phone. I don't hear his side of the conversation, and his expressions are hard to read. But as he glances back to his companion quickly before he's resuming the conversation, I gather it's got something to do with her.

Once finished, he continues to the bar and waves Hank over, heaving a heavy sigh as he does so.

His tight expression makes me ask, "Problems?"

Leaning forwards with his elbows on the bar, he turns his head. "No, not really. Well, it wouldn't normally be an issue. Word's got around pretty fast that I'm back and I've been offered a rush job in Vegas. Someone dropped his bike and wants the decal restored. Before next Saturday!"

"Huh. Weekend biker."

He gives a small grin. "Yup. I did the original paint job for him last year. I just didn't expect to get work this early." Again he throws a look over his shoulder to the woman in the wheel-chair.

I realise immediately where his problem lies. "You don't want to leave Wheels alone?"

Lifting up his hands and putting them down again in a 'what can I do' gesture, he replies, "I'd hoped to be here to help her settle in. She's shit scared of what I've brought her to." He sighs. "But the work would be good. Especially if I get exposure at the Vegas rally, but I don't like the thought of leaving her alone, not just yet. I knew I'd have to, but she's out of her depth, hasn't settled in, and on top of that she'd just been given some devastating news."

I throw him a quick nod, enough to let him know I've already heard about the contract out on her. "How's she takin' it?"

He heaves a sigh and shrugs. "Just like you'd expect. She's scared stiff. Despite St John-Davies' henchman paying her a visit, I don't think she believed he was so serious about finding her." He nods at Marsh and orders two coffees and two brandy shots to go along with them. "From what Josh told me about her friend, Zoe Baker, and the lengths she'll need to go to keep out of his reach, St John-Davies doesn't like to lose. My reading of it is, whatever the value of Sophie to him, by running she's issued a challenge."

"And he's someone who doesn't like anyone to get the better of him."

"That's my interpretation." Horse winces, agreeing with my assumption.

As Marsh busies himself with the coffee machine I examine Horse. Wondering not for the first time why he's taken Wheels under his wing and, like last night, whether there's more to it. Man's lost his wife, but he could be getting over that by now. And he's reluctant to leave her alone. "You fuckin' her?" I ask him bluntly.

His head shoots around sharply. "No I'm bloody not!" he scoffs. "She needed help and I was in a position to give it to her." He seems disgusted at the very thought. Then he touches his earring, twisting it around in his ear and gives me more. "She reminds me of Carrie, my wife. Not in looks, but that fucking accident. Carrie never had a chance to live her life, Sophie does. I don't want anyone to take that away from her."

The relief that shoots through me when he admits it's only a platonic relationship is out of all fucking proportion. Trying to ignore my irrational reaction, I try to give him some reassurance. "No one knows she's here, I trust Mouse on that, so I don't see a problem with you going to Vegas. I know how you don't like turnin' a client away. We'll look out for her." Thinking quickly, I could put a prospect on her, give her the feeling that she's being protected. And I open my mouth to suggest just that when different words come out before I have a chance to filter them. "If you're worried about leavin' her alone, what if I keep eyes on her for you?" Why the fuck am I offering to do that? Don't I have enough to do as VP without babysitting a cripple? But it's too late to take them back. Horse looks like I've answered his fucking prayers. This job in Vegas must be important to him. "I can't ask you to do that."

"You're not askin', I offered. It will only be for what, a week?"

"Should be, hopefully less. It's too good an opportunity for me to want to miss. I'd like to leave this afternoon if possible, get a head start on estimating how much needs doing." His hand slaps me on the back. "Thanks, Wraith. That would be a load off my mind knowing you're watching out for her." His eyes scan the room that's almost empty this time of day, but I know what he's thinking.

"Drum's scared us all off of her," I assure him. "She's off limits to everyone. No one's gonna take advantage of her."

He shrugs. "Can't help worrying about her. It's more her nervousness about being here than not trusting your brothers."

"Come on," I pick up my drink and help him out by carrying the shots as Horse takes the two coffees, "let's go break the news."

When we get back to the table, I notice Wheels has a little more colour in her face now. Hearing a contract's out on you, particularly for someone like her, must be shattering, but looking at her I can see she's starting to deal with it instead of letting it overwhelm her. But when Horse explains his predicament, her face falls again. She looks down into her coffee laced with brandy, and her lovely sleek blond hair flops forwards over her face. My fingers itch to brush it back.

Horse quickly tries to put her at ease, divulging our solution, and her gorgeous blue eyes come to meet mine. Fuck, I don't think I've seen such expressive orbs before, and they seem to be seeing straight into me.

"You're the vice president, you must have better things to do than watch out for me." She tells me what I already know, her face creasing, but whether she's worried about herself or me, I can't say.

She's right, but I brush it off. "You won't be a bother, and you're safe here, Wheels." Even as I reply, I wonder how true that is. Protected from the man who's trying to find her for sure, but safe from me? My cock starts to grow hard as I wonder about the wisdom of spending extra time with her—it certainly doesn't seem bothered she's missing a leg. The rest of her makes up for that. *But she's off limits, to you, to everyone.*

Horse drains his drink. "It's hopefully only for a few days, Soph. You've met Crystal, and Wraith can introduce you to the other old ladies. They're a good bunch. And I'll be back before you know it."

I can see she's not happy, and it's understandable she'll be uncomfortable and most probably disorientated in an outlaw biker club that has to be so alien to anything she's ever known. But now she impresses me, pulling herself up straighter, showing a little more backbone than I've seen so far, she nods at him. "Horse, don't worry about me. You've got me here safely, I can't ask more than that." Reaching over she puts her hand on his arm. "Now I know about the contract and how far Ethan will go to find me, well, but I think you're right. He'll never think of looking for me here. So thank you. Now you go to Vegas and do your job." She gives him a warm smile and I wish it had been directed at me.

"Well, if that's settled, I'll go get my stuff sorted and be off." His eyes question her.

"Yes, you go, Horse. I'll be fine." Again, the corners of her mouth turn up as she reassures him.

The fact she makes no protest confirms their tentative relationship, and it's clear she doesn't feel placed to make demands on a man she hardly knows. But what he's done for her so far has made her feel comfortable with him, and I've yet to prove myself to her. Subtly I adjust myself under the table. If she gets sight of her very physical effect on me, I doubt I'll get far earning her trust.

Horse finishes his coffee and stands up. He nods his goodbye to her and then beckons to me. "A word?"

Telling her I'll be back shortly, I awkwardly get to my feet and follow him as he takes his empty cup and glass to the bar. These Brits have good manners; I'd leave mine for the prospects to pick up.

I follow Horse around the corner into the games room—in the middle is a pool table and to the side the arcade machines. Only one in use this time of day, and I give a quick grin as I see Adam thump it and swear loudly. Obviously he's not doing well. Adam's the only brother who seems to prefer personal time playing games rather than using the sweet butts. But he's a good man, despite his strange addiction.

A cough brings me back to my companion. After checking we're out of Wheels' line of sight, he passes me a small box and tells me quietly, "These are her painkillers. Only give her them when she needs them. I'd prefer not to leave them with her. Just as a precaution. I'm not certain I trust her. Especially if things get too much now that she knows about this darn contract."

My brows rise as his words sink in. As I realise the implication, I can't help stepping back until I'm able to cast a glance at the woman sitting at the table. A *suicide risk? Fuck, what have I taken on?* Perhaps it's not surprising knowing what she's been—is—going through. At least the thought has the same effect as an icy shower on my cock. Here I am thinking about getting into her pants while she's obviously in her own hell. I make a mental note to keep a careful eye on her, and subtly to let at least some of my brothers know to be aware so they can watch out for her too. Jerking my chin as a signal I understand, Horse turns and leaves.

I watch her as he goes, her eyes tracing his path across the clubroom, her growing tension at the loss of his company palpable.

Essential now, after what he's confided in me, I know I need to make her feel more at ease. Leaving her alone for too long would be a mistake. Returning to the table, I make a suggestion, "Why don't I give you a tour of the place? We're not your average biker club, you know."

A small smile comes to her face. "Not that I would know what that looked like anyway." She laughs softly. "But thanks, Wraith. I'd like to have a look around."

Thinking once again how pretty she is when she smiles, I finish up my beer as she drains her coffee. Having some experience watching one of my brothers in a similar situation, I've noticed she's been wheeling herself and understand it's important not to take her independence away, so I check, "Shall I push, or d'you want to do it yourself?"

Her head tilts to one side as if she's surprised I've asked, then she throws me a grateful nod. "I'll do it myself, thank you."

Without giving myself away, I glance quickly at her bare arms. There's hardly any muscle on them, so I doubt she's done much more than moved her wheelchair around her home up to now. I'll watch for any signs of fatigue and be on hand to help if she needs me. But for the present, I'll let her have her way. She's such a tiny thing; I could pick her up and carry her, no problem. Hmm, that's given my cock ideas now. Fucking thing! But I can't go there. *Uh uh.*

"This way, then." I walk by her side as I take her around to the back of the club. Now we're not bothered about too fancy a site, but over the years we've made real inroads into clearing a lot of the buildings that were too fire damaged to restore, and now there's a good-sized area outside where we have a few fire pits and hold barbeques when the weather's accommodating. And, our pièce de resistance, one of the original three swimming pools in full working order. Kept that way by the prospects of course. Having to clear it of used condoms and bottles after a party isn't much fun.

She halts her wheelchair and turns to look up at me, her eyes wide. "A swimming pool?"

"Yeah, it gets put to good use in the warmer months."

"Wow! I see what you meant about not being a typical biker club."

"Weather will be heatin' up soon; perhaps you'd like to take a dip?"

She huffs as though I've said something stupid. *Fuck, I forgot about her leg.* I keep my thoughts to myself, though I suspect it wouldn't be as much a problem as she'll be thinking it is. Not like the brothers haven't seen that stuff before.

I let her take in the view for a moment, and then indicate another pathway. It's a bit rutted and potholed in places, so I lend a hand to help her manoeuvre over the worst of it. I lead her across to our garage, one of our legitimate businesses, and one which is always busy, either with brothers sneaking in repairs to their bikes or doing paying work for customers. Situated just inside our ten-foot boundary fence, we don't have to let citizens far into the compound when they drop off their vehicles for service. Like any other day, it's buzzing with activity. Slick and Tongue work here, together with Bullet and Rock, and Buster when he can be bothered. *Which reminds me of that conversation I need to have with Drummer about his recent behaviour.*

We pause for a moment as she takes it all in, her first lesson that the club's not all about play. Then I draw in a sharp breath and glower when I see the only man in the club I have a dislike for has downed tools at our approach and coming over with a leer on his face. Hearing a small sound I look down, and I can't miss the way the woman beside me draws back into her chair as he draws closer.

Even the sour look on my face doesn't stop him coming right over to us. "So this is what all the fuckin' fuss is about." He sneers down at her.

"Aren't you supposed to be workin'?" It comes out as a snarl. There's something in his expression I immediately take exception too.

He actually ignores me. "Got a great lookin' rack there, babe, how about you and I getting it on together?"

I want to hit him for noticing. He shouldn't be fucking looking. "Buster, have some fuckin' respect. And get back to work."

"Fuck." He deigns to look at me. "You Tucson boys are on my back the whole fuckin' time. In San D we used to have fun."

"This Tucson boy is your fuckin' VP, Buster. And it's time you remembered that!" I don't like getting riled in front of Wheels. This isn't the nice calm afternoon I had planned for her, but I can't let him get away with disrespect.

He's got a fucking death wish or something. He just doesn't get the message. "I'll come find you later, shall I? You and I get to know each other better, babe?"

While I'm taking in a breath to blast him with my thoughts on that matter, Wheels answers for herself. The words are directed at him, but there's a message for me there too.

"Sorry, Buster," her words say one thing though she doesn't sound particularly apologetic as she pauses to wave her hand down indicating her body, "I'm not into any of that nowadays. I can't anymore." She sounds brave, but as I rest my hand on her shoulder I can feel her trembling. She's scared of him, and I must admit, I'm gutted on her behalf. And on my account, is it true that she fucking can't have sex? Surely not? Did she also suffer injuries to her pelvis?

I have to put my wants and desires behind me as Buster just won't fucking give up! "You've got a pussy, ain't you? And a mouth? And I s'pect you're hidin' a pretty little ass under there. That's all I need, babe."

I can't hold back. My fingers clench, and my fist comes out, catching him hard on the chin, rocking him on his feet. As he goes to swing at me, Slick and Rock, who must have emerged sometime during our confrontation, step forwards and grab hold of him, each holding an arm.

"You don't fuckin' hit the VP," Rock hisses. "And you asked for that one. Now apologise to the lady and remember she's under our protection."

"Apologise?" he yells, and then points down. "To that? She's not a fuckin' ol' lady, she doesn't belong to anyone. Which means she's another cunt waitin' to be filled." He sneers and turns to look at us one by one. "Just because I ain't so particular as the rest of yers…"

This time it's Rock who takes him down before he can finish his sentence. Buster hasn't got a chance. Unlike the rest of us, and another example of the way he disregards instructions from his prez, he doesn't spend time in the gym or sparring. Slick nods to let me know they've got this, and sends a knowing look Wheels' way. I give him a chin lift; he's right. I need to get her out of here. Buster won't be looking pretty by the time they've finished. *Just another thing to add to my long growing list of issues with the fuckin' man.* He'll be lucky if he keeps his patch if he keeps on like this.

Thank goodness I didn't assign a prospect to watch over her, they'd never have been able to stand up to a fully patched member. I certainly don't want Buster's unpleasantness anywhere near her again. I'll make sure I, or one of my trusted brothers, are on her at all times. Just until Horse gets back.

Having pushed her away so we're out of sight and hearing of the altercation which will be taking place at the garage, I hunker down in front of her and take her hands in mine. She's shaking. "Buster's a pain in the ass, darlin'. There's not one other brother who'd disrespect you like that. Slick and Rock will be teachin' him a lesson he's not gonna forget in a hurry. Put him out of your mind, darlin'." In truth, I'd like to be back there taking my turn. This is not the impression of the club I wanted her to take away from our tour this afternoon.

She wipes a tear away that's escaped from her eyes, and looks at me beseechingly as if she wants to confide in me. But as she turns away with a shake of her head, I understand she doesn't know sufficiently well enough yet to trust me with her innermost thoughts and fears. But I'm not stupid, I can guess how she feels—vulnerable.

Unable to stop myself, I put my hand to her cheek. "Trust me, darlin'. I'll make sure that you never have to deal with him again. He's going to lose his patch if he's not very careful, and after I speak to Drum, I reckon that's gonna be made very clear to him."

"I don't want to get anyone in trouble," her voice trembles.

"Not on you, darlin', he's doin' that all by himself."

I take charge, pushing her back to the clubhouse where I'm pleased to see Sandy, Viper's old lady and manager of our restaurant, and Carmen, a hairdresser who belongs to Bullet, sitting huddled around a table. I draw her closer and make the introductions. Soon they're chatting about the subject that seems to intrigue her, how their old men got their handles—Viper, because he's been our undercover snake in the grass on more than one occasion, and Bullet because he rides his bike faster than his proverbial speeding namesake. She seems to be fascinated with the tales behind them. I shift uncomfortably, hoping she never learns how I got mine.

Deciding I can leave them to visit for a while, I make my way to see Drummer. After filling him in, he's incensed at Buster's latest fuck-ups and promises to talk to him about his now precarious position in the club. Then, returning to the main room and after checking that Wheels is happily laughing with the girls—our old ladies are a great bunch—I find Peg at the bar and join him. As our sergeant-at-arms, he also deserves to know about Buster's behaviour, so I give him the gist of it.

When I've explained how it all went down, Peg shakes his head and echoes my thoughts. "I can see we're gonna be takin' his patch one way or another before he's done assin' about." Changing the subject, he points to Wheels. "You babysittin' her now? I saw Horse leavin'."

Sighing, knowing out of anyone he'll understand, I tell him of her apprehension about being here in general, and that the disagreeable exchange with Buster certainly didn't help her feel at home. I'm in the middle of explaining when Sandy comes up and touches me on the arm, pointing over to Wheels, who seems to be doubled up in pain. But it's her prosthesis she seems to be rubbing. I crease my forehead in surprise.

"Everything okay, Sands?"

"Yeah, we were gettin' on fine and then her leg started hurtin'. She wants help to get back to her room so she can find her painkillers," Sandy tells me, her eyes full of concern and worry for her new friend. Sandy's a good girl.

I reach into my pocket and take out a box, at the same time beckoning Hank over. "Bottle of water," I tell him.

Reading the dosage, I push out one small yellow pill into my hand, then taking the bottle, give them both to Sandy. "Here, Horse gave me her stuff to look after, give her that."

Thanking me, she does. As Sandy returns to the table and gives the medication to Wheels, I don't fail to notice the look of surprise that's flicked towards me, and embarrassment on her face as she realises Horse put me in charge of her medication.

Peg is also watching her. "Nasty thing, that."

"What?" I swing back to him.

"Phantom pains." As it's obvious I don't understand him, he continues, "People think it's all in the head when a missin' limb starts hurtin'. But it's not, ya know? It's nerves and the like sendin' the wrong signals. Very real and painful. But there're ways to help." Then his eyes narrow, not much gets past our sergeant-at-arms. "Why have you got her pills?"

As he's one of the men it would be good to have in the know, I fill him in on Horse's concerns.

He looks down into his beer, deep in thought for a moment, and then draining his drink leaves the empty glass on the bar and purposefully strides over to where the girls are sitting. "Skat!" He waves his hands at Sandy and Carmen. They throw him identical surprised looks, but he just stands there, arms folded, waiting to be obeyed. With huffs, they pick up their glasses and move away. Wheels puts her hands on her wheels, preparing to go too.

"Not you." Another terse instruction. Wheels looks up at me. I nod, hopefully comfortingly. Peg is not the gentlest looking man, or with the most polite manners. Standing my height, with shortly shorn hair and a long thick beard, I know how menacing he can appear. A good trait in a sergeant-at-arms.

He stares at Wheels for a second, as if taking her in. I'm expecting he'll talk to her about her pains, but no, he takes an entirely different tack. "My name's Peg, Wheels. Know why they call me that?"

She gazes back at him, then looks down, shaking her head in confusion. "No," she answers softly.

"Well," he begins, and then again surprises me, "Blade, our enforcer, well, let's just say a knife's his weapon of choice. And

Buster likes to use his fists. Me, I'm a little more imaginative than that. You see, when I like to get information from someone, or just want to see them die rather painfully, I stake them out with pegs and let the sun do its work. Works like a charm."

"For fuck's sake, Peg!" I round on him, seeing Wheels has gone white as a fucking sheet for the second time today. My fists curl at my sides, and I'm going to hit him if he upsets her any more. *Way to make her feel at home here, Peg!*

Suddenly Peg's hand thumps down on the table, and he leans forward, ominously getting right in her face. "Why the fuck do you think they call me Peg, little girl?"

She shakes her head, her eyes widening as she goes from believing his story to doubting him in a second.

"Why d'you fuckin' think?" Without giving her a chance to reply, he lifts his leg onto the table and pulls up his jeans revealing what I already know is underneath—though most of the time forget it's even there—a titanium prosthesis leading into his motorcycle boot.

I've seen her eyes open wide before, but now they seem to take up half her face. She gawks at the artificial leg, her hand appears to reach out by itself to touch it, and then she turns her gaze to him. "But… But how?" I realise as he does, she's not asking his history when she adds, "You ride a motorcycle?" It's half statement, half question as her gaze flits from his artificial leg to his face.

"That I do," he tells her. "Lost my leg in Afghanistan, a land mine. The other was pretty badly damaged too."

"What, how…" She's trying to stammer out a question and at last finds what she wants to ask. "How did you…"

"Get to walk again?" he pre-empts what she's trying to say. "Sheer fuckin' determination." He puts his leg down again. "Meet me back here at six. And no fuckin' excuses."

CHAPTER 7
Sophie

No excuses? Just who does this man think he's talking to? My eyes follow him as he turns abruptly and walks out of the room, and I know my mouth has dropped open. I glance at Wraith, who's looking as bemused as me. *What the fuck was that all about?*

There's tension behind my eyes, and my head starts pounding as my body shakes. Not only have I been transported to what seems to be a different universe, in one day been told there's quite possibly a killer after me, and I've also been insulted by one of the club members. Now their sergeant-at-arms has shouted at me. And all on the top of jet lag. It's too much.

"Wraith, I want to go back to my room, please. I need some time alone." I'm fighting back tears, annoyed at my weakness. In truth, I want to go home to my own familiar surroundings in England, bury my head in the sand and forget all this is happening to me.

"Hey." Wraith crouches down in front of me. "I think Peg's tryin' to help you."

"He's a bully. If that's his way of helping I think I'll pass!" I retort, but my hearts not in it. "Just let me have some down time, will you?" I wish Horse was here. Not that I know him that well either, but he's been the one constant over the past few days.

Wraith's hands touch mine and the day gets even worse when I feel his warmth on my fingers. My body's reacting to him, and if I wasn't on the verge of crying before, I would be now. I look up at him, his brow creased in concern, dark brown eyes staring into mine as if trying to read what's hidden in the depths there. He's a strikingly attractive man—he could have any woman he wanted. He might be the first since the accident to arouse feelings inside of me, but he'd never reciprocate them in a million years. Like everyone else, he's just feeling sorry for me. For a second the idea of him looking at my disgusting stump fills me with horror. I couldn't stand to see the inevitable revulsion on his face.

Briefly, he squeezes my hand, regards me intently, and then gives a quick nod as he comes to a decision. "Let's get you back then."

I want to be out of this clubhouse, away from the bikers that unnerve me, so I make no protest as he takes charge, pushing my wheelchair. It doesn't take long before we reach the suite where I'm staying, and after one last concerned look, Wraith leaves me alone.

In my room, I transfer myself to the bed and lie back, my arm over my eyes, fighting to keep back the tears which have threatened all day. What have I done to deserve all this? All I did was give Zoe the money that should have enabled her to get away. If I'd known how Ethan would retaliate, would I have still gone ahead and helped her? I'd like to say yes, but a selfish part of me is screaming that there's no way in hell, and I admit to wishing she'd never come to my door that day. Then I'd still have my leg and wouldn't be in this position. *Why do bad things always happen to me? When will the world decide I've suffered enough?*

Gradually my jumbled thoughts slow. The jet lag and the gruelling events of the day have taken their toll, and I drift asleep. I'm awakened abruptly by a loud banging on the door.

"Who is it?" My voice shakes and my hands grow clammy. *What if Buster's come calling?* Although I said I was okay about Horse leaving, I wasn't really. *God, I wish I didn't feel so helpless and alone.*

But then comes a familiar voice. "It's just me, Wraith. It's five-thirty, and Peg wants you to meet him in half-an-hour."

Remembering how the burly man had yelled at me, that's the last thing I want to do. "I don't want to go," I call out, sounding as petulant as I feel.

"Can I come in?"

I heave a heavy sigh. "Yes, okay."

The door opens, and Wraith enters. He comes over and stares down at me, his face is set, his lips pursed. "I think you do, sweetheart. You'd have to be a braver fucker than I to ignore an instruction from our sergeant-at-arms. Come on, let's get you up and sorted."

Shit. It doesn't look like I'm going to get out of this. Why does everyone think they can just push me around? "I don't need help," I reply tersely, pulling myself to a sitting position to demonstrate the point. Pausing just for a moment for my equilibrium to orientate as I move from horizontal to vertical, I reach for my wheelchair and shift across. "Just give me a minute to use the bathroom and I'll be with you." I don't want to go. Half of me wants to protest, and half of me is scared not to see what Peg wants with me. I don't know the rules here, and without Horse I'm at the mercy of these intimidating men.

And that's why just before six o'clock I'm back in the bar area of the clubhouse waiting for the man who'd been so abrupt and scary earlier. My hands twist in my lap, and I chew on my lip as I wonder what on earth he could want with me? To try and take my mind off unanswerable questions of what Peg's got planned, I glance around the room. There are a number of bikers around, some I recognise, some I haven't met yet, as well as a few girls already scantily clad. I notice the latter seem particularly interested in me, and not in a good way, unlike the old ladies I was introduced to earlier who'd made me so welcome. I begin to get suspicious about their role in the club, but if they think I'm looking to get between them and their men, well, they'll soon realise unless it's someone who *'ain't so particular'* as Buster, I'll be no threat.

On the dot of six Peg strides into the room. Had I not seen his prosthesis with my own eyes, I'd never have known he was wearing one. He walks so confidently and surely as he heads straight to me, throwing a chin lift to Wraith before addressing me.

"Good, you're here. You wouldn't have wanted me to come and get you. First rule, darlin', don't cross me and we'll get along just fine."

His opening words don't offer much comfort, and I regret coming out of my room.

"You're scarin' her, Peg." Wraith points out the obvious.

For an answer, he just nods, and his lips curl up into a not very attractive smile. It does nothing to calm my fear. And it only worsens when he walks behind the chair and starts pushing me. When Wraith takes his place alongside, Peg pauses.

"Leave her with me, Wraith."

Wraith frowns. "I don't know if that's a good idea."

Peg stares him down. "It wasn't a request."

I find my voice. "I'd like him…"

Now Peg's eyes flash. "You've had it easy up to now, Princess. Now you're gonna do things my way. Wraith stays here."

"I promised Horse…"

"I'm not going to fuckin' hurt her, man."

The two men stare at each other, and to my disappointment, it's Wraith who backs down. And then I'm left alone with this daunting man as he wheels me away to God knows where.

Wondering where the hell he's taking me, and for what reason, I'm surprised when he takes me out to the back of the club, wheels me over to a picnic bench and parks me beside it. He sits himself down, his bum on the table, feet on the seat. Putting his elbows on his knees, he rests his chin on his hands and stares at me for a moment.

"You had phantom pains, earlier," he starts, "they can be a bitch. Anyone told you how to deal with them?"

It wasn't what I expected him to say. His tone isn't sympathetic, just matter-of-fact. Lifting and lowering my shoulders, I tell him, "My physio suggested some things, but…"

"But," he takes over without letting me finish, "you don't want to think about the part of you that's missin', do ya? You spend your days wishin' it hadn't happened, and fuck, I can relate to that, Princess. But it did, and now you've got to learn to live with it. Or without it more's the case."

Christ, what's up with me and the waterworks today? Tears prick at my eyes. "You don't understand."

"Like fuck I don't." He raises his voice. "I gotta show you my fuckin' leg again?"

I shake my head, letting him know there's no need for him to do that.

Reaching over, he places his fingers under my chin and raises my face until I'm looking at him. "I'm gonna tell you how this is gonna go. You're going to do everythin' I say, got it Princess?"

He frightens me, so I don't dare disagree.

"Right. It's happened babe, you've lost your leg."

"Part of it," I correct him. "From below the knee."

"Sounds much the same as me." He nods. "You've got to move on and deal. Instead of ignorin' it, try to imagine it, crunch your toes together. Go on, do it now."

"I haven't got any toes," I whisper.

"Imagine them," he instructs.

I'm worried what will happen if I disappoint him, so I concentrate and try to do exactly what he says. My facial muscles tense with the effort.

"Good girl."

For some reason his approval warms me.

"If it's easier, do the same with the other leg. That's it, good. Now raise and lower both legs and scrunch those toes together."

I do what he says.

"Good. Now it helps some people. The problem is, your brain can't accept you haven't got a physical limb there, so it can help if you fool it into thinkin' it's still there. It can help with the pain, Princess. Keep doing that a few times durin' the day, *every day*, and maybe it will help. It does for me."

"Okay, thank you." I start to feel grateful that someone who knows precisely what I'm going through is taking their time to help. I'm sure he's got better things to be doing. "People don't understand how much something that's not there can hurt."

"Exactly!" His face creases into the first real smile I've seen from him. "I know how fuckin' hard it is to come back from somethin' like this. But I'm telling you now, you can get up out of that chair and walk again."

I start shaking my head to tell him he's wrong, it's too hard, but again he's there before me.

"Your prosthesis is hurtin' you, you can't balance, and your other leg is too weak to support you. Yeah, I've been there too. And that's why I'm gonna help you."

He jumps down off the table—jumps! Without even a wobble, and grabbing the handles of my chair, starts pushing me again. I let him do so in silence as I digest how he understands exactly how I feel. Sure, I'd met other amputees at the hospital, but I'd steered clear of them. Peg's right, I've been avoiding accepting what's happening, preferring to wallow in misery rather than dealing with it. Perhaps it's time to make the switch?

Taking me around to the back of the club, he opens a door and pushes me through then flicks on some lights. My eyes open wide—it's not what I expected at all. "A gym?" There are all sorts of equipment in this large room, and a boxing ring in the middle. At the moment we have the place to ourselves.

"Yeah, Drummer likes his men to keep fit." He points to the area in the centre. "We have sparrin' matches once a month."

"You spar?"

He humphs. "Of course I do. I might not be as nimble as some of the others, but I can hold my own." Then he's moving me again, over to some equipment at the side of the room, a set of parallel bars, and it's then I know what he's got planned. It's a similar setup to the one at my physio's. I'd seen it once, the only time I'd attended a session.

"Right, now let's get you to your feet."

My physio would have encouraged me to support myself and use my arms to get myself onto the equipment, not so with Peg. His broad arms reach down and he manhandles me out of the chair, holding me until my hands grasp the bars. When he's sure I've got my balance, he lets go.

My knuckles turn white as I try to take all my weight on my arms, afraid to rely on my legs to hold me up. "I can't do this," I rasp out.

"Yes you can. And you will. Relax and get your legs under you."

He's moved the wheelchair out of the way. My arms are shaking with the effort to hold myself up. He steps away, a statement that he'll be no help at all.

Gingerly I put weight on my weakened leg.

He's noticed. "Good. Now balance on the prosthesis."

With some difficulty, I do that too.

His next instruction is to walk to the end of the bars. One glance at his set features shows me he'll take no sympathy on

112

me, and the only way to get out of here is to do what he says. Slowly, very slowly, I shuffle along until I reach the end. When I get there, I look up with a smile of achievement.

He comes across and his hand touches my shoulder. "I'm going to work you hard, Princess. It will take time to build up your strength and balance, but one day you'll be walkin' again, and you can lose your fuckin' handle. You want that, *Wheels?*"

There's something about the way he speaks, the conviction he puts into his tone, that has me believing someone for the first time since my accident. I feel I have to say something to him. "Peg, I…"

But he's moved away again, his posture one of dismissal. "Now fuckin' turn yourself around and walk back again."

Sergeant-at-arms? He ought to be a bloody sergeant major!

He keeps me going until my muscles are screaming out in protest. Only when the sweat's pouring off my brow and my lungs are heaving does he relent, helping me off the bars and back into my chair.

Waving at the equipment he tells me, "The boys put these in for me after I came back from Afghanistan. I know what you're goin' through, darlin'. And it's gonna be the hardest fuckin' thing you've ever done in your life. But just promise me one thing?"

Still breathing heavily, I glance up at him curiously when he doesn't continue and prompt him, "What?"

"You'll have your first fuckin' dance with me!"

A laugh bursts out of me. It was the last thing I'd expected him to say.

And I'm still grinning when he pushes me—I haven't the strength or energy to propel myself—back to the clubroom. Wraith jumps off his bar stool and comes over, anxiety in his gaze, which goes between Peg and me before he stares intently into my eyes, then checks me from head to toe. I know he can see I'm still flushing red and sweat is still beading on my brow from the effort Peg made me put in.

"You alright?" He's still checking me over.

Peg snarls an answer for me. "Of course she's fuckin' alright."

My reaction might have called him a liar, as involuntarily I let loose the tears which have been threatening all day. But instead of being those of frustration or self-pity, I can feel the difference. They're of hope.

As Wraith moves closer I reach out my hand to reassure him. "I'm fine." Then looking him straight in the eyes, and although my words are punctuated with sobs, I manage to stammer out, "Peg's going to get me walking again."

Wraith's face beams as he hears the elation in my voice, and he slaps Peg on the back.

The unaccustomed exercise has awakened my appetite, so when my biker protector suggests we join the others for dinner, I quickly agree. All the old ladies are there—Carmen, Sandy, as well as Crystal, and I'm amazed to see how gently the rugged bikers treat little Amy, even curtailing their colourful language at the fierce glares from her mother. Surprisingly, I have a good time, joining in with laughing at inappropriate jokes and innuendoes, and even find I'm getting used to responding to the tag, Wheels. *And perhaps, with Peg's help, I can rid myself of that name.*

I'm surprised when Carmen walks past me and seems to ruffle my hair. Now I might be in a wheelchair, but I'm not a bloody child. I glare up at her.

"Whoops, sorry. Occupational habit." She takes the seat beside me and sits down, her eyes examining my bob. "I'm a hairdresser."

Ah, that makes sense now.

"That your natural colour?" She's staring at my roots.

"Yes." I'm lucky to have been born the colour blond most people get out of a bottle.

"Well, if you want a trim or try somethin' different, just give me a shout."

"I'll do that," I agree. I didn't expect the club to have a resident hairdresser on site, and I must admit, I could probably use her services soon.

I lean a little closer to her, and while I've got her attention I decide to take advantage. "Can I ask you something?"

"Of course!"

"The girls that hover around the clubroom, who are they?" I ask quietly, having noticed they don't join the rest of us for meals, and I've come to the conclusion they're probably not old ladies at all.

She laughs. "They're sweet butts, or club whores."

Dart's overheard, though I tried to be quiet about it. "They're here to provide their services to us."

My eyebrows rise. "Do you pay them?"

"No." He grins. "They get food and lodgin' for taking care of us."

"And by that, I don't suppose you mean cooking and cleaning."

Now he laughs. "Not sure their talents would run to that."

"Nah, they've got other talents, like suckin' dick," Slick butts in.

Well, he's made their services quite clear. "How many of them are there?"

"Four who live here—Jill, Chrissy, Allie, and Pussy. And on the weekends we have girls up from Tucson too. We're well taken care of." Dart takes over the conversation again.

What the hell kind of name is Pussy? I don't ask as I really don't want to know, but at least I've a better understanding of their place in the club now.

When Wraith finally takes me back to my room I enter feeling tired, but for the first time in months, with optimistic thoughts of the future. Perhaps I could have gotten back on my feet again if I'd kept up with my physiotherapy, but it had all seemed so pointless. But I didn't have someone with the determination and the understanding of Peg to give me the kick I needed. I go to bed even looking forward to the day ahead.

Over the next week, I start to get used to living at the club. Being alone was no hardship for me. I'd learned to amuse myself back home reading and keeping my own company, but here I'm not given much chance to be on my own. Wraith would drag me out of my room, and there was always someone around in the clubhouse. I started to get to know the brothers, some more approachable than others but, with the exception of Buster, all treated me with respect. I grew particularly fond of Dart, who's always giving me a cheeky wink, and also Rock, though it takes me longer to get used to his habit of constantly cleaning his gun. At first, sight of the weapon made me shudder, but somehow, seeing how the brothers openly carry arms does give me a feeling of safety. If somehow Hargreaves turned up here he'd certainly meet his match. One constant who seems to live in the clubroom is a biker named Adam. Once I really examined him and noticed the huge bulge in this throat that certainly looked like he'd swallowed a real apple, no one had to explain how he got his name. Not that I have much to do with him, he spends his time glued to one of the arcade machines.

I fast become friends with the old ladies and, feeling guilty about eating their cooking, soon start to try helping them out in the kitchen, though being in a wheelchair I'm limited as to how far I can assist. I never thought I'd be envious of someone lifting pots and pans off the cookers before, but now I certainly am. But something's different now, I'm not looking at things thinking *I'll never be able to do that*. No, I watch them knowing that with

Peg's encouragement and gruelling exercise regimen I'm gradually getting strength back into my injured leg. I'm starting to believe one day I'll actually walk.

When Horse returns he only stays a few days before he's off again, full of apologies for leaving me again. But he goes off with a lighter heart as I'm able to convince him I'm fine here among my new biker friends. It sets a pattern for the next few weeks. Whenever Horse is away, Wraith steps in to keep me company, but I know it's only because Horse has asked him to. Otherwise he keeps his distance, I suspect grateful to be rid of me as a burden. And if my heart beats a little faster when I'm in his presence, I'll be keeping that little fact entirely to myself.

With regard to the contract, I don't become complacent, but the gentle giant, Mouse, is keeping tabs on things and making sure I'm updated. As the days pass I stop looking over my shoulder, as there's nothing to suggest anyone is any closer to finding me.

I only have two problems with staying in the compound—one is quite obviously Buster, who makes crude gestures at me when no one else is looking, suggesting his 'invitation' is obviously still on his mind. I could have told Wraith, but I didn't want to get Buster into any more trouble than he's in already. And Wraith, as VP, must surely have better things to do with his time than worry about me.

The other issue is the club whores.

I'm sitting alone in the clubhouse, engrossed in a great novel on my iPad, when I become aware that someone's taken the seat opposite me. Glancing up I'm surprised to see it's Chrissy, one of the sweet butts who have, up to this point, avoided talking to me. She's staring at me, waiting to get my attention. Deciding I don't need any more enemies, I greet her with a smile, still unable to get my head around how they can let any man who wants to, touch them. Sure, I used to enjoy sex, but who I did it with and when was always my choice. I couldn't imagine anyone submitting willingly to Buster, but I've seen enough now to know that's what they have to do. And sometimes to multiple men on the same night, or even at the same time. Still, it doesn't seem to bother them, so to each their own.

"Hi, it's Chrissy, isn't it?" I've had the dubious pleasure of seeing Viper's cock disappearing into her mouth while Beef's hammering into her from behind. I left the clubhouse pretty quickly that afternoon. I'm not a prude, far from it, but some performances, in my opinion, should take place behind closed doors. Like in a broom cupboard, for example. A grin comes to my face at the memory.

She acknowledges her name with a dip of her head, then gets down to what she's come here for. "You ain't anyone's ol' lady."

She's telling me what I already know. "No, I'm not," I agree pleasantly.

"Only women in the club are either ol' ladies or sweet butts," she tells me. "Don't understand what you think your place is here."

"Well, I'm not a sweet butt," I cough out.

"Nah, none of the brothers would want you like that." She points to my leg, the one with the prosthesis.

She's right, but I don't appreciate her pointing it out to me. I shrug. "Your point?"

She shakes her head. "We don't know what you're doing here."

"As far as I'm aware, the club has given me protection."

"Only because of Horse, and he ain't even a full member. You better watch yourself, sweetheart. And don't get too friendly with Wraith. He's mine, you feel me?"

Is she threatening me? And I don't recall Wraith even passing the time of day with her in the time I've been here.

"Me and the others, we take care of the brothers, you understand? Don't need another bitch here."

Seeing as she's just said that none of them would want me anyway, I don't understand why she's bothering to talk to me. I'm saved when Slick approaches our table. His eyes go cold as he sees her talking to me.

"Get lost, Chrissy," he rasps out. "Wheels ain't one of your kind."

"She's not an ol' lady neither." Her face scrunches in disdain.

Slick grabs ahold of her long dark hair, wrapping it around his fist and pulling her head back so she's forced to look up at him. "She's more akin to them than your whore ass," he says in a voice that would brook no argument. "So get back and don't forget your place. Reckon Tongue's lookin' a bit lonely over there."

His voice isn't quiet, and the man he's just suggested looks up with a leer. His tongue comes out and waggles suggestively as he crooks his finger towards Chrissy. She looks aghast at the suggestion, which I don't understand. *Isn't her job to service any of the men?* As he releases his hold, she gets to her feet, and with an unhappy look on her face, giving a final sneer in my direction, goes off towards Tongue.

Slick stares at me for a moment. "You okay, Wheels?"

I nod and reassure him, "I'm fine, thanks."

"You don't want to get in with the likes of them."

I've realised that. There's a hierarchy to the club women— old ladies are at the top, club whores at the bottom, and never the twain shall meet. Me, on the other hand, as Chrissy pointed out, I've no freaking idea where I belong.

Slick or someone must have had a word with the sweet butts because they leave me alone after my conversation with Chrissy. But that doesn't stop them from glaring at me when they think no one is looking.

CHAPTER 8
Wraith

P eg's a good man, and I'm pleased he's taken Wheels under his wing—kindred spirits I expect. Out of all of us, he understands her best. When he's not out on business, every day for the last couple of months he's worked with her helping her to build up her strength, but what's even better to see is that she works with him too, putting in so much effort that even he's surprised with her progress. While she still uses her chair, particularly when she's tired, he's encouraging her to use her crutches, and the more she does, the more she smiles.

Peg explained the amount of damage in her one whole leg resulted in such muscle wastage it will take some time to build the strength in it up to where it should be, but in time he expects her to be able to throw her crutches away. And I can't fucking wait.

There was such a visible difference in her mood from the first time Peg started helping her, that before Horse set off on his second trip away from the compound he returned her medication to her. I saw him do it, and couldn't miss the way her mouth broadened into a grateful grin when she realised he trusted her again.

I can't forget that day when I saw her wobbling into the clubroom on those crutches and not using the chair. Damn, if I didn't grow harder than steel as I saw my first glimpse of her fine ass. Even out of the chair she's not tall, probably around five-foot-two or so, but even so, her legs go on for miles, and did I mention that ass? Christ, I just want to hold my hands around it, squeeze it, and pull it down over my eager cock. She's got an hourglass figure, just the kind I like. And I wasn't the only one staring. A small growl came from my throat when I realised my brothers weren't immune either.

We've no issues about continuing to give her our protection. It doesn't take much to keep her amused and happy—most of the time she's with the old ladies for that. Mouse has found no indication that anyone knows where she is, and we've all taken a liking to her. When she lets herself go, she's got a wicked sense of humour and isn't shy in coming forward. But something tells me she's still fighting her mental battles, as well as her physical ones.

And me? Well, I'm fighting myself. I want her like I've never wanted a woman before, only with her it wouldn't be a one-time fling. A woman like Wheels would expect more than that. I don't know if I'm ready to take an old lady. But the thought of sinking my cock into her... Fuck it. She only has to walk into the room and I'm hard again. I can't deny the day may be coming soon when I'll have to step up and mark my territory and to hell with the consequences. Sessions in the shower aren't doing it for me anymore, I need the real thing. *Drum would kill me if he knew what I was thinking!*

"Hey, Wheels!" Dart calls out. "Over here, sweetheart."

As she gives him a little wave and slowly makes her way across to the table he's sitting at with Rock and Beef, I notice Chrissy staring at her, contempt written all over her face. The sweet butt nudges Jill, who's sitting beside her and whispers into her ear. Jill also turns and sneers. My lips tighten. Slick had a word with them some time ago, but they're getting increasingly envious over her comfortable relationship with the boys, and the fact she's on her own two feet today has made them worse than ever.

I've got to shut that shit down fast. This is a landmark day for Wheels, having the confidence to leave her wheelchair behind, and I'm not having jealous bitches spoiling it.

As I stomp towards them they look up, the artful smile on Chrissy's face fading once she sees the expression on my own. I pause before speaking, folding my arms across my chest, letting them see my distaste. "Don't think I don't know what you whores are bitchin' about. And if I hear you say one fuckin' disrespectful word about Wheels you'll be out of this club before you can fuckin' blink. D'you feel me?"

"But Wraith, we weren't…"

"Yes, you fuckin' were Chrissy. Don't bother fuckin' denyin' it."

She casts a glance at Jill in case she'll help her; Jill just shrugs, Allie and Pussy look the other way. Chrissy tries another approach, putting out her hand and resting it on my arm. "Wraith, how about you an' me get together? It's been a while and you know I could make you feel soooo good."

I look down at the hand touching me with disgust. Yes, I used to go there, but fuck knows why. And I know I have absolutely no desire to go there again. The longer my stare rests on her skin, the lighter her touch becomes until she gets the message and pulls it away. I decide to lay it on the line. "Yes, we fucked. But I don't wanna fuck you again. Got it?"

If I thought it was possible, I'd have sworn there were tears in her eyes. But I had to be wrong. Sweet butts should know better than to think they can get involved with members—no one's going to take an old lady that all the other brothers have sunk their dicks in.

I have one last thing before I go. "Lay off Wheels," I growl, and then look between the four of them until I see the resignation in their faces, letting me know they've got the message.

A roar of laughter from across the room draws my attention. Wheels, now seated with a drink in front of her, is grinning broadly. Bullet and Blade have joined them, and Peg's hovering behind. Dart's tapping a cigarette out of a pack and lighting up. Wanting to find out what's going on, I make my way over.

"What's the joke?" I ask to the table in general.

Dart's still smirking. "Blade just asked for a cancer-stick," he starts, and I know that's not unusual. He's apparently given up, or at least has given up buying his own.

"Okay…" I encourage, knowing that can't be the end of it.

Laughing again, and causing sniggers around the table, Dart continues, "So Wheels asks if he always bums fags."

Bullet's now doubling up.

"It's not that funny," Wheels says, though she's giggling too.

"I didn't believe English people really said that shit!" Blade manages to stammer out.

Wheels glances up at me, her lips curling up, and then turns to Dart. "No need to get your knickers in a twist."

"Ain't wearin' any, babe," he replies, and for some reason that sets the table off again.

"Say somethin' else, sweetheart," Blade encourages her.

"Nah." Wheels pulls her crutches towards her and makes a show of getting onto her feet, but she's still grinning. Peg puts out his hand to help her. "I'm going for a slash now." At the looks of incomprehension thrown towards her, she clarifies, "I'm going to spend a penny," then adds, waving her hand towards the heads, "Going to visit Aunty Loo."

Rubbing his hand over his face, Blade laughs. "Christ, she talks a fuckin' different language."

"Oh stop taking the piss," she throws over her shoulder as she walks away.

Fuck, I'm chuckling too now. She's in her element here. Why haven't we seen this side of her before? My problem is I like this new feisty Sophie that's emerging, the one not afraid to have a laugh with my brothers. And so does my cock. I've managed to stay away from her for weeks now, but it's getting more difficult as each day passes. And that ass! Fuck, I'd have to be blind not to want to go there.

Peg comes to stand beside me. "She's doing fuckin' well. Been hard fuckin' work for her, but she's getting' there."

"She's improvin' mentally, too," I told him, and his slow, steady nod shows me he agrees. "It's the independence that she needs. I know, I went through the same fuckin' thing."

Tapping on my arm, he indicates he wants me to move aside so we can get some privacy. "What's happenin' with that contract out on her?"

"Mouse is keepin' his ear to the ground, but nothin' seems to have changed. St John-Davies has probably traced her to Phoenix, but she could have ended up anywhere in the States for all he fuckin' knows."

Again his slow nod. "Let's hope it stays that way. So far she's not caused trouble for the club." He's echoing my thoughts from earlier.

The more I'm around Wheels, the harder it is to keep my hands to myself. For some reason, as Wheels has improved the sweet butts and even the townies who come up to the clubhouse at weekends have ceased to interest me to the extent that since I first set eyes on Wheels, she's become the only one I've wanted. For the first time since my teens, my hands been seeing far too much action, preferring to jerk myself off to thoughts of the woman I can't have rather than sinking into any that I can. If any of my brothers knew they'd be laughing their fucking heads off.

And the following Sunday it only gets harder to keep my distance when we hold a club barbeque. The sun's shining, grills are grilling, little Amy's running around and getting in everybody's way, and *she* comes out wearing a tight tank top which showcases her boobs perfectly. Fucking Wheels! My cock stands immediately to attention and I lose track of what Drum's saying to me.

"Wraith!" My name in a sharp bark draws my eyes back to him.

His own are narrowed as he notices what distracted me. "She's a fine lookin' girl."

I laugh. "You've only just noticed?"

"No, but I'm not lookin' with my cock."

Luridly I thrust my hips a couple of times. "Can't help it if I've noticed her tits."

"As long as lookin's all you're going to be doin', VP." He sounds suspicious.

"It's alright, Drum, I ain't goin' there. She's got too much baggage." Oh, but fuck I wish I could.

"Hmm." He's still giving me one of his searching looks, and now I'm uncomfortable, believing he sees far too much. Thankfully he changes the subject. "It's all gone quiet on her front, and I ain't talkin' about her rack." He doesn't have to explain he's still talking about Wheels, and his choice of words considering our previous conversation has me giving a brief smile. "But I want to be prepared for trouble. Peg reckons we should double our stock on ammunition and get in a few more guns. He's suggestin' some of the Mac 10s."

I give a slow whistle through my teeth as Drum mentions the small handheld machine guns capable of firing 18 bullets a second. Even a blind man would have a hard time missing a target with one of them. The spray action can affect accuracy, but still, despite that it's a good bit of kit. "Nice," I tell him. It sounds like he's preparing for war, but I know the brothers will be pleased to have new toys. "Got a supplier?"

"Eduardo," he replies.

Looks like I might be taking a trip down to the border shortly. The thought of a good run is welcome; the direction and the complications of getting guns across from Mexico, not so much.

He sees I've caught on. "Thought you and Peg and a couple of the prospects, Spider and Marsh perhaps, could go?"

"Yeah, Prez. When you thinkin' off?"

"Next week?"

I consider what else I've got going on, but am certain he already knows my plate's pretty much clear. "Yeah," I tell him, "I'm up for that. But you expectin' trouble?"

"Not that I know of. Just don't want anyone to catch us with our pants down."

It makes sense.

Hank comes up with fresh beers having noticed we've got empty bottles in our hands. Mentally I give him an extra point for observation. He's a good lad, and I reckon almost ready to patch in. Indicating with my beer, I'm interested to know what Drum thinks. "Hank, eh? He's almost been with us a year now."

Not a speedy response from Drum, but I didn't expect one, the prez isn't someone who speaks before thinking. "I reckon he's almost there. He'll make a good fuckin' brother. Give it another month and bring it to church. What about the others?"

Now it's my turn to take a few seconds to think. "Marsh is good, not been here as long as Hank so let's leave him a while longer. Spider... Still can't make him out. Seems to have a bit of a knack at not being around when you need him."

Drum nods. "I've noticed. Brothers have been sayin' they think we've only got two prospects."

"I'll gee him up a bit. Perhaps partner him up with Hank for a while to show him how it's done."

A slap on the back and Drum's obviously going to move on. "Only thing left for us to do is come up with a road name for

Hank. Think on it, VP, while you ride to Mexico. Oh, and one last thing, any more trouble from Buster?"

Even the name makes me frown, although he's been attending church and minding his own business lately, there's something about the man that's just off. I can't put my finger on what it is, just that his overall attitude is wrong. But my gut feeling isn't enough to cause a brother to lose his patch, so I have to give an honest answer. "No, he's behavin' himself," but can't resist adding, "For now." Something tells me he'll be fucking up again sooner or later.

CHAPTER 9
Sophie

When Horse brought me to the Satan's Devils' clubhouse I thought it was the worst place I could possibly have come to. But my eyes have been opened over the couple of months. With the exception of Buster, who gives me the creeps, all the other brothers have been great towards me. Some I still don't know that well, particularly Drum, the president, who seems to keep himself to himself, but Dollar, Blade, Dart, Rock, and Heart and, of course the studious Mouse, have all become what I'd call friends. None of them have made me feel uncomfortable, but neither have any of them made any type of pass at me except for mild flirting with no promise of a follow up. Ruefully I look down at my incomplete leg—obviously no one wants to fuck a woman with missing parts. It's obvious in my previous life, before the accident, I never had any trouble getting a man, or even two for the night. Now it seems I'm destined to be alone for the rest of my life.

The lack of attention from most of the men doesn't bother me in the slightest, as none of them evoke feelings I'd want to follow up on in any event, well, with one exception. And that's the man who I seem to have the least effect on at all, Wraith. Each time I see him, oh fuck it, or even hear his voice, it starts places tingling inside me, letting me know certain parts of me haven't shrivelled up and died like I hoped they would. When he comes into the room my nipples start to harden, and moisture dampens my underwear. But while he's friendly enough, apart from the times when Horse is away, he doesn't seek out my company, and only talks to me when he has to, to be polite.

Shit, Soph! Why are you thinking about sex? Just remember how mortified you'll be when a man sees your stump. Think about the humiliation when he realises what a turn off that is.

Looking around my room, which has become to seem like home to me, I eye my wheelchair, which I still use as the muscles in my legs get tired walking for too long, and when, as is becoming increasingly common, my stump gets sore from using the prosthesis. Bless Peg, who's explained to me the size of the stump changes as healing continues, and that I might need a new prosthesis soon. But for that I'll have to return to the UK, and God knows how long it will be before they deem it safe for me to go back. Personally, I wonder if Ethan has forgotten all about me. Mouse is reporting nothing seems to be moving with that contract on the dark web, though it hasn't been taken down, which remains worrying. Zoe's still missing—the reward on her fucking head is now astronomical, so perhaps he is still desperate to get her back, which means he could still be looking to find and use me.

Wraith's been gone a few days. Fuck, why am I thinking about him again? God knows, but the days seem to drag when he's not around. Even though I'm torturing myself, I love just being in the same room as him, and miss him when he's not here. He's on a run of some sort, but what for is club business, and none of mine. I got shot down when I asked. Peg's out too, and a couple of the prospects. Unusually, Horse is away at the same time, but I've grown comfortable here, so I'm not worried that I'm left on my own.

Despite my taskmaster being gone, I've been keeping up with my exercise. Not that whiling away an hour in the gym isn't enjoyable. If I time it right—and I've become a master at doing that—I can be there at the same time as some of the brothers working out, and that's a sight to keep me moving. Rippling fit bodies lifting weights or doing bench presses or the like. What a sight for sore eyes!

Wraith's due back tonight.

Why the fuck should I care?

Sitting down on my bed, I undress for the night and visit the bathroom to do the necessary. I did a lot today, helping with breakfast and dinner as well as spending time in the gym, so I'm dead tired and can't wait to get under the duvet and fall asleep. No one else is in the suite—Horse has gone to Texas to do some work and won't be back for another week.

After rubbing cream in my sore stump, I slide beneath the covers and close my eyes. As expected, I'm soon out like a light.

It's pitch black in my room when a noise wakes me. I don't know how long I've been asleep, and at first am disorientated, but I quickly become aware of a shuffling sound, followed by coarse swearing. *Has Horse come back early?* Feeling a flicker of apprehension and switching on my bedside light, I pull myself up and try to interpret the sounds. But it doesn't sound like Horse's voice outside. A chilling shiver makes me shudder. *Who could it be?*

And then my door bursts open, so hard it hits the wall and rocks back on its hinges. And the man who enters is the very last man I want to see. It's Buster.

My mouth drops open in surprise and horror. "What are you doing here?" I hiss. "Please get out of my room."

He swaggers into the room, rolling as though he's drunk. "Shut your mouth, bitch. Unless I tell you to open for me." He gives a spine chilling laugh at his own tasteless joke.

OH! SHIT! "Please leave." Trying again to get him to go, I start to reach for my wheelchair by the bed but he knocks it away, picking up my prosthesis and hurling it at the wall for good measure, and following it with the crutches. I eye up the distance, knowing the only way I can get to my chair is to crawl.

"I've been waitin' for this, seeing you flaunt your fuckin' self around the club. You think you're better than the rest of the whores but you're just a fuckin' cunt like all the rest. And now that I've got you on your own, we're gonna have us some fun."

NO! This can't be happening. Shaking, I glance at the bedside table but he's quicker than me, grabbing my phone and throwing it on the floor out of my reach. I pull up the duvet so it's tight around me, not quite able to believe what his intentions are. Surely he doesn't mean to...

"You naked under there and waitin' for me?"

"Get out!" I say it again, my only weapon within reach is a pillow, and I throw that at him anyway.

It hits him, but only makes him laugh again. "Though I'd love to have a pillow fight, baby, I've got other things planned for you." He smooths his hand over the bulge in his jeans and rubs himself through the material. Then he moves swiftly over to me. "Be grateful, bitch. The others might not be able to bring themselves to fuckin' touch you, but I don't mind ya a fuckin' cripple. That's good of me, eh? You've got a cunt and that's all I want. Well that for starters, then it will be your mouth, and I can't wait to get inside that tight juicy ass you've been tauntin' me with."

NO! There's no doubt about it, he intends to rape me. No! *This can't be happening.* Quickly I run through my options, realising fast that there's nothing I can do. The suite I'm in is slightly away from the rest, if I call out it's doubtful anyone would hear and come to help. Shit! There must be something; I can't let him do this.

"I'm not one of your whores." I try to reason with him, keeping my voice as calm as possible although my heart is beating wildly, blood draining from my face as I try to think how I can possibly evade the inevitable. As he's taken my supports away, I'm trapped. I'm on my own and I can't move. I can't let him use me like that. My heart's beating so fast I think it's going to jump out of my chest, and I'm finding it hard to breathe. *This can't be happening!*

"Of course you're not a club whore—no one wants a cripple. You should be grateful I'm prepared to overlook your fuckin' defects," he sneers, his bloodshot eyes zooming in on me. "Be grateful that I'm here." He cups his crotch in his hand and thrusts his hips forwards and back a couple of times. "You're fuckin' lucky. I'm gonna give you what you want. Bet you're gaggin' for it, ain't you? Bet you're gonna be fuckin' tight as hell as it's been a long time since anyone wanted near your broken fuckin' body."

As he steps closer, I again try to reason with him, this time unable to keep the tremble out of my voice. "It's not what I want. I don't want this. Please, please leave. Please don't do this."

"Oh, I like you beggin', bitch. But I thought I told you to keep your fuckin' mouth shut!"

He's at the bedside now, and while exercise has helped my arms get stronger, I'm still no match for him as he wrestles the duvet out of my grip. I'm wearing a tank top and shorts, and as his hands go to rip my clothing off of me, I let out a piercing scream, only to get the back of his hand across my face. He's wearing rings that cut my skin.

I try to fight, to push him off me, but he's too strong. He tears my top and throws it down. His hands start roughly kneading my breasts, and then his mouth's on them—he's sucking and biting. His hand reaches lower as I scream again.

CHAPTER 10
Wraith

We got back from Mexico with the M10s without problem, which relieves the shit out of me. So far I've managed not to do time, but that's the risk we take travelling and packing so much heat. Relieved to have got home without being pulled over, I've spent the evening with my brothers at the bar, but while my body was there, my mind was elsewhere, with Wheels. And for some reason I'm remembering that first day she'd spent in the club. When Peg had taken her off I'd been worried he'd upset her—I knew he wouldn't physically hurt her, none of us are into harming women—but he can be a funny motherfucker, and I thought he might upset her. I'd noticed a fragility about her, and his no-nonsense approach might have been too much for her to take.

But I'd been so fucking proud of her when he brought her back—he seemed to have given her a new determination and made her believe walking again was possible. Something that over the past few weeks she's darn nearly achieved. I'd like to see her without chair or crutches and on the back of my bike. I still. *Fuck. Where did that come from?* I've never had a woman on the back of my Harley before. Shaking my head, I try to concentrate on the conversation going on around me to get the woman out of my head. My thoughts are definitely leading me into dangerous territory tonight. I've never wanted an old lady, and there ain't no bitch gonna be riding behind me.

It's getting near two am. Sandy's gone home, and Viper's taking advantage, his cock eagerly being sucked by Allie. Rock's being greedy with one hand kneading Jill's tits and his other already down Pussy's panties. I suspect either we'll be in for a show shortly, or maybe not if he takes them back to his room.

I feel someone come up behind me and a hand come around and grope my junk. Well it's certainly not going to be one of my brothers. Spinning around expecting to see the other club whore, I'm not surprised to find it's Chrissy.

"When you gonna take me on the back of your bike, honey?" Her voice strangely echoing my earlier thoughts, however she wasn't the one I was imagining with her arms wrapped around me, breasts up tight against my leather...

She's shattered the image in my head, which annoys me. Roughly I push her hand away. "Ain't never gonna have a bitch on the back of my bike, babe."

"Course you are," she murmurs at me.

As usual she's made a bee line for me when she's not servicing one of the other brothers, but her fake blonde hair and tits and her sharp features do nothing for me, even though I've given into temptation on occasion when I need to shoot my load into the nearest hole. I thought she'd stay away after that last talking to I gave her, but no such luck. Reckon she's a few sandwiches short of a picnic for my message not to have stuck. My thoughts of Wheels have, as normal, sent blood flowing south. As Chrissy's hand wanders, her full red lips curve up in a smile as she touches my hardened cock. For a second I consider using her to get some relief, but I'm not that desperate tonight. And last time I was with her she was making it obvious she wants more from me than any brother would be prepared to give. A property patch. Well, she's not going to be getting that. Best not to mislead her.

134

Pushing her away hard enough, she gets the message. I watch as she pouts, but doesn't move away. Oh well, I can't be bothered to play this game tonight. If she's going to hang around I'll have to be the one to leave and make myself scarce. After the long ride today I won't be that sorry to get into my bed. *Uh uh.*

I'd had a good time tonight, unwinding in the club and catching up with my brothers on what's gone on while I've been away, particularly over the last half hour after loud-mouthed Buster decided to take his leave. God, I hate that fucker. Thinking of him pushes Chrissy out of my head, and I resolve when Drummer's back tomorrow I'm going to be having another little chat with him about our newest patched-over member. Not that he's done anything in particular, but during our trip it was interesting that Peg's view of him is about the same as mine. Neither of us trusts him nor believe he's a good fit for the Tucson chapter—maybe we can get him to go back to Cali. Yes, I'll need to have words with Drum in the morning, see if there's some way we can get him out of our hair.

Leaving the club room, something guides my feet away from the direction of my room. Telling myself I'm only going to get a breath of fresh air before turning in, I carry on up the track, walking up towards the guest suite where Wheels is staying. I've overindulged tonight, making up for the need to stay sober on the road while carrying such a risky cargo, so I'm a little unsteady on my feet as I make my way up the small incline to the building she's in, and my earlier, very inappropriate thoughts of what I'd like to do to her come back into my head in blazing technicolour. That rack she's got hiding, I'd like to see that for myself, put my hands all over it...

Suddenly a panicked scream fills the air. My inebriation disappears in an instant, and my hand goes to the gun at my back. Pulling it out I walk briskly forwards, another scream guiding

135

my way. That was no scream of pleasure, and it's coming from Wheels' suite.

Adrenalin kicking in I start to run, but reaching the door I find it's locked. There's a key somewhere in my pocket but I don't want to delay searching for it in my drunken state, so kicking out sharply I smash the wood into smithereens. Moving swiftly across the central sitting area I shove open the door leading into Wheels' room.

WHAT.THE. FUCK? Charging over to the bed I grab Buster by his cut and throw him off Wheels, my right arm arcing up and pistol whipping him as I do so. With all my strength and rage behind it, he's out like a light.

Multi-tasking, I take my phone out of my pocket as I leap forwards, pulling the hysterical woman into my arms, taking just a moment to console her and yanking up the duvet to cover her nakedness. "Shush, it's over now. It's me, Wraith." I'm not even sure she recognises me through her tears until I feel some of the tension leaving her body. "Did he…?"

A shudder and shake of her head tells me hopefully I got here just in time. I press a key on my phone, it's answered quickly. "Peg—I'm with Wheels in her room. Get here quick, Buster tried to fuckin' rape her."

The man in question starts stirring at my feet, and leaving her I go and give him a sharp kick to his nuts, he doubles over. At least he's immobilised for a moment.

Only moments later, Peg, Viper, and Dart dash in, their faces turning dark as they take in the scene.

"Motherfucker!" Peg takes a swing at the wall with his fist, his palpable rage rolling off him.

"Fuckin' bastard!" Dart unwittingly copies my earlier kick and I give a very male wince when he too kicks Buster in the balls.

Viper just stands and stares, his eyes wide in disbelief.

136

I just want Buster out of here for Wheels' sake, she doesn't need to see him any longer than she has to. "Get him out, and take him to the storage room," I snarl. This is it, the end of Buster in the club, and the end of him completely if I have my way. As Peg and Viper grab him by the arms and drag him out to take him to the location indicated, the area with the innocuous designation where all manner of unsavoury actions take place, I'm so angry I can't trust myself to follow them now. I'll kill him, and to take the life of a patched member without the club having voted on it wouldn't go down well. But to try to rape a woman who's even more defenceless than most—I simply don't have the words to express my repugnance.

And anyway, my first duty of obligation is to the woman still crying uncontrollably in my arms.

"She okay?" Dart has lingered, his face taut with concern, his voice almost breaking with worry.

"I don't know." Honestly, I don't, not yet. A horrendous thing to happen to any female, but to her? It hasn't escaped my notice that her wheelchair is on its side against the opposite wall of the room, the crutches and prosthesis lying out of her reach next to it. "Can you go get a bottle of vodka?" Probably not the best answer, but it might help.

With a sharp nod, and a quick glance at Wheels, he leaves to do as I asked. I know it will be killing him too, he's got a soft spot for the woman who's been attacked tonight in the very place she should have been safe. And it won't just be him. I know all my brothers have taken to her by the way they behave when she's in the clubhouse.

Now, how to comfort Wheels? I shift her so she's held more comfortably in my arms. "Hey, sweetheart. I've got you now, he's gone, and I swear you'll never see him again." I try to get through to her. "I promise you darlin', he's gone." I smooth my hand up and down her back, not caring that her tears are soaking through my tee. When her sobs stop being quite so forceful I decide to find out exactly how far Buster had got. "Here, tell me, did he fuckin' hurt you, darlin'?" I'm hoping to get some response from her and that she'll tell me I got here in time. Fuck, if he laid a finger on her...

When her hand comes up to wipe her eyes I think I'm beginning to get through. As she lifts her face it's then I notice the blood trickling from the side of her mouth, and that her cheek's split open. My breath catches in my lungs, and as gently as I can I turn her to face me. "He fuckin' hit you?"

"Yes," her voice catches. Her hand comes up to touch her cheek to check the damage, but I cover it with mine and pull it down.

"May I?" I hover my other hand over the cheek where it looks like a ring caught it. I've seen that type of injury often enough before—hell, we all wear rings that double as knuckledusters. But I don't want to take liberties or to scare her more, so ask again for her permission to examine it closer.

She gives such a tiny little nod I almost miss it. But taking it for consent, the only thing she's consented to tonight I remind myself, I felt my fingers lightly against it, making sure I don't hurt her more than she is already. It doesn't look deep enough for stitches.

At that moment, Dart comes back into the room, and thank fuck he's had the sense to bring the first aid kit with him. I ask him to put on the main light, and he brings the small case over to me, then I hear his sharply inhaled breath.

"He's a dead motherfucker," he breathes. "Never liked the fucker anyway."

At least I wasn't alone in that! Someone else as well as Peg was of the same opinion. Maybe that vote would go my way.

Keeping my voice as gentle as I can, working hard not to let my anger show, I tell her what I'm about to do. "Here, sweetheart, you don't need stitches, but I'm gonna clean that up, okay? And put a plaster on." I'm going to use the butterfly strips to hold it together, hopefully she won't be left with too much of a scar—she won't want a reminder of this night.

As I take an antiseptic pad and start gently dabbing at the blood, I get around to my main concern. "Did he hurt you anywhere else?" She goes to shake her head. "Be still now, and let me do this. But I want an answer, babe."

Her voice has a little more strength in it now, but she still stutters as she replies, "He... he...groped me, roughly. My breasts, he bit me. He had his hand down my underwear but you stopped him before...before..."

As tears start to fall again, I pull her to me and hold her close. Behind I can hear Dart swearing, and a thump tells me he's probably copied Peg's earlier action and has hit the wall with his fist. I can't fucking believe any member of the Satan's Devils would even think of doing something like this. It's not what the club stands for. And I blame myself for not acting on my instinct to get him kicked out of the club before he went this far. The warning signs had been there. Why hadn't I acted on them?

"If he bit her she might need a tetanus shot," Dart interrupts my thought, making a good point.

"Can you show me, sweetheart?" I know I'm asking a lot. Her hands are gripping the duvet to her like a shield.

Warily her gaze flicks over my shoulder to where Dart's standing, but after only a moment's pause she pulls down her cover. She doesn't have to expose much, there are clear teeth marks on the top curves of her luscious and perfectly natural looking breasts, not deep enough to break the skin, but nasty bruises are already forming. Dart whistles air in through his teeth, takes out his phone, fiddles with it for a moment, and then hands it to me. I take a picture of the marks and cover her up again, then take a photo of her face.

Proving his usefulness, Dart hands me a glass with clear liquid, which I'm pretty certain isn't water. I pass it into her shaking hand. "Drink this, it will help settle you."

She takes a couple of swallows, the neat vodka making her cough, but it works to make her loquacious and it all comes pouring out. "I was completely powerless, Wraith. He broke in. I locked the door, honest, but he must have got a key from somewhere. He came in, kicked my wheelchair away…"

"Hush, now." I grit my teeth, knowing I'd been right but not feeling any the better for it; it was her helplessness that bothers her the most.

Her hands grip my tee, her fingers curling and uncurling. "Thank God you came, Wraith, I couldn't have stood it if he, if he…"

"Hush," I repeat, she doesn't have to put it into words. We all know what his intentions were. "You'll never have to see him again, babe." I reiterate my earlier promise.

"What… What's going to happen to him?"

"We'll make sure he never gets his fuckin' hands anywhere near another woman, sweetheart," Dart answers for me.

"I can't stay here. I've got to get away." She's pulling back, pushing herself from me. "What if someone else…?"

She thinks someone else in the club would take advantage of her? I have to get that thought right out of her mind. Gritting my teeth, I tell her, "You don't have to worry about that! None of the other brothers would even fuckin' dream of comin' near you, babe. You're safe here. I fuckin' guarantee it. None of them would lay a finger on you."

But instead of calming her, my words seem to make her more agitated and she lets go of me completely, her shoulders slumping in defeat. And just when I'm about to ask her what's wrong, she wails, "That's what he said."

"You, what?" Dart and I say virtually the same thing at the same time. I'd like to hope she just meant they'd have too much respect for her, but something in her tone makes me believe she meant it an entirely different way.

She shrugs, and the way she shrinks back into herself is almost like watching her will to live seep out of her as she explains with a catch in her voice, "He said no one would go near a cripple like me. So I suppose I have to believe you."

My anger, which had been replaced by sympathy for the woman in my arms, returns with a vengeance, and the thoughts which had been plaguing me all night come rushing to the fore, making my words come out unfiltered. "He's a fuckin' liar, babe. He's twisted and doesn't know what he's fuckin' talkin' about. *I* want you. Christ, how I want you."

I ignore the whistling sound Dart makes behind me as myriad of emotions flick over her face at my admission—hope, disbelief, fear. I hurry to reassure her, "But the one difference with me, babe, is that I'd want to be fuckin' sure you wanted me too. I would never force you. But whatever happens, I'll protect you, you feel me? I'm gonna fuckin' be here for you babe. Whether you want me or not. But I won't touch you without you sayin' yes."

She looks at me as though she can't believe me, her brow furrows. My declaration has given her something to process, so I gently pull her to me and brush my lips over her hair, hoping to convey my sincerity with actions, not words. She sobs once again, reminding me she's sore and in pain. I ask where she keeps the Tramadol, then open the bedside table and take the box out. I know you're probably not supposed to drink with the medication, but I'm hoping it will ease her pains, and if it makes her sleepy, that's what she needs tonight. Still bemused and uncertain by my admission of my desire, she washes it down with vodka. Another possibly not so good idea.

"I'll be off now, man. Unless there's anythin' else you want?" A shuffling of feet lets me know Dart's taking his leave, and I turn to nod at him, seeing him pause by the door. "Wraith, what you said here. I ain't gonna tell anyone, okay?"

Thanking him—Drum would have my ass if he knew—I turn my attention back to Wheels. "I'm stayin' with you tonight. I'll take that chair over there, but I'm not leavin' this room, okay? Now, settle down and close your eyes, you'll be safe, I said I'll protect you." As my voice murmurs on, she shuffles down the bed and rests against the pillow I recovered from the floor. Her eyes close, and then flick open again and she looks around the room, her pupils wide and staring.

"It's alright, babe. I'm here. I'm gonna switch off the main light, and then go sit on the chair."

But before I can move, she grasps me. "Stay here. Hold me. Please."

I don't need much encouragement—the thought of how far Buster might have gone, even killing her to cover his tracks as he must have known what the penalty for her rape would have been, is devastating. I could have lost her before I even had her. With a shudder, I get to my feet and darken the room, but leave on the bedside light. My heart's beating so fast just imagining what could have happened had I not got here in time, and my teeth clench together as I think about the morning to come and what I'll have to do. Lying down beside her, I gather her into my arms, smoothing my hand down her back until her breathing slows.

She wakes once more during the night, with a heart-rending cry, but I pull her closer and gently kiss her hair, her eyes, and cheek on the unharmed side of her face until she drifts off to sleep again.

We're woken to voices outside. As I go to leave the bed, wanting to open the door and check who's there, she pulls at my tee, holding me back. Her eyes look at me warily in consternation. "Wraith, what you said last night. I know you didn't mean it. It's alright, I know you just said it to make me feel better."

Leaning over, I place a chaste kiss to her forehead. That she's having difficulty believing me makes me want to smile—there's hard evidence of it if she cared to look, but I keep my amusement from my face. My face as serious as I can make it, I try to impart my sincerity. "I meant every word," I tell her. "Every fuckin' word. And whatever happens, or you want to take this further or not, well, darlin' that's completely up to you. But never doubt exactly how I feel. And exactly how much I fuckin' want you."

She lets me go, her brow creasing as she considers my words.

Opening the door, I find quite a crowd waiting outside. Sandy and Carmen have covered dishes on a tray, and Blade, our enforcer, is standing behind with a jug of coffee and mugs, and behind him is Dollar. I wave them all in. She gives Blade a wary look, and one look at his reddened face wearing a deep scowl, rage rolling off him in waves, tells me why. I remember Peg explaining how he got his name. With Blade, it's all true, and I wouldn't be at all surprised to find Buster at the mercy of some of his handiwork later.

The women bustle in and take over, helping Wheels to sit up, fussing over her, helping her to sit and putting the tray of bacon, eggs, and waffles on her lap. The first thing she goes for is the coffee, almost seeming to inhale it, and when Sandy offers one to me I take it without hesitation and do the same.

Blade takes me to one side. "Emergency church at ten," he tells me quietly. Checking my phone I see it's just gone nine now. "I've brought the prospects with me. They'll stay with Wheels until you're out."

I'm glad he thought of that.

"You okay, darlin'?" Looking up I see Bullet staring at her carefully, and the thought flits through my mind that I don't like him doing that. He catches sight of my eyes narrowing, but waits until she nods, then after a moment's further consideration he turns away and joins Blade and myself.

"I s'pect I know what you want, Wraith. I'll be votin' that way myself. Fuckin' motherfuckin' coward going after a defenceless woman." I lift my chin in thanks at Bullet.

"I'm with you, man. He's sick." Blade's not wrong in my opinion.

After slapping my back, both men leave. I watch her with the women for a second, seeing how strained her face is, as though having to keep up the pretence that's she not suffering any after effects of her ordeal is draining. I decide to rescue her and wheel her chair across to her and pick up her crutches and prosthesis to give her a feeling of independence, as well as a gentle hint to the girls.

"You ladies wanna give her some space now? To get dressed and that?"

Sandy creases her brow and her mouth purses—it looks like she wants to stay, but Wheels lays her hand on her arm. "Thank you for coming to see me, but I'd like to put this behind me. Once I'm dressed I'll come down to the club room to find you."

So, picking up the tray—the food on which I notice has hardly been touched—Sandy and Carmen leave us alone.

Making my way to the bed, I sit down, bringing myself once again to her level, believing she'll find it less intimidating. I study her for a second, she looks tired and drawn, and the smile she'd managed to summon up for the girls has disappeared. I'd do anything to put that smile back.

After a moment, I explain what's going to happen. "I've got to go to a meetin' for a while. It shouldn't be too long. The prospects are outside and they're not gonna let anyone in without checkin' with you first, until I get back. That okay with you, babe?"

"Which ones?"

"Hank and Spider."

A little smile. "I like Hank."

I do, too. The jury's still out on Spider. He can be a lazy fucker. Another moment of consideration, and then she says bravely, "Okay. But, Wraith, you won't be too long, will you?"

I shake my head. "I'll be as quick as I can be. You get showered and dressed, and I'll be back before you know it. If you feel up to it, the prospects will take you down to the clubhouse. The ol' ladies will be there to keep you company."

She nods, but slowly. I'm reluctant to leave her, but there are things that need to be done. After placing a gentle kiss to her forehead, I leave her, go back to my room, change, and freshen myself up. Slipping back into my cut sporting the patch I'm so proud to wear but that was so sullied last night, I make my way through the club room and into church.

CHAPTER 11
Wraith

Not everyone is here yet—I'm a little early, but Drummer is sitting, waiting at the head of the table. And someone has already filled him in on all the events of last night. Drummer might go through women like a knife through butter, but would never take anyone but a willing partner. And that goes for the rest of us.

"Lucky you were passin'," he tells me, his face as dark as I've ever seen it. "Bastard wouldn't have stopped."

Suppressing a shudder, I don't even want to think what would have happened if I hadn't been there, or if I'd left it to later to leave the bar. I suppose I should thank Chrissy for chasing me out when she did. Not that I'm going to, but if she hadn't have come on so strong and I hadn't wanted to get away, well, I agree with Drum, Buster would have raped her. And maybe wouldn't have stopped there.

"I'll get a prospect on her until Horse gets back. Give her some kind of fuckin' comfort. She must think we're a load of animals."

"No need for that. I'll be with her." The words come out before I can censor them.

His eyes narrow. "Like that, is it?"

I shrug, trying to recover some ground. Drum hasn't rescinded his instruction that none of us should touch her. "I don't like a guest of ours being put in that position. I think we owe it to her to show we're takin' this seriously."

"It's serious, brother," he assures me. "Very serious. And there's gonna be serious fuckin' consequences too."

During our short conversation, the seats around the table have been filled, except for the one of course. Friday is usually the day for church, and we'll still be holding our regular meeting later, but all members have made themselves available for this special meeting after getting the call. This morning there's just the one important item on the agenda—what to do about Buster. The only missing member.

Drummer bangs the gavel and gets attention on him. "Right, the way gossip spreads around this place like wildfire I think we all know why we're here. Before we go through the options, I want to let you know what the bugger Snake had to say when I had words with him earlier."

I sit up, my interest caught. Snake is the president of the San Diego chapter, where Buster had transferred in from.

"Seems like he hadn't been exactly straight with us. The patch-over request came from Buster himself, but if he hadn't had jumped, he would have been pushed. And quite possibly had his fuckin' patch taken away."

"He cause trouble down there?" This from Slick.

"Too fuckin' right. Apparently, the club whores had complained about him. Seems he was inclined to be rough."

Now that's something. Those girls take a lot from brothers who can get pretty rowdy at times—for them to complain suggests he'd been particularly brutal with them.

"Snake wasn't surprised by what I told him, and I have his go-ahead to do whatever we think we should. Not that I need it of course." No, as Drummer is president of the mother charter, he outranks Snake. "Now, anyone got anythin' to say?"

Rock lifts his hand, the one not twirling his gun around on the table. "He's been showing outright disrespect for the VP and other officers, Drum. As well as to the girl. His fuckin' attitude is off. Last night was fuckin' despicable, but this would have come to the table eventually in any event."

"And he's been disrespectin' the fuckin' club too. He missed church a few times with no fuckin' excuse. Before we go on, anyone want to say anythin' in our brother's defence?" As Drummer's eyes flick around the table, no one stirs.

"VP, you witnessed the incident, what's your proposal?"

Before I can speak Dart puts his hand in the air. "You might all want to see these." He throws copies of the photos he'd taken last night of Wheels' face and the bite marks clearly visible on the top of her breasts. "Luckily Wraith stopped him before he went any further." As the pictures do the rounds, various miens of disgust appear on my brothers' faces.

I tap my fingers on the table. I know what I want, and hope my brothers will support me. "I want his patch, Drum." As Drummer goes to speak, I hold up my hand. I haven't finished yet. "And I'm sick of breathin' the same fuckin' air as that sadistic bastard. I want him dead."

There was an audible intake of breath from around me. I couldn't put it any plainer than that. Mutterings started but were quickly brought to a halt when Drummer slammed his meaty fist down. "Okay then, there are two motions on the table. First, we vote on takin' his patch."

He starts with me, a definite 'Aye' purely for form's sake as everyone knows the way I'll be voting, and continues around. There was no dissension.

"Right, Buster, the man we used to call brother is out, and out bad." That, at the very least, would mean the large Satan's Devils tattoo on his back would be burned off. Drum pauses for a moment as Heart records the result of the serious vote in the club's record book.

The prez wipes his hand over his face, and then says in his most solemn tone, "Second motion, that we send him on his way to Satan."

I could hardly get the word 'Aye' out of my mouth fast enough, but for such a decision with such grave repercussions, it doesn't surprise me this time the vote takes a little longer, and can't help but be relieved as one after the other of my brothers gives the same vote as me. It comes back around to Drummer, who, with a glance in my direction, gives a resounding 'Aye'.

As Heart scribbles again, Drum nods slowly. "Right, we're all in agreement. VP, you, Blade, and Peg will take the lead. Any other brother wantin' to help Buster on his one-way fuckin' trip to Satan feel free to join them. I want this sorted by church this evenin'. As the VP so eloquently fuckin' put it, it offends me to be breathin' the same fuckin' air as that bastard."

With a final bang of the gravel, church is dismissed.

I'm warned how many of the brothers follow Peg, Blade, and me as we make our way to the place with the innocent misnomer of storage room. As I glance behind I see faces flushed with rage, a couple of brothers have their arms moving to and fro in practice swings, and others have fists clenched by their sides. Slick is thumping one hand against the other. The man waiting for us was in for a great deal of hurt. His exit from this life isn't going to be easy. *Uh uh.*

Deferring to their VP, it's me who opens the door and flips on the lights. He'd been left hanging by his arms from the rafters in the dark—why waste electricity on a man who'd everyone expects to soon breathe his final breath?

Stepping inside it becomes clear that whoever had strung him up had already got a few licks in. Buster is dangling shirtless, and there were nasty bruises across his chest, which I hope are hurting.

As we enter, he lifts his head, and any hope he might have had evaporates at the expressions on our faces. But he tries. "Aw, fuck, come on brothers. You don't wanna do this."

I step in front of him, bouncing on my feet, hardly able to contain my rage. Did he really think we'd give him a pat on his motherfuckin' back? "We don't need fuckin' brothers like you, Buster."

He spits on the ground. "All this about a fuckin' bitch?"

Heart, his affable personality absent for once, comes up alongside me. "We care about our fuckin' women, you mother-fucker."

"I'm gonna lose my fuckin' patch over this? Jeez. Bros over hos, guys." He shakes his head as though he can't believe it.

He doesn't seem to have a clue how badly he's fucked up, but one look at my tight features gives him the answer.

I want to get back to Wheels and don't want to string this out. "Blade, get the blow torch and the rum." We keep a bottle of 100% proof rum here for just this purpose. Luckily, we rarely have occasion to use it.

The fire in Buster's eyes slowly died as his pupils dilate in horror. "Hey, I'll get the ink blacked out. No need for this. Hey, come on, guys, you don't want to do this. Snake will vouch for me."

"Snake thinks the same as us, that you're a fuckin' animal that needs to be put down." I nod to Blade, knowing as our enforcer he'll know what to do, and I see no need for any delay.

Blade passes the bottle to Peg, who begins making sure Buster's back is covered in the flammable liquid, while Blade gets the blowtorch going. Without giving the hanging man a chance for any more filth to come out of his mouth, he touches the flame to his back. Now the air is filled with the sounds of screaming and the odour of burning skin as the full back patch tattoo is burned off. The smell makes me want to gag, but I stand stoically until the flames have died away.

Buster's conscious, but in a whole lot of pain, and he's about to take a lot more. Moving off to the side I take the baseball bat that's conveniently sitting there and take the first hit, smashing into one knee cap and then the other. He's now holding his full weight on his arms, tears of pain flooding down his face. His eyes search out mine, and I give a crooked smile, knowing that now he realises we're not just taking his patch, he's a dead man.

Buster spits blood, then in a gurgling voice gasps, "She's just a fuckin' crippled whore…"

Slick gives him no time to spout any more poison. Taking the bat from me, he chooses the ribs. One by one my brothers step up until Buster's nothing more than a dangling mess of broken bones. He's flitting in and out of consciousness.

I hold up my hand. There's no point continuing, more pain probably wouldn't even register, and I'm anxious to get back to check on Wheels. I jerk my head towards Blade and he nods back. Getting out his namesake from his belt, he swipes his finger along the side as though checking how sharp it is, it will be like a razor—he keeps it that way. Now he steps forwards and starts carving over the would-be rapist's torso. He's quite artistic is Blade, so I give him the time he needs and enjoy the last few screams which turn to whimpers as the blood pours out, and then there's silence. Blade cocks his head towards me, and I give him a quick jerk of my chin. He knows what has to be done, and ends it by slicing the blade across Buster's throat.

It's done, over. And I for one will sleep easier in my bed tonight.

"I'll send the prospects down to clean up. Blade, you stay here and watch them." Blade throws me a chin lift. He'll make sure the body is burned along with his cut and buried up in the forest behind us. After one last glance back at the dead man, I leave the storage room.

CHAPTER 12

Sophie

Before my accident I used to love sex—I mean, I *really* enjoyed it. I suppose some people would call me promiscuous, but I've never seen it that way or thought it was wrong. If I saw a man I liked and believed he could give me a good time, I went for it. No one would criticise a man who acted the same way, so why should I be the one to feel ashamed? After getting burned so badly the first time I knew I would never again be in the market for a relationship, so why not get my physical needs fulfilled in different ways?

A brief smile comes to my lips as I recall some of my experiences in rather unusual places, the illicitness of our activity seeming to fire the pleasure. The men I'd been with wouldn't have walked away with their heads hung low, so why should I?

But all the times I've hooked up with men, it's always been my decision. A handsome man giving me a come-on, and I'd be there, but only if I wanted him to. Never has someone tried to take it from me by force.

Since my accident all that's changed. Sex is no longer important to me, the fear of rejection dampening my libido. I know there's no point flirting suggestively as I'm too ashamed of what my body has become. I don't even get aroused reading my books, and the batteries on my vibrator are still as fresh as the day I put them in before it happened, before Ethan St John-Davies arranged for me to lose my leg.

Now I'm a victim of attempted rape, saved at the last moment by a man who says he wants me, even with my physical limitations, though I'm not sure whether I believe that or whether he just said it to make me feel better. I spent a good part of last night sobbing into his shirt, but my tears were not so much down to what Buster had tried to do, instead it was that I'd been absolutely powerless to stop him. I'd had no means of fight or escape. That he had known that makes me angry—what kind of man takes advantage of a helpless woman? That he nearly succeeded makes me scared. What if it happened again? The fear which had been in the back of my mind since Horse brought me here, that I was at the mercy of these tough, leather-clad men with violence running through their veins, assails me.

But what else can I do? Where could I go? There's a bloody contract out for me so I can't go home, and I'm not sure how safe it would be for me alone in a foreign country. As last night showed me, I can't exactly run away if I'm in any danger. A woman in a wheelchair or even on the crutches which I'm now starting to use more regularly sticks out like a sore thumb!

Suddenly a vision of Peg comes to my mind. Not only has he learned to walk again, but he also does so with such ease that it's hard to see he's got an artificial leg. I'm never going to get my leg back, but if I keep up with the exercise I will be able to regain my independence. If I could walk properly again, it opens up a whole new world to me. And people would be less able to take advantage. Then my motivational thoughts start to fade. Whether I can walk with my prosthesis or not, I don't wear it to bed. I'd still be just as helpless unless... Unless I have a weapon to hand. That's what I've got to do, get Wraith to get me a gun, or even a knife. Something I can have close by so I'm able to protect myself. I'm sure Wraith will help me.

The decision made my positivity return. Electing there's no point dwelling on what might have happened, I need to get my strength back and some form of protection so nothing of the sort can happen again. I wheel over to where my prosthesis is lying on the floor next to my crutches, which Wraith had neatly grouped together after that bastard had thrown them away. Picking it up, I go back to the bed, transfer from my chair, and start strapping it on.

It's an hour later when Wraith returns. I'm sitting in the wheelchair, the prosthesis lying over my lap. Seeing the fresh tears in my eyes, he misinterprets them.

"Hey, darlin'." He rushes to my side, putting his arm around me and pulling me to him. "You don't have to worry about him ever again, I promise."

Wiping my hand over my weeping eyes, I give a little shake of my head. Incapable of forming words, instead of speaking I pass my prosthesis over to him. My constructive thoughts of a while ago having been totally swept away.

He takes it from me and gives me a curious look, then glances down to examine it more carefully.

I see the exact point he realises when his eyes narrow and his lips grow thin. "Shit," he exclaims as he notices the crack in the socket which should form a snug fit between my stump and the device. "That fucker do this?"

"Must have happened when he threw it against the wall."

I don't have to explain what this means. I don't have to tell him that the independence I was slowly regaining has now been lost to me. Or that I'm stuck in this bloody wheelchair until I can get a replacement. Oh, I might be able to hop short distances on one leg and my crutches, but for anything more I'll need a prosthesis. And fuck knows when I'll be able to get that. I don't have to say a word, he understands without me spelling it out. Wraith hugs me closer and rests his chin on my head. After a moment he pulls away and takes his phone out of his pocket.

He dials, then I hear him say, "Peg, can you come to Wheels' room? Yeah? Great."

I don't know why he's asked the sergeant-at-arms to come to the suite, or what he'll be able to do. And depressed as I am, I don't bother to ask.

"We'll sort it," he tries to reassure me. "Don't worry."

Swallowing down another sob, I cry out, "But how? We came so quickly I didn't get travel insurance and don't even know if they'd cover something like this if I had. I'll need to go back to England to get a new one. And if it's anything like the last time, that will take a couple of months."

He tries to calm me by stroking my back. "We'll fix this, darlin'." But I know there's nothing he can do. I'll have to go back to England and run the risk of Ethan catching up with me.

Peg must have moved fast because hardly any time passes before he's knocking at my door. Wraith goes out to meet him, taking the offending item with him. I hear deep voices murmuring, but can't make out the words. I sit alone, rubbing my arms with my hands as if I'm cold, feeling as though I've lost my leg all over again. I'm still staring down, vacantly looking at nothing when I hear them come back in. Life just seems to be one blow after another.

Walking over to me, Peg puts his hand under my chin and turns my face up to his. "Not your fuckin' day, is it darlin'? But don't worry, we've got this."

"There's nothing you can do," I tell him despondently.

"Hey," he speaks more sharply now. "I told you we've fuckin' got this. When have I lied to you, darlin'? Now pull yourself together and show me the woman who's worked so hard to get walkin' again."

The confidence that there's something they can do and the brief pep talk he's delivered starts lifting my spirit once again.

Peg understands prostheses. "Can you repair it?" I ask hopefully. I don't see how, but perhaps he knows a way.

But he shakes his head, confirming what I expected. "No, it's important that cup is a good fit and a repair ain't gonna cut it. That's a pretty standard one you've got anyway. We can probably do better than that."

"It was on the National Health." I just took what they'd given me, of course. And at least it was free.

"Yeah, the standard issue I expect. But I think there's a lot more choice out there. I'll set up a meet with the people I use and see what they recommend." Peg's talking about it as though it's no problem.

But he's ignoring the one thing I'm most worried about. "Peg, I won't be able to afford to replace it over here. I don't have insurance." I can't see any way around it.

Wraith laughs. "Hey, babe, don't worry about that."

The force with which he rejects my concerns makes me look up.

Peg's on the same wavelength. "Reckon the club owes you a new leg. Least we can do. You are under our protection, and that motherfucker should never have gotten near you."

What? My mouth opens as I stare at them. *Does he really mean it?* I never thought for a moment they'd replace my prosthesis for me. But the thought they'll change their minds when they realise the cost dashes my hopes.

"In fact, I'll go make an appointment now," Peg says. "I don't see that there'll be a problem getting Drum to agree. Then, before leaving, turns to me. "Wheels, don't worry, darlin'. We'll sort everythin' out for you. We'll have you back walkin' in no time."

As the sergeant-at-arms leaves the room, Wraith tells me, "Peg's a good man. He's battled his own demons and I've watched him go through exactly what you are. And if he says you're getting' a new prosthesis, darlin', just trust him to sort it out for you. Now, shall we go and see what we can rustle up for lunch?"

I'm still mulling over them paying for a new prosthesis for me, but even if the money's taken care off, I'll be waiting for months if it's anything like it was in England. Leaning forward, I put my head in my hands, wondering how this day can get much worse. Then Wraith's words sink in. He wants me to go to the clubhouse with everyone able to see I'm missing a leg? At least with my prosthesis I can pretend to be a whole person. "Can we just have something here?" I ask, hoping he'll understand.

But he doesn't. "What happened last night ain't on you, there's nothin' to be worried about."

So it's down to me to explain. I lower my eyes, embarrassed, and mumble, "But everyone will be able to see…"

The light dawns. "That you haven't got a leg? Hell, we already know that babe. And no one's bothered about that, I can assure you."

"But it's horrible…"

"Hey, stop that now." He brushes his hair back and then stands, stroking his beard. "The fact you're missin' a leg doesn't define you, babe. If someone has a problem with it, then it's on them, not you." He moves until he's standing right in front of me and takes both my hands in his. "You're a beautiful woman, Wheels, just take a good look and you'll see exactly the effect you have on me, and most of the other men here if they're not dead."

Raising my eyes, his swollen cock bulging at the material of his jeans is blatantly obvious. Swallowing rapidly, my stomach clenches and I feel myself getting wet in response.

I know Wraith would be true to his word and wouldn't force me. Involuntarily my breathing has increased, and a flush has come to my cheeks. He must see how he affects me. If I told him I didn't want him now, I'd be lying.

Falling to his knees, he curls one hand behind the back of my head, looking into my eyes, checking he's reading me right. Satisfied with what he sees, he brings his lips closer to mine. And then waits.

Can I? Can I risk his rejection? He might say it doesn't bother him, but what if it does? But how can I not take the chance? I want him as much as he says he wants me, and have ever since I first saw him. The old Sophie would have been there weeks ago. Knowing he's caught me with my defences down, I take the leap. Closing the distance between us, I bring my mouth to his and move my lips gently over his.

He takes over, applying more pressure, then murmuring, his voice a vibration I feel as well as hear, "Open for me."

Trembling slightly, I let him inside, tentative at my first kiss in months as though I'm a teenager on her first date. Our tongues touch, sliding and mating together. He doesn't hurry or rush me, just lets me get used to his unique taste. His lips are soft as they brush against mine—so gentle for such a big, tough man—and his beard brushes against my chin. As I breathe in, his unique scent fills my nostrils—some sort of cologne mixed with motor oil, and also, strangely, an acrid lingering odour of smoke.

He pulls me more tightly against him and deepens the kiss. My breasts brush against his chest, my nipples peaking as my arousal heightens. With one hand on the back of my head, he fists it in my hair, and with his other he reaches up to caress my cheek. My arms go around him and I hold him close, feeling the soft worn leather of his cut beneath my fingertips.

I open my eyes to find his gazing into mine, deep brown with flecks of gold, his pupils dilated with pleasure.

His touch is sweet, unhurried. I'm relishing everything about it. I don't think I've ever been kissed so tenderly before, though the tension in his body tells me he's holding himself back. *What would it be like if he released all that passion?* A shiver of delight runs down my spine and my womb clenches.

But he takes it no further. Slowly, he breaks away, nipping at my bottom lip before removing his mouth completely from mine, leaving me slightly bereft.

His eyes crinkle at the corners and the sides of his mouth turn up. "Now…" He looks ruefully down at his crotch where it's easy to see his cock bulging at the denim of his jeans. "Do you still fuckin' think I find your missin' leg a turn-off?"

I feel myself redden, and half turn away. "You haven't seen it yet."

"Believe me, babe," he smirks, "when I get you naked your legs are going to be the last things I'll be lookin' at."

Feeling almost inebriated, drunk on his taste, I giggle, realising for the first time in months the thought of exposing myself to a man doesn't worry me quite so much.

"And if we don't get to the clubhouse, that might happen sooner rather than later, and darlin', our first time? I don't want to rush it."

"You're quite sure of yourself, aren't you?"

"Yeah." Now it's his turn to smirk.

And I have no inclination to contradict him.

CHAPTER 13

Wraith

After a little persuasion, Wheels agrees to come to the clubhouse with me. Not too many people are around, but Carmen's in the kitchen, so I get Wheels settled by a table and go grab us some food. While I'm loading the plates, I feel a touch on my arm. Glancing up, my eyes meet Carmen's for an instant and see them narrow as she glares at the person behind who's put their hand on me.

I stiffen, and am not surprised to hear a breathy voice. "Hi Wraith, can I help you with that?" Her hand moves from my arms to the front of my jeans, and her fingers try to grasp my now, thankfully flaccid cock beneath the material. It had taken a while to go down after that kiss which, if I hadn't already been on them at the time, would have brought me to my knees.

Incensed, I swipe her hand away. "You do not touch a brother without invitation!" I snarl. "If anyone wants in your overused hole they'll let you know."

Chrissy's cheeks flush red, in anger or embarrassment—I neither know nor care. All I want is her grubby mitts off me and to get back to the woman I want. But as always, she doesn't realise that I've had enough.

"I've got two workin' legs, Wraith. Remember what it feels like when they're wrapped around you? The cripple can't give you what I can."

My hands clench into fists before I remember that I don't hit women, but if she carries on like this I'll be making an exception. Quickly spinning around, I take hold of her shoulders, squeezing tight and give her a little shake. "Bitch, if I hear one more disagreeable fuckin' word out of your mouth you won't like the consequences."

Eyes filling with fake tears, she tries once more. "But Wraith, I love you. We were so good together."

She thinks she loves me? Christ, she'd love any brother she thought would give her the patch. And she's set her sights on the wrong one here! "Good together? We fucked. End of story. Now if you don't fuckin' get lost, I'll throw you out of the clubhouse myself."

With an exaggerated sob, she seems to get the message at last and turns and walks away. I hear slow clapping behind me, and rotating around again see Slick standing there.

"Bitch has got a hard-on for you, Wraith."

"Fuck knows why," I tell him. "And that's not the first time I've told her to leave me the fuck alone. In her head she thinks we had somethin' between us." I run my hands through my hair in exasperation. I hadn't fucked her for weeks, having run as soon as I picked up the sign she was looking to be an old lady.

"Bitch is forgettin' her place here. Seems like we need to remind her. Drum would fuckin' kick her out if she tried it with him." Shaking his head, Slick gets his phone out, checking the time. "Church in fifteen minutes," he reminds me.

"I'll be there. Just give me a few to eat this."

Carmen walks towards me. "Tell Wheels to come in here while you're in church. Amy's comin' over shortly with Crystal. We'll keep her company and try to take her mind off last night. I might see if she wants me to give her hair a trim, make her feel better."

I thank Bullet's wife—the old ladies are a supportive lot who seem to have taken Wheels under their wing. Then, at last, I return to Wheels with her lunch, happy she's not going to be left alone to stew while I'm gone.

"Wraith, the club whore..." Running my hand through my hair, I know she'd seen my altercation with Chrissy and I'm going to have to give her an explanation.

"Ain't fucked no whores since you've been here, Wheels. And that's the fuckin' truth. Some of those bitches want to get their claws into a brother and build up their services as being somethin' it's not." I break off, and then add forcefully, "Believe me, darlin', anythin' that bitch assumed was all in her fuckin' mind."

I know how the club runs is still something she doesn't completely understand, but she's been here long enough to know the club whores have to make themselves available to anybody, and being bikers, we take advantage. Of course we do, or I did, until I met Wheels.

But instead of harping on about Chrissy, she's picked up on something else I said.

Putting her hand on my arm, a touch that this time I welcome, she says quietly, "Why haven't you been with them since I arrived?"

I breathe in deeply and tell her the truth. "Because you took my fuckin' breath away, darlin'. I've just been waiting until it was the right time."

She sucks in air through her teeth, and the light fades out of her eyes. There was something about my reply that she didn't like. And for the life of me I don't fucking understand it. But I don't get the chance to delve into what it is, as Slick passes by, slaps me on the back of my head and tells me it's time for church.

Entering the meeting room a couple of minutes later, I am still wondering what I'd said to cause the unexpected reaction, but have to put it out of my mind for now as I see everyone is already here. One less seat around the table now, of course. And that gives us a problem—Buster used to work at the strip club we own in Tucson, which now means someone else needs to be deployed there. Beef volunteers, we all agree, and Drummer's gavel bangs down confirming it. Nudges, winks, and outright crude comments fly around the table, but to be honest, Beef will probably be able to keep his hands off the strippers better than Buster could.

It's the usual Friday night meeting. We run through the state of our other businesses, which all seem to be in relatively good health, discuss a run that's coming up the week after next, and then Drum asks if there's any other business.

Before I can open my mouth, Peg starts, "Buster broke fuckin' Wheels' prosthesis. She's helpless without it. I want to take her to Utah to my specialist to either get it fixed or preferably to get a new one. I think they can give her a better one than she's using at present."

"Lucky he's already dead," Slick starts. "What kind of sick fuckin' bastard does somethin' like that?"

Murmurs of agreement go around the table. "Hope you made him hurt!" Mouse drops in.

I assure him we did.

"She got insurance?" Drummer asks.

Peg and I shake our heads in unison. "I'm proposin' the club coughs up for it. She was under our protection after all." I make my suggestion.

"We shouldn't have to protect a woman from our own fuckin' members," Drummer snarls out, he runs his hand over his beard as he thinks for a moment. That's our prez, not rushing into a decision. Although if we're in a tight spot he can call the shots pretty damn fast. It's not long before he speaks again. "I agree with you, VP. Club should foot the bill."

"Thought that would be the case. I've already made a provisional appointment for Monday. I propose I'll take her up there Sunday night and stay over until Wednesday. They're usually pretty quick there, and have a two-day turnaround."

My eyes widen. "Wheels said it took months to get her first prosthetic."

"Prosthesis," Peg corrects me. "She's got a prosthetic limb, but the actual artificial leg is called a prosthesis. And that's the British health system for you! Taking ages and supplying shit, but then, she wouldn't have had to pay for it," Peg answers me.

Drum bangs the table. "I don't want a fuckin' debate on semantics or on the English National Health. Just do it, Peg. But take someone with you. We can't forget someone's very interested in getting a hold of her, and I'd be happier if you had back-up."

"I'll go." The words came out of my mouth, but I don't recall making the decision.

Peg and Dart both throw me knowing grins, then jerk their chins at the other brothers around the table. I narrow my eyes, not getting the joke, but knowing I'm the butt of it.

Drummer's looking at me carefully, his brow furrowed, then he smirks. "Ok, VP, she should be *safe* with you and Peg." The emphasis suggests he doesn't think I'm just offering out of the goodness of my heart. But it's a relatively quiet time for the club, so he doesn't seem too bothered about losing his VP for a few days. Then, after giving it further thought, he adds, "Take a prospect with you."

Mouse's fingers tap on the table and the way he's shifting in his seat shows he's got something to say. Prez has noticed. "Spit it out, Mouse."

After clearing his throat, our computer geek speaks up. "I've been monitorin' the dark web. The contract's been taken down."

"Could he have given up?" Dart leans forwards, interested.

But Mouse shakes his head. "Nah, it's more likely that someone has taken on the job."

"Can you find out who?" I put in.

Mouse grins. "Have I ever let you down? But it just might take me a bit of time."

Drum leans back in his chair, his finger moving around, indicating all of us. "Right, I'm takin' it we're all in agreement that the club coughs up for Wheels' new fuckin' leg?"

There's no dissent, and Heart writes it in the book.

"So recorded. Church fuckin' over!" Drum bangs the gavel for the final time, and we get up to go and party.

When I get to the clubroom I see the old ladies have disappeared, and the club whores and hang-arounds are out in force, the latter being girls coming up from Tucson for the dubious delights of sharing their bodies with bikers. It always amazes me how there are so many who treat us like rock stars, always hungry for biker cock.

I'm pleased to see Wheels is nowhere in sight, and assume she's been here long enough to know she doesn't want to be at a full-on biker party. But I need to make sure she's safe. I take out my phone and text.

Wraith: You okay? Back in your room?
Wheels: Yes, I'm fine.

Though I'd trust any other brother with my life, the incident with Buster has unnerved me, so I feel relieved. Knowing I've no wish to sink my cock into any pussy other than hers, I don't want to stay and get involved with any of the whores or visiting girls, but I could do with a drink or two.

Wraith: I'll be in the clubhouse for a while.

Wheels: No problem. Hank's with me.

Hank's with her? Inside her room, or does she mean outside? The prospect better not be in her fucking room. Or her bed. Suddenly that drink doesn't look quite so attractive anymore. Christ! I can trust the fucking prospect, can't I? He's not going to be doing anything to upset a brother. Especially his VP. *Pull yourself to-fucking-gether!*

Slick comes up and shoves a bottle in my hand and, recognising I'd look a pussy to run off right now, I take it, but can't get rid of the niggling question of just how closely Hank might be watching her for me. He's a handsome bugger, and not far off Wheels' age. If he wants his patch he better go nowhere fucking near her. He won't be getting my vote otherwise.

The beer takes the edge off, but I need more. It's Friday night, and however much I want to personally check that the prospect's behaving himself, I've got to keep up appearances at least for a while. Otherwise, every motherfucker here will know where I'm going and suspect exactly what I'm planning to do. At the bar, I find Peg in his regular place and wave at the bottle of Jack. Marsh fills a shot glass and I down it in one gulp. Then, after rapping twice on the bar, Marsh gives me another.

Peg's watching me. Easing himself up on a stool, he leans his elbow on the wood. "Be fuckin' careful with her," he warns me.

I crease my eyes, not quite understanding.

"Wheels," he clarifies. "It's a fucker of a thing to get over, losin' your leg. It takes time to adjust."

I settle on another stool. Peg knows what he's talking about, and it might help to listen. "She thinks seein' her stump would be a complete turn-off."

"And she's right."

"What?" I didn't expect him to say that.

166

He nods slowly. "For some people it is. I've had women who don't want anythin' to do with me once they've seen it. As if my cock ain't enough to compensate."

"Her leg doesn't bother me." I might not have seen it yet, but I've watched my brother put on his prosthesis before.

"It probably won't, her pussy will take all your attention. But to her? If you're going to be the first man other than her doctor to see it, she'll be worried. If you don't handle it right, man, you could damage her."

I huff a laugh. "You reckon I want in her?" Drum hasn't lifted the restriction he imposed on us all, so I've got to take care who I admit my intentions to—even Peg.

"I've seen you around her. I know you do. And otherwise," he pauses to take a swig of his beer, "why did you volunteer to come seven hundred miles to fuckin' Utah? Just step up and own it, brother. I ain't gonna tell Drum."

A grin starts to come to my face, there's no point in denying it —Peg's known me too long. And then my smile disappears as I see fucking Chrissy coming up behind him.

Her arms try to encircle his large body and she leans forwards to whisper into his ear, but plenty loud enough for me to hear. "You wanna take me back to your room, big fella? Have some fun?"

Peg's eyes widen, and he glances at me. While a club whore and therefore expected to give her favours to all the brothers, the brothers know she usually focuses her attentions on me. Peg certainly does, and as her hands reach around to his groin and blatantly rub against his cock, he tilts his head and throws me a silent question. Realising he hadn't heard our altercation in the kitchen earlier, I simply lift my chin. If he can get her off my back and keep her away from Wheels, I'll be quite happy.

"Don't mind me." I wave my drink in salute.

The sergeant-at-arms gets off his seat and gathers Chrissy to him. As he leads her off, she throws a pleading look at me over her shoulder, letting me know she was trying to make me jealous. Huh, she's failed, and now she's going to have to eat the fruit of her labours. I find I could care less.

One more shot of Jack, and that's me done for the night.

CHAPTER 14
Sophie

Despite my concerns about being out in public with my jeans flopping around my non-existent leg and visibly having no foot, I'm not the public spectacle I feared I'd be. Crystal, wearing yet another colourful pair of leggings, this time with trees and parrot-like birds, keeps me entertained with telling stories of the men in the club, while Carmen, to my delight, gives my hair a much-needed trim. Little Amy's an absolute delight. Once Carmen had finished with me she climbed on my lap and pulls at my now tidier locks, eventually getting bored and dropping off for a nap in my arms.

"So," I glance up at Carmen, "how did Slick get his name?"

Now with her hairdressing duties done, she's helping out again, popping the lasagne Crystal's just prepared into the oven. She turns to me with a smile. "He hit some oil once and laid his bike down. Slid down the road apparently."

"Ouch." I'd thought it was something to do with his bald head. These men are cruel not letting him forget something like that.

Amy starts fidgeting and Crystal comes to take her now wide awake daughter from me. The rest of the afternoon passes quickly as we start discussing anything and everything. I realise I've never really had this, girlfriends who I could just relax with. Soon we're involved in a discussion trying to decide which men of the club are the better endowed, and I'm having a great time, at times almost bent doubled-over with laughter. It's only spoiled momentarily when the club whore Wraith had chased off comes over with a sneer on her face, but before she can open her mouth Carmen shoos her away.

Slowly the club room begins to fill up with women—women who didn't come over to talk to the old ladies. As well as the whores, other scantily clad girls appear, up from Tucson my new friends explain. And later, as I look over and see Chrissy with the other sweet butts waiting for the men to come out of church, I feel a moment's envy at her long, beautiful, and fully functional legs plainly on display under her short and almost indecent skirt. It makes me wonder about Wraith's firm declaration that he hadn't been near them since I'd arrived at the compound. I can't understand it—surely he'd prefer someone who was whole?

Knowing I wouldn't want to be around when the men came out of church unless I wanted to watch free live porn, after eating a plateful of the delicious pasta and helping where I can with the clearing up, I decide to go back in my room. Crystal's already left with Amy, and Carmen's now getting ready to leave.

"I'm off now, Carmen."

After nodding at me, she beckons to someone outside the kitchen and Hank walks in.

"You ready to go, Wheels?" he asks in his cheery voice.

"You coming with me?"

"VP's orders, so yeah."

I admit, although they assure me Buster won't be bothering me again, I was feeling a bit nervous about going to my room alone, so I'm not going to complain about having him along. Though I soon make it known he doesn't have to push me, and he takes up his place walking alongside.

Being accompanied by someone I don't really know is a bit awkward, so to remedy the fact I decide to break the ice and find out more about him. "So, Hank, what made you want to join the Satan's Devils?"

He glances down at me and then gives a small shrug. "Was lookin' for somewhere to belong, I guess. Grew up in foster homes, never really stayed around anywhere for long. I dunno, the brotherhood seemed to call to me. And I love Harleys, of course. Got myself a real beaut, been restorin' it for a while now."

"What's it like to be a prospect? What do you have to do?"

Another shrug. "Anythin' the brothers ask me to do." His mouth snaps shut.

"Like?"

He grins and laughs down at me. "Ain't tellin' you that. Club business."

"So you're basically a runaround. Doesn't that get wearing?"

His smile disappears. "Ain't gonna say some days aren't harder than the rest. Didn't much enjoy today."

His eyes are no longer on me, so while I can wonder what unpleasant job he'd been called on to do, he won't be telling me. And anyway, we've reached my suite now. Unlocking the door for me, he stands back so I can wheel myself in.

"I'll be stayin' out here until someone relieves me."

"Why not come in and wait, Hank? You'll be more comfortable inside."

"Huh! A bit of comfort ain't worth riskin' my patch over."

Tilting my head on one side, I tell him, "Well, if you're sure, but the offer's there in case you change your mind."

"I won't," he replies, shortly, and shuts the door firmly behind me as I go in.

Shaking my head, thinking I'll never understand how it all works here, I cross the small sitting area and go into my bedroom. Moving from my wheelchair to the bed, I get out my book and try to get engrossed in the plot, but quickly find my mind wandering. Easing myself back, I soon give up on the fictional hero and close my eyes.

Wraith's a handsome devil of a man, tall and strong, built with bulging muscles and a body I'd love to explore. But have I got the nerve? I shudder. How would I feel seeing his reaction to my ugly stump and the scars on my other leg? What if he turned and ran? I used to be so confident in my own body, knowing that all I had to do was flirt a little and my target would be mine for the taking. But now? Am I prepared to take that next step?

Wraith had said he doesn't mind, that he doesn't care I'm not a whole woman anymore. But what if he can't hide a shiver of revulsion when he sees me? What if actually seeing my injury in the flesh is a real turn off for him? Could I survive that? Or would it destroy me, simply confirming what I've known all along? *But what if it's possible? To have Wraith for just one night?* That's all I want after all.

It can't be more than an hour later before voices outside the building break into my thoughts. I hear Wraith, and it sounds like he's dismissing Hank. I'm surprised, I hadn't expected to see him this early, if at all tonight. Despite that curious statement that he'd been waiting for me, I can't understand how he could resist the heady selection of girls back in the clubroom. They aren't damaged like me.

A minute later, and there's a knock on my door. I pull myself up straight. "Come in."

Wraith enters. He stands in the doorway, studying me for a moment. "The prospect stay outside?" he growls.

Creasing my eyes, perplexed at his lack of greeting and the bizarre question, I give the honest answer. "Yes, I asked if he wanted to come in, but he grunted something like he was okay where he was."

Wraith's taut features visibly relax. "Good."

"I thought you'd be at the party…" I know the guys like to go a bit wild on Friday nights after church.

Now he breaks into a real smile. "The only party I want to go to is right here, with you."

I look down at my hands, twisting together in my lap, not convinced this is a good idea.

He's over to me in a moment, sitting beside me, his fingers under my chin, turning my head to face him. "Hey, I've got some news for you. You're comin' to Utah with Peg and me on Sunday—he's got an appointment for you with the specialist he uses the next day. You'll get a new prosthesis, and we'll be back by Thursday."

My brow creases and I shake my head picturing the astronomical sum that would cost. "I told you, I can't afford to go private."

He smirks. "Club voted, babe. We all agreed we'd pick up the tab for it."

Now my eyebrows rise, it seems to be too good to be true. "Really?" They'd do that for me? I'd hoped, but even after Peg and Wraith had suggested it, I hadn't really believed it.

"Yes, really. Peg say's they're real quick there too. You'll have the fittin' and cast taken on Monday, and by Wednesday should have a new leg made."

"Wow!" I can't believe it. "It took a couple of months just to get the appointment in England, and then weeks until I got the prosthesis."

"Money talks, babe. Money talks." He's still holding my face toward him, now he leans forward, and after just a second's hesitation his lips come down to mine. Despite my uncertainty and inner warnings, I can't help but respond.

All at once there's a loud slamming of the outer door, and then a lighter knock on the door to my room.

"You there, Soph?"

"Fuck it!" Wraith exclaims at the same time as I call out that I am. We pull apart as Horse enters the room.

He eyes us suspiciously, his face tightening as he sees we're sitting so closely together. "Looks like I came back just in time," he tells us, his arm muscles tightening suggestively.

Wraith stands abruptly and takes a step towards Horse. "No, I was the one who got here in bloody time," he sneers. "You would have been far too late!"

Horse shakes his head and closes the gap between himself and the biker. I draw in a breath, seeing both tall and equally well-built men standing head to head, worried they're about to come to blows. "What are you fucking talking about?"

I wish I could get to my feet and put myself between them, but I'm bloody helpless as usual. All I can do is shout. "For goodness sake! Stop it, you two! Calm down! Horse, you don't know a thing about what's gone on."

The Englishman at least glances in my direction, and lowers his arms to his sides. "Well why don't you fill me in then?" He tosses a glare at Wraith.

"She was almost fuckin' raped last night," Wraith explains, his posture slowly becoming less combative. He goes on to explain what happened, and who was responsible.

Horse's anger rises to the fore again. "Where's this mother-fucker now?"

"In the fuckin' ground! I made sure of that!"

I can't suppress my gasp, knowing that could only mean one thing. I didn't understand when Wraith said he wouldn't bother me again that he meant they'd killed him. What kind of man does that make him? I draw back as far as I can, as though to distance myself. Did he actually do it himself? Could the man I'd been on the brink of giving myself to commit murder?

Wraith turns around, his face falling as though he realises he's perhaps said too much. Horse pushes past him, comes to sit beside me and pulls me into his arms. His smell is familiar and safe as he rests his chin on the top of my head, his hands stroking my back. I relax into his comforting non-sexual and non-threatening touch.

Watching us, his gaze flitting from one to the other, stroking his beard with his hand, Wraith breathes out a long breath. Then, throwing up his hands in a gesture of defeat and giving a mumbled curse, he leaves the room.

For a moment Horse and I sit in silence, then Horse pulls back, and unknowingly mimics Wraith's gesture as he cups my chin in his hand and gently turns me to face him. "Are you okay, Soph?"

I don't answer immediately. Bikers, club whores… I already knew this was a different world. I hadn't given much thought to what they were going to do with Buster. I suppose in the back of my mind I thought they'd either kick him out of the club or report him to the police. But take his life? For what he did to me? And possibly by Wraith's hand? The hand of a man who, if Horse hadn't interrupted, might now have been making love to me?

"I don't know, Horse." My voice is just a whisper. "I can't believe Wraith or any of them did that. That they are capable of it."

"Oh yes," he replies. "Don't kid yourself, love. Any of the men here are capable of killing." At my sharply indrawn breath, he taps his fingers to my forehead. "And that's why I thought you'd safe here." Then he adds with a bemused shake of his head, "Or you should have been."

"But I don't want anyone to kill to protect me."

"You're in an outlaw biker club, love, it comes with the territory I'm afraid. Or actually, in this instance I'm glad. I'd have killed that bugger myself if I'd been here. I'm so sorry that happened to you, I'm sorry I left you."

Wondering whether he really would have murdered someone or if it had been a figure of speech, I try to console him. "You're not to blame, Horse. There's only one person to blame, and apparently he won't be bothering anybody ever again."

"Hey sweetheart, don't cry."

Until he pointed it out, I hadn't noticed that tears were running down my face.

He realises why in an instant. "You and Wraith have been getting close, haven't you?"

My confirmation comes out on a sob.

Rubbing my hands over my leaking eyes, I breathe in a sharp breath. "I don't think I can stay here, Horse. Please take me away."

Horse sighs. "I can't do that, babe. I wouldn't be able to protect you anywhere else. And you certainly wouldn't be safe on your own. Remember the contract that's out on you?" He leans forwards, putting his elbows on his knees. "They live by different rules here, Sophie, rules you don't understand."

"Explain to me, then," I cry out. "Justify how killing a man can be right?"

"A man who tried to fucking rape you!" Horse swings around, his eyes narrowed and gazing into mine intently. "If Wraith hadn't stopped him, just think about that. He could have hurt you badly, or killed you." As I go to speak he puts his fingers over my mouth. "Call Wraith, get him back here, and let him have his say. Talk to him, let him explain how the MC works."

His words have brought back what happened yesterday, and I shudder remembering how Wraith had saved me in the nick of time. *How far would Buster have gone?* I really can't sort out my thoughts, my mind's racing and I don't think I can cope with any more. Speak to Wraith? No, not now.

"Not tonight," I tell him, wiping the backs of my hands over my eyes to clear the last of my tears. "I just want to forget everything, to go to sleep." I want to be alone to try and process everything that's happened. "Aren't you going to go to the party, Horse?"

Tilting his head to one side, he looks into my face and ignores both my protest and my question. "Call Wraith back."

He seems to think it's important I speak to Wraith, but I'm not even sure I want to see him again. Or stay here.

As Horse sits, patiently waiting, giving me time to digest what he's said, I try to make sense of everything that's happened. Apart from Buster, nothing that Wraith or any of the others has done has made me feel the slightest bit uneasy staying in the club—leaving aside the free sex shows that is. But now I know they live a different way of life, far closer to *Sons of Anarchy* than I believed. *Buster wouldn't have stopped.* Would I have wanted to live with the fear that he'd come after me again? A violent shiver makes my entire body shake. *Or want Buster walking around forcing himself on other women?*

No, of course I didn't, but I expected he'd go to prison. *But they don't like involving the police.* Instead they meted out their own brand of punishment, extreme in my view, but it doesn't necessarily mean they go around killing at random and for no reason. Perhaps it's not good to let my imagination run wild. Perhaps Horse is right. If I gave Wraith a chance to explain, maybe I'd be able to understand him and the life he lives a little better. As an answer, I reach to the bedside table and get my phone.

Wheels: Can we talk?

I stare at the phone, willing him to respond, suddenly having a vision of him being with Chrissy or one of the other whores, or perhaps a Tucson girl has caught his eye? My gut clenches as I realise how much that thought hurts.

Horse pats my hand as my phone remains silent. A short while later, I give up looking at the screen and put it back where it was on the bedside table.

"Well, so much for…" I break off as I hear it vibrating on the wood and the accompanying ping.

Wraith: Be right there.

CHAPTER 15
Wraith

What did she think we were gonna do to that motherfucker?" I ask Peg, realising how much I've fucked this up.

Peg moves his head side to side. "She ain't from here, is she? The club, heck, the U.S. is completely alien to her. You need to speak to her, explain."

"Doubt I'm going to get the chance." She'd looked so disgusted with me, as if I was something she'd scrape off her shoe.

"Why'd'you tell her?" Drummer's scrunched up eyes show his displeasure. "She knows too much now."

His words chill me. He doesn't have to spell the ramifications out. "She's not gonna tell anyone." Well, I think I'm certain on that, but there's part of me acknowledging maybe I'm just hopeful. "I didn't mean to tell her, it just came out when Horse and I were gettin' into it. I didn't come right out and say it, but she read between the lines."

"You got to make sure she's gonna keep quiet." Drum's normal level of irritation has increased to the point where I know it's the real thing.

How the fuck do I do that? "Who would she tell? She's here at the compound, she won't be going out anywhere alone."

Drum's eyes open wide and a vein visibly throbs in his forehead. "She's got a fuckin' phone, hasn't she?" His hand thumps down on the bar. "Get back to her and sort this mess out, VP.

Make her see sense." He doesn't need to add what the implications are of me failing to do so.

Stretching my head back on my neck and rolling my shoulders, I think there's nothing I'd like to do more. But will she even listen to me? Before I can say anything else, my phone vibrates in my pocket. I read the message and respond, a tentative smile on my face.

Slapping Drum on the back I tell him, "I'm gonna see her now."

"About fuckin' time," he grunts.

It only takes a few minutes to get to her room, and that's not enough time to decide how I'm going to approach what needs to be said. It's one thing to try and explain why Buster had to meet Satan, it's quite another to clarify that it's likely she'll be going the same way if the members don't trust her. I'm just hoping I can stop it from going that far. Fuck.

On the way into their suite, I find Horse waiting for me, pacing the small connecting seating area. "Don't you fucking hurt her," he starts. "I'm trusting you, Wraith."

In response, I glare at him. He knows how the club works, and the penalties for exposing club business, but how can he think I'd harm her? I raise my chin, acknowledging what he's said. For a few seconds we have a standoff, then, with a small shake of his head he steps aside, allowing me to enter.

Walking across to her bedroom door I knock on it lightly. After I hear her voice, I go inside.

Closing the door behind me, I lean with my back up against it and watch her warily, trying to assess her mood. Her head's bowed and she's using her blond hair like a shield, though I'm still able to see her eyes are red and watery, and I hate that I've made her cry.

"Oh, Wheels..." I go over to her, kneeling in front of her and taking her hands in mine.

She pulls away from my touch. "My name's Sophie," she tells me firmly. "I'm nothing to do with the MC."

Staying where I am, I look down while gathering my thoughts together. "You might have been here for gettin' on a couple of months, but you still don't know much about us, or our lifestyle, do you?"

Her eyes flare. "Your *club business?* Oh no, no one's told me about that. But I know about how you use women, the club whores, the girls from the city. Now I know you *kill* people."

Pulling myself to my feet, I indicate the bed. She shrugs, and I take that as permission to sit. I don't get too close to her just yet. Putting my elbows on my knees, I cup my face in my hands, stroking my beard. "We're a one-percenter motorcycle club, Wheels." She might hate the name, but it has kind of stuck. "We have our own rules that we live by. We don't recognise citizens' rules."

Her brow creases, so I continue, "Citizens are what you are, anyone not part of the club or our lifestyle."

"Outlaws." She spits out the word as though even saying it leaves a nasty taste in her mouth.

I ignore the way she's said it, just confirm that she's right. "Yeah, we live outside the law."

"So you're admitting what you do is illegal?"

"Ain't going to lie to you babe and tell you we're whiter than white. But we run a lot of legit businesses—the strip club, a steakhouse, a construction company, and the garage. Most of the members work in one or another. Some things aren't so legit, but that's club business and I ain't gonna be tellin' you about that. And I can assure you that neither the club whores nor the city girls are forced to do anythin' they don't want to do, that's a given. They come because they want to be here. Nor do we go around randomly killin' people. That's not who we are, darlin'."

Throwing a sneer at me as I refer to our more nefarious dealings, she goes quiet for a moment. When she starts speaking again she gets to the point. "I don't know what I expected you to do about Buster, but I didn't expect you to kill him."

"I never said we did."

"Not in so many words, but you implied…"

"I said things I shouldn't," I pull on my beard, "I regret that."

"Why?" she snaps. "Because you didn't want me to know the sort of men you are?"

"No," I rasp back. "Because you didn't need to know and what you don't know can't hurt you. Look," I run my hands down my face, "let me try and explain how we work. Not just anyone can join the club. Someone wants to, well they need to be sponsored as a prospect, and while they're prospectin' they do anything they are asked *without question*, usually for at least a year, and sometimes more. If they prove their loyalty to the club and their willingness to do anythin' for the club, even give their lives if necessary, they become members. Once a member you're a member for life. And members do whatever's needed for the club, including dying for it if necessary. There's no getting out, or not very often. Unless you're kicked out, and that ain't pretty."

She's mumbling, and I have to ask her to speak up. "It sounds more like a prison sentence. What's the benefit?"

That's easy. "The club is a family, and we call each other brother as that's what we are to each other, brothers. Maybe not related by blood, but just as close—if not closer—than if we were. We'd give our lives for each other." I pause, and then tell her the plain truth of it. "And for those under our protection."

Her eyes flash. "I'd never ask that…"

"I know you wouldn't. And I'd have hoped it would never come to it, but that's what we sign up for when we join the MC. And that's why we take the betrayal of a brother so hard." I pause again. "The Satan's Devils may not be saints, but we don't hurt women. We run a strip club, yeah, but the strippers are salaried dancers, not prostitutes. We don't trade in flesh. I ain't gonna lie to ya, some MCs do, but not the Satan's Devils."

She shudders and I move a little closer to her. "What did you want? To get the law involved? D'you know what would have happened if you'd reported Buster to the cops?" It's a rhetorical question, so I don't wait for her answer. "I'll tell you. They'd have looked into it, sure, but it would have been a question of whether they'd believed you or accepted my story as the witness. He might have been arrested, been taken to court. He might have got himself a fancy lawyer and got away with that shit. And you'd be dragged through the mill. They might not have been able to bring up anythin' in your sexual past in court, but a clever counsel could have found ways of alludin' to it. They could probably make a virgin look promiscuous."

She turns her face to mine and looks at me properly for the first time since I entered the room. Her hand comes up to touch my face. "He could have got away with it? That's what you're saying? So your form of justice made sure he was punished."

"Yeah, babe. Perhaps not the citizen way, but we made sure Buster wouldn't hurt another woman ever again."

Again she goes quiet for a moment, and then asks, "How did he get into the MC if you're all about keeping women safe?"

That's a good question, and I think on it for a moment. "He transferred in from the San Diego chapter several months ago. To be honest, they seemed well rid of his shit. From what I knew of him, he'd never have got his patch if he prospected here."

"It's all so strange to me, Wraith."

"It must be, darlin'. It must be."

Now I can't help myself. I pull her towards me but feel a slight resistance as she tries to keep a distance between us. But from the intent expression on her face, she's not trying to evade my touch, she's got something else to say.

"I hate being so helpless, Wraith. If I'd been able to move, I might have been able to get away or to fight. I've been here thinking about it." She touches my beard with her hand, an almost unconscious action. "I don't want to be so weak and defenceless anymore. I'm going to work on getting my strength back once I've got my new prosthesis. It was my vulnerability that made him think I was easy game."

I can't help but admire her. She's fighting back, not letting what happened defeat her. "I'll give you all the help I can, darlin'."

"And Wraith?"

"What is it, babe?"

"I want something to defend myself with—a gun or a knife. Some sort of weapon." She looks down at her hands and then glances up. "I suppose, if I could have, I'd have killed him to keep him from touching me." She gives a short self-deprecating laugh. "Which makes me no better than you."

"Heat of the moment, darlin'. You might have been able to if you had to defend yourself, but someone like you wouldn't do anythin' in cold blood." And that's the difference between us. Not that my blood had been anything but red hot when we dispatched Buster.

As she considers my words, I reach down to my waistband and extract the knife I carry there and press it into her hands. "Ain't gonna give you a gun, darlin', not until I've taught you how to use it. But for now, keep this close if it makes you feel safer."

She stares at the weapon I've placed in her hands, and I can almost see her thinking what she'd have done had she had it on hand the previous night.

"Darlin'," I start, but she puts her fingers to my mouth and I have to resist flicking out my tongue to taste them.

"I won't say a word about what's happened. I won't get your club into any trouble." The determination in her face makes the breath leave my body and my tension rolls away at the words I needed to hear. The assurance that protects both her and the club.

Turning to face her, I take the hand that's touching my face and hold it firmly in mine. With my free hand I stroke her hair, then fist it, pulling her towards me. "I want you." I force myself to ignore the gash on her face left by Buster's ring. There's no place for him here, not anymore.

She takes a sharp breath, her pupils dilate, and I can feel her pulse beating fast. "I'm scared," she admits, honestly.

I know without her telling me she hasn't been with a man since her accident, and even without Peg's earlier warning, I know the reason for her fear. Talking about it isn't going to cut it. I have to show that I'm not going to reject her just because she's not complete anymore. Keeping my eyes fixed firmly on hers, and a tight hold of her hair so she can't get away, I release her hand and move mine down, over her body, running it down her leg until I reach the stump, below which the rest of it was amputated. As she gasps, I softly trace the injured limb through the material of her jeans with my hand.

"It ain't gonna put me off, babe," I murmur into her ear as she tries to move. "It's part of you."

While she's trying to comprehend what I'm saying, I allow her no more time to think. I move my mouth over hers. Teasing her with a gentle touch, then becoming more forceful, pushing my tongue against her lips until she opens and lets me inside. Still fisting her hair, I strengthen my grasp so she's no chance to get away. If she fought me I'd let her go, but she doesn't, and I know tonight she needs me to take control. As she begins to respond to my kiss, our mouths mash. She tastes so sweet as our tongues slide together and our teeth clash. The odour of arousal starts to pervade the room. *She wants me too.*

Releasing her leg, I sweep my hand up to her breasts, feeling them through her shirt. Her nipples are peaked, ready and waiting for my caress. I need to feel her skin, so letting go of her hair and pushing up her top, do exactly that, and as I touch the soft, smooth skin of her globes and then push her bra down, I gently twist their hard tips and her breathing speeds up.

"I need to see you." I hardly recognise my voice as my own. As I loosen my hold on her, she pulls back, giving herself just enough space to take her upper clothes off. Brushing her hands away, I remove her clothes myself, too impatient for a slow striptease. I throw her shirt away, and without pause reach around her back to take off her bra. As it falls, I struggle to breathe at the first sight of the perfection in front of me. Two round, perfectly sized globes, flawless lily-white skin covering breasts big enough that I can't wait to get my throbbing cock between them, topped with rosy-brown nipples just waiting for my attention. I can't hold off any longer to feast on them.

Forcing myself to pay no attention to the bruising left by that fucker who tried to rape her, and bowing my head, I use my mouth and my hands, feeling, plumping, kneading that tender flesh, taking those turgid peaks one at a time into my mouth, teasing them with my teeth. When I give a small nip, she gasps and throws back her head. I can't get enough of them. And all the time I'm suckling and fondling blood is racing south, swelling my cock to a hardness I've never felt before.

Her eyes close, her mouth opens, and her breath comes in pants. While her breasts are enticing, I need to move this on before I disgrace myself in my pants like a teenager. Pulling myself away, I gently push her back onto the bed, swinging her legs up so she's lying flat.

Now my hands go to the button on her jeans, quickly unfastening it and pulling down the zip. A waft of musky scent is released, and my nostrils flare.

Then her hand covers mine as if to stop me. Her eyes have opened, worry clear to see there, her features are taut. Staring into her face, I forcibly move her hand away.

"I *don't* care." I try to impress on her that the sight of her injuries won't pour cold water on my ardour.

A little nod, but there are tears hovering close, waiting to fall at the first sign of rejection.

Moving down the bed, I gently ease off her jeans and have to suppress my reactions. If I let my memory of that fucking video come back to me, if I let my anger at her senseless mutilation overwhelm me, she'll read my reactions all the wrong way. Removing the shoe from her good leg, I free her from her jeans entirely.

Glancing, I see her eyes have squeezed shut, a tear has escaped and is rolling down her face. Bending over I place a soft kiss on her stump, and then trace the red lines betraying the injuries on her other leg, wincing inwardly at the pain she must have gone through. I can see the muscles, though getting stronger still look weak, and realise she's still got a long journey until she has sufficient strength even in her one remaining complete lower limb for her to walk completely unaided.

She's waiting for me to react, to say something—to gasp in disgust or to voice fake platitudes. So I do neither. Instead, I nest myself between her legs, pushing them open wider and indulging my eyes on her perfect pussy and neatly trimmed pubes. The club girls keep themselves bare, but suddenly I love the sight of her pale bush, only slightly darker than the hair on her head. Then when I've seen enough, I huff a warm breath over her already hard clit, and she arches off the bed. I grin and start to indulge.

She's so wet and ready for me as I lap up her feminine essence, loving the sweet musky taste. I dip my tongue inside her pussy, keeping an arm across her to hold her still for me, the other hand playing with her clit. After toying with her I bring my secret weapon into play, swiping my bearded chin between her folds, tickling and teasing that tight bundle of nerves.

Her hands are grasping the bedcovers tightly as her whole body tightens. She's close, so I use my chin, rotating and pressing down hard while taking my free hand down and putting a finger against the tight hole of her ass. It's enough to send her over. She screams and begins to thrash. I hold her down and am relentless, squeezing every last contraction out of her. When she comes down, I pick up the pace again, and a second orgasm follows soon after. It's only when her body goes limp that I raise my head.

Now it's my turn.

While her lungs heave to take in air, I stand and remove my clothes, throwing her a wicked grin as I do so. The corners of her mouth turn up, and then it widens with appreciation as she watches me take off my shirt, revealing skin covered with colourful tattoos. But she can examine those later—now I've got one thing and one thing only on my mind.

As I quickly divest myself of boots and take down my pants, her eyes flash with excitement as my cock is freed at last, and her husky gasp incredibly makes me swell even more.

Before throwing my jeans to the floor, I take out a foil packet and extract the condom. As I give myself a couple of tugs, I feel the veins throbbing in eagerness to get into what I already know is a very tight hole.

Pre-cum glistens at the tip, and she's licking her lips as she notices. *Time for that later. Oh yeah!*

Quickly I roll the condom down my dick. Then I position myself, my tip poised to slide inside her tight pussy. Automatically I pull her right leg up so it's bent, her foot resting on the bed, and it's then I see the flare of panic in her eyes, the redness burning her cheeks. Not knowing how the fuck I'm still able to think with the right head, but understanding any moment of awkwardness will ruin the moment, in one smooth move, reaching for the spare pillow, I fold it and put it under the thigh of her left leg.

Now that she's situated exactly how I want, I push inside.

Fuck, she's tight!

I pause to take a deep breath, trying to get control when all I want to do is thrust into her with one smooth stroke. My cock doesn't care she's not club pussy, someone to pound into chasing only my own release. Somehow I manage to restrain myself, taking it slow, pressing into her slowly, advancing and retreating, gaining ground each time until at last I can hold it no longer, and I drive inside until I'm up against her cervix. At her little gasp I wait, giving her time to get used to my size.

The fit is so snug I can feel little contractions of her vaginal muscles teasing the hell out of my dick. My arms are rigid, resting one either side of her body. Her hands come out to touch me, gripping my forearms. Her mouth is open and appreciative moans come from her throat as her eyes roll back in her head. She wriggles against me, and that small movement almost makes me lose it and shoot my load.

Now I let myself go, pulling out then thrusting inside. Making sure to hit that special place inside her each time I move over it. My balls are churning, my cock's swelling, and I have to force myself to hold back, waiting until she's with me. Moving one of my arms I put my fingers to her clit, strumming until I feel her tighten. She's gasping now, little cries and wails coming from her mouth, sounds that almost push me over the edge. And then she's there.

At the first fierce contraction of her muscles, she takes me with her. She screams at the same time as I roar my completion and feel the cum shooting from my balls, through my cock in wave after fucking wave of ecstasy. It seems to never end as I continue pumping until, at last, I'm completely drained.

I collapse over her, pulling her into my arms and holding her tight. Emptying my balls into club pussy has never felt as rewarding as this, and at that moment I know I won't want to let her go. She may not know it yet, but I'm claiming her. *She's mine!*

CHAPTER 16
Sophie

My heart's pounding, I'm panting as I try to get oxygen into my starved lungs. In all my previous hook-ups and one night stands, never have I come so hard or at the same time as the man I've been with, nor have I felt so satisfied or sated after. He's lying close now, propped on one arm to keep his weight off me, but I can't hold him tightly enough. I want more. I want it again. Me, who never goes back for seconds.

But hell, that was better than I could have dreamed. If his re-action was anything to go by, the visible evidence of my disabil-ity didn't turn him off, and how the fuck did he know what to do to find a comfortable position so quickly? I'd been embarrassed, not sure what to do, but it was as if he'd instinctively known.

For some reason, the tears which have been threatening sud-denly start to fall, and I sob loudly.

He pulls out of me, ties the condom and chucks it away to deal with later, then takes me into his arms, his hands caressing and soothing me, his head resting on mine, and I feel him softly murmuring everything will be okay over and over again, giving me the time to try to process what's happened between us. Slowly my eyes dry and I'm at last able to control my sobs.

"That was…" I try, but can't describe what's just happened between us.

He rolls off me, pulling me into his side. "Yes, it was," he replies with a short laugh. It seems he, too, can't put the experience into words.

We lie without speaking for a few moments, then I feel a prodding against my stomach. Pulling myself up on my elbows, I look down to see his cock once again hard and ready to go.

"Really?" I raise my eyebrows.

He smirks. "See the effect you have on me?"

Suddenly his strong arms encircle me, and I seem to be thrown through the air and land on my stomach. I'm giggling as he puts one hand under me, pulling me up while with the other he's arranging the pillows under my belly, positioning me so my arse is in the air, and with a gentle touch between my shoulder blades, pushes my head down. Turning my face, I rest on my uninjured cheek.

"Don't move," he instructs as he fumbles with his discarded jeans.

I have no intention of doing so, waiting with expectation as I hear the tearing of a foil packet, a moment's silence, and then his cock's pushing at my entrance again.

"Now I'm going to take you like the big bad biker I am, babe. You ready for my cock to give your pussy a poundin' like you've never had?"

Christ! His words are turning me on, and I know I'm already dripping wet and ready for him. "Give it your best, big boy." Some of my old moxey is returning to me, but as he lines himself up and fills me with one fast stroke, part of me wonders whether it was wise to taunt the beast.

Thrust after fierce thrust his cock hammers into me like I've never experienced before. My muscles start to tighten and I can feel my womb clenching. He puts a finger on my clit, and presses another to that forbidden entrance, my virgin arse which I haven't allowed a man near before. Then his well lubricated finger slips inside, and I wonder what I might have been missing as it shoots my arousal higher than it's ever been.

I hear someone giving a keening cry and realise it's coming from me. My thighs start tightening around him, my whole body shaking out of control as he takes me to heights I've never got close to.

"Come for me," he shouts, and my body obeys him as it seems every muscle in my body pulsates in frenzy before locking and then releasing as I come so heavily I don't know if I'll ever recover. I feel him lose his rhythm and thrash inside, and hear his own triumphant bellow of completion as he goes rigid and starts to come, and then little pumps as he fills the condom.

Grateful for the pillows holding me up—my body has no strength left to support itself—I feel his now flaccid cock pulling out as he draws away from me, and fleetingly I wonder what he's going to do now. Will he leave me? Is that it? Just like I've left so many men before? Or should I take the initiative and ask him to leave?

Then the sobering thought hits me, and the fear I might be nothing more than something to cross off his own bucket list perhaps—a fuck with a cripple—floods over me. I'm relieved my face is hidden in the pillow, so if he thanks me and leaves he won't see my reaction. I shiver, not from cold, but from the loss of his body heat surrounding me. *I don't want him to go.* And that's a thought I'll have to deal with later; I'm incapable of doing so now.

"I can hear you thinkin' from here," he tells me. There's warmth in his voice.

"If you're leaving, just go."

"Oh, Wheels, if you think I'm just going to walk out of here like you're one of the club girls you're very much mistaken, darlin'." Suddenly his naked body is next to me. He manoeuvres me, lifting me to remove the pillows and turning me over. "That was the best fuckin' experience of my life, babe. I'm claimin' your ass, you know."

I'm really not sure what I think about that. He might have put his finger there, but surely he's too big? And I'm too knackered now for anything more—he's completely drained me. So I glare at him. "No one's ever... Not back there."

He squints at me in confusion. "What the fuck you sayin'?"

"My arse," I clarify. "No one's ..."

He interrupts me with a roar of laughter. "While I want that, one day, I'm not just claimin' your *ass*, babe, I'm claimin' *you*! All of you. You're mine, okay?"

I'm his? Oh fuck! No! I sit up and look down at him, my eyes wide. "What?" I might not know much about club life, but from what I do know, he's talking about something serious. And permanent. And I don't want, can't have that.

"Wraith, we hardly know each other."

He flings an arm back beneath his head and stares at me intently. "Yeah, I know." His eyes briefly close, then he opens them again. "But I know I'd kill any brother who'd lay a hand on you. I want that pussy all to myself."

I don't understand myself as I get possessive. "I don't want that cock in any other woman either. Or I'll cut it off." *Fuck, why did I say that?*

He chortles at my threat, and then the corners of his mouth turn down. "It don't want in any other pussy after you, babe."

It's too tempting, shaking my head in bemusement at my actions, confused with the thoughts in my head, I take the easy route and accept the invitation of his open arms, snuggling down beside him. I have to stop this, have to tell him to leave. I don't cuddle after sex. I get up and leave, or kick them out of my bed. I *can't* do this. Can't lead him on.

Then the devil sitting on my shoulder whispers into my ear— it probably won't take long for him to get bored with a disabled lover. Why not take advantage of him and just enjoy him for now? I'm not committing to anything, but can't deny a few more bouts of amazing sex with a rugged biker wouldn't go amiss.

But it seems he's got plans, and he lets me in on them as he wraps his arms around me. "I want you on the back of my bike, darlin'. Never wanted a woman ridin' behind me before."

"I can't…" Now he's just crazy. Has he forgotten I've only got half a leg?

"Not yet, but you will. You need a new prosthesis, then you're going to work building your strength up. Fuck, Peg *rides* a bike with one whole leg, it'll be a piece of cake for you to ride bitch." Now it's his turn to half-sit up and look down at me. He smooths his hand over my face and it feels a strangely intimate gesture. "I know it will be a lot of hard work, babe, but I'll be with you. Every fuckin' step of the way."

I cover his hand with mine, and turning my mouth plant a soft kiss on it. I honestly don't know what to say, but right now I can't find the words to explain I won't want him to stay around. And if I could, I don't think I'd be able to bring myself to utter them. He'll get fed up with being lumbered with me soon enough, and maybe I won't have to say a thing.

"Don't know about you, babe, but I'm well and truly fucked. Come, let's get some sleep now." He pulls me so I'm spooned against him, his front to my back. A hand comes up to cup one of my breasts, and I feel his breathing slow and deepen. It's been a heck of a long time since I slept with a man's arms around me. I tense, waiting for the memories to come and remind me why I shouldn't be doing this. But the lingering odour of our joining surround me, and the gentle rising and falling of his chest mean there's no room for another man in this bed. As Wraith fills my mind and senses, giving space to no other, my body gradually relaxes as I follow him into an exhausted, extremely satisfied and surprisingly dreamless sleep.

Saturday morning dawns, well, we miss the sun rising, and it's nearer midday when Wraith eventually wakes me with another bout of glorious lovemaking, leaving my disused muscles slightly sore and my resolve to end this sorely challenged. After getting dressed, he walks beside me as I wheel myself down to the clubhouse for something to eat. He towers above me, making me remember last night's promise to myself, to get back on my own two feet—well, one of them and a new prosthesis.

After Friday night's party, the clubhouse looks like a bomb's hit it. The prospects are bustling around, waking bodies, picking up bottles, and generally clearing up. That they do so stoically without complaint reminds me what both Hank and Wraith had told me, that to prove themselves worthy of being patched in they need to show they'll do anything needed. I try to steer through the mess on the floor and avoid Hank's overzealous sweeping, smiling back at him as he winks at me, knowing I'd made a friend the night before. I hear a growl from Wraith at the familiarity, and he pauses and mumbles something to the prospect before following me into the kitchen, where I found none of the old ladies are around. Presumably, they're keeping out of the way until the place is tidier.

Peg and Drummer, together with Blade and Dart, are already in the kitchen, looking like they're nursing sore heads and all with large coffee cups in their hands. Immediately the aroma makes my mouth water. Wraith barks a laugh when my eyes fixate on the coffee machine, and taking pity on me, goes to get me a much needed dose of caffeine.

Indicating the table where his brothers are sitting, he goes over, pulls away a chair, and sits in the empty one beside the space he's created. I take the hint and wheel myself over to him, reaching out for one of the two mugs he's put on the table. Taking my free hand, he brings it to his lips and places a kiss on it.

Embarrassed, I glance around. Peg's smirking, the other two brothers are grinning, but Drummer looks over sharply. "You and I got to talk, brother?"

Wraith's still got hold of my hand, and he squeezes it gently. "Yes."

"My office, thirty minutes."

"I'll be there."

As the prez marches off, Dart's face splits into a wide grin and pumps his fist in the air. "Yes! I called it!"

Astonished, I watch as the others start handing money over to him. Seeing my expression, he clarifies, "We placed bets on when you two would get together."

As I breathe in sharply in indignation, I've no time to explain in my view we're *not* together, because Wraith pre-empts any words coming out of my mouth when he turns to me and asks, "Hungry?"

Staring at him, seeing his face as relaxed as I've ever seen it, despite the meeting he's soon to be having with his president, I realise to disillusion him in front of his brothers wouldn't be fair, so I just nod. To be truthful, after all the activity last night and this morning, I'm starving.

He goes to get us an overfilled plate each and brings it back to the table. The food's good, but not up to the old ladies' standard. I suspect the poor prospects probably had to do the cooking.

When I've had my first rasher of bacon and downed a good part of my coffee, I glance around the table. Everyone's scoffing their food, seeming not to care it's a little under par.

"What time we leavin' tomorrow, Peg? You got a suggestion for somewhere to stay?" Wraith speaks around a mouthful of egg.

I listen to their plans for my trip to Utah tomorrow. Apparently, there's a fairly decent motel close by the clinic they're taking me to, which Peg has used before. But I'm stunned to find it's a seven-hundred-mile trip and will take about thirteen hours to get there. I forget just how big the USA is. On the map, it's just one state up, and we'll be heading almost right to the north. We'll have to leave early in the morning to get there in good time.

When we've finished eating, Wraith gives me a nod and stands. After he's ascertained I'll stay in the clubhouse to wait for him—Carmen's just arrived so I won't be the only woman here—the two men leave the room. I'm a bit concerned about what's going on, having a good idea it's me they're going to be talking about. I just hope Wraith isn't putting anything on the line for something I know won't be going very far.

But he's coming to Utah. Lowering my head into my hands, I wonder what the hell I should do. Should I end it before we leave? See if someone else would come instead? Or, asks the little devil sitting on my shoulder, should I just admit that I haven't had enough of him just yet?

As the kitchen starts to fill, I come to a decision. I'll be breaking my own rules by doing so, but I'm going to indulge myself, just for a few days. Surely that can't hurt?

CHAPTER 17
Wraith

ntering Drummer's office, I take the seat that he's waving to in front of his desk. My prez stares at me for a moment, tapping his fingers on the desk in front of him. I wait for him to get whatever it is off his mind.

"She ain't from our world."

Shaking my head, I agree with him. "Know that, Drum."

"She ain't a sweet butt neither."

I nod. "Know that too."

"So anythin' I should know?"

Stroking my beard, I try to explain. "Don't rightly understand what it is myself, Prez, but she's different." I breathe in and take the plunge. "I want to claim her."

He's shaking his head. "Leavin' aside the fact you went against my direct instructions, she's a civilian, she don't know anythin' about this life." His fingers still.

"I've been talking to her about it, explainin'."

"Talkin's one thing, livin' it quite another."

"Know that." I realise I have to give him more. "She wants a gun, wants to learn how to defend herself. She doesn't want to leave herself vulnerable to any more Busters."

His eyes widen. Her desire to be able to protect herself showing that she may be more suited to our world then he thinks.

"I'll take responsibility for her," I add.

"Horse got that."

"Not anymore."

"He know it?" Drum's eyes narrow.

"Not yet," I admit. "But I'll talk to him."

His fingers start tapping the table once more, a rhythmic drumming that might have got on my nerves had I not known it meant the prez is deep in thought. I know why he's worried, bringing an outsider in is always risky. Despite how careful we try to be, there's always a chance club business will be overheard, or two and two put together about some of our comings and goings, and we need to be able to trust people we have in the clubhouse. I feel Wheels is solid, but the brothers will need to be convinced of that too. Because what I'm suggesting is that she becomes a permanent fixture.

Suddenly both of Drum's hands slap down on the desktop. "You've got a week. Bring it to church on Friday, and you better have somethin' to persuade us by then."

Not quite sure how I'm going to achieve that, but thinking maybe I'll have the time to talk to her in Utah, I nod my head to agree. I'll think of something. And Peg, our sergeant-at-arms, will be with us the whole time. His view will count for a lot. His role means he's responsible for the safety of the club and its members.

Drum's still watching me intently, and I gaze steadily back. "Now there's the question of going against me. Ain't gonna be able to let that go."

I hold my breath. I deserve to be reprimanded. It wouldn't be a good example to the others if he lets me get away without any form of punishment, even though apparently everyone could see it coming. While I don't think he'd go so far as to have my patch, I could lose my position as VP.

He makes me wait for it, then says, his lips curling, knowing he's making me suffer. "Standard fine."

200

Letting the air from my lungs out as a sigh of relief, I nod my agreement, knowing how lightly he's let me off. A fifty-dollar fine is nothing to me.

"You got everythin' sorted for your trip?" He's moving on.

"Peg's dealin' with the specifics, I'm just going along for the ride." And one heck of a long ride it's going to be. The kind I live for. Why would anyone be in an MC and not love the feel of the open road beneath them and the wind in their hair? Too long inside and I start to suffocate.

"And for the woman's protection," he reminds me to keep my mind on the job.

"Yeah, but I'm not expecting trouble. No one knows she's with us, or about her going to Utah."

"Always expect trouble, VP," Drum tells me, his face twisting into a smirk. Then he gives an imperious wave and I'm dismissed.

He didn't need to tell me that I'm going along to keep Wheels safe. I've personal reasons for doing that. So after leaving his office, I continue my original plan and walk down the corridor and knock on another door, pushing it open as soon as I get an answer. Inside there's a desk covered in all manner of shit —empty bottles, cans, an overflowing ashtray, and in the only clear space in the middle, a couple of monitors which the occupant is gazing at intently. Using my hand to waft away the smoke that has a distinct odour of cannabis, I step inside.

"Hey, Mouse," I greet my brother. "Any chatter about our girl?"

"Your girl." He grins. "Couldn't you have waited a bit? Lost me a heap of money." Word has obviously already got around.

I don't want to encourage him so I ignore his comment. "Just wanted to check whether there's any need to be concerned about our trip?"

"Nah, Peg's already asked me. It's a bit of a risk as he had to give them her full name and details so they could get hold of her medical records from England, but I've checked the clinic and surprisingly their system's reasonably secure. And someone would have to know she needs a new prosthesis at exactly this point to be checkin' all such places. Bit of a long shot—even if I was the one doing the searchin'. And we've provided a decoy address as a temporary one. I've used a hotel in Phoenix. There's nothing to connect her with the clubhouse. Even Peg uses his own address rather than the club one when he goes there." Like a lot of the brothers, Peg has a home closer to the city, as living in such close proximity to each other can get wearing at times. To date, I've not seen the need, but that might need to change now.

Mouse jerks his head towards the screen in front of him. "I'll keep an eye on things while you're gone. If anythin' comes up that looks worryin', I'll let you know."

Satisfied, I thank him and leave him to it. Mouse is an interesting character, half Navajo, and his grandfather was one of the Navajo code talkers in the Second World War. Reckon he's got code in his blood.

Returning to the kitchen I'm not pleased to find there's a definite chill to the atmosphere, and that Chrissy is hovering around Wheels.

I enter just in time to hear the club whore say, "Just stay away from my man, you feel me?"

I see red. "What the fuck?" I'm across the room in seconds, my hands taking hold of Chrissy's shoulders and shaking her violently. "What fuckin' garbage are you spoutin' to my woman?"

Chrissy looks up at me, tears in her eyes. In a dramatic gesture she wipes them away. "But Wraith," she starts in a simpering voice that grates on me like nails being scraped down a blackboard, "you and me, we…"

"How many fuckin' times do I have to tell you? There's no fuckin' 'you and me' you stupid fucking slut," I roar, unable to believe she ever thought there was anything between us. "There never was! We had this out yesterday. You're a fuckin' sweet butt."

"But..."

She just doesn't know when to shut the fuck up. Disgust wells up inside me as I realise my hands are still on her, and I throw her away from me, not caring she stumbles and ends up on her ass. Instead of helping her up, I lean over her, my features taut with anger as I shout right into her face. "You are nothin' but a whore. You get me? A convenient hole. There was and never will be anything between us. Now get the fuck out of here and never, ever speak to Wheels again!"

As I've been shouting she's been inching away from me, the tone of my voice at last getting through to her. But she has one more try. "But I love you, Wraith."

"You don't know the fuckin' meanin' of the word. Love? You love the idea of being an ol' lady and don't fuckin' care whose bike it is you're riding on." I straighten, my hands going up and tunnelling through my hair.

"Get out, Chrissy." It's Heart—he must have entered sometime during the altercation. He's standing in the doorway, his daughter Amy with him. He's got her turned into her body, his hands covering her ears. Crystal's here too, and she goes straight over to Wheels, her arms encircling my girl giving her the comfort I should be.

Slowly Chrissy stands, giving me one last pitiful look and then her gaze turns to Wheels. Although she tries to hide it, I don't miss how her expression changes in an instant to one of pure hatred, putting all my senses on high alert. She's stupid, but not so much that she does anything other than walk straight past, pushing Heart and Amy aside as she leaves through the door.

"Fuckin' bitch," Heart snarls as he kneels down to make sure his daughter is okay.

Leaving him to deal with his family, I go over to Wheels. Crystal is talking to her in a low voice, but loud enough for me to hear.

"Don't let that slut get to you, Wheels. She's had her claws into Wraith for ages."

I hunker down so I can look her straight in the eyes, and reach for her hands and take hold of them. I answer the question she doesn't have to voice out loud. "She ain't for me, babe. Whatever claim she thinks she has, she's very mistaken."

She returns my gaze and I can't read anything in her eyes. Fuck, has that bitch ruined this before we even had a chance? As I look into her steel blue orbs I haven't a clue what she's thinking, and then she goes and surprises the fuck out of me when she laughs.

"I'm not dense, Wraith. You've got a past, I've got a past. But as long as you're not going to be fucking around while you're fucking me, I couldn't give a damn about who you've slept with before."

Her strong words made me chuckle, and I let out a breath as my tension slips away, but I have to set her right. "Babe, there wasn't any sleepin' involved. No one's stayed the night with me—except when I was blind drunk and wasn't conscious to know better. I fucked the sluts. End of story."

I expected her face to soften as she realises what an exception I made for her last night, and one which I'll be repeating often if I get my way, but instead she gets a faraway look in her eyes, and once again I get a feeling of unease. Am I reading her wrong? Isn't she in this as much as me?

But then the moment of uncertainty is gone as she makes a suggestion, "Take me back to my room?" It's phrased as a question. She fucking winks at me and the cheeky grin accompanying it suggests she wants to stake a claim, and I'm all for that. My cock strains at my jeans, clearly saying it's up for that too.

Back in her room, we waste no time getting our clothes off. It's a race to see who gets naked first and I end up hopping around with my pants around my ankles, having forgotten to take my boots off first. Fuck, I can't get enough of this woman—and it's only been a few hours since I've been inside her. With the club whores, I never went back for seconds without a good long gap in between, wanting variety rather than a repeat performance. But with Wheels it's completely different. Already I suspect I'll never want another woman again.

Before sliding inside her hot, slick, welcoming channel, I feel the need to justify myself. "Wheels," I start, "Chrissy…"

"Just shut up about her and fuck me!"

She doesn't have to tell me twice.

The rest of the day goes past much like it started, sex until we were completely drained interspersed with short forays out for food. Oh, and one trip out for me when I heard Horse return. I told him my intention to claim her and, after questioning me as though he was her father rather than her friend, he agreed that responsibility for her would pass to me. To be honest, he'd have met my fist if he'd come up with any objections. Ain't letting anyone get in my way. *Uh uh.*

I simply can't get enough of this woman, and by the time we fell asleep I'm utterly exhausted. So much so that when after I wake her early Sunday morning—in a predictable way—I swear my balls have shrunk and are feeling sore, and a thirteen-hour bike ride doesn't hold its usual attractions.

We set off early at five a.m., but even so, given the breaks we'll need—mainly due to having to stop to fill up the bikes—will not be arriving at our destination until late in the evening. Peg's driving the cage, the nondescript SUV we keep for such trips, and I and the prospect are on our bikes behind.

Drummer's choice of Hank made sense. I'm on my pride and joy, an FXR, the Harley citizens didn't like the look of what wasn't a popular model, but its sturdy frame makes handling a breeze at speed. Hank's on his beautifully restored and heavily customised older model Night Train. Both bikes have the larger five gallon tanks, which means we won't be needing to stop quite as often. If Marsh or Spider had come along we'd have been stopping more often, as their bikes are fitted with the smaller tanks with only just over half the range.

As we're travelling out of area we make our first stop just before the border of our territory, taking off our cuts and replacing them with sweatshirts carrying the more discreet SDMC lettering—enough to let those in the know realise who we are, but making sure no one else would bother us. Hopefully it means we shouldn't randomly get pulled over by the heat, or appear on the radar of a rival MC. We take the opportunity to fill up with gas, and as we pull away I yawn deeply, feeling a fleeting envy for Wheels and her opportunity to sleep on the way, but I don't begrudge her. She looked worn out this morning. And I can't help the sense of pride that fills me. *I did that to her.*

Before we head off again I glance over at Hank, who's delaying getting back on his ride.

"Come on." I'm impatient to get on the move again. Peg's leaning out of the window of the cage, an irritated expression on his face.

Hank's shaking his head, now kneeling and patting his hands around the ground under his bike.

"What the fuck is it, Prospect?" I'm starting to wonder whether he's got a problem. I hope not, I don't want to delay.

"Lost my gremlin bell," he murmurs, so quietly it's difficult to hear him.

"For fuck's sake, buy another one!" We've a long distance to go and I'm eager to get started.

With one last look around, Hank, with a look of desolation on his face, finally puts on his brain bucket and sunglasses and we're ready to go.

All that fuss about a damn toy!

Initially following the I-10, we head up towards Flagstaff where we take Highway 89. Our destination is a city near the northern border of Utah, so basically we'll be heading straight up all the way. Once on the freeway Peg puts his foot down, and I sit back to enjoy the ride, twisting the nut to hold the throttle in position to give my hand a break. In my head, I'm planning road trips Wheels and I could take once she's sorted out with a prosthesis and that fucking contract is done and dealt with. I can't wait until she's at last able to ride behind me without fear of anyone coming after her. Sedona and the Grand Canyon come to my mind or, in the other direction, Tombstone—visitors from England always seem fascinated to visit the O.K. Corral. Knowing this is her first trip to the U.S., I'm sure there's plenty of other places she'd like to visit as well. Closer to home is the Arizona Sonora Desert Museum. But does she even like things like that?

I've got a lot to learn about her, so don't know what she's into. But for the first time in my life I'm looking forward to finding what makes a woman tick—other than the obvious of course. The options going around my head keep me occupied for a good part of the journey, and as we're not particularly expecting trouble today, I take the time to indulge in my thoughts.

It's easy riding, a hundred odd miles on the I-10, then a hundred and fifty on the I-17. When Peg turns on his indicator after a couple of hours on the road my tanks starting to get pretty empty, and I imagine Hank's is the same. Peg pulls the SUV over in front of the coffee shop, and as I pull up alongside the pump, I see him get the wheelchair out of the back, unfold it, and lift Wheels out. I want to deck him for manhandling my woman, but suppress that desire understanding it's a must. By the time she's seated and is wheeling herself inside, I've finished filling up so I move my bike up beside the SUV and go to meet her, helping her find her way to the disabled bathroom while Peg buys some drinks and orders breakfast for the three of us.

Joining us at the table, Wheels stretches her arms and rolls her head on her neck. "The thing I hate," she starts to tell us, "is not being able to walk around and stretch my legs."

Peg places his hand on hers, and when she turns to face him, replies, "You will soon."

Then he catches my glare, laughs loudly, and puts his hand back where it belongs—anywhere but on her.

I move my chair so I'm sitting closer beside her. The waitress comes to fill up our coffee cups and later returns with the food.

"Jeez, what's this?" Wheels is looking at her plate with wide eyes, then she glances at me. "How the hell am I supposed to eat all this?"

With a start, I realise it's the first time she'd been out of the compound since she arrived from England more than two months ago. Lots of things are going to be strange to her. And what she's got in front of her is a typical American breakfast, so I shrug. "Eat what you can." I can't suppress a grin when in the end she eats it all, her moans of pleasure at the combination of maple syrup, pancakes, and crisp bacon going straight to my dick. Finally, she seems surprised at her clean plate.

"Hey, Prospect, who's killed your dog?" I notice the usually ebullient Hank is surprising quiet.

Lifting his shoulders almost to the ears, he drops them again in a gesture of defeat. "Can't believe I lost my gremlin bell."

I bark a laugh. "Is that all?"

He tosses me a frown. "Don't want to break down and hold you up."

Fuck, he really does believe that shit. I give him a playful thump on his arm.

"What's a gremlin bell?" Wheels asks, her head tilted to one side.

Peg answers, "Gremlins love to cause trouble to bikers, darlin'. They live on yer bike causing all types of problems or making you lay it down. The bell keeps them away. Gremlins can't take the ringin', you see? Drives them mad, so they drop off your bike, wait on the roadside, then hop on someone else's."

She grins, and leaning over pats Hank's hand. I notice he moves his away fast and casts a glance my way. Now he's more worried about his VP's woman touching him than his fucking toy, so I suppose that's all too good.

Breakfast over, we get swiftly on our way. Eventually, after a couple more stops, the long ride comes to an end and we back the bikes into a straight line in front of the rooms Peg has pre-booked. I doubt any of us will have much trouble getting to sleep that night—except for Hank, of course, who has to stay alert to watch over the bikes.

The next morning we set off for the clinic. Taking pity on the prospect and leaving him at the motel, I stay outside while Peg and Wheels go in to do their thing. It feels cold to me, only about half the temperature we'd left in Tucson, but I'd wrapped up warm knowing what to expect, and at least the sun is shining. After a while, I visit a coffee shop over the road where I can sip a hot drink while still being able to keep an eye on the bikes. Not that I expect anyone would fool with them around here, but hey, who'd want to take a chance?

At last, I see familiar faces coming through the glass doors and am pleased to see a huge great fucking smile on Wheels' face, knowing without her having to tell me that everything had gone to plan.

"They're going to get it done by Wednesday!" she tells me excitedly once I'm within earshot. "It's going to be much better than the last one. Lighter too."

Leaning down, I pull her into me and kiss her lips, the cold air and enthusiasm giving a flush to her face.

"That's great, babe," I tell her. "Fuckin' ace."

CHAPTER 18
Sophie

There's obviously something to be said about going private. Everyone at the clinic had been so solicitous and helpful. My new leg's going to be lightweight titanium, and I won't even have long to wait to get it. Certainly not as long as I would have had to in England. Peg was great too, so encouraging, telling me how he motivated himself to get up and moving again. Apparently, it was the draw of his bike he couldn't resist. He just kept that vision of riding again in his head, which helped him focus on getting his strength and balance back.

Oh, to walk on two legs again without the aid of crutches! I can't wait!

The guys were great. After the clinic we picked up a now refreshed Hank, and drove out to visit various local spots which were suitable for my wheelchair. The scenery here is beautiful, and I looked longingly up at the mountains, some of the highest peaks still with snow on top, wishing I could go up the hiking trails which seemed to be advertised everywhere. I might never be able to ski, of course, but to ride a buggy through the snow, that would be great. *One day*, I promise myself, *one day*.

But the best of the day is yet to come. As soon as we return to the motel after dinner, Wraith draws me into the room, shutting the door firmly behind us. He lifts me out of my wheelchair and holds me to him. As best I can, I wrap my legs around him, my arms hugging him tight.

He stares into my eyes for a moment. "Fuck, I've missed you today."

"You've been with me almost all the time." I laugh.

"Yeah, but you haven't been naked."

I'm still laughing as he takes me to the bed and remedies the situation immediately by stripping me bare. "Babe, you're fuckin' beautiful. These tits? The best I've ever seen." His eyes gleam as he places his large palms over my breasts, fondling and caressing them. His fingers go to my nipples, tweaking and twisting them until I'm writhing as pleasure shoots down my spine. Once my nipples are peaking he sits back to admire his handiwork, then pushes my globes together. "Fuck, babe, can't wait to slide my cock between these beauties."

The devotion he's lavishing on me is making it almost impossible for me to speak, so I simply moan in response.

When his eyes meet mine they glint wickedly, and his finger comes out to touch my lips. Gently he circles them, slipping his digit inside, pushing my teeth apart until my mouth drops open. I smile at him, thinking I know what's on his mind.

"Got somethin' to put in there, babe. You up for that?"

Biting down on him, I manage to awkwardly get out the words, "You want me to suck your cock?"

His eyes blaze as he gasps. "Fuck, yeah, darlin'. Fuck I do."

He shifts up the bed, and lifting my hands I undo his button, then his zip. As soon as it's free, his large cock bobs out as though happy to be out of its confines. He lifts his hips and helps me push the denim over his hips and shuffles up some more.

Taking him in both hands, I use a moment to study him. He's perfect. The head of his cock, glistening with pre-cum, is bulbous and purple, paler skin punctuated with bulging bluish veins covering the rest of his shaft. As my fingers explore, it twitches in my hands. Teasing him, I tighten my grip, but only a little, and start running my hands up and down the long, thick rod, my tongue coming out and licking my lips in anticipation of having all that inside me.

He can't hold back a groan, and I see his hands jerk as if he wants me to get a move on.

But I want to torture him a little longer. Now, pulling him a little towards me, I lick the moisture at the tip, making sure to slide my tongue along his slit, lightly enough to tantalise. His salty taste and musky smell evoke a rush of wetness between my legs, and I moan against his skin.

"Fuck! You trying to kill me here, babe?" he growls, as he feels my breath and the vibrations of the sounds I'm making.

Taking pity on him, I pull him closer, taking the head in my mouth, sucking him in.

"Fuck!"

Knowing I must be doing it right, I take in as much of him as I can, using one hand to keep pressure on the length of him I can't take inside, and with the other I start to massage his heavy balls. Hollowing my cheeks, I draw him in further, as far as he can go without me gagging. Again I moan, and start a rhythm of sucking, laving with my tongue and swallowing.

"Oh Christ, yeah babe. Fuck!"

I keep it up, squeezing his balls gently as I start to feel him swell in my mouth. But he pulls out.

"I want in your pussy!"

Swiftly moving back down, he wastes no time putting his mouth to my clit, sucking and swirling his tongue around. Already aroused, I feel myself tightening in just moments, every muscle tensing as he adds to my body's excitement when he slides his fingers inside me, curling up to that spot which will send me over the top.

"Fuck, you're ready for me, darlin', aren't you?" His words, mumbled against me and his warm breath against my tender flesh, shoot me higher."

"I... I..."

"Come for me, babe."

His encouragement is all I need. My whole body stills, then starts to shudder as I reach the peak and soar over. Jesus! Every single time it gets better! It's as if he's learning my body and how it reacts. I can hardly catch my breath as I come with a scream I'm unable to suppress even while knowing the walls of the motel are paper thin.

Now he's reaching for a condom, his eyes glow knowingly as he rolls it on in one smooth movement, and then he's inside me, his large cock pushing through my tight folds as I adjust to let him in.

My eyes roll back in my head. I'm still shaking from that first intense orgasm, and as he starts slowly sliding in and out it ramps up my arousal all over again until soon I'm coming for a second time, my muscles contracting around him.

"Fuck, I'm not gonna last," he roars, picking up the pace, making the headboard slam against the wall.

I didn't think I was capable, but he's hammering into me now, and a third orgasm starts before the second completely fades.

"Wraith!"

I scream his name as he shouts out, "I'm comin' babe!"

He loses rhythm, pushing into me with short, hard bursts, emptying himself into the condom. His arms are taut as he holds himself above me, his face strained, his eyes closed. Then, as I watch, he opens them and bestows on me a beatific smile.

"Fuck, it just keeps getting better."

Reaching up a shaking hand, I stroke his cheeks. "For me too," I tell him. "For me too."

Suddenly we hear a knocking on the wall, and a muffled voice shouting, "Glad it was fuckin' good for someone."

Then he collapses down and rolls me over into his side, both of us shaking with laughter.

"Fuck off, Peg!" he calls out, making me giggle even more.

After having to sit through a good light-hearted ribbing over breakfast the next morning, we set out for a day's sightseeing. Limited to where they can take me, we end up at a petting zoo, one of the few attractions in the area that's on the flat. I had a riot of a time watching the two burly bikers oohing and ahhing over baby goats and the like! I was slightly surprised they didn't insist on taking one home! Poor Hank had once again been left watching the bikes, but he took it all good-naturedly in his stride, and Wraith told me it was no more than he'd expect—he'd had to do similar when he was prospecting. Feeling sorry for the prospect, I made sure to take him out a burger from the stand in the zoo before we left. He'd taken it from me gratefully after a cautious glance towards Wraith. Peg made as if to take it away from him, and even I had to giggle at the disappointed look on his face, but then the sergeant-at-arms relented, and we waited until he'd eaten before setting off.

Another bout of delicious lovemaking that night, which made me grateful for my wheelchair the next morning, not sure I'd be able to walk on unbowed legs even if I had two of them to stand on. But along with the pleasure, I had the niggling thought at the back of my mind, how long should I be letting this go on for? I'm leading him on and giving him unfair expectations. But I can't bring myself to pull away, not just yet.

A message first thing tells me the clinic has my prosthesis ready for collection. When I have it fitted, it moulds snuggly to what's left of my leg, much better than the old one. But apparently the stump changes in size as healing continues, and I might have needed a new one in any event. But my new prosthesis should last for the next two to three years. They give me spare socks to cushion it, an explanation, and a leaflet—which I take politely though I'd had similar instructions in England—on proper stump care, and we're ready to leave.

The clinic visit hadn't taken long, and it's only just eleven o'clock, and the guys decide to head back today rather than staying until tomorrow as originally planned. So we don't hang-around, just returning briefly to collect our things and settle up at the motel, and soon we're setting off for the tedious drive back.

The journey goes smoothly, but I grow fidgety, and I'm grateful for the stops we have to make every couple of hundred miles for the bikes to top off their tanks. Feeling more awake than I did on the way there, to relieve my boredom I get Peg talking. He tells me how he lost his leg, and how he survived the emotional aftermath, leaving me in awe of his strength, having picked himself up and got on with life again. But when I express my opinion he shuts me down, admitting being angry for the first few months, believing life had treated him unfairly. Although he also divulged he was better off than his comrades who'd lost their lives in the same blast that injured him. It makes me feel ashamed that I'd thought of ending my own, and I realise he is right. Life is still worth living, even if it means making adaptations and having to work so hard at what for the able bodied is easy.

Having someone who understands, who can give me so much advice and encouragement, is great. Much better than the physios who I felt couldn't appreciate what I was going through. As we drive past Phoenix with only a couple of hours left to go, I make up my mind not to let my disability stand in my way or rule my life. The woman coming back from Utah has a far different outlook than the person who went.

We make one final stop just south of Casa Grande as the I-10 meets up with the I-8, and pull off into the same service station we stopped at on our way to Utah. Before filling up for a final time, Hank and Wraith join Peg in getting their cuts out of the back of the van and putting them on, now back on the Satan's Devils' Tucson Chapter ground. It is, Peg tells me, the usual place they tend to stop for that very task.

Wraith takes a moment to come and give me a hug and a kiss that makes Peg whistle loudly. Hank just grins at us, shaking his head before going back to his bike. And that's another thing that's changed during our trip. Having enjoyed the company of all three bikers during our days away, they've become people I'm proud to call friends despite the revelations I've recently been given about the way they live. Then I slap down the thought as one in particular seems far too close to becoming much more to me than that. And I can't let that happen.

Before we get back into the SUV I take one last lingering look at the biker who's given me so much pleasure over the last few days, admiring the figure he makes as he sits on his bike, waiting for us to get moving. Even before my accident I'd have counted myself fortunate to have attracted the interest of the likes of him, and as it is, I can't believe he's not just able to overlook my disability, but embraces it. As my eyes greedily soak him in, I try to harden my heart. This ends soon. It has to.

Peg slips the gears into drive and we pull away. I think back to the previous night and shift awkwardly in my seat as I remember Wraith's talented mouth and hands, and wonder whether I'll ever find anyone to match his calibre in the future, or if anyone else will ever accept my deficiencies in the same way.

Forcing myself to strengthen my resolve never to tie myself to any one man, I dredge up my nightmare to remind me there's nothing else I can do.

As the final miles pass, Peg and I drive on in a comfortable silence with just the radio playing a rock station, but turned down low. We're tired, and both of us just want to get back to the club. It's dark, past midnight now, as at some of our stops we'd had to take the time to fill our hungry bellies. I feel stiff, and my missing leg is aching like a bitch, so I concentrate on the exercises Peg had told me about. Despite the fact my new prosthesis is more comfortable than the old, my stump's started feeling sore. No, I can't wait to get...

The loud sound of gunfire coming out of the blue makes me jump. Peg looks in his mirror and swears loudly seconds before the SUV starts lurching to the right. He tries to fight it, but more gunshots sound, and despite his best efforts, the vehicle's swinging around onto the hard shoulder, throwing me hard against the seat belt. Stunned, my chest hurting, I see Wraith shoot up in front of us, gesticulating wildly. As Peg's yanking the steering wheel with one hand desperately trying to keep an iota of control, he's grabbing his phone with the other.

"We've got trouble," he says into it without introduction. "Just south of Casa Grande. Five or six bikes, firin' at us. If we make it we'll be comin' in hot."

If we make it?

I hang onto the door with all my might as the SUV lurches and bumps up over the ground at the side of the road and comes to a jarring halt. Peg jumps out, yells at me to keep my head down, and slides a gun out of a hidden compartment in the central console. Before I duck, I see Wraith's produced a weapon from somewhere on his bike and is running up to us, gun in hand and at the ready. They both start firing.

It's at that point I realise I haven't seen Hank. Where the fuck is he? Has he been hurt? A glance in the mirror shows me his treasured bike lying on the road behind, but no sign of the prospect. *Christ, I hope he's okay!*

Shots keep being fired, ringing out loud over the sound of engines idling. Wraith and Peg exchange words which I can't hear over the hammering of my heart and the rushing of air in and out of my lungs. My whole body's trembling. Suddenly my door's wrenched open and Wraith reaches in and pulls me out. "You'll have to hang onto me, darlin'." *Hang on to him where? How?*

It all becomes clear when he carries me to his bike, puts me on an uncomfortable flat seat on the back, and in a smooth motion gets himself on in front.

"Arms around my waist. Hold fuckin' tight."

I can't do this, I can't be on a motorcycle. Not like this, and especially not in the middle of the night while strangers are firing at us. But Wraith doesn't give me a chance to object. His engine already running, we roar off at a frighteningly fast pace. All I can do is hang on for dear life. Somehow my right foot has found the foot peg, and I tense the muscle in my other thigh knowing I can't let my prosthesis touch the wheel. The only time I've been more scared was when the car ran over me.

As the firing fades into the distance, I hear the thunder of bikes chasing after us. Wraith rides like the wind, and I'm hanging on to him so hard I think I might hurt him, but at that moment that's the last thing on my mind. I just don't want to fall off! I close my eyes so I don't have to watch the road disappearing at a sickening fast rate beneath us, worried that at any moment we might be shot, or he might lose control of the bike. Or both.

I don't know how long it is in reality, but it feels like hours before we meet a pack of bikes coming the other way. Wraith slows and comes to a halt beside the leader, the rest stream past us, giving chase to our pursuers who've made a swift about turn and are zooming off in the direction we'd come from.

"Peg's back there—tyres shot out on the van."

"Hank?" I recognise Drummer, the president.

Wraith shakes his head. "Think he took a bullet. He came down pretty hard. But I saw him take one of them out first."

Drummer swears, loudly. I put my hand to my mouth. Oh no, sweet Hank. And Peg. Both of them who I now count as good friends. I start praying they'll be okay.

"You alright, sweetheart?"

It takes me a moment to realise Drummer's talking to me. In response I can only shake my head. I feel like I'm going to be sick and am about as far from alright as I could possibly be.

After giving me an assessing look, he instructs Wraith, "Take her back to the clubhouse. Get her settled. I'll go see what the damage is."

As Drummer speeds off into the night, Wraith takes no time getting on his way again. This time a little bit, just a tiny smidgeon, slower.

I can't talk to him until we get back to the compound. When he lifts me off the bike I'm shaking in his arms. He carries me straight into the clubhouse where a couple of members have remained. I recognise Dollar and Heart. As soon as we enter, they send the sweet butts on their way. Wraith lowers me into one of the seats around a table and goes towards the bar. Dollar has already moved to his side.

"Vodka for her." Wraith puts in his request. The treasurer already appears to have something brown and strong in a shot glass for Wraith.

I hear them talking quietly while the drinks are prepared, punctuated by loud swearing and exclamations. But Wraith doesn't forget me, and soon appears with my drink in hand. I'm rubbing my leg where the muscles locked from me clenching it so hard to stay on the bike. He sees, and his face twists ruefully.

"Told you I'd get you on the back of my bike. Next time I'll sort it so you'll be more comfortable."

I'm not at all sure I want there to be a next time. My heart's still feeling like it's going to jump out of my chest, and violent shakes keep going through me. My ears are still ringing from the gunshots and loud engine noises. But I'm alive, and I'm safe. Unlike the others.

I take a long drink, splutter at the neat vodka, and then put down my glass. Staring at the table, unable to look at anyone, I ask shakily, unable to stop trembling, "What about Hank and Peg?" I'm so worried about those we left behind.

At that moment Wraith's phone rings, and he holds up his hand before answering me. "Talk to me," he says simply.

"Ah huh. Thank Christ for that!"

"Fuck it." This comment is accompanied by him slamming his fist on the table, making me jump.

"Shit. Got it. I'll wait here for you."

"Nah, she's okay. Fuckin' shaken up."

"Yeah. I'll get Doc here."

Then he finishes the call. Dollar, Heart, and I all look up at him expectantly. Leaning over to me he pulls me into him and rests his chin on my head. Holding me tight, he speaks over me to the others. "Hank's dead." I gasp loudly and fasten my hands in his shirt as he continues, "Peg's took a fuckin' hit but not before he took a couple of them out as they rode off after us."

I can't believe it. Hank, who had such hopes of joining the MC; Hank, that lovely man who'd been so friendly to me. And Peg? He's already been through too much. How badly is he injured? Is he going to die too? The gruff, scary sergeant-at-arms who'd done so much to help me come to terms with my disability. The thought that any of us had been killed tonight is horrifying. A huge sob escapes from me, quickly followed by another as my adrenaline rush fades and everything hits me. *It could have been any one of us. Or all of us.*

Wraith is nodding at someone as he smooths his hand over my hair, and Dollar gets out his phone. I can't think of anything but the near miss we've all had—or that Hank had lost his life. It doesn't seem real. Once they start I can't stop the tears, they keep falling. My glass is refilled and put into my hand, and then I hear another, familiar voice in the room.

"What the fuck's happened?" Horse is on my other side, his hand on my shoulder, his fingers tightening until they're almost digging into my skin as the men explain.

"Horse, can you take her back to her room and stay with her until I get there? I need to wait for Drum," Wraith's voice rumbles over me.

I try to shake my head, wanting to hear the details myself when the others get back. "I want to stay here."

"Shush, darlin'. There's nothin' you can do tonight. Let me find out what's going on and I'll come to tell you, okay? Go with Horse now. He'll stay with you 'til I get there. Hush now, it'll be alright."

It can't be alright. Hank's dead. Still trying to get my head around that fact, I protest again, "I need to know how Peg is. How bad is it? Will he be okay?"

"Soon as I know I'll come tell you." After a kiss on my brow, Wraith gently removes my hands from his shirt and eases away, giving Horse room to reach down and pick me up.

Cradled in Horse's strong arms, I try once more to object but Horse stops me. "They know what they're doing, babe. Just let them do what needs to be done."

"But Hank…and Peg?" I protest once more.

"Hank's gone," Horse tells me softly, repeating what I already know but can't quite accept. "He's gone. And we'll just have to wait on news on Peg."

CHAPTER 19
Wraith

Throwing back another shot of Jack, I hear the main door to the clubroom loudly banging open. It interrupts my dark thoughts and, having checked who's entering, my eyes close briefly in relief as Drummer comes in, his arm around and supporting Peg, who's at least on his feet. Doc, the ex-Army medic who we pay a fucking enormous retainer to for these very circumstances, and who'd arrived only moments before, rushes over to help.

In his usual fashion, the sergeant-at-arms brushes him off. "Church first." Peg's in pain but doesn't want to delay club business.

But this time he doesn't get his way as his president overrules him. "You're fuckin' bleedin' all over the place, man. Let Doc have a look at you."

Grumbling, Peg lets himself be led off to the room we reserve for medical emergencies but don't, thank the fuck, often have to use. Last time it was when Slick cut his hand open doing some shit on his bike.

Drum's eyes follow the Doc and his patient until they're out of sight. He stands in the centre of the club room, his hands tunnelling through his hair and then his palms wipe down over his cheeks. Now his gaze, full of fury, lands. "Where's Wheels?"

"I sent her off with Horse. There ain't nothin' she can add to this. Fuck, she's a mess."

Slowly he nods. "Wouldn't expect her to be anythin' else. At least you got her back here okay." He rolls his head on his shoulders and breathes deeply. "We'll give it a minute and see what's going on with Peg, and then it's church." He glances around the room as he mentally adds up the number of bodies, and his slow nod of satisfaction shows he sees almost all the brothers are present. We're a tight-knit community, the majority of us normally bunking down on-site, with only Heart, Viper, and Bullet, the members with old ladies, regularly living separate. But even they've come from their beds tonight. The sweet butts have been sent packing. Mouse is the only one missing, but that's as per norm. We'll drag him out of his bat cave when we need him.

I raise my chin toward Drum, but the quick shake of dismissal makes me curb my impatience. He'll want to think this through for himself before updating all of us at once.

By the time the prez has helped himself to a couple of shots of his top-shelf whisky, Peg's come out with Doc, the former's arm is in a sling, and I wince knowing how much he'll hate that. But at least he's alive. And walking.

Mumbled conversations around the room cease as Peg stands in the middle, all brothers questioning him with their eyes. He gives a nod to Doc. "Doc sewed me up. Bullet went straight through. Will just have a wing clipped for a while. Now let's get to church."

Doc flinches and glares a little. "Now what did I tell you, Peg? You should be restin'. You've lost a lot of blood."

"Yeah, yeah." Peg tosses him a scowl of his own. "I'll get my head down later, got things to do now."

"Thanks, Doc." Drum goes over to both men, and I know he'll realise it would be a lost cause to try to argue with his sergeant-at-arms. "We'll get him sorted after church." His warning stare suggests that Peg will be given space to be brought up to date, but after that will be following doctor's orders. Then he turns to Doc again. "D'ya mind poppin' up and taking a look at the girl, Wheels? Wraith brought her in fast and she was pretty shaken." Then, after Doc agrees, without wasting any more time, Prez shouts out to the rest of us, "Right you buggers, church. Now! Let's get this over with so Peg can get his fuckin' head down."

Relieved Drum was looking out for my girl—I'd have asked Doc to pay her a visit if he hadn't—I follow my brothers into the large meeting room, having shot off a quick text to Mouse summoning him in. His office is only a couple of doors along so he enters almost immediately. I notice that on his way in, Prez has indicated that the prospects are to join us. Unusual, but totally understandable, as one of their own has gone. The brothers all find their seats. Marsh and Spider stand at the far end of the table, casting anxious glances at each other.

Without preamble, Drum gets down to the first order of business, his face bleak as he looks around the room. "Our prospect, Hank, gave his life for the club tonight. He'd been with us almost a year and this vote would have come to the table shortly in any event. Now, I'm fuckin' proposin' we posthumously give him the patch, bury him as a full member. Let's vote."

There are overwhelming shouts of 'Aye' accompanied by the sound of fists banging on the table as brothers don't even bother to vote in turn.

Drum bangs the gavel hard on the wooden table top. "Motion carried."

His stern face gentles as his gaze falls on Marsh and Spider. Spider's the same age as Hank, Marsh just a couple of years older. "Your brother died a fuckin' hero," he tells them, his voice sombre. "He died a true Satan's Devil."

More thumps on the wood and a general murmuring of agreement.

Drum gives us all a moment to digest his words then instructs, "Prospects, you're dismissed now." They might be called on to join the fight, but as they've not yet proved their loyalty to the club, club business and the decisions we'll make here tonight are not for their ears. I watch them leave, knowing while they want to stay to hear the discussions, they understand their place and will accept being left out. It's something we've all been through.

The prez waits until the door shuts behind them. Then he looks at each of us in turn before announcing, "Rock Demons."

"Fuck it!" I slam my hand on the table. The reason he's named the ruthless rival MC club based in Phoenix can only be that it was them responsible for killing Hank and injuring Peg tonight. I'd been too much in the thick of it all to see their cuts. The Devils and the Demons have had an uneasy peace for years, and I can't immediately think why they would turn on us all of a sudden.

Mouse is busy tapping on his ever-present laptop. We ignore him, it's what he always does.

Peg raises his good arm, and Drum throws a chin jerk, his way of giving him permission to speak.

"It's my fuckin' fault, Prez, I'm sorry, I should've fuckin' known better."

"You fuckin' what?" It's not only me who throws out the question as various echoes with slightly different phrasing go around the room.

Peg's looking downcast. "You should take my patch for this. It's my fuckin' job to watch out for the club. I've got sloppy—we should never have been using the same fuckin' place to stop and put on our cuts."

Slick is shaking his head. "But we've stopped there for years."

"Precisely!" Peg looks white, but cheeks blaze red. "Fuck knows why they wanted us, but they knew exactly which rest area we'd be usin'. All they had to do was wait and then follow."

"It ain't all your fault, Peg," Mouse interrupts, causing a hush to come over us all. "It was like lookin' for a needle in a haystack before we got a lead, but now I know who I'm searchin' for and I can tell you that the Demons got a nice sum put into their bank account recently. Looks like they're the ones who picked up on that fuckin' contract for the woman. They wanted the girl."

Talk bursts out again; Drum calls us to order. "Makes sense, a fuckin' Phoenix chapter when she would have been traced to landin' at Sky Harbor. And they could have spotted Dart and Slick pickin' her up."

I shake my head. "If they had, they'd have been on us long before now. She's been here nearly three fuckin' months. How the fuck they found it out now I don't know."

"Did you have a tail up to Utah, VP?"

I'm already going back over everything in my mind. "I was checkin' out for that, but no, Prez, I'm pretty fuckin' sure we didn't. How could someone follow us seven hundred miles and neither me nor Peg spot them? Nah, somehow they knew enough to lie in wait until we were on our way back."

Peg's head is in his hands. "I shouldn't have stopped there…"

"Brother, this ain't on you. We've learned the lesson now, but ain't had trouble with the Demons since I got in this fuckin' chair, so I'd have made the same call."

"I was there," I back up the prez. "Peg, I was there to fuckin' keep her safe, and *I* didn't give it a second thought."

Other brothers back us up. Stopping there was a habit for us all when we'd been out of state—one we'll change now. Yeah, a sloppy schoolboy error, but one any of us would have made. And one I *had* made. It wasn't all on Peg.

The sergeant-at-arms is still shaking his head, but Drum's moving on. "Right," the prez starts. "What I still can't understand is how the fuck they knew you'd be on the road tonight? The VP's got enough experience to know if he's picked up a fuckin' tail, and he's right, he and Peg would have had to be blind not to spot one all the way to Utah and back. Anyone got any fuckin' ideas?"

Beef's shifting in his seat, Drum's sharp and narrowed eyes don't miss it, settling on him. "You got somethin' to say, Brother?"

His fingers tapping on the table, Beef looks up, his face looking drawn as he starts to speak. "Hate to say this, but that bitch Chrissy was mouthin' off at the Running Horse a couple of nights ago. The day you went to Utah, Wraith." He's referring to one of the bars we often frequent in town. It's near the strip club and brothers often stop by there. "Heard her mention Wraith's name, but she shut that shit down pretty quickly when she saw me."

Fuck, that bitch! If she let anything out about Wheels being here, she was sharing club business. "Who the fuck was she blabbin' to?"

"No idea. Didn't recognise the motherfuckers. But a biker type. Didn't think too much of it at the time, and as I said, she got a glare from me and moved away from him quickly."

The prez's face grows as dark as a thundercloud as the implications sink in. He brings his fist down hard on the table. "Right, first thing tomorrow I'll be talking to that fuckin' whore. You'll want to be with me, VP," Drummer growls out menacingly.

Too fucking right I'll want to be in on that conversation. And if she betrayed my girl…

"She's targeted you for a while, Wraith. Would suit her to get the woman out of the way." Slick's only telling me what I'm already thinking.

Fuck. If she betrayed me, she betrayed the club.

With no other suggestions how our whereabouts had been discovered, our suspicions of where the leak that led to Hank being killed had come from seem to be confirmed.

With a glance at Peg, who's clutching at his shoulder, Drum wants to move things along. "So it looks like the Demons have taken the fuckin' contract you found on the web." He throws a nod at Mouse as if to confirm where the information came from. "I said we'd give our protection to her as long as there was no blowback on us."

For a second I'm unsure where he's going with this. My heart speeds up. *He's not going to suggest throwing her to the wolves, is he?* If he is, there's only one thing I can do.

I start opening my mouth to claim her publicly, so they won't have the choice of removing the protection of the club owing to her relationship with me, when he continues, "Now they've killed one of our own, this fight's at our fuckin' door. That changes things."

"Too right it fuckin' does." Rock glares, his gun out on the table in front of him, his fingers spinning it. "No one kills a fuckin' Devil and gets away with it." There are general grunts of agreement.

"It's our war now, Prez," Slick butts in. "We're not backin' away from this."

Drummer's face is set. "I hear yah all, but we need a fuckin' vote. All those in favour?"

After we'd gone around the table there was no need for a vote to count any against, all were prepared to fight, and that meant Wheels would continue to be safeguarded. I can only hope we make a better job of it than we have so far. Slowly I let out the breath I didn't know I'd been holding, as I realised if the vote had gone the other way I'd have found some way to protect her myself. No fuckin' way would I have allowed her to be taken by

229

the Demons and then placed into the clutches of a man who end up hurting and killing her. Just no fuckin' way.

"Right, we're on lockdown as of now. Bring the ol' ladies in—Heart, you'll have to have Amy here, okay? Which means the rest of you fuckers mind what you do around the little squirt."

Drum's a hard bastard, but sometimes he shows his softer side. Heart throws him a grateful look.

"Peg, Mouse," the prez continues, "we all secure?"

The man who looks after our security systems, as well as being the go-to computer guy, nods. "As long as the front gates are locked a fly couldn't get into the compound without me knowin' about it."

"I'd like to get Spider workin' with Mouse. He's got an interest in security and seems to know his stuff. We need eyes on it at all times." Peg looks drawn and tired, but he's contributing just the same.

"Agreed. And I want two men on the gate every fuckin' minute, a prospect and a fully patched brother. Need someone sharp to make sure no fucker gets in."

"What about the businesses?" Dollar has an eye to the money.

"Business as usual until we know what's in their heads. Can't see them directing a hit on our earners right now. Have to assume they want the woman, not an all-out war.

"I think that's right," Peg interrupts. "They didn't stop to finish me off, just tore after Wraith and Wheels."

"So we keep open for now, but keep our ears to the fuckin' ground." Drum pauses and wipes his hand over his chin. "What do we know about their club numbers?"

"I think they're a bit smaller than us," Peg replies. "But that's old info, and things could have changed.

We've got fifteen full members and now only two prospects.

We spend a short while tossing around what we know of the Demons, which isn't a lot since we've kept to ourselves for a few years now. But know thy enemy is something we need to get a handle on, so we come up with a few ideas about how to do that. Peg's noticeably looking worse for wear now, as are we all. The adrenalin rush of getting Wheels back in one piece while knowing I was leaving my brothers behind is starting to fade now, and I'm coming down with a bang. Tonight's been hard on us all. We might be an outlaw club, but we've not had a member killed by another club for a very long time. Tonight's action is the start of something all of us will be prepared to fight for, and we're going into it knowing Hank may not be the last to give his life.

Knowing his club, Drum reads us all pretty well and starts to wrap up. "Okay, brothers. That's all we can do for tonight. We'll get together tomorrow to go through some specifics. But before we do, I think the VP has something to say." He cocks an eyebrow in my direction. He'd given me until Friday to get my thoughts straight about Wheels; now he seems to be moving it up the agenda.

As we'd hurtled back at speeds a Harley wasn't really meant to go, with Wheels literally hanging on for dear life behind me, the fear for her safety had given me clarity on what she means to me. We'd escaped this time, literally with our lives, so I have absolutely no problem letting my brothers know where I stand. Giving a cough to clear my throat, and even in these circumstances unable to keep the smile from my face, I had no problem telling them. "Yeah, well, I'm claimin' Wheels. As my ol' lady."

Now it's common knowledge I'd starting fucking her, but I'm probably one of the last they thought would take the next step and put my head in the old lady trap, so the indrawn breaths

CHAPTER 20
Sophie

Hank's dead. And Peg's injured. After the great time I'd had in Utah and all my positive thoughts on the way back, I was still shaking when Horse got me back to my room. What the bloody hell have I got myself into? What kind of trouble is the club in that they'd get into a gunfight on the road?

And why did they chase Wraith and I almost all the way back to the Tucson clubhouse? What would have happened if the rest of the club hadn't met us halfway and run them off? Just how close was my own brush with death tonight?

My leg's throbbing and my chest aches from where the seat belt cut into me. As thoughts churn through my head, suddenly my pains take second place and I grow cold as the dreadful notion hits me. Was it me they were after? There is a contract out on me after all.

A gasp escapes my lips, drawing Horse's attention, and he's by my side in seconds. "What is it, babe? What's up?"

"Was it my fault, Horse?" As his brow creases in confusion I continue, "Were they after me? Is it my fault Hank died?"

"Oh babe." He pulls me to him and I lean into his comfort as he gently brushes his hand down my hair. "I don't know. Let Drum and the boys sort it out. There's no point thinking on it; we don't know what the club's up to at the moment. And even if it was to do with you, the club offered you protection…"

"They offered to hide me, Horse, not die for me."

"Hey, wait until we know more before you beat yourself up. And no, nothing was your fault. Even if St John-Davies was behind it, that's not on you, sweetheart. You're an innocent in all this, caught up in someone else's dirty business."

"I was so happy, Horse, coming back from Utah. I had hope that I could get my life back on track for the first time in months."

"That's great to hear! And hang onto those feelings, Sophie. Whatever the reason for tonight's shooting, don't let go of those positives."

"But I can't, can I? If I wasn't here, Hank would be…"

"You don't know it was anything to do with you. And even if it was, do you think Hank would want that? Don't you ever fucking say that you shouldn't be here, babe. Hank went down fighting for his club, doing what he'd signed up to do, just like any soldier in war. You're alive, don't think of fucking wasting what he did for you. Whatever the reason for the attack, he died to give you the chance to get away. You owe it to him to live, and live full."

Hearing him put it like that makes me feel even guiltier. "Don't waste your chance at life, some don't have it so good. My wife…"

I knew his wife had died, but not what had happened to her. "How did she die, Horse?"

I think it's only to help take my thoughts off the horrific night I've had that he opens up to me, and his words explain why he's helped me so much.

"She was in a hit and run, babe, just like you." The catch in his voice tells me how much he loved—still loves—her. "She was dead on arrival at the hospital. They could do nothing for her." Taking his arm away from my shoulder, I see tears shimmering in his eyes, then he buries his head in his hands. "I'd give my life to have her back, for her to have survived. Whatever parts of her were missing, I wouldn't care. She never had a chance to carry on, Sophie. Unlike you. Life may have thrown a fucking big curve ball at you, but you've got to pick it up and run with it." As I reach out my hand to touch his arm he covers it with his own. "Soph, I know things look bleak right now, but do it for me, will you? Live and enjoy life. Take the chance that my Carrie never had."

It explains so much—why he was so intent on helping me and why he was so angry when he'd found out I'd been tempted to end it all.

While I'm still trying to process what he's told me, there's a knock on the door. Horse goes to open it and a man walks in carrying a bag. I've never seen him before, but I gather why he's here as I hear Horse greet him.

"Hey, Doc. Good to see you again."

"Drummer sent me up. How's the girl doin'? Hear she's shaken up after what went down."

As Horse has lowered his voice all I can now hear are murmurings, and I'm impatient to talk to him myself. If he's a doctor he's probably treated Peg. I'm desperate to know how he is. But luckily I don't have to wait long, and Horse brings him over. At well over six foot and dressed in biker leather, but without the cut the others wear, he's unlike any medical person I've ever seen before. But despite his size, he has gentle-looking grey eyes under a shock of unruly brown hair, and his welcoming smile puts me at ease.

I ask as he's crossing the room, "How's Peg?"

"Honey, he's okay. He had little more than a graze. A few stitches and he'll be right as rain before you know it. Don't you worry about Peg, hun. He's a tough old bird."

I didn't realise how much I needed to hear that news. My head falls forward into my hands, and for some reason tears start streaming down my face. I'd been so worried that the sergeant-at-arms would die too.

"Now, let's take a look at you, honey. How are you feelin'?" Doc sits down beside me and gently takes my hand, his fingers going to my pulse. Then he puts his hand under my chin and turns me to face him, staring into my eyes. "Hmm, you've had a rough time tonight, haven't you?"

Pulling myself up straight I answer, "I'm alright, it's, it's…"

"You're a strong woman, Wheels, I can see that. But after what you've been through I think you might need a little help gettin' some sleep tonight. Are you on any medication?"

"Tramadol," I tell him. "For the pain."

"Taken any today?"

I shake my head.

"Right, well I'll leave you a sedative. Take it and you should get a good night's rest. You've had a shock, honey. You're probably runnin' on fumes now, and you'll come down hard. Take it or not, it's up to you. But my advice is to try to get a good sleep and leave your worryin' until the mornin'."

It's probably sound advice. I'm not sure how else I'd be able to close my eyes without seeing Hank laughing and joking in front of me, or the bike I'd seen lying on its side.

It's not long after the doctor leaves us that Wraith comes in. He's looking so serious.

Throwing a steely gaze at him I tell him, "If you're going to tell me it's club business I'll bloody kill you, Wraith." I'm frightened he's not going to let me know what's going on. But he beckons Horse over, who pulls up a chair, and Wraith sits down beside me, the third man to sit in that exact same spot tonight.

He takes a deep breath and then moves his hand over mine, turning so he can talk to me directly. "It is club business, but there are some things you need to know," he begins, his fingers tracing my knuckles and fingers. "It was a rival club, the Rock Demons out of Phoenix that came after us."

"Why? Have you had problems with them before?"

Now he touches his fingers to my lips. "Give me a chance to explain, huh?"

Okay, I'll shut up for now.

"We already knew a contract had been put out on you, that St John-Davies wanted you found. But until tonight we didn't know who'd taken up the challenge. Now we do."

"The fucking Rock Demons," Horse spits out.

"Seems that way."

Immediately I know what I have to do. "I've got to go." It's the obvious suggestion. Either the club will chuck me out or I'll go of my own volition.

"Fuck that! You're going no fuckin' where." Wraith's grip on my hand tightens.

"But I've brought trouble to the club. Hank..."

"You brought no fuckin' trouble, babe. The Demons brought that all by themselves. Hank knew the score. We've made him a full member, by the way. He'll be buried with a patch."

It warms me to hear that, but I wished he'd been alive to become a proper member of this new family he'd been hoping to find. "But..."

Again, Wraith interrupts me. "The Demons have started somethin' they shouldn't have. We're not going to let them get away with this."

I gasp. "You can't fight over me!"

"No, not over you, babe, though we're not gonna let them get their fuckin' hands anywhere near you I swear that, but because they killed one of ours. They're all fuckin' dead men walkin', they just don't know it yet."

I've started a war. Whatever he says, this is down to me. If they hadn't tried to take me, the Satan's Devils wouldn't have been involved. I can't let them put other people in danger because of me. "Wraith, I can't let you do this. I'm going to go. I can't put anyone else at risk. I'm not worth it."

"This is happenin', darlin', whether you want it to or not, whether you stay or go. I can tell you that. Killin' a brother is not somethin' we take lightly. And..." He pauses to sweep his hand down my cheek, around my chin, across the hollow of my throat, and ending up resting over my heart. A shiver runs through me, which intensifies as he tells me in a solemn voice, "You ain't going nowhere. You're mine now, I've claimed you in front of the club. Your mine to protect. My ol' lady."

I'm lost for the right words and don't completely understand. "That sounds permanent, Wraith?" I whisper it, my voice rises, making it a question, but I've been around the club long enough to know that's exactly what it means.

"Fuckin' right, it is. Good as a marriage in my world." He confirms it, his lips curling into a smile as he waits for my elated response.

My eyes widen. *Oh my God, what has he done?* "You should have asked me first, Wraith." My voice comes out on a whisper.

He smirks, and I realise he has no fucking idea what a mess he's made of everything when he leans forwards and asks, "Wanna be my ol' lady, darlin'?" And without waiting for an answer, presses his lips to mine. Still shocked at this turn of events, I automatically respond, my mouth already moulding to his as though he's trained me. His hand goes to the back of my hair and pulls me closer to him.

A coughed laugh interrupts us. "I think this is my cue to leave," Horse tells us.

Wraith pulls away, but only very slightly. "Night, Horse."

His mouth back on mine, I don't even notice the door closing. Our tongues dance, but slowly. I give into his kiss, knowing it's the last time I'll be this close to him, knowing I'm going to have to hurt him. But I relish his touch for another few minutes, storing up memories for the lonely times to come.

My hands tighten around his. Oh God, what do I do? I want nothing more than for him to hold me, to make love to me again. Just one last time. But once more wouldn't be enough. And that's when I know it's time, and that I have to tell him, have to explain and make him understand why I can't risk it all again. Why I can't do this.

Gently I put my hands on his chest and push him away.

Taking a deep breath, I raise my eyes to his. "Wraith, I need to tell you something."

He's trying to pull me back to him, and his eyebrow raises as I press back, pushing him away. Something in my expression communicates he knows he's not going to like it. His eyes narrow. "What you want to say have any bearin' on us?"

Nodding, then using the words, I confirm it. "Yes. Everything."

"Then tell me, darlin'." A slight hardness has come into his voice as if somehow he already suspects what I'm going to say. "But if you're gonna say you can't stay because of some false notion that by going you'll stop what's been started, you're wrong. And there's no safer place for you to be than with me, babe. If you go, I'll fuckin' go with you. I've told you, you're my ol' lady."

Breathing in sharply once again, I get it out there. "I can't be your old lady. I don't want to be claimed. We've got to stop this now, Wraith."

"Fuck, woman. What the fuck you talkin' about?"

"Us." I point to him and then to me. "I'm finished with us, Wraith. I don't want to do this anymore. It's been great…"

Wraith stands, he kicks at the chair Horse had been sitting on and sends it crashing to the ground. "What the fuck are you sayin'? It's been *great?*" He runs his fingers across his beard. "What have you done with the woman I've been fuckin'? Where is she?

'Cos you obviously weren't the one in bed with me. *Great?*" He stops, paces, then swings back. "What we had together was fuckin' incredible! Once in a fuckin' lifetime incredible!" Again he steps away, moving to the wall and putting his fist through the plasterboard. His head rolls up, then down to his chest, then again he comes over to me and his voice calms. "Am I pushin' you too fast, darling? D'you need a bit of time to think this through?"

How can I make him understand? "No, I don't need time. I should never have let it go on this long," I cry out, desperate for him to believe me, to go away and leave me alone to wallow in my misery. "I only wanted a one night stand. I didn't want it to turn into anything more."

"A one fuckin' night stand?" His hands fist in his hair and his face reddens. "You only wanted one night? You wanted me to treat you like a fuckin' sweet butt?"

I can feel tears leaking from my eyes. His rising anger is palpable, but I know he won't hurt me. He doesn't have to, I'm hurting myself.

"Wraith, I…"

He kicks the fallen chair again and stomps around the room. Returning to me he leans over, his hands on the bed on each side of me, trapping me. When he speaks, it's right into my face.

"I fuckin' claimed you, woman. In front of my brothers. I went up against my president's instructions. I went out on a limb for you and was prepared to take the consequences. I thought there was somethin' special between us. Never dreamt all you wanted was another notch on your fuckin' bedpost."

He pushes away again, his hands clenching and unclenching by his sides. "One biker going to be enough for you? Or are you going to go through the rest of my brothers now? You want to become a club whore?"

His words are like arrows of pain shooting through me. I hurt, even though he's not physically touched me. But how can I truthfully say it's nothing like that? While I'm not going to be chasing after his brothers, one night was all I ever should have had with him. *See what happens when you break your own rules.*

"Wraith, I didn't mean to hurt you."

"Hurt me? You think I'm fuckin' hurt?" He spits the words at me. "Well, you were a good fuckin' lay, bitch. Glad I found out what you really are before we got in any deeper."

He turns and leaves, slamming the door hard behind him.

CHAPTER 21
Wraith

Stomping my way back down to the clubhouse I'm unable to understand what the fuck had just happened. For the first time in my life I put my neck on the line for a woman, and this is how she fucking rewards me? Told me she just wanted a bit of fun and nothing serious. What the fuck? *Wasn't that my line?*

I kick out at everything movable in my way, and even some things that aren't—at least my steel toed motorcycle boots are protecting my feet. Tension radiates through me and I'm lucky I don't meet a brother on the way, as just one word might mean he'd get my fist in his face. I can't go inside like this. It's late, or early, whichever way you prefer to look at it, but there'll still could be someone around, and right now I'm not in the mood for company. I circle the clubhouse, making my way to the picnic tables out back and sit on one. My fingers probe in my back pocket for the packet of smokes I used to keep there before I remember I'd given up two years ago. Fuck, I could kill for a cancer stick right now.

My head falls into my hands. *How could I have read her so wrong?* Thinking back, the signs were there, how she reacted any time I hinted this could be something more than just a few fucks between us. I'd assumed she'd been on the same page. *How could I have been so mistaken?*

Slowly my rage starts to fade, replaced by some other emotion that I'm reluctant to name. At first, I was attracted to her, but then different feelings began to grow, and I'd been certain they were reciprocated. *Had I been wrong all the way along?* Those little touches, those loving looks. Had she really just been using me for my body? Fuck, what a turnaround this is. *Is this my punishment for the way I'd always push the club whores out of my bed after sex?* What fucking payback to find she's acting like a female me.

I lace my fingers behind my head. What a fucking day all around. Being shot at, losing Hank, the decision to go to war with the Demons. She'd clung to me during that madcap ride back to Tucson, and while the circumstances weren't as I'd imagined for her first ride, I loved her being on the back of my bike. Her arms tight around me, her breasts squashed up against my back.

But she'd been scared, terrified. While I'd been running on the endorphins triggering my flight or fight response, pushing my bike to its limits, feeling the exhilaration which comes along with that, she'd been petrified, hanging on for dear life. Then she'd found out about Hank and Peg, and I'd laid on her the reason for the attack. While none of my brothers would put the blame at her door—they'd answer to me if they did that—the truth is, if it wasn't for that fucking contract on her, Hank would still be alive. That's one fuck of a lot of guilt for her to be saddled with. And I'd just thrown the old lady label in there as if it weren't nothin' at all.

Unlocking my hands, I wipe them over my tired eyes, then cup my cheeks. No wonder she doesn't want to get more involved with an MC. Pushing her tonight was the worst fucking timing. My reasons? I could have seen her taken or killed today, and I didn't want to waste a moment of our time together. But looking at it from her side, asking her to be my old lady when she'd watched one of my brothers die might just have been a stupid fucking thing to do.

But she hadn't said any of that. She'd told me she wanted me for nothing more than entertainment in bed. As I run over our conversation, although the night carries a chill I begin to sweat, my heart rate increases, and my hands start to shake. How fucking dare she say the things to me that she did? My emotions tonight are swinging like a pendulum as rage sweeps through me once again.

As my teeth start to grind I know right now I could kill someone, or fuck. My cock's still rock hard, as I'd expected to be inside her by now. Expected to claim my old lady in every way I could. Getting to my feet, deciding I'll find another whore to address my needs, with just a few paces I weave around the fire pits and enter the clubhouse, which by now is fucking empty, not one single bitch is hanging around to scratch my itch. For Christ sake, this has been a total fuck-up of a day.

Briefly, I consider waking one of the sweet butts—it's nothing more than they'd expect, they're well compensated for their services—but suddenly it seems too much bother. Electing on a different solution, I reach behind the bar and grab a bottle of Jack, not bothering to get a glass. Taking myself off to my room, I throw myself on the bed and lift the bottle to my lips, knowing the only thing left to do tonight is to seek oblivion.

The next thing I know I'm being woken by a banging on my door and the empty bottle falls off the bed. My head is throbbing, and I feel like shit, and immediately I regret the remedy I chose last night. Why does drowning your sorrows seem such a great fucking idea until you wake the next day?

The banging comes again, and then the door opens.

"The fuck you doing here? Thought you'd be with your ol' lady? That was the first place I looked... What the fuck's happened to you?"

Wishing he'd speak a bit more quietly, I answer Peg with a snarl, "Ain't got no fuckin' ol' lady."

Peg's eyes widen and he takes a step into the room. He gives me a long hard stare. "What happened? You fuck it up, Brother?"

Right at this moment I can barely remember my name, let alone the details of last night. "Just leave me alone, Peg."

But he doesn't go. Instead, he steps closer, invading my personal space. "What did you say to her? You hurt her and I'll..."

As his voice trails off, I realise how protective he is of her, bound as they are by a common disability.

A quick shake of my head, which I immediately regret, I get my rebuttal in quickly before he starts using the fists our sergeant-at-arms is famed for. "No, Peg. She wasn't the one to get hurt."

His mouth drops open as the penny finally drops. "She turned you down?"

"Yes." Saying it is less painful than nodding.

His head cocks to one side as though shocked, and his hand comes up, cupping his chin. "Well, fuck me. You two were tight back in Utah. I thought she was into it as much as you. What did she say?"

"That she only wanted me for a one night stand."

A laugh bursts out of him. "Thought that was your line."

The bright light is hurting my eyes. "Seems all she wanted was a good fuckin'."

"Jesus." I know Peg will understand, offering to make her my old lady was a fucking big step for me to take. That she turned and threw it back in my face hurts. A lot. He glances around him, then grabs the chair and sits down. Leaning back, he crosses his feet at the ankles and folds his arms. I sigh. He's settling himself in for the long haul, and I don't feel up to this right now.

"I'm sorry, Wraith." He sounds sympathetic.

I believe he truly is, but I'm dreading the reaction of my other brothers, knowing they'll be mocking me. The VP turned down by a woman—fodder for one heck of a lot of ragging.

After a moment, Peg speaks again. "Yesterday must have been fuckin' hard for her," he starts. "Perhaps you shouldn't have pressed so soon."

That's the hope I'm clinging to. What the fuck? As the thought hits me, I realise at least one part of me is willing to go down on my fucking knees and beg if it meant I had the chance to be with her. And I don't do that. Someone fucking rejects me, throws the biggest compliment I can ever pay them back in my face? I don't go back for fucking seconds.

"Get yourself showered and dressed, and get a prospect to clean that puke off the floor." *Puke?* Leaning over, I see the drying puddle on the carpet. *Shit!* My arm goes over my head—I really laid one on last night. Why the fuck won't Peg just go and leave me to wallow? "I'll keep my fuckin' mouth shut until you go and have a fuckin' conversation with Wheels. If you want her, don't let your pride get in the way. Last night, fuck…" His hands run through his shortly shorn hair. "She might think differently now that she's slept on it. Losing Hank hit her hard. Give her another chance, man."

Give her another chance to turn me down? I don't fucking think so. "No, she's made her choice. I don't go back, Peg. Ever." *Uh uh.*

He leans his head back, closing his eyes briefly before turning back. "If I'm readin' her right, there's somethin' she's not tellin' you, somethin' that's behind her rejection. Find out what it is before you slam that door for good."

"I don't fuckin' care what's in her head. She's made her choice." I'm repeating myself, but he's not getting the message.

Another long assessing stare, then he shrugs as if dismissing the subject. "Came to tell you fuckin' Chrissy's just turned up, sweet as pie and acting like normal. Drum wanted me to come get you."

Shit! The last thing I want to deal with this morning is that fucking bitch. Or is it? My lips curl up into a parody of a smile that would make grown men turn and run. Perhaps dealing with a traitor is *exactly* what I need. I'm not in the mood to be forgiving.

Telling Peg I'll be there in a few, he at last leaves me alone. Dragging myself to a sitting position, wincing at the pain in my head, I grab a couple of ibuprofen from the bottle I keep in the drawer for just such occasions as this, and swallow them dry. When I can cope with being vertical I stand, swaying, still slightly drunk. I run through the shower and dress, careful not to step in the pool of vomit on the floor.

My head finally clearer, I'm ready to deal with the business of the day. Fuckin' Chrissy—if she'd been the one to betray my club, to betray my... No, not my, *the* woman, I'm not going to be merciful. Fuck knows how everything would have turned out if we hadn't been ambushed, if Hank hadn't been killed, and if Wheels hadn't become terrified of her association with the club.

The first sign for Chrissy that she might have fucked something up comes when Peg drags her with a tight hold on her arm into the meeting room we use for church. Prospects are rarely invited in, club whores, never. He stands her at the end of the table, not offering her a seat, and with a terse command to stay there, comes to take his seat on the opposite side of the prez from me, throwing a nod to Blade, who's already in his customary place. As I speculate how Drummer is going to play this, I watch her, my eyes cold. Any man would tremble being called in front of his prez, sergeant-at-arms, enforcer, and VP. Chrissy's gone from cocky to terrified.

"Sit down." Drummer gives her the permission which Peg hadn't. I keep my expression neutral, but am surprised at the softness in Drum's voice—he's even dredged up a smile for her from somewhere. Peg raises his eyebrow at me.

"Sweetheart," Drum starts, the endearment sounding strange, but it seems to relax her, "we'd like your help with somethin'."

Of course, he's not the president for nothing. His welcoming approach and encouraging smile put her at ease. I'd have just interrogated the bitch, but taking the lead from him, I lean back, folding my arms and making every effort to gentle my features. I don't think it's working, but for once her focus isn't on me.

"Of course, Drummer, anythin'," she simpers in reply. She pulls her back up straighter, and her lips curl up. Stupid whore.

"Last night, Hank was killed." Drummer frowns as he gives her the bad news.

Now her lips turn down. "I heard. What a shame. Still, he was only a prospect."

My fingers are curling into fists, nails digging into my palms. *Only a prospect? How dare she disrespect a man who gave his life for the club?* It's hard to keep my temper under control. Throwing a look at Drummer, I see his leg impatiently bouncing under the table, and can see he's just as angry as me.

"He'll be buried a fully patched member," Drum informs her, still managing to keep his voice even.

"Oh. That's good." The inadequate statement shows she's stumped for anything to say. "How can I help you?" The moronic bitch is puffing herself up with importance. Club whores *do not* get called into this room. If we need their input on anything we'll fuck it out of them.

Now Drum starts to get down to business. "It seems we're up against the Rock Demons, and you might be able to help us with that. Heard they've been comin' into our territory and you might have seen them at the Running Horse."

If I hadn't been watching her carefully, I might have missed the flicker of fear that comes into her eyes for a second.

She takes a moment to respond. "I was there the other night. Yeah, saw some bikers there, but I didn't know who they were. They weren't wearin' cuts."

"You spoke to them?"

She shrugs. "One of them bought me a drink, so I sat with them a while."

Drum leans forwards. "And what did you speak about?"

Another dismissive shrug. "We were just shootin' the shit, you know? They were flirtin' with me."

Now we give her board, lodging, and spending money for the services she provides to the brothers, but as long as she keeps herself clean, there's nothing to say she can't go with another man. But someone from another club?

Drummer's face is growing dark, and I can see a vein twitching in his forehead. Familiar signs that any moment now he's going to lose his shit and the whore will shortly find out what it means to be brought in front of the president of the Satan's Devils. Both of his legs are bouncing furiously now as he leans further forwards.

"We know you were talkin' to them about club business. Beef overheard some of it. Now you've got two choices—keep on pretendin' you didn't let anythin' loose or fuckin' fess up and tell us exactly what you told them." As she goes to speak, Drum holds up his hand. "I'm tellin' ya now, take the first route and you'll get a fuckin' bullet in your head." To emphasise his point, he takes out his gun from his shoulder holster and lays it on the table.

And take the second she'll end up the same way, but hopefully we'll have got some useful intel first. I exchange looks with Peg. We both know what's going to have to happen. Not that we like it, killing women is something we'd never normally do. In fact, I can't remember the club ever doing it before, certainly not in my time. But Chrissy can no longer be trusted, as a club whore she probably picked up too much knowledge for us to just set her loose.

Drummer gives her time to think about her position. Apart from the automatic twitching of his legs, his physical signs of anger that she can't see, he simply stares her down. As he does so, the blood slowly drains from her face and she goes paler by the second, and her gaze flits down to the weapon lying threateningly within the prez's reach. As though to back him up, Blade takes out a knife and starts using it to clean his nails. Peg leans forward and puts his clenched fists on the table.

That's enough to get her talking. With a narrowing of her eyes, she rounds on me. "It's all your fuckin' fault, Wraith. You should have been fuckin' me, not that fuckin' cold crippled bitch." As my mouth falls open she continues in a whiny voice, "I've been good to you, Wraith, so why did you toss me aside?"

Luckily I'm saved from answering as Drum slams his fist down on the table. "No fuckin' excuses. Whatever the VP did or didn't do is no concern of yours. You're a club fuckin' whore of the Satan's Devils, and should know better than to shoot your mouth with anyone."

"I didn't know they were from the Demons!" But her eyes flitting away, unable to meet ours, show that she did.

"Now I won't be askin' again. What did you fuckin' tell them?" His tone is chilling and quiet, almost worse than if he was shouting.

Tears start coming from her eyes as the predicament she's got herself in dawns on her. Lowering her head into her hands, she tries to wipe them away. "I would never betray the club," she starts.

"But you did," Drummer interrupts.

A loud sob, and then she starts to tell us what we want to know. "I didn't mean to, I was just so angry. Wraith had been so awful to me." Her voice breaks. "They bought me a couple of drinks and then started askin' if I'd seen a cripple around."

I have to breathe a deep breath to stop myself from blurting out that she's never to call Wheels that again. She's not even discussing her as though she's a real person. Suddenly I find myself hating the handle we've given her—she's more than that fuckin' chair she's been imprisoned in and is fighting so hard to get out of.

Chrissy carries on, and now that she's started it seems she's not going to stop. "I just told them she was here. I didn't say anythin' about the club."

"And what fuckin' else? I want it all, Chrissy." Drum knows there's more to come.

"Well, I might have mentioned that she was gonna go to Utah to get her leg fixed. But Wraith," she looks at me with a longing look, and then throws an apologetic glance towards Peg, "I never thought you or Peg would be going with her, I thought you'd just send prospects. So when they asked when you'd be comin' back, I told them the stop off you usually used…"

"You fuckin' bitch!" Drum stands and thumps both fists down on the table, making the wooden top jump. "Is that all? Did you say anything else?"

Shaking now, she points a trembling hand towards me. "I might have told them she'd stolen my ol' man, that he was giving her his protection…"

"And put Wraith right in their fuckin' sights! You stupid, stupid bitch!" Drum kicks his chair away from behind him and starts to storm out of the room, turning as he reaches the door, "VP, take Blade and Peg with you. You know what you gotta do?"

Chrissy goes completely white now as she realises the death sentence that's just been passed. *Fucking Ace—I've got to kill a woman? Much as I hate her and know it's got to be done, I'm not sure if I can handle it. Oh, I'll do it, my prez has told me to. And there can be no other way out of it for her.* Peg is looking intently at his hands, as if already seeing her blood on him. *I know this will go against the grain with him too.* Blade doesn't look any happier.

The betraying whore is staring at us in horror. She knows there's nowhere to run.

Then, behind her, I see Drum take out his second gun from the back of his jeans and without her knowing lines it up on the back of her head. Pop, pop. Two shots and she falls dead on the table.

I feel like collapsing with relief. *The traitorous bitch is dead, and not by my hand.* "Thanks, man." My grateful comment is heartfelt.

Drummer is still standing behind her body, his face drawn. "Not in any of our natures to kill a woman, boys. But my ass is the one sittin' at the head of the table, so I wasn't gonna ask anyone else to do it." He looks down on her lifeless body for a second, blood slowly leaking onto the table. "Get the prospects in here to clean up the mess. When that's done, get the boys together for church." He spares me a nod. "You're gonna have to watch yourself, Wraith. They might be comin' through you to get to her."

It doesn't seem to be the right time to tell him Wheels has given me the elbow and whatever, the damage is already done. Thanks to Chrissy, the Demons think we're an item, whatever the truth of it is.

Peg and I leave soon after Drummer, pausing outside the room when the sergeant-at-arms puts his hand on my arm. "You okay?"

I nod, I fucked Chrissy, more than the others I admit, but I didn't have any particular feelings for her. And anyway, apart from her recent behaviour, her betrayal would have killed any compassion stone dead.

"I'll get this taken care off."

I thank him, knowing he means he'll make sure she's buried far up in the forest where her body will never be found. Just like Buster. Seems we're digging far too many graves recently. I lean against the wall, my eyes closing as I come to grips with what's just gone down. It's a dark day for the club, but it couldn't have turned out any other way.

When I look up again, Peg's got mischief twinkling in his eyes. "You ready to see your woman, now?"

I open my mouth to refute the ownership he's assigned to me, then shrug as I realise any anger towards her had dissipated during the unpleasant meeting I've just sat through. "Yeah, I'll go see if we can talk."

He slaps me on the back and we start walking away. "Never thought I'd see you twisted up about a bitch, VP. But if she means that much to you, don't let her get away. There's more to it than she's lettin' on, I tell ya."

In the clubroom, Peg calls the prospects towards him, and I leave him to it. I've got somewhere else I need to be.

CHAPTER 22

Sophie

After Wraith had left I'd taken the pill Doc had given me last night. God knows what was in it, but I fell asleep quickly and woke late feeling surprisingly refreshed, albeit with a slight grogginess in my head, which was soon sorted by a couple of cups of coffee.

When Horse had brought in the nectar of the gods, I'd answered his query about how I was feeling with a brief okay, and turned away before he could ask why Wraith wasn't here with me. Taking the hint, he'd left me alone, but there's probably no way I'll escape an inquisition later.

Lying on my bed, my arm thrown back over my head, I walk through the events of the day before, my stomach rolling when I remember that Hank was dead—such a sweet man to have died so young. Then the latter events of the night caught up with me, and with a groan, it hit me just how awful I'd been to Wraith.

He hadn't deserved to have been dismissed without explanation. My cold rejection had hurt him, but how could I explain? I've never told anyone before, never got close enough to have needed to. No, I'd always run before the trap started to close. *But not this time.* And I'm hurting, really hurting. I already miss him. My heart feels like it's been broken, the thought of never being with Wraith again is almost as bad as...

No. I am not going there. Not even thinking about it. But the tears pricking at my eyes tell me I'm a liar, and I start to wonder if I may have made a mistake. The need to protect myself as overwhelming as always, just this time I'd left it too late and already got too close. I admit that now. I should have stuck to my normal pattern of one night and done, but I hadn't been able to do that with Wraith. I'd been too greedy, wanting more. Wanting as much as I could get.

But he would have left me too. Just like... He might not have wanted to, but he's not exactly in a nine-to-five safe job. Yesterday was a prime example of the dangerous ways in which he lives his life. And now his club is going to war because of me.

It's safer for everyone if I just leave—then their fight might be averted and I wouldn't be faced with seeing Wraith every fucking day. And if I've injured him as much as it appeared last night, it would make things easier on him too. I know just how much it takes for one of these men to commit to an old lady. He must really care about me. Yes, it's best if I go.

I can't see any alternative. Though I'm limited, there must be somewhere in this vast country where I can hide. How the hell did anyone find out I was here, anyway? Shaking my head, I realise there's no way of knowing.

God, my heart aches when I think of the biker who I allowed to get too close. How could I have started to fall in love with him in such a short time? I've always protected myself better before. I never wanted to feel like this ever again.

As I pull myself out of bed, grab my clothes and get ready for the day, I sigh, dropping my head into my hands. I'm lying to myself if I think I can just leave and forget him. It's too late. *I already love him.* And love destroys.

Horse makes another couple of attempts to get me to talk under the auspices of bringing me more coffee and breakfast, but I'm not in the mood for sharing. I keep quiet, hoping he'll go and leave me alone, as if I open my mouth I know I'll give myself away. Or I'll succumb to those tears I'm fighting back, sorrow at the trouble I've brought to the club's door, and for everything I'm leaving. Horse has been good to me, but he won't approve of my plans to get away and would try to argue me out of them. My resolve is weak enough as it is. If I'm going to act on it I need to do it soon, and quickly, like ripping off a band-aid. I know it's going to hurt, but sticking around will just be more painful for everyone.

At last, Horse tells me he's going down to the clubhouse. Without delaying, I google on my phone then make a call, arranging for a taxi to collect me from the compound. I have to ring a few, the first couple of companies didn't want to come as far as the gates, offering instead to pick me up at the end of the half-mile long track that runs up to it. But the fourth is more biddable, and agree they'll be there in half an hour.

Quickly I stuff a few clothes into a bag. Somehow during the night they must have brought the van back and, thank God, my chair, which was brought to my room while I was sleeping. I don't want to rely on my crutches in case I have to walk long distances, so I'm loath to leave it behind. But that means I can only carry the basics. With one last look around my room, my heart breaking at the memories of Wraith in my bed, I fix my crutches on the back of the chair, and with my bag on my lap start to wheel myself away from the suite that has become my home.

Going down past the clubhouse isn't difficult. I'd hoped not to meet anyone on the way, and for once luck was with me. The whole place seems deserted. Perhaps they are all in a meeting? That suits me fine. I don't want to make any goodbyes, and I know Horse, for one, wouldn't agree that my leaving was the best thing to do.

Congratulating myself on getting away, I come to the gates. As I approach them, Slick and Marsh step out from the shadows.
Oh. Shit!

Slick looks at me, pointedly glancing at the bag on my lap, and cocking his eyebrow. "Where d'ya think you're going, darlin'?"

I decide to play it straight. "Could you open the gates for me, please? I've got a taxi coming to pick me up."

At that moment a car pulls up outside, with a glowing sign on the top. Slick has a silent conversation with Marsh over my head. As the prospect steps towards the gate, I'm assuming he's going to open it, but he doesn't, just waves the taxi driver to roll down his window.

"Now what ya leavin' for, darlin'"

Heaving a sigh, I reply honestly, "I don't want to bring trouble to the club. If I'm not here, the Demons won't have a beef with you anymore."

His eyes narrow. "I could care less about the fuckin' Demons, darlin'. But you're under our protection and you ain't going nowhere. Christ, where did you think you could fuckin' go?"

"It's none of your business." Disgusted with myself I feel tears at the back of my eyes at this obstacle in my way. Who's he to thwart my plan to keep them all safe? "You can't keep me prisoner here."

He laughs, he actually bloody well laughs! And to my horror, I see Marsh has finished his conversation with the taxi driver and seems to be passing him some money. The car's engine starts, then the taxi makes a U-turn and drives away.

"Noooo!" I cry out in exasperation.

Slick smirks. "Watch her, prospect." Then, getting his phone out of his pocket places a call. "Got your ol' lady at the front gate, Wraith. She'd called a fuckin' taxi and was makin' a break for it. Thought you like to know."

Another sneering look towards me. "Quickest time I've known an ol' lady to call it quits, Brother."

Then, "Yeah, she ain't going nowhere."

I slump my head forward. Why the fuck can't anyone else see the trouble I'm bringing to them by staying here? And the second thought following close behind, why did he have to ring *Wraith*? He's the last person I want, can stand to see. Then I sit up again—perhaps it's all for the best. Surely, after the angry words last night, Wraith will want me gone as much as I want, need, to get away.

That I'm right seems to be confirmed when Wraith comes storming along the driveway with Peg by his side, his hand which isn't in a sling on the VP's arm as though holding him back. The reminder of the sergeant-at-arms' injury fuels my determination to leave.

"Just tell them to open the gates," I shout out when he's within hearing.

His face contorts with rage. "You're not going fuckin' anywhere, Sophie."

He called me Sophie?

But I can't think about that for now, waving my hand at Peg I direct my next plea to him. "You of all people should know it's safer for everyone if I go away."

Peg stops just in front of me. "Ain't safer for no one, babe. We're at war with the fuckin' Demons whether you're here or not. They killed one of ours, remember? Can't let them get away with that."

I can see how they'd want revenge, but it would have to come at a cost. "Surely you don't want others to die?"

He shrugs. "If that's the result, so be it. We all know that when we take the patch."

My gaze turns to Wraith, who's looking no more relaxed, and the notion that he might be the one to lose his life causes such pain inside me. I know I can't allow them to stop me from getting away. "Don't ask me to stay here and watch you die, Wraith. Don't. I can't do that." My plea comes out as a whisper.

Suddenly he's moving Peg out of the way and crouching in front of me, his eyes radiating pain as he stares into mine. "Don't ask me to watch you leave here and get yourself killed, Soph. 'Cos that's what's gonna happen if you go out those gates. Don't ask *me* to do that."

I grasp at straws. "But Ethan only wants to talk to me."

He shakes his head. "Yeah, talk to you with his fuckin' fists. You got anythin' he wants to hear?"

I look down. "I don't know where Zoe is. I can't tell him any-thing."

"So he'll kill you. And it's my guess as he's a known abuser, he'll enjoy takin' his time about it." He reaches out and touches my hands and I can feel him shaking. "You want me to stay here thinkin' about that happenin' to you? You think I'd be able to stand that? Darlin' that would kill me faster than a fuckin' bul-let."

Suddenly Peg huffs a laugh and we both glance up. I think we'd both forgotten he was there. "Well, look at you two love birds, each wantin' to die for the other." He places his hand on Wraith's shoulder and squeezes it. "Bout time for that talk you were gonna have," Peg suggests to Wraith.

"I…"

But I can't tell him how much I don't want to have any type of conversation, as Wraith stands, then leans with his face right up against mine. I feel his breath on my face as he tells me, "Not one more fuckin' word, Sophie. What we've got to talk about is gonna be done in private without these fuckin' clowns around."

As he steps back I see it's not just Peg, but also Slick and Marsh who are avidly taking in our every word. Knowing I've got no option, I sink back into the chair and let him wheel me away back to my room, which not so long ago I'd thought I'd left for the last time.

He takes me inside, leaving me by the bed and getting my crutches off the back of my chair and placing them close to me, giving me the option of staying where I am or moving. He goes over to close the door then leans back against it, and I take a moment to study him. His anger seems to have left him. Instead, he looks tired and drawn, and something makes me want just to hold him. I sit on my hands to stop myself from doing something stupid, like reaching for him.

He sighs deeply, his chin resting down towards his chest, and then he crosses the room, pulling up the chair and sitting opposite me, keeping the distance between us.

"Before we have the discussion we need to, I've got somethin' to tell you," he starts. He's clenching and unclenching his fists, and I can't work out whether it's sadness, anger, or like I'm doing, stopping himself from reaching for me.

I nod and wait for him to speak, tears threatening once again as now, despite his impassioned plea by the gates, he seems so remote.

Taking a deep breath, he starts to explain, "Chrissy, the sweet butt, betrayed the club. She told the Rock Demons that you'd be going to Utah, so they were on the lookout for our return."

"Chrissy? The one who wanted you?" I can't believe she'd done that.

"That's her. But you don't need to worry about her anymore." There's such a finality about his pronouncement it chills me.

"Do I want to know what happened to her?"

He shakes his head. "Better you don't ask, darlin'"

I don't want to know, but I can guess. Chrissy had caused Hank's death, could have killed us all, or, in my case, delivered me into the hands of a vile abuser of women. But fuck, if I hadn't have come here three people could still be alive. I'm still having nightmares about Buster.

Wraith's studying me carefully. "This ain't on you, so don't think it for a moment. Bitch was jealous, fuck, she'd have been jealous of any woman I looked at more than once. She thought she was somethin' special to me. Well, she was fuckin' wrong about that. Whoever I wanted would have been a threat to her. That she was someone who'd betray the club, well, we didn't see that comin'. But seems it was somethin' waitin' to happen if I stepped out of line."

He pauses, watching to see if I'm accepting his explanation.

"Did you…"

"Did I kill her?" Now he does reach over and takes my hands. "No, darlin', it wasn't me. And thank fuck for that. I'd never want to hurt a woman. It was quick, she didn't see it comin'."

For some reason, it pleases me he hadn't got his hands dirty, but it's still hard to take the swift retribution dished out by the club. That they can take a life so easily chills me. But then again, perhaps more merciful than a prisoner kept waiting on death row for years.

"Sophie," he starts, and my eyes widen as he again uses my name and doesn't call me Wheels. I don't know what to make of it. "Soph, can we talk? About last night? I know I was wrong to push you so fast, particularly after everythin' that went down."

I start turning my head from side to side, wanting him to know that while terrible, it hadn't been the events of yesterday that made me push him away.

But he misunderstands. Reaching out, he brushes the strand of hair that's fallen over my face back behind my ears. "I know you're worried about what might happen, but we're taking every precaution to keep everyone safe." He turns my head up, his dark eyes staring into mine. "You don't need to worry about us, about me. No one's going to be taking unnecessary risks. We're on lockdown. All the ol' ladies are here—and that imp, Amy." He studies me for another moment. "I rushed you last night, but this is me givin' you space. No pressure. I want you, babe. I want you as my woman, but if you need time to think about it, take it."

I'm still not ready to tell him all the time in the world wouldn't change my mind, so I focus on the one word I didn't comprehend. "Lockdown?"

"Yeah, if the club's threatened we pull everyone in."

And that's down to me. My problems are disrupting everyone's lives. "It would be so much better if I leave. Just let me go, Wraith."

"No," he states, firmly. "I told you at the gate that you wouldn't have a chance out there. Club's given you their protection. We'll get these bastards off your back and then you can think where you want to go. You're going nowhere until it's safe, I promise you that. No one is going to let you leave. And, once everythin's cleared up, I hope you never want to."

I sit, sadly shaking my head. "It's all my fault."

He heaves a deep sigh in exasperation. "Soph, put that out of your mind once and for fuckin' all. You can't take it on yourself. If Buster hadn't broken your prosthesis we wouldn't have left the compound, and at the end of the day, it's on Chrissy. If she hadn't set her sights on me, the Demons would never have found you. That's down to her, babe. And she got what she deserved for it."

"But…"

"No buts. Do you want to blame your friend for havin' left Ethan, or fuck that, getting' together with him in the first place? You're innocent in all this. It ain't down to you. You might as well say you shouldn't have been born."

I contemplate what he's said. I suppose it's like the butterfly flapping its wings on the other side of the world, with the resultant ripple effect. While I don't think it exonerates me completely, he's right, none of this was directly my fault in that I did not cause it to happen.

Something in my expression shows he's, at last, got through to me. He lowers his lips to mine, and as he gently moves his mouth across them, I'm unable to resist. It's the gentlest kiss I've ever received. Moisture floods between my legs. There's just something about him that arouses me, so I moan, and despite myself, press against him, wanting more.

"Told ya I was going to give you space darlin'." He stands and walks to the other side of the room. "But it's just so damn hard keepin' my hands off of you." He adjusts himself in his jeans with a rueful smile. "See what you do to me?" He pauses for a moment before continuing, "Babe, my timin' was all wrong, but I'm fallin' hard for you, and unless I've been readin' you entirely wrong, I reckon you're doing the same. Now are you going to be brave enough to admit it?"

"Wraith, it's not your timing. Whenever you asked me, the answer would have been the same."

As his eyes close and his face shutters, I know I have to try to explain. "You're right, I'm afraid. But it's not what you think."

His eyes snap open again. "Gotta give me more, darlin'. Tell me what you're afraid of." He sounds as if whatever it is he'd fight it for me, but he can't take on my demons, they've got too great a hold over me.

Taking my crutches, I struggle to my feet, and already knowing me well he doesn't offer to help, just patiently waits until I've got my balance. Then I cross the room to him. He's so much taller than me, I have to crane my neck to look into his face. Taking a breath, I put it out there in the only way I can, giving it to him straight. "I'm too fucking afraid of having my heart torn out, of going through that devastating pain all over a-fuckin'-gain. I wouldn't survive it!"

His dark eyes blaze. "Someone hurt you, darlin'?" he rasps out. "Babe, trust me, that's not what I'm going to do."

"They didn't fuckin' hurt me. They *destroyed* me!" I cry out, and before I know what's happening I'm enclosed in his strong arms and tears are flooding down my face. He sweeps me up, my crutches dropping to the floor as he carries me to the bed and sits down with me in his lap, gently rocking me back and forth like a baby until my sobs turn to hiccups, and then, at last, stop.

After giving me the time to compose myself, passing me tissues from the box on the bedside table to clean myself up, he says gently, "Tell me what happened, Sophie. Give me somethin' I can understand."

CHAPTER 23
Sophie

I take several deep breaths as I try to compose myself and prepare to relive everything I've buried so deep, the things I try every day to forget that only a handful of people know. Not even Zoe had an inkling of what was in my past. As he tightens his fingers around mine to give me his support, I know I have to get it out. My mouth opens and shuts a couple of times, then I swallow and at last manage to speak, delivering my life story in a monotone, trying to keep emotion at bay.

"My mother died when I was three years old, breast cancer. I was brought up by my father. He was okay, did a decent enough job. I was clothed and fed, but I suppose I missed a mother's love."

"Soph…" His hand reaches out and smooths down the side of my face.

"No, please, if you interrupt me I won't be able to do this." I watch until he nods, showing his agreement.

"Eight years ago," I resume, "when I was just seventeen, I met a man. He was a little older, he'd just turned twenty-one." I pause, remembering how much more mature he seemed at the time, but looking back I know he was really so young, too young. "He worked on a North Sea oil rig and had done so since he was eighteen. He'd come down to spend his time off in London. I met him in a pub, and we got talking. We clicked immediately, and on his next shore leave he came back and we spent the whole three weeks together. I lost my virginity to him, and it was hell when he had to go back."

I glance at Wraith, wanting to see whether he's hurt that I'm talking about another man, but the expression on his face is one of concern, for me. So I continue, "He worked two weeks on the rig, then had three weeks off. He got in the habit of flying down to see me and staying in the area for all of his leave. After three months he asked me to marry him, and I agreed."

"You were very young. Hell, was that even legal?"

"In England we can marry at sixteen as long as we have parental consent, so yeah, it was all legal."

Wraith looks concerned. "So your father was okay with that?"

I laugh shortly. "My father had just found another woman. I didn't know about it at the time, but I think it influenced him when Mark asked for his blessing. It suited him for me to be out of his way. He actually put it into words—I had the whole of my life in front of me, being older he'd not got as long left to enjoy.

"We got married as soon as we could and got a small bedsit. Mark wanted me to finish school and go to uni. I'd applied to Aberdeen so I could move up and be near him. Anyway..." My voice breaks and more tears fall as I get ready for the final straight. "We'd only been married a month when there was an explosion on the rig..."

Now he reaches for me, his arms holding me tight as I start crying again, unable to stop the tears running down my face. I know I don't need to explain that first terrible phone call, the waiting while they tried to find the missing men and all the time hope fading until finally the confirmation had come that Mark had been one of the unlucky ones. My beautiful, loving husband gone, and I would never see him again.

Another few minutes, another few tissues passed and used. When my tears dry up he doesn't press for details, but just asks me, "Did you move back to your family?"

"No, my father had already remarried and my step-mother didn't want to be saddled with a teenage daughter. So I stayed in the bedsit, ended up going to uni in London, and that's where I met Zoe."

"I'm so sorry you had to go through that." He rests his head on the top of mine.

It's times like these I wish I could stand and pace around the room. But with my crutches lying on the floor on the other side of the room, all I can do is pull out of his arms and sit up straight. "There's a reason I'm telling you this, Wraith."

"Thought there would be."

"Mark was the first man I loved." I nearly added 'only' man, but I changed it, realising that now it wouldn't be true. "He was my first in every way, and him leaving me like he did, well, I knew I'd never get over it. So I vowed never to put myself in that position again." I swallow a couple of times, getting up the nerve to tell him who I am. That might be enough to put him off me.

"When I went to uni, well, there were lots of men. Boys really, more my age than Mark's. They kept asking me out, and I knew I'd never want to get involved. But Mark and I had been very sexually active—his days on leave we spent mainly in bed and I missed," oh God how I'd missed, "being physically close to someone. So I thought if I used men for sex and didn't have any kind of other relationship with them, that I wouldn't get hurt again."

Again I watch to see if there is any judgement. There's not. "So that's what I did. I even made a joke of it—one and done. That was me. And I had fun. It didn't matter to me whether it was a quick hook-up in a broom closet at work or if I went home to someone's bed. But I never stayed the night, never allowed myself to get close.

267

"It was the only way I could protect myself, you see. I can never forget getting that phone call, finding out Mark was never coming back."

"Oh darlin', you were so young. Just seventeen, not even an adult." Wraith isn't going to let me get away with keeping myself at a distance. His strong arms come out and encircle me once again. "But you can't live your life in fear of what might happen."

"I like sex," I tell him, adamantly.

"Suspected that, darlin'," he says with a chuckle. "Not sure what gave it away."

I slap him lightly on the arm. I'm trying to have a serious discussion here. "Since Mark, until you, I never spent the night with anyone."

"I can say the same. No one interested me enough. That's partly how I knew I had to make you mine."

"But Wraith, I can't be yours. I can't go through that again. If I let you in… If anything happens to you, I'd die too. I wouldn't be able to survive that kind of hurt again."

He sighs and kisses my hair, and despite my thoughts and what I'm telling him, I'm not immune to his touch. He's quiet for a while and then he asks, "Do you think this lonely life is what Mark would have wanted for you?"

"I'm not lonely…"

"Yes, darlin' you are. Didn't you like sleepin' with me? Wakin' in my arms?"

Too much! "But Wraith… What you do with the club, especially now… If I took a chance on you, how long until I find out you've died in a shoot-out somewhere? Or just came off your bike? You'd give your life for the club, you've already told me that."

The door to my room opens and Horse appears. "I was passing, couldn't help but hear." He's not looking very apologetic. He walks across and crouches down by my feet, looking up at me. "You and me, Soph, we're not very dissimilar, though I was older than you were. I was married, you know that. And the love of my life died. But I've never regretted those three happy years I had with her. Not for one fucking moment."

"I don't regret knowing Mark." Do I?

"Think you do, babe. That's why you're not willing to take the risk again. You're not remembering any good times, only the bad." Horse can't be right, can he? Would my life have been better had I never known him? Mark had shaped all my actions since his death.

I challenge Horse, "But you don't want to get involved with another woman, Horse." His situation seems to back mine up.

He laughs. "I've just never found someone who could hold a candle to my Carrie." His lips turn down as he grows serious. "But if I found someone who was right, just like you've found Wraith, I know up in heaven she'd be cheering me on. And if there was a woman that perfect, I'd jump straight in with both fucking feet." He gets to his feet again. "Sorry for the intrusion."

"Nah, thanks, man." Wraith throws him a chin lift as Horse leaves us alone. Then he turns back to me and says quietly, "Darlin' that's a sad fuckin' story, and I understand you a whole lot better now. But don't let the past rule your future. It's time to move on from the loneliness you've imposed on yourself. Take a chance on me, babe. I can't promise you anythin', but while we're together we'll be havin' a lot of good times, probably a few bad too. No one can give any guarantees, whether they're an outlaw biker or a citizen. But I want you on the back of my bike. I want you as my ol' lady. For however long we got."

I stay quiet for a moment, thinking. It's a lot to think about, a lot to take in. But eight years have passed, and I'm not a teenager anymore. Maybe now is the right time to move on. "I'm not even sure how to do a relationship, Wraith."

Now he chuckles and then leans his forehead down to touch mine. "Guess we're both gonna be feelin' our way there, darlin'. I've no fuckin' idea either." Then he gives a barked laugh. "A broom closet, eh? Have you left any places where you haven't done it that we can share?"

I huff as though I'm affronted, then, suddenly, while I know that neither of us might have a clue how we're going to make this work, there's something that we already do pretty damn well. I throw myself at him, unbalancing him so he leans back on the bed, pulling me with him. He's not a stupid man, and knowing the time for words has ended without wasting another moment, his hands come up and he starts to ease off my shirt and bra slowly and reverently, his lips kissing his way from my neck down to my breasts, pausing to tease my nipples until they peak for him. Then, pushing me gently to the side, he undoes my jeans and pulls them down, removing my shoes before taking them off completely. His hands then go to my prosthesis that I haven't yet removed, and his eyes question me.

Giving a quick nod, I give him my permission to touch it, to remove it. And he does so confidently, as if it were just another article of clothing. I'd worn it for a long time yesterday as well as this morning, and the stump is reddened and sore.

He notices. "You got anythin' to soothe this, darlin'?"

"The stuff from Utah is still in the van, but I've got some old cream from the UK." I show him where it is in my drawer, and without comment, he gently rubs it in for me. I could never have imagined anyone would want to look at, let alone touch what remains of my leg. But as his tender administrations soothe me, I lie back and think that his easy acceptance is helping me come to terms with the loss more than anything else has ever done.

Placing the cream back on the table, Wraith then slides down my body, and as his talented tongue gets to work, I smile to myself. There's a bubbling feeling inside of me that I haven't felt before. And as my muscles start to tighten and just before I'm lost in the ecstasy only he seems able to bring, I recognise it for what it is—*I'm happy.*

CHAPTER 24

Wraith

I return to the clubhouse with more of a spring in my step than I had on the way up. Sophie isn't immune to me at all. It's her fucked up history that stopped her taking that leap and admitting it. Now I know that I'm fighting the ghost of her husband, I'll be able to plan my campaign to get her permanently on the back of my bike. No, it's not even a ghost I'm up against, it's the hurt that losing him so quickly and dreadfully caused her.

Trouble is, as I told her, there are no guarantees in this life I lead. All I can hope is that I won't be leaving her via a wooden box as well. But I'm too selfish to accept that as an excuse to step away. There can be no warranties given, however we choose to make our way in the world.

I arrive just in time as Peg is calling the members together. It's hard not to pick up on the sombre mood in the clubroom, killing the bitch Chrissy quickly was kinder than marching her up to a grave in the woods, but it meant we couldn't keep it quiet. But from the whispers I heard as I passed through the room, it seemed the message had got around. Betray the club and you'll have to accept there'll be bloody consequences. The sweet butts are whispering amongst themselves, and for once, not pestering the brothers.

Drum casts a worried glance towards me as I enter, and I raise my chin, showing him I understand. Until Horse and Sophie arrived we'd had years of peace. Now we're about to have a council of war to prepare to do battle. It's the kind of thing we've tried hard to avoid. The last time we came up against another club was back in the days when I was a prospect, all of ten years ago now.

One of the last to take my seat, I look around at my brothers, appreciating the looks of determination on their faces. We have each other's backs. I can only hope all of us will be left standing at the end of this.

The gavel's banged and church is called to order.

"Right, talk to me." As Drum lays the meeting open, we're all aware there's only one topic he's asking about.

"I'll start arrangin' Hank's funeral." I take the chance at the having the first shot. "All the out of state chapters will be invited. We should give him a good send-off."

"Won't that attract the Demons attention?" Heart is frowning.

Drum laughs. "If it does there'll be over a hundred of us against them. If they try to take us there, we'll slaughter the motherfuckers."

Peg growls, "And massacre them is what I want to do." As he rubs his shoulder, I notice he's no longer wearing the sling, and wince on his behalf. But he's got much better colour today—he bounces back fast, our sergeant-at-arms.

"Do we know exactly what that bitch whore told them?" Rock asks the question, fidgeting with his gun as usual. I realise they all need to be brought up to date. I leave it to Drum to explain that she told them Sophie was here, and that she was my old lady. Oh, and the info about the Utah trip of course.

"I've never trusted the fuckers," Beef throws in. "It was only a matter of time before we came up against them head on. Been hearin' some rumours about human traffickin' up that way."

Tongue snarls, "With you there, Brother. Drugs are gettin' out of hand too. That could be why they were in the Running Horse."

Beef nods. "Could well be. Wouldn't put it past them to try to sell on our territory."

Now we're not into any business to do with women—our strippers get a good wage and are under no coercion to work for us. Likewise, we avoid hard drugs like the plague, would never deal. That kind of shit gets the attention of the wrong people.

"Blade, any thoughts?"

Blade doesn't say a lot, but when he does we all listen. "I think we should hit them hard. Take out the whole fuckin' bag."

Peg obviously agrees by the way he's bobbing his head.

"VP?" Drum asks for my view.

My fingers play on the table as I give it some thought. "If it's done clean, with little risk to us, I'm with the plan. But they'll be expectin' us to retaliate for Hank, so let's bide our time and lull them into a false sense of fuckin' security. Then we make our move."

"You just want time to get your dick wet with your ol' lady!" Trust Slick to put that in.

"If we're going to hit their clubhouse I'd like to get some eyes inside," Mouse offers. "Any way we can get someone who could put some cameras in there for us?"

"It's a good idea," Drum says, thoughtfully. "But it's a risk. Don't see how any of us would get an invitation. They know all of us." After a brief pause, he resumes, "I could ask for a meet with Stick, their prez, to discuss retribution for Hank, but I doubt they'll let me roam free."

"You're not fuckin' walking into that den of motherfuckers," Peg roars out. "Or anyone else for that matter, so keep your fuckin' mouth shut, Wraith."

I snap my lips back together without speaking, deciding I wasn't going to waste breath offering to go instead of Drum after all.

"We don't know much about them, but what I do know is I wouldn't trust 'em. Anyone going in is at the risk of being held and ransomed for Wheels. That's who they want after all."

Bullet's made a good point, and we all nod. He nudges Dart and points to the packet on the table. Shaking his head, Dart taps out the last smoke and rolls it over to him.

Slick speaks up next. "The sweet butt, Jill, she's been talking about a friend who'd like to get in with the club." He glances around to see if we can guess where he's going with this. "She's got no connections to us at present, but if she offered her, er, services to the Demons, she might be able to get inside."

I'm shaking my head, hating the idea of sending a woman into that particular den of iniquity. Who knows what the fuck might happen to her?

It's Drum's turn to tap on the table now. "Could she be connected to us at all?"

"Nah, she's been here a couple of times as a hang-around on party nights, but that shouldn't be enough for them to link her with us."

"So has almost every girl in Tucson." Tongue nods at Slick. "They just can't resist." He waggles his tongue in his customary manner to make sure we all get the point. We do.

Cigarette smoke drifts across me, and I breathe in that shit. I might have given up, but sometimes even secondhand it still does the job.

"O...kay." Drummer has made his decision. "Slick, talk to the girl, make sure she knows what she'll be getting' into. If she's agreeable, we'll get her set up in Phoenix. Would be too strange for a Tucson girl to want into their club, but if she's in the locality and wants to make it with bikers, it won't look odd." His fingers rap on the table. "I'll need two of you fuckers to be close by when she goes in. Get her a burner so she can ring us if she needs help. And she'll have to tell them all about her mama and pa who're going to raise merry shit if she doesn't check in at home."

"Pa being you, Drum?" The empty packet of cigarettes gets thrown at Slick.

"So we stay on lockdown and prepared. Don't want those fuckers comin' waltzin' up to our door and findin' us with our pants down. Slick will liaise with this girl and see if she's up for this shit. Tell her she can be a sweet butt and all the brothers will reward her with as much biker cock as she wants. And then some." Drum pauses for the roars of laughter to subside.

"Too fuckin' right!" Adam tosses in, the first time he's spoken at the meeting. Adam is known for being silent and his huge, great fucking Adam's apple that bobs as if it's a living thing when he swallows. Throwing him a glance I see him playing with something in his hand.

"Me! I'll make the sacrifice!" offers Beef.

"Hey, brothers, she might look like the back end of a cow," contributes Dart. Leaning forward, he extracts a new pack of cigarettes from his back pocket and retrieves his lighter from Bullet.

"Don't give a fuck what she looks like. Long as she's got a mouth and tight pussy, they all look the fuckin' same in the dark!"

Drum glares at Rock, and gradually the table simmers down. "Mouse, you get some of those miniature camera gadgets, and if the girl's agreeable, make sure Slick's got them to pass to her. Right, that's it. Let's hope things calm down a bit for tomorrow night's church."

Church again, fuck we've had a few too many of those lately. But tomorrow's Friday, so we'll be back to our regular timetable.

I watch Dart light up and blow smoke before saying what I know is going to be very unpopular. "Can't have the hang-arounds up tomorrow. If we're gonna be sendin' in a fuckin' Trojan horse the Demons might be thinkin' of doing the same thing."

Collective groans and moans, but no one says anything, they all know that I'm right.

"Good point, VP. We can't be too fuckin' careful. Make sure everyone knows it's a closed house. Ok, if that's it, let's break up this hen party, ladies."

I'll give it to the prez, he knows how to send us out grinning.

"Er, Prez. I found this outside." Adam tosses whatever it was he'd been fiddling with onto the table. We all look at it in stunned silence. My eyes settle on Peg's, and we both wince. It's Hank's fucking gremlin bell. Now I'm not a superstitious man, but the fleeting thought goes through my mind that things might have worked out differently if it had been on the young prospects bike that day.

"Fuck it." Peg sums it up succulently, and the look he throws me suggests he's thinking along the same lines as me.

I don't want to touch it, but know what I have to do. Reaching forward, I pull it toward me, and after holding it in my hand for a second I put it in my pocket. I nod at Drum. "I'll put it in his coffin."

"Good call."

It's a sombre end to the meeting as we all take a moment to remember the man we'd lost.

When I finally leave the room, Peg's waiting for me in the hallway. "That fuckin' bell."

"Yeah." I shake my head.

He sighs and rests his hand on my shoulder for a second. Then he straightens, and shakes it off, making a rapid change of subject. "So how did it go with Wheels, you talk to her?"

Touching Peg's good arm lightly, I wave him over to a table in the corner, then holding up two fingers towards the bar, alerting Marsh to the fact we need beers. Putting my elbows on the table, I lean towards the sergeant-at-arms, now seated opposite me. "She's had some shit in her life, Peg. Got married very young, lost her husband a few months later in an explosion on an oil rig."

"Fuck."

"Yeah, well, she made up her mind not to get involved with anyone after that."

"So until you, she stayed faithful to a dead fuckin' man?"

I bark a laugh. "Quite the opposite! She's been fuckin' around, likin' the variety."

"She's a whore?"

"No more than any of us. Nothing worse than I've ever done, using someone just to get some release."

He's shaking his head, looking a bit disgusted, but fair's fair. We take what we can get from whatever willing women we find, who are we to criticise someone else doing it just because they're a member of the opposite sex? "You okay with that?" He sounds dubious.

"Don't see any problem with it. I'm no fuckin' hypocrite."

He's quiet for a moment as he considers it. "As long as she's got a tight pussy, I s'pose."

I toss him a glare. "Don't go there."

He laughs, the fucker. "So all's sorted then?"

"I fuckin' hope so." Marsh delivers the beers, and I take a large swallow then wipe my lips on the back of my hand. "She's feeling guilty she brought all this to our door, Peg."

"Yeah, I get that. Shit happens. We agreed to give her protection. If it wasn't for that bitch Chrissy, she'd have been safe here. Ain't Wheels' fault."

"The Demons might have come knockin' in any event. Sheer fuckin' luck they took the contract."

"That reward was too darn attractive. Should have guessed he'd look for her in Arizona since she flew into Phoenix."

"Yeah, we underestimated how fixated this St John-Davies guy is on her." I think for a moment as an idea occurs to me. "What if I get her out of here, take her somewhere he can't find her?"

Peg's head moves side to side, my off-the-cuff plan not sitting well with him. "You'd have to steer clear of any of our other chapters, first place they'd look. Don't really know where you could go and be safe. Hey, you got company."

Not sure what he's talking about, I turn my head to see Sophie coming into the clubroom on crutches, her face creased with the effort. When she catches my eye, she smiles and continues our way. Peg stands like the gentleman he is and pulls out a seat for her. I take hold of her crutches as she eases herself into it.

Peg avoids any mention of our altercation by the gate. "You're lookin' good there, darlin'." He nods at her crutches so she knows what he's talking about.

She thanks him and reaches out her hand to take mine. I place our entwined fingers on the table. I'm making a point for all to see, and feel a sense of elation when she doesn't pull away. Then her eyes flick around the room, settling for a moment on little Amy, who's playing with her dad and the other old ladies who are drinking coffee around one of the other tables. She turns back to me.

"Look at this." She circles her hand to take in all the room. "It's ridiculous, everyone here because of a threat to me. I know you don't want me to leave, but I feel so guilty being here."

Peg glowers, and suddenly he's the sergeant-at-arms, not the friend she's come to know. "We talked about a lot of things in church, but not one of the brothers suggested the solution was for you to go, Wheels. So just suck it up. You're here under our fuckin' protection, and that's where you're going to fuckin' stay. I don't want to hear another word about you leavin' else you'll be soundin' like a fuckin' ungrateful bitch!"

It wasn't just what he said, but the way in which he delivered it. Wheels pales, as his words sink in, and I hope to goodness that she's going to let it drop now. But she doesn't. "I don't understand why," she says, quietly.

He's still frowning, but his face has softened. "Because you're one of us now. You're with Wraith, aren't you?"

When she nods, confirming it in public, I feel like we've crossed the final hurdle.

"Too fuckin' right, you're mine now," I growl. Oh to hell with it. I scoop her out of her chair and onto my lap. Putting a hand on each side of her head, I gaze into her gorgeous, bright and sparkling eyes, and though it might be wishful thinking, it looks like a shadow has gone. Almost reverently I touch my lips to hers, and then apply more pressure, pushing my tongue inside. Her perfume assaults my nostrils and a rumbling comes from my throat as I fist my hand in her hair, pulling her closer. The taste, the scent of her, driving me crazy.

"Looks like Wraith's got himself an ol' lady!" Peg announces loudly to the whole room.

Ignoring the shouts and hollers, I lose myself in her. Not letting go of her hair, I loosen one finger and hold it up. As the comments get more ribald, we at last come up for air. She's laughing, and her cheeky grin shows me she's going to fit in here. I don't know if she's thought all this through or whether it's sunk in yet, but this is her home, and where she's going to stay. Forever if I have my way.

Peg's still sitting there, smirking at us. He's got his phone in his hand and holds it up to show me the screen.

"You were fuckin' timin' us?"

"Yup. Should have taken bets on it. Quite a record you set there, VP."

Sophie bats his arm. "Peg! How could you?"

"Any takers for how long they're gonna disappear for?" Christ, Slick's getting into the act now.

"Three hours fifteen!" Adam calls out, though he's not taken his eyes from the game he's currently battling with.

Sophie's face is glowing red, but she's not upset at all, and in fact, she's laughing so hard she's hiccupping. I decide taking some personal time is a fuckin' good idea. Standing, I go to lift her into my arms, but Peg stops me.

"Six o'clock, Wheels. Meet me in the gym."

"She'll be too tired to exercise," I tell him, grinning.

"Not if you do all the work," he replies, his eyebrows waggling up and down suggestively.

CHAPTER 25

Sophie

Despite Wraith's reassurance, the feeling of guilt remains that I'm the cause of the club being on lockdown, but to be fair, it must be in my head as no one makes any comment to make me feel that way. If anyone, it seems to be Chrissy who draws their ire. She betrayed the club after all, and most of the blame gets apportioned to her, but I can't shake the feeling that deep down I'm responsible.

Life goes on. Every night Peg has me working to build strength in my legs and to get my balance until it gets to the point when I can walk a few steps confidently without using the crutches. Despite recent events, my confidence is returning along with my independence, and I can feel the old Sophie starting to emerge. I'll never get my leg back, but my man doesn't give a damn, and that's all that matters to me. There can't be many men in the world prepared to put up with a one-legged woman.

Being an official old lady has raised my status in the club, and now I have a role to play. Along with the other brothers' women, I help plan, organise, and cook for Hank's funeral, and with Wraith, make sure the prospects have prepared as many of the guest rooms as possible. I've been warned there'll be many people from out of state who'll need to be fed and housed.

This morning Wraith had presented me with a cut of my own, and at first I was taken aback to see what is known as a 'property patch' on the back. But having got used to the other old ladies proudly wearing their cuts which, in their world was akin to a wedding ring, tears came to my eyes as I realised it signified how much I actually mean to Wraith, and the woven words, 'Property of Wraith', give me a warm feeling. He's given me strict instructions to wear my cut at the funeral—that way the men from the other chapters will know I'm taken.

I'm happy that Hank will have such a good send-off. I'm still grieving over his death, but as I remember my conversations with him I hope that somehow he was able to see how much he was respected by his brothers. The men give the prospects hell, but deep down they're already members of the club, especially one that had proved himself like Hank. The young man had no parents or siblings to mourn him, yet there will be hundreds of people to send him on his final journey. That was what he'd been looking for—a family where he belonged. I can only hope that somehow he knows that he found it.

A week after that terrible night I ride behind Wraith—who's now fixed a more comfortable passenger seat on his bike and a sissy bar so I feel more secure—in his position at the front of the procession just behind the president, who in turn is following the hearse. Up ahead is a police escort, but no one's out to cause trouble today. Peg's up beside us with Blade and Dollar behind him, and then the rest of the Tucson chapter. The way to the graveyard is lined with what must be a hundred men on Harleys from other chapters, all revving their engines as we pass. The sound is deafening and, I hope, loud enough to get through to the dead.

The funeral itself is a simple one. After the coffin is lowered into the ground in one of the plots reserved for the Satan's Devils, I take out the single rose that I'd carefully kept safe under my jacket and throw it onto the coffin with tears in my eyes. *Thank you, Hank. Thank you for protecting me.*

Then, leaning on Wraith's arm, I pick my way carefully across the grassy ground and back to the bike, and we make the return journey, followed by some two hundred bikes back to the clubhouse, once again escorted by the police, there to make sure there's no trouble along the route.

By now I've learned the full story of how the Satan's Devils came to acquire the compound where the club is based, and today they must be thankful for it. The large club room which used to be the reception of the old resort opens out into a huge dining room, and after that, there's the patio area where barbeques have been set up and are now scenting the air with tantalising smells of burgers and other goodies cooking. It's a lovely day today, with temperatures heading into the eighties, or as I still have to do the conversion, the high-twenties Centigrade. The prospects have cleaned and refilled the pool, and splashes tell me there are already a few people taking advantage of it.

Music is playing and space has been cleared for a dance floor in the clubroom. I'm in the kitchen mixing up a bowl of coleslaw to take outside when the container is taken from me as an arm snakes around my waist, and I know it can't be Wraith as I can see him chatting to a member of another chapter outside. Wearing my cut clearly designating me as belonging to my bearded biker, I'm not too disturbed, but swing around to see who it is.

"Peg! You startled me."

In his gruff voice, he tells me, "You owe me! And I'm here to collect."

My brow furrows as I try to think what on earth I promised him, but can't think of anything, so my eyebrow raises in question. "What?"

The sergeant-at-arms gives, what for him, passes as a smile. "Your first dance."

Dance? I cock my head to the side. A raunchy heavy metal tune is playing, and there's no way I'd be able to boogie along to that, I'd lose my balance and fall on my arse for sure. Narrowing my eyes, I'm just about to tell him when that song finishes, and while not a slow ballad, the next song is at least something we can shuffle too. As Peg holds out his hand, I start to grin, realising he's planned it. My fingers loop around his and he gently pulls me into his arms. And then I recognise the tune playing, it's Bruce Springsteen's 'Man's Job'.

"See," he starts with a smirk, "I told you I'd get you up and dancin'."

Listening to the words, I narrow my eyes. "This song, really?"

He laughs. "So? I like The Boss. Anyway, just fuckin' with Wraith." And then he's singing along, "Lovin' you's a man's job, baby, loving you's a man's job."

I laugh. For a moment we dance together. I'm not too sure that description fits the swaying and lumbering that we're doing, but it's so much more than even just a few weeks ago, and something I thought I'd ever be doing again. Now I've become thankful for even the little achievements I make each day. I curl my hand around his head and bring it down so I can reach my lips to his cheek.

"Thank you, Peg, for everything you've done. I don't know where I'd have been without you pushing me."

"We all need a little help, sweetheart." Suddenly, his eyes crease, and he gives a laugh. "Reckon your man ain't too happy with me."

"What the fuck, Peg?" comes a holler.

Suddenly my dance partner is wrenched away by a very angry Wraith, and I stumble and have a problem getting my balance.

"Wraith!" I yell, to get his attention.

His fist is pulled back ready to hit Peg, but luckily my scream distracts him and he reaches me before I fall onto the floor.

"Fuck, babe. I'm sorry. You alright?" His eyes stare into mine. "What the fuck you doing lettin' Peg put his hands on you like that?"

Why shouldn't I dance with another man? While being amused at his possessiveness, it also makes me angry. "Why shouldn't I? He's the one who made it all possible."

"I don't like seein' you in another man's arms." Wraith gives his explanation with a small smile. "Even one of my brothers. And 'specially this fuckin' song."

"That first day, when he forced me to start exercising, he told me he'd have my first dance with me. I didn't believe him then as I couldn't see this day coming," I explain, my eyes narrow, not appreciating his jealousy.

Now Wraith understands, and he smooths his hand over his beard as he makes his apology. "Oh darlin', I'm sorry I got annoyed. But I'd like to dance with you too. You know I always like you in my arms."

And I like being in his. As Peg steps away with a smirk, Wraith takes his place, and we gently move to the music. Then I get the devil in me. My man's holding me tight, he's not going to let me fall. Holding up my arms, I wave them in the air, leaning back and shaking my hair out. I get a feeling of elation. *This is the old Sophie!* Wraith's laughing and getting into it—he turns me around, I bend towards the floor. All the time he's holding me secure and I love every minute. *I love him.*

Then as the song ends he turns me to face him again. His hands run up and down my back, then go down and squeeze my arse. With one hand on his shoulder to balance myself, I move the other down and reciprocate his touch. As he pushes against me, I can feel his hard cock pressing into my stomach.

I then hear his voice as he whispers into my ear, "I need you. Wanna blow this joint?"

I thought he needed to be around as he's the VP and there're so many visitors. "Shouldn't you be here?"

"Yeah, but my patch looks good on you. Been dreamin' of you wearin' that and nothin' else since I gave it to you this mornin'."

Hmm, the thought of just the leather vest caressing my skin while Wraith fondles other parts of me sends a tingle down my spine. But just as I'm about to agree we're interrupted as the music's abruptly turned off.

"VP! We've got problems!"

At Drum's voice, Wraith spins around. After making sure I've got my balance, he leads me to a picnic bench outside where Sandy and Carmen are sitting. He goes off fast to see what's going down.

"What d'you reckon that's all about?" Sandy's noticed him go, her eyes creased with worry.

Carmen and I both look at each other and say at the same time, "Club business!" We both laugh. It's hard for an independent person like myself, but over the weeks I've realised that sometimes I just have to curb my curiosity, as there are many things the men don't want us to know.

But it seems like this time we're going to get involved, as members of the Tucson chapter rush over to us, telling us to go inside. Men are pulling out guns and the party atmosphere has completely disappeared. Shots are being fired from the direction of the front gate, then a silence descends over the compound. Then, only shortly afterwards, we hear the roar of bikes going away from the club.

Sombre men flood back in, and not just a few of them cast a glance in my direction. So many that I feel my cheeks going red, not happy being the centre of attention. I start to stand, wanting to find Wraith and see exactly what's going on, but before I can move, Wraith, Drummer, Peg, and Blade come back together, talking animatedly. I don't have a clue what they're saying, but nods are being thrown in my direction.

Then the group breaks up, and the next thing I know is that the music stops and Peg steps forward, climbing on a table. As he hollers for silence, gradually all other voices die down.

Cupping his hands to his mouth, he yells out, "All patched members to the clubroom now. Prospects, ol' ladies, and kids to go outside."

As the men start moving in the direction he's ordered them, I exchange looks again with Carmen. But before I can speak, Wraith comes over and puts his hand on my shoulder.

"Drum thinks you need to be here for this, Soph."

Even though the day is warm, I feel myself going cold. The looks thrown my way left me in little doubt the shots fired had something to do with me. "Has anyone been hurt, Wraith?"

"Nah," he reassures me quickly, "we just fired a few in the air to get a message across."

He takes my arm. "Here, let's get you up. They'll be waitin' for us." He patiently waits for me to get my balance, and then holds my arm as I walk across clubroom floor.

Going into the bar area isn't something that generally worries me now that I've got used to all of Wraith's brothers, but it's a bit different today when I'm entering as the only woman among over a hundred leather-clad bikers, many of whom turn and give me strange looks as I walk in. Wraith puts his arm around me. I move closer to his side and keep my head down. He leads me to the bar, which for once isn't manned by Marsh or Spider, and where the other officers from Tucson are waiting.

A chin jerk to Wraith, acknowledging our arrival, then without further delay Drum jumps nimbly up onto the bar. Seeing the president of the mother chapter ready to speak, gradually the sound of men's voice recedes, and the room goes quiet.

"Thank y'all for giving me your attention. You might have noticed we had some visitors just now, and while I've got y'all here, I'm gonna fill you in on what's been going down in the mother chapter. I'm gonna let our VP, Wraith here," he indicates Wraith, who jumps up on the bar beside him, "Wraith will give you the deets, but I'll just tell you our fuckin' uninvited guests were the fuckin' Rock Demons out of Phoenix."

As Drum jumps down a roar goes around the room, and I take it the other MC is not a friend to any of the Devils, whichever chapter they come from. With the amount of sound it's hard to make out individual words, but 'pieces of shit' and 'motherfuckers' come distinctly to my ears.

Wraith whistles loudly, getting everyone's attention. Again, silence gradually descends as he begins to speak. "This is Hank's day, and I've no wish to spoil it. We'll go outside and raise a glass to him in a few, but Drum and I agreed while his untimely death has brought us together today, we should take advantage of it."

I'm impressed at how he's so good at public speaking. He pauses until the nods and cries of assent die down.

"As you know, the Rock Demons put Hank in the ground, but the person they are after is my ol' lady here, Sophie." He waves his hand down towards me. Now I'm five-foot-two in a room full of tall, imposing men, so it's hardly likely they'll be able to see me. But they crane their necks just in case. "Now don't worry Soph, I'm not gonna ask you to come up and join me."

Thank goodness for that—I'd never be able to get up there. But Peg does the next best thing, wrapping his arms around my waist, he hoists me up into the air. Now comments of 'you lucky fucker' and the like are thrown around, and I feel my cheeks burning red.

"That's enough, Peg," Wraith growls, and I'm grateful when my feet are back on the ground. Drum, showing his thoughtfulness, shoves a bar stool my way and I sit myself down, pleased to take the weight off my feet.

"Now, Sophie here came to us for protection. There's a man hungry to get hold of her and he ain't no ordinary man. He's put out a fuckin' bounty on her, a contract to get hold of her." Another pause before carrying on. "Just so's you know, he's had a hold of her before. Sophie lost half of one leg, and the other was badly fuckin' damaged time. You see her on her feet today due to sheer fuckin' determination. When she first came to us she was in a wheelchair."

Another rumble of voices goes around the room. Peg takes the opportunity to lean over and speak into my ear. "And my fuckin' bullying. He could have mentioned that."

Wraith starts again, "To cut a long story short, she's become my ol' lady, and this chapter has vowed to keep her safe. The contract out on her was taken up by the Rock Demons, and they've just come to cut us a deal. If we hand her over to them, they'll kindly split the bounty with us, fifty-fifty."

"What's the fuckin' amount on her head?" someone shouts out.

"If it's gonna make any difference to you, two million dollars," Wraith replies.

What. The. Fuck? I gaze up at him, askance. Surely they'll want to take that offer. No more killing and the club a million dollars richer? My face falls as I accept my fate.

I turn to Peg, who's still standing next to me. "You're going to hand me over, aren't you?"

Suddenly it's Drummer's voice thundering in my ear. "No we're fuckin' not."

"But be sensible, Drum." I try to forget the fact it's my life we're talking about here. "It's the only way to avoid bloodshed."

An evil looking grin comes over his face. "It's going to be the fuckin' Rock Demons' blood that will be shed, sweetheart. Now listen up and don't make me regret invitin' you to our meetin'."

Faced with the full blaze of his steely eyes, I shut up.

Wraith's grinning down at me. "Now we ain't inclined to take their very generous offer. But I'm willing to listen to other views, so I'll ask. Does anyone here think we should take a million dollars and throw my ol' lady to the fuckin' wolves? To be tortured and killed? If ya do, speak up now."

Not one hand is raised, not one word of dissent. Then a voice shouts out, "Devils protect our fuckin' women."

General snarls of agreement support his words. I start to get a warm feeling inside, yet can't help thinking it's not a very sensible decision.

"Now, Soph here has concerns about whether we'll be able to take the Rock Demons on." When the next blast of shouting dies down, he continues again, "She'd rather give herself up then see any of our members get killed."

The men standing closest to me throw me looks of respect but shake their heads. One man I don't know puts his hand on my knee. "You won't be doin' that, sweetheart," he murmurs.

Wraith glares down, his eyes flashing with anger. "Hooper, will you kindly take your hand off my woman?"

A burst of laughter rings out, breaking the tension, and the man who apparently answers to Hooper steps briskly away. Drum uses the opportunity to jump back up on the bar.

"I wanted Sophie here 'cos I know she's been feelin' uneasy about the support she's getting' from the club. But now I think she's convinced of our commitment, our protection. I don't believe she needs to hear any more. Sophie, can you join the girls outside now? And remember, guys, she's wobbly on her feet so please can we clear a path for her to go through?"

Cheeks burning, worried I'm going to fall flat on my face, I slide off the stool and start making my way out of the room. When I stumble, an arm comes to support me. I turn quickly; it's Wraith.

He's grinning at me. "Just seein' you safely outside, darlin'."

It takes us a while to go across the clubroom, as we're stopped every few steps with men I've never met before in my life swearing they'll keep me safe.

Before I make it all the way out, a hand comes out and rests on my shoulder. As I swing around I hear Wraith growl, "You and I gonna have a problem?"

Glancing up I see a bearded, rugged giant. A stunningly attractive man, although I don't usually go for redheads. His hair, a deep ginger colour is shoulder length, half pushed tidily behind his ear, and half is flopping over his freckled face. His green eyes sparkle at Wraith, who, despite his tone, is grinning.

"Just wanted to tell your girl that she's got our support."

Slowly the smile drops from Wraith's face and he grows serious. "Thanks, Brother, that's good to hear." Quickly he turns to me and explains, "Sophie, this is Red, President of the Vegas Chapter of the Satan's Devils."

Red inclines his head towards me; he has to leave down a long way. "When your problems are sorted, sweetheart, get your man to bring you to see us. We'll show you a good time." His voice is a sexy growl, which does something to my insides, making me feel guilty as I'm hanging off the hand of my man.

Although I'm starting to feel claustrophobic in the midst of so many large and imposing men, I take the time to spare him a quick smile, hoping he'll put down the blood that's rushed to my cheeks to the heat of the room, and simply tell him I appreciate the offer.

Then, at last, Wraith gets me to the door.

CHAPTER 26
Wraith

I have to admit I wasn't totally on board with Drum's suggestion that Sophie be dragged into our meeting, knowing it would be overwhelming to be the only woman in the midst of a hundred rowdy men. But she handled herself well, and the fact that she was an attractive and tiny little thing had helped sway the others to our side. I was as proud as punch walking her out through the room. Seeing my name on the back of her cut hasn't grown old yet, and I suspect, won't for some time, or even ever.

I take her over to the picnic table, noticing she's favouring her right leg, suggesting that her prosthesis must be making her stump sore. She's been on it for a long time today. I help her sit down and hear her quiet sigh of relief. Nodding to Carmen and Sandy, I know they'll take care of my girl. After bending to give her a deep kiss and leaving my hand on her shoulder for a moment before lifting it, I return and make my way back to my prez's side.

As I re-enter the club room I have to push my way through the exodus of the rank and file—just as we agreed earlier, all members would hear the background to what's going on, but strategy would be determined by officers only.

Now much emptier, presidents, VPs, sergeant-at-arms, enforcers, and treasurers and secretaries have pulled up seats or are sitting on the tables. Drum's called the prospects in and they busy themselves making sure everyone has drinks before they're dismissed once again.

Once only the most experienced officers are left, Drum calls the meeting to order.

"Grateful for your support, brothers." His gaze slowly goes around the assembled crowd, a nod for each of the presidents. "Now let's thrash around some thoughts on how to get these bastards out of our hair once and for fuckin' all."

In the end, it all hinges on how much we can find out about the Rock Demons, and Mouse's plans to get eyes on them goes down well. After an hour or so kicking around ideas, Drum and I get what we were aiming for. Support by way of manpower if we need it once we know the kind of numbers we're up against, and agreement that they'll lock down other chapters of the Demons when it's time for us to go in. We do come away with the useful information that not all chapters of the Demons are involved in trafficking, and that retaliation for taking out the Phoenix chapter might not be as bad as we fear, though obviously we wouldn't be making friends. But we couldn't give a fuck about that.

We shoot the shit, drink some more, then the meeting breaks up. Some wander back outside to the party and some stay to catch up with brothers they haven't seen for a while. Although the reason for coming together today is a sombre one, a chance for the chapters to meet up is always welcomed.

Taking Drum's arm, I clasp my hand around his forearm, an action that's reciprocated, and with a chin lift I thank him for his part today. We don't need words as he gives a sharp nod in return, and then once more I'm heading outside.

As I come up behind her, those words, 'Property of Wraith', stitched onto the back of her cut have me hardening in my pants, and while it looks like she's enjoying herself, I know it won't be long before I'm dragging her back to my room to have a party of our own. But making my way through the throngs of people I haven't seen for some time, especially since they all want to offer support to help me keep my old lady riding behind me, takes time. I'm getting impatient to get back to her when a beefy hand lands on my back, almost making me fall. I swing around, fast.

"Red, you fucker."

He grins lopsidedly. "Never thought I'd see a bitch on the back of your bike, Wraith."

My face creases. Red and I prospected together, then he went off to Vegas while I stayed here. It's the kind of bond that never dies. "How d'you like being prez?" He only got the position last year when the previous president of the Las Vegas chapter succumbed pretty darn fast to cancer. Mind you, he'd smoked like a chimney for years.

Red's grin fades. "It was easier being VP."

I know where he's coming from—there's no way I covet the responsibility of Drum's position.

"But gettin' back to your girl, you gonna introduce me properly?"

My face shutters as my suspicions start to grow. "What exactly are you askin', Red?"

He opens his hands in a gesture of innocence, but there's a glint in his eye. "She's a beautiful woman, and you're one lucky motherfucker. Shame about what that bastard did to her though. How's she copin' with just one leg?"

I sigh, waving over to a spot behind the grills where no one seems to be making out, and it looks a good place to have a word without being overheard. Soph looks up as I walk past, so I hold up five fingers, and she smiles and gives a little wave of her hand to show she's okay with waiting for a few minutes.

There's a convenient log, so as Red sits down I rest my leg on it, leaning over with my hands on my knee. "When she first came here she was in a wheelchair," at last I start to answer his question. "Horse suspected she was suicidal."

"Shit!" He wipes his hand over his chin and adds sadly, "Gets to some like that."

"Yeah, that's what Peg said. Anyway, Peg has been helpin' her—huh, he bullied her and came on strong so she couldn't turn him down. But he got her exercisin' and now walkin' again. She's just about getting there as you can see." I jerk my head backwards, and his eyes follow and look at my girl.

"Peg would be the right man to help." He knows our sergeant-at-arms.

"Yeah, didn't help that one of our members tried to fuckin' rape her. Threw her prosthesis against the wall and fuckin' broke it."

"You what?" Red gets to his feet and slams his fist into his palm. He flexes his muscles and looks around, narrowing his eyes. "He still fuckin' breathin'?"

"No."

"Thank fuck for that."

I drag my hand down my beard. Truth is, I've known Red a very long time, was really close to him at one point, and still regard him as one of my best friends. So I tell him the rest of it. "Bastard put some fuckin' bad thoughts in her head—that no one would want her as she wasn't a proper woman."

He huffs a laugh. "Bit twisted seeing as he obviously did."

"Yeah, but it was only what she'd been thinkin' all along, so that's why I acted when I did. I'd been wantin' her for weeks but puttin' it off until it was the right time. Red, she's got to me. Haven't wanted anyone else since I saw her."

"You're a lucky devil you did see her first." He claps his hand on my shoulder, then pushes me slightly so I turn to face him. "Want any help convincin' her she's a fuckin' stunner?"

When I'd seen Red, memories of our past had come back to me. I knew I could trust him, in ways I wouldn't trust anyone else. Hoping I'm not going to regret this, I huff and say, "Come on then, but remember whose patch she's wearin'." I stomp my way over to the picnic bench. Bullet and Viper are hovering close by, and at my arrival, scoop up their women and leave. I jerk my chin towards them, knowing they were waiting until I was here to take care of my girl myself.

Red pushes past and takes the seat beside her. He looks down at the leg she's ruefully rubbing. "That painin' you, sweetheart?"

I see her face reddening; he's embarrassed her.

She looks to me as though for guidance. "You getting' tired, darlin'?"

She seems grateful I've noticed. "A bit." She pauses, then motions to me to come closer so she can whisper into my ear. "I'm getting fed up with everyone treating me like a freak in a carnival."

Red hears and rears back before I can react. "You're no fuckin' freak, sweetheart. And the only reason anyone's lookin' at you is 'cos you're fuckin' beautiful."

I'm grateful to him, but Sophie stares him down. "The first thing you mentioned was my leg, Red." She remembers his name from my introduction earlier; he apparently made an impression on her.

He raises his hand and gently touches her cheek. "It's been a long ass day, and you looked like you're in pain. You ain't got to hide that from anyone, girl. Fuck, most of us are in awe at what you've suffered and come through." As he smooths his fingers down her skin, he rests the tips for a second on the scar Buster left and flicks his eyes to me. I give a short nod in response, and see his face tighten.

Watching as she leans into his touch, I see her quickly straighten and look at me. Her mouth has dropped open and her eyes widened. Her breathing speeds up and her flush deepens. Quickly I reach out and reassuringly caress her hair while my eyes connect with Red's. The fucker's smiling, and out of her sight he's reached his hand down to his crotch, pointedly adjusting himself.

I stake my claim. Leaning forward and taking advantage of her open lips, I sweep my tongue inside. My grip on her hair tightens and I pull her into me, delving as deep into her mouth as I can. A slight waft of oranges comes to me from the shampoo she uses, but beneath that, the scent of something that's all her. Her taste teases me—my cock, already lengthened, swells almost to the point where it's painful, and my balls throb, seeking release.

She gasps into my mouth, but I hold her in place, and her lips move more urgently over mine. Opening my eyes, I see, as I'd expected, Red has his hands on her hips, and his fingers gently caressing her. My nostrils flare as I slowly end the kiss and stare at my girl.

"Who do you belong to?" I ask, my own breathing speeding up.

Still held prisoner by my grip on her hair, she looks directly at me and gasps out, "You, Wraith."

Throwing a glance at Red I see his eyes are dilated, and there's a look of hunger in his eyes.

Suddenly I'm scooping her up in my arms. "My room's closest," I tell them both.

She hugs me around my neck, holding on and holding me close. As Red gets up to follow us her eyes widen. "Wraith? Red..."

She weighs nothing at all, so it's easy for me to turn her so her hips are straddling my waist and carry her that way. Automatically she rubs her pelvis against me. Pausing my stride, I check for signs of concern, but she's perplexed rather than afraid.

"Red's comin' with us. If you're okay with that?"

She throws a glance over my shoulder at the other man, and just when I think I'll need to prompt her to respond, she turns back to me and I can see her pupils dilate as she whispers into my ear, "Are you okay with it, Wraith?"

Only with Red. And only because I'm confident that whatever sexual feelings she might have for the Vegas President don't hold a candle to the depth of her emotion for me. So I kiss her and whisper into her mouth, "Yes."

She leans into me, her eyes feeding on the man following us.

I get to my room, unlock it—with the numbers here today I'm not going to trust leaving it open—and take her inside. Red closes the door behind us.

CHAPTER 27

Sophie

One minute I was sitting talking with Carmen and Sandy, and the next Wraith comes up with that stunningly attractive man I'd seen in the clubroom. When Red seated himself beside me it was so close I could feel the warmth of his leg next to mine. Too close, invading my personal space, but instead of feeling trapped, a shiver of anticipation ran down my spine.

It was like a bucket of cold water being thrown over me when he commented on my missing leg, as though that was all I was. But then, the reminder that I'm a cripple was swept away, and things became blurred as Wraith was kissing me, and I felt Red's hands touching me, holding my hips, his fingers finding the skin between my top and jeans and gentling circling, and I was spiralled into a level of arousal that was out of this world.

It took me only seconds to know that if they both wanted me, I wouldn't be able to resist. *But Wraith wouldn't want to share me, would he?*

Then I was in Wraith's arms and being carried to his room, and Red was following. Over Wraith's shoulder, I could see his face, his fair skin darkening, his eyes narrowed, his lips pursed as though fighting to keep control. He was walking, legs slightly apart, drawing my attention to what's hidden beneath the denim of his black jeans. And it's quite a lot. My eyes widen and rise to his at the size of the package he has difficulty concealing, and he smirks in response.

Wraith checked with me, but I had to check back. My love for Wraith isn't going to waiver, but the chance to have this other man too? The one I'd felt such an immediate reaction too? The old Sophie would never have given up an opportunity like this, so why should the new version? It wouldn't be my first time with two men.

Then it hit me as we entered Wraith's room.

Suddenly my hands are beating on his shoulders. "Stop, Wraith, no."

Wraith freezes and gradually allows me slide to the floor. When I've got my balance he lets me go, stands back and tunnels his hands through his hair. "Fuck, Soph. I'm so sorry. I thought you might want this." He turns away and hits his fist against the wall. "Shit, I've fucked this up."

"I'll go." Without hesitating, Red turns to walk out of the door.

"No," a hoarse cry comes from me, not wanting them to think they'd upset me. "Wraith, my leg!" That's why I'm not the old Sophie! That's why I can't do this, can't think of another man seeing me."

"Oh, babe," Wraith's back by my side and I feel a body come up behind me.

"Don't give a fuck about what you've got or not got, beautiful. Don't matter none to me," Red's sexy rasping voice rumbles into my ear.

Wraith's hands brush my hair back from my face, studying me. "Get that out of your mind, darlin', Red ain't gonna care."

But my fears of a man rejecting me have come back in force, those cruel words Buster threw at me never far from the back of my mind. I know I'm still desirable to Wraith, he's convinced me of that time and time again, but to anyone else?

301

Red is gently kissing my neck, his teeth gently nipping, then his tongue soothing, but I stiffen at his touch, not wanting to see the disappointment in his eyes. Then he whispers to me, "Show me, trust me."

Staring at Wraith, I know I can't let this go further without showing Red what he's going to be dealing with. Pushing the man in front of me away, and stepping out of the grasp of the man behind, I half walk, half stumble to the bed and perch myself on the side. My hands go to the button of my jeans, and I hear two sharp intakes of breath as I start to undo it.

I close my eyes, unzip by touch, and ease my bum up to remove my jeans to my hips. Slowly I draw the denim down.

The unique smell of my man reaches me, and I know it's his gentle touch that takes over, taking off my shoes, then my jeans following. I feel him undo the straps around my prosthesis, and can't help the sigh of relief when it's off. I've been standing too long today.

Then another man's touch, his hands feeling coarser, smoothing down my thighs.

Taking a breath to fortify myself, I look up to see Red staring down at me, nothing but sheer male appreciation shining from his face. As Wraith slips onto the bed behind me and pulls me back into his body, Red steps forwards, taking my hand and resting it on his crotch. He feels hot to the touch and hard, and every bit as big as my eyes told me he was.

"Ain't turnin' me off none, girl." He's grinning but breathing hard, as though it's an effort to get air into his lungs. "It's hot." As he waves at my stump his words make me inhale sharply, and then he clarifies, "You're fuckin' brave, that's clear. That's what I see, sweetheart."

Then, his eyes fixed on mine, he removes his cut and slowly slides off his shirt, revealing a muscular body underneath decorated with colourful tattoos. Unable to let out my indrawn breath, I let my eyes absorb the sight in front of me. He's gorgeous. His skin is fairer than Wraith's and glistens with a slight sheen of perspiration due to the heat of the day, freckles abound, making me want to reach my fingers out and trace them like a child joins the dots of a puzzle.

Behind me, Wraith divests himself of his top, pulling me to him so I feel his warmth against my back. Then he reaches around, and taking the ends of my shirt, pulls it up over my head.

Now it's Red's turn to stare as Wraith undoes the front fastening of my bra, letting my breasts fall free. "Fuckin' beautiful," he rasps.

I feel myself grow wet at the two hot bodies surrounding me, my nipples peak as though crying out for attention, and Wraith doesn't disappoint, his hands coming out to tweak and caress them, sending a tingle directing down my spine to my clit, which begins to throb. I can't stifle the moan that his touch, and the greedy eyes of the man in front of me, elicits.

Red's hands go to the top button on his jeans, and lazily he undoes it then flicks the next through the button hole. He takes his time, and I can't pull my eyes away as one by one the buttons reveal what he's been hiding underneath. Unconsciously, I lick my lips in anticipation as his massive cock springs into view, hard and ready.

Part of my brain kicks into gear and I glance towards his face. "You clean?"

"Yeah, got tested recently and I never go ungloved."

"You can trust him, sweetheart," Wraith whispers in my ear.

Now Wraith scoots off the bed, toes off his boots and removes his jeans and boxers entirely. With a wry glance as though he's lost a race, Red stops his slow striptease and lets everything drop. Coming back to the bed, Wraith centres me on it and lies to one side, pulling my front towards him. Red slides next to me, his warm chest up against my back.

Wraith kisses me deeply, and then turns me to Red, who takes his turn. His taste is different, and his tongue swirls around mine in an unfamiliar dance, but is not at all unpleasant. As they take turns, slowly rolling me between them, their hands roam until I'm not sure which one is touching me where.

I hear murmurs in two different voices telling me how beautiful I am, telling me how sexy I am, how they can't wait to be inside me, and I feel two hard cocks pressing against me, reassuring me of the truth of the words coming out of their mouths. It's beyond hot, their touches almost scorching me.

Then Wraith's familiar hand finds my clit, and a different set of fingers probe inside me, curling around, seeking that special spot inside.

"Fuck me, she's so wet."

"That she is." Wraith kisses my neck, nipping it and sucking, marking me as his.

And then I can't think anymore—my senses are on overload, mouths at my breasts, hands everywhere, fingers touching, probing, stroking, and strumming. My muscles contract and I can't get a breath as I reach higher and higher until Wraith gives me permission. "Come for us."

I come, hard. So incredibly hard. I'm keening as they keep it going on and on and on, taking me to the peak a second and even a third time before finally letting me come down, my body shaking and quivering as small aftershocks keep assailing me.

"God, did you ever see anythin' so beautiful?" Red asks, his voice in awe.

"Three times a day," Wraith answers, making me give a small giggle.

"Lucky bastard."

Wraith rolls me towards Red, then reaches across and fumbles for something in his drawer, moving back, he tosses something towards his friend. As I hear foil packets tear, I gaze from one to the other, new sensations flooding me as I watch them each roll on a condom, their motions practised and precise.

Pulling me down on the bed, Wraith positions himself between my thighs, pulling my hips up, his tip now poised at my entrance.

Red kneels by the side of my head. "Will you suck me, sweetheart?"

Grateful he's using a condom, I nod my head, incapable of forming words. As Wraith pushes inside my pussy, Red teases my lips with his cock. I open my mouth and take him inside.

Wraith pushes in, and Red lets me take the lead, taking him inside as far as is comfortable, using my hands for his remaining length, stopping him from going too far. Once he's sure I'm controlling how much I can take he starts to thrust, and Wraith does the same.

Breathing in through my nose I take in Red's unfamiliar musk, and the thought I'm sucking a man I don't know coupled with the cock of the man I love thrusting into me sends my arousal sky high once again. Sounds of manly grunts fill the air, together with my smothered pleas to give me more.

Wraith thrusts, Red pushes in, almost in time with each other. Their moans of enjoyment, the odd words of 'fuck you're beautiful' and 'yeah baby, right there' spur me on. My muscles start contracting around my lover's cock as I suck Red in as deep as I possibly can, taking his heavy balls in my hands and rolling and squeezing them gently.

I feel Red swell and hear him shout out a warning to Wraith. I feel Wraith start to pump harder, feel him start to jerk and come, and that's enough for me to shatter at the same time.

Holding the condom to him, Red pulls out of my mouth, then leans over and gives me a deep, long kiss. As he pulls away, Wraith's mouth takes his place, and as his cock deflates and slides out of me, he holds me tightly to him. I snuggle close, my arms around his back, holding him tight.

A sound of rustling, a belt buckle clanking, and I look up to see Red getting dressed.

"Gonna leave you lovebirds now," he says, then leans, putting one arm on the bed. "Soph, you were amazin'. You *are* amazin'. Never let anyone tell you otherwise for a moment. And Wraith's a lucky, lucky bastard to have you all to himself." He stands, rests his hand on Wraith's shoulder and pats it. "Thanks, Brother."

He grabs his cut and shirt, and still half naked, leaves the room.

Neither of us speaks for a while when Red has gone, but perhaps we don't need words, as Wraith runs his hands up and down my back. After a moment he says softly, "Soph, you're a beautiful and desirable woman. I've said that, and Red has shown you too. Now are you going to fuckin' believe it? 'Cos I'm tellin' you now, ain't gonna let any other brother into our bed to get the message into your head."

"That was for me?" I'm still trying to process why my possessive man let another touch me.

"All for you, darlin', and Red's the only fucker who'd I'd let near you."

"You've known him a long time?"

"Years. We prospected together."

Then it hits me, the way they worked so well together. "You've shared women before?"

I feel the bite of jealousy as he replies, "Yes. But not for a very long time. And I ain't gonna be sharin' again."

Pulling himself up, he leans over on one elbow. "Did it work, Soph? Do you understand that you're more than your missin' leg, that if my brothers knew what I'd offered Red, they'd be fightin' over themselves to get into this bed? Not that I'm gonna fuckin' let 'em."

I'm quiet for a moment as I think, and then speak my thoughts aloud. "After my accident I convinced myself no man would ever want me again. And then, what Buster said…"

"Have you thought for a moment that Buster wanted you? He told you he was doing you a favour, but fuck woman, he was hard for you from the first moment he saw you, which must have told you somethin'. Sure, his verbal arrows hit the target, playing on your insecurity, but babe, he wanted you—though damn him for it and I hope he's burnin' in hell. I want you, most of my brothers would love to be where I am, and Red was droolin' from the moment his eyes landed on you."

"I'm making more of it than anyone else, aren't I?"

"Won't lie to you, Peg's said his injury turns some women off, but only the shallow ones, darlin'. The ones who can't see further than their own fuckin' noses."

I stare into his gorgeous eyes, so full of love for me. How many men would have invited even a close friend into their lover's bed just to prove a point? Slowly I nod my head, my mouth turns up as my eyes start to crinkle. "Men who'd be turned off aren't the ones I should be worried about, are they?"

Leaning over, he places a chaste kiss on my forehead. "No, darlin', that's my point. And the ones who'd want to fuck you, well, they're the ones who'll have somethin' to worry about if they even look at you too long, as they'll find themselves meetin' the business end of my fist. Ain't going to be any more experiments, babe. Never. You are all mine."

"I don't want anyone else." It's true. It was fun including Red, but Wraith is all I need. For the first time, I've let myself acknowledge the emotional contact with a man, and sex comes second to me wanting to be part of his life.

I pull his lips down to mine but pause before we meet. "Thank you for tonight, Wraith. Thank you for showing me I'm still a woman."

"Think you were the only one havin' doubts about that, Soph."

CHAPTER 28
Wraith

The Rock Demons know that Sophie is at our compound. Since the ultimatum that was delivered on the day of Hank's funeral, there's been no further movement on either side. We're watching them, just as we know they'll be watching us, each waiting for the other to make the first move. But that doesn't mean that we've been sitting with our thumbs up our asses. No, we've been putting the groundwork in place.

At church, the following Friday, we get the update we've all been waiting for. After the usual business is out of the way, including Beef's report that the new dancer he's taken on at the strip club is working out well and drawing in the punters, and Dollar's confirmation that takings are up, we all sit up straighter as Drum gets to the main point of the meeting, the Rock Demons.

Slick holds up his hand, the one without the lit cigarette in it, and takes the floor after taking a long drag. "Jill took me to meet her friend, Ella. She's a fiery lass, got some spark in her. Tucson born and bred, and wants in with us."

"Did you try her out, Slick?" Blade smirks before leaning back in his chair and folding his arms.

Slick stares him down. "Could have done, she's hot for biker cock, but that's not what I was there for."

"Get to it, Slick. Everyone else pipe down." Drum puts a stop to any other snarky comments.

"Spoke to her for a while." Slick takes another drag then continues without further prompting, "I reckon she'd fit in okay here. That spark she's got, well, she'd stand up for herself with the other bitches, but she shows a lot of respect for the men."

Now it's Drum who interrupts, his steely eyes centred on Slick. "She able to damp down that fire? Demons don't allow the women the leeway we do."

"Reckon so." Slick nods thoughtfully. "I explained what we wanted her to do. She's smart enough to know she's got to play the part and act dumb, but she's confident she'll be able to get the cameras planted."

"She know she might have to get down and dirty with the Demons? She can't go in as a hang-around and stay on the sidelines."

Another nod. "Yeah, if it's dick and it's attached to a biker she's happy with that. As long as they don't get too rough."

"Can't make no guarantees on that, but we'll do what we can to get her out of there before they have her pullin' a train." Drum is obviously not happy about sending a woman into the rival club, particularly the sort of club which might have all members lining up to take a turn at the new girl, but we've talked about it all ways to Sunday and can't come up with another plan. We can't take them on without knowing more about them. And this is the best way to get the intel we need.

"Ok." Drum looks at me. "VP, we set up from your end and ready to go?"

I lift my chin. "Yeah, we've rented a one room apartment in Phoenix near their clubhouse, nothing fancy, and it's ready for her to move in. The Demons' base is a ways out of town, so I've got her a cheap beater to get back and forth."

"Have you met this Ella?"

"Nah," I tell him. "The less she has to do with any of us the better. Slick's been the only contact, and he's always visited her without his colours."

"I got the cameras, and Slick's got instructions how to set them up. They're tiny and will be difficult to spot. Unless you are lookin' for them, you'd never find them," Mouse tells us, tucking his long hair behind his ear.

"Difficult? I hope it's fuckin' impossible," Drum growls. "As the new girl, this Ella would be the first one they'd suspect."

"Got that covered, Prez." Slick draws our attention again. "She's to go there, get herself accepted, then when she feels it's safe—probably late at night when they're passed out drunk, she'll drop the cameras discreetly and then get the fuck out of there. We'll pick her up and bring her back here."

"She got the burner phone?"

"Yeah, Marsh and I will be up in Phoenix near enough to move quickly once she's clear and ready get out. If she has any problems we're prepared to go in."

A thought makes me want to grin, but I push it down. Slick seems mighty fixed on doing this himself, when it hasn't been put up to vote who'll be watching her. And selecting Marsh? Well, he's the one of the two remaining prospects that I'd trust with something like this. Seeing as he doesn't want to take any chances, I think the woman might have made more of an impression on him than Slick's letting on. Glancing at Drum, who raises an eyebrow at me, I gather he's also thinking along the same lines. But like me, he says nothing. At the end of the day, we've all got a lot of respect for the girl who's taking such a risk on our behalf, and it's up to us to minimise it.

Picking up the gavel, Drum just finishes up. "Ok, Slick, I'll leave it in your hands. Send her in as soon as she's ready. Report back to Mouse when the cameras are set up and he can start monitorin'. Mouse, you keep us informed. Shame she won't be able to put one in their fuckin' church, but that's too much danger if she tries that, so don't even ask her. Hopefully there'll be some loose mouths in their clubroom." He bangs the gavel down. "Church dismissed!"

For the next two weeks the waiting game continues. Sophie continues to get better at walking without her crutches and makes it down to the club room herself without any help. I'm so proud of her, and since that night with Red—the night I admit I enjoyed but never want to repeat—she seems more confident in herself. She's started wearing makeup again, and while, in my view she doesn't need any, as she's beautiful the way nature left her, I take it as a sign she's more accepting of herself.

We've finished up a few more of the fire damaged rooms, meaning Horse has been able to move out of the suite—a good thing, as I've virtually moved in. Well, why not admit it, I have. There's not one night that we've spent apart. I've been toying with the idea of buying a house off the compound where we can start to build a life together, following the example of the other brothers with old ladies. But that will have to wait until there's no longer a fucking price on her head. Some days I'd love nothing more than to throw her on the back of my bike and take off on many of those sightseeing trips I'd planned in my head, until I remember the danger in her going out of the club. Once was enough to risk for that until we put the fucking Demons in the ground.

It's two weeks later when I'm walking into the clubroom and Slick calls me over. "Hey, VP, come 'ere a sec."

He's got a woman beside him. She's got long auburn hair that reaches down to her ass, and a fringe coming down almost hiding her eyes. As I move closer, I see her shoulders are hunched, and as she raises her head to look at me, I see a darkening bruise across her right cheek, and her left arm is held tight across her stomach. And when I get closer, the haunting look in her wide eyes hits me. Without him having to introduce me, I know who she must be. This is the woman we sent into the Demon's club. But I wait for him to confirm it.

"Wraith, this is Ella."

I hunker down in front of her, lifting my hand to push back her hair, wondering whether she's got any more injuries. She flinches before my fingers can reach her face, and Slick puts a possessive arm gently around her.

"Sorry, darlin'," I tell her softly while vowing those bastards will meet a painful death.

I flick my eyes towards the man at her side. "She get caught?"

Slick shakes his head, "No. Cameras should be transmittin' now well enough. This is just how those bastards treat their women."

"Doc look at her?"

"I've called him, he's on his way in. Reckon you've got a broken rib, don't ya, babe?"

Ella nods, and I growl, "Fuckin' bastards."

Turning back to Slick, I ask, "Drum know?"

"Not yet, was just going in to see him."

At that moment, Jill runs into the clubhouse, making a beeline for her friend, obviously already having been told she's here. Her eyes widen in horror at the sight, and she demands to know what's happened.

I'm impressed when Ella looks up at her and, after throwing a small smile at Slick, tells her, "I was mugged."

I stand and step back, allowing Jill to move in and comfort the battered woman, then jerk my chin towards Slick. After he makes sure Ella will be alright left with Jill, he takes the hint and follows me to Drum's office.

Slick updates Drum about Ella and apprises him of her condition. Drum's eyes narrow, and his first thought is for the girl.

"She'll be stayin' here now, too risky her going home. I'll be lookin' out for her." Slick's eyes challenge his prez and VP.

"Of course she's fuckin' staying here. She's under our protection now, Slick. Girl's done a solid for the club." Drum seems astounded he'd think anything else.

"You let Mouse know?" I ask.

"Yeah, texted him as soon as she was out." Slick pulls a pack of cigarettes out of his pocket and lights one up.

"Any problems her leavin' their club?" Drum wants all the details.

"No. She phoned me about eight o'clock this mornin'. Pretended she was callin' her ma and findin' out she was sick. They didn't bat an eye when she left, as she said she needed to go see her."

"What's the story, Slick? If they didn't catch her plantin' the cameras, what's with the state she's in?"

"Couple of the bastards were rough with her last night, she protested, and they both clocked her for it." As Slick gives me the details, my hands clench and unclench, and I can see Drummer's leg start bouncing. "She was gonna wait for a better time, but couldn't take much more. So she hid the cameras around the bar once it was empty, then waited for her chance and got out."

"She's a brave woman."

"Yeah, she is that, Prez."

Drum's fingers tap on the table and we give him the space to think. He then looks directly at Slick. "So she's gonna be a new sweet butt once she's healed?" He raises his eyebrow.

I have to hide my grin when Slick sits up straight and almost roars his answer, "No she's fuckin' not."

Drum chortles. "Thought things were goin' that way. She yours?"

For a moment Slick looks like he's a rabbit caught in the headlights, then he too gives a laugh. To be honest, Slick was probably last on my list to get himself an old lady, but that's what he seems to have gone and done. And probably he'd thought the same about me. Christ, we're going down like flies.

"Fuck, Prez, hadn't really thought that far. 'Cept I ain't gonna want any other brother touchin' her." His eyes narrow at the thought.

"She feel the same way?"

Slick's face falls. "Think she's had enough biker cock to satisfy her for now. Fuck, I think it's gonna be hard just gettin' her into my bed."

Our prez nods, his face grim. "Give her time, Brother. I'll make it clear at church it will be hands off."

I throw a snide look at my brother. "Welcome to the club," I tell him.

He huffs a laugh. "Suppose I am a member, now. Fuckin' pussy-whipped. Who'd have thought it?"

When we get all the brothers together at church there's no dissension about leaving Ella alone—we were all too much in awe of what she'd had done for us. Especially when those cameras started feeding back interesting video and audio of the inner workings of the Rock Demons club. There appeared to be about twenty of them in all, but it was hard to make out how many of those were prospects. Ella had placed the cameras well, but it was impossible to make out the differences on the cuts or recognise all the faces, so we could have been double counting at times.

They were, as we had hoped, not close-lipped around the bar. Not so much when the sweet butts were about, but when it was just their members they inadvertently let slip some extremely useful information for us.

The Rock Demons had big plans. Not only did they want to take Sophie, but they wanted to take us all out, take over our clubhouse, and start up their own Tucson chapter, another city as an outlet for drugs. That was the reason they hadn't yet made another attempt to grab my woman—they were getting themselves organised for the bigger hit. And before they made a move on us, they were carrying on with business, waiting for a gun shipment to arrive and preparing for a drugs run to Vegas.

But we were going to hit them first.

That they discussed their plans so openly was nectar to our ears. Drum got onto Red and made arrangements that he would take out the drug-running group as they entered his territory. That was going to be child's play as we had all their routes and waypoints given to us straight from the horse's mouth. As Dart suggested, the members going on the drug run were probably sampling their own product and had got over-confident on their home turf.

The gun shipment was more of a worry. The members involved in that were obviously more experienced and played their cards closer to their chests, only letting slip the timing, and not openly discussing the route or destination. So we decided on going in before it arrived.

Five members of the Demons were going to Vegas the week after next, and Red would deal with those. That left, to the best of our knowledge, fifteen we'd need to take out.

We started to make plans.

Three days before the final twenty-four hours the Demons would be breathing air, we have another emergency church. We've been meeting almost daily this last week to make our final plans, Drum not wanting to leave anything to chance. Mouse is tapping on his laptop, as usual, the info he's been able to pull down from Google Maps vital in planning our three-pronged attack.

"So, VP, you'll be leadin' the first group here." Drum points to the map we've got set out on the table. "Dart, Slick, and Tongue will be with you." He moves his finger to another weakness in their defences that we've identified. "Blade, you'll be..."

"Hey!" Mouse's shout interrupts the prez; Drum glares at him. "What the fuck is it, Mouse?"

"Ethan St John fuckin' Davies is dead."

"What?" That was not the news I expected to hear, but the best fucking news ever as far as I was concerned.

"Yeah." Mouse's eyes aren't on me, but on his laptop screen. I watch them scan left to right as he takes in some news article he's reading. "There was an attempted coup in some fuckin' Arab country. Somewhere in Ezirad, though fuck knows where that is. Hang on, it doesn't say much, the emir—is that a king or somethin'?—well, Emir Kadar issued a statement sayin' he regrets the death of the prominent businessman who got caught up in the fightin'."

"Here, let me have a look." I go around the table and lean over his shoulder. As I dare to touch his beloved laptop to turn it towards me, Mouse actually snarls at me. I ignore him, speed reading the contents, though there's not a lot more than Mouse has already told us.

"He's right, it's Ethan St John-Davies alright. There's a footnote explainin' who he is. There can't be two of his name who run ElecComs."

"The man who took the contract out on Wheels? Hey, man, this means she's got nothin' to worry about now." Peg looks excited on her behalf.

"Yeah, there can't be a fuckin' bounty anymore if he's not around to pay it." Even Beef's nodding enthusiastically. My brothers have all taken my woman to their hearts, and I'm overwhelmed with the relief they're feeling for her.

"It says here he leaves no heirs," I'm still reading it through, "so I think it's safe to assume the contract died with him." Thank the fuck.

"Demons going to be shittin' themselves at missin' their chance. Ain't heard any chatter yet, Mouse?" Rock questions him.

"News is just hot off the press—they might not be so quick on findin' out about it. Will be interestin' to hear what they have to say. They left it too long to make their move."

"Sloppy bastards."

"That as may be, but we shouldn't underestimate them, and we can't forget their other plans. Still, it's some better fuckin' news for once." Drum bangs the table to get our attention. "VP, you'll want to be off to tell Wheels the good tidin's. But brothers, this doesn't change our plans one iota. Demons already killed one of ours, and it probably won't make a difference to their plans to get rid of the rest of us. Attack's still going ahead in three days."

He bangs the gavel. I leg it out of there fast, the biggest smile on my face.

CHAPTER 29
Sophie

Wraith is pushing up into me, gently pulling out and then thrusting in again as though he's got all the time in the world. He's keeping me on edge, so close to coming, but not quite being able to go over. I'm floating in a state of ecstasy, so aroused, yet feeling so loved.

He keeps on with his slow slides, and gradually my muscles start to contract, squeezing around him.

"Fuck, I can't hold off," he groans out. "You're stranglin' my cock, darlin'."

I can't even answer him. Rapidly approaching my peak I let him do all the work, and then I'm there.

"Let it go, I've got you, babe."

He's spent so long bringing me here that my orgasm is not so much intense as a strong but gentle wave washing over me, seeming to go on for ever. I moan loudly as I slowly come down. Wraith slows his movements, my muscle spasm triggering his release.

"Fuck, oh fuck," he shouts into my ear, and gives a last few sporadic thrusts. "Oh, fuck darlin'." Bringing his forehead down to mine, he releases my hands, which he'd been holding above my head and takes his weight on his arms. I pull him down to me, wanting to feel his warmth, chest to chest. It was the sweetest lovemaking I'd ever experienced.

It felt like he was saying goodbye.

Tears form at the corners of my eyes. "I don't want you to go."

"Darlin' we've been over this." He nuzzles my face and gently wipes away the tears with his fingers.

"Ethan's dead, there's no need to go after the Demons now." He hasn't shared club business with me, he's told me nothing other than that Ethan's died, but slowly the mood in the club-house has been changing over the past week or two, and I know something big is in the cards. Something that involves all the members, and which has had men looking solemn and cleaning their weapons as if they're getting ready for war. The arrival of a dozen brothers from other chapters without celebration or party-ing reinforced my fears.

Wraith hasn't replied, he's now kissing my neck.

"Where are you off to today, tell me that at least."

All he'll say is that one of the prospects will be staying with me. Everyone else, except for Mouse and Adam, who'll remain in the clubhouse to protect the women, is going on a run. Yes, with all their weapons prepared and ready. I'm not stupid. Go-ing after the Demons was something I knew they had planned.

He takes my lips and murmurs against them, "Love you, darlin'."

"Wraith…"

He pulls away with a rueful smile. "Got to get going, Soph. Can't leave the boys waitin'."

"Please don't go. I've a really bad feeling about today, Wraith." A feeling I'm never going to see him again.

He doesn't answer other than giving a sad little shake of his head, then just goes to the bathroom and has a quick shower. On his return, he dresses quickly, and I see him put a gun in his shoulder holster, and another in the waistband at the back of his jeans, and then a third, which he spirits out of nowhere and straps to his ankle. He's usually armed, but never as much as this before.

With an air of finality he comes over to me. "I'll see you to-night, darlin'. I don't know what time…"

"Text me, Wraith. Let me know you're safe."

He sighs deeply. I know he wanted to keep me away from this. He didn't want me to worry. But the clues have all been there. Something big is going down, and my man will be right in the thick of it. He has to be, he's the VP.

I care about the other men too, some more than others—Peg, of course, but also Dart and Slick, who seems to have suddenly got himself an old lady. But it's my man I need to come back home.

Without giving anything away he tells me, "We got this, babe, but I'll text you. Soon as I can, okay?"

Then with one last kiss, he's gone. As he closes the door I hear him greet someone outside, telling them if they ever want their patch to keep a close eye on me. It'll be the prospect who they're leaving behind.

Silence. Now the tears start falling in earnest, and all I can think of is saying goodbye to Mark that last time, the day he left for the oil rig, telling me he'll be back in three weeks' time. Remembering that awful telephone call, the waiting, and then the confirmation of his death. And today feels exactly the same, like that dreadful bleak period when I'd been waiting for news.

I can't lose Wraith. But I've a terrible sense of foreboding, of déjà vu. I've been here before, and it's a place I never wanted to visit again, ever. This, this was why I tried to protect my heart. I'd failed miserably at that and am now paying the price.

Closing my eyes, I try to go back to sleep. If I can sleep the day away it will go faster. But the ploy didn't work last time I had to play the waiting game, and it's clearly not going to work now. My mind churns ten to the dozen, and I can't switch it off.

It must be half-an-hour later that I hear the roar of bikes starting up, usually the sound doesn't reach up here, but there must be thirty or so bikers going out today—our club and the visiting members—so the thunderous noise carries. And then it's silent again, and the lack of sound hangs heavy in the air, an ominous quiet broken only by the chirping of cicadas, as though something is going to happen.

I can't just lie here.

Realising the women, Adam, and Mouse will be in the club-house, I decide to get up and go join them. Moping around here on my own won't help ease my mind. At least there I'll be in the thick of it and with whoever's the first to get any news when it comes in. Now being familiar with Mouse, at least I know he'll be monitoring everything as it goes on.

It's my best course of action if I want to keep in the loop. So forcing myself up, I take a tissue and blot the last of my tears, blowing my nose to clear it, then reach for my prosthesis, knocking my crutches as I do so. As they crash to the ground a worried voice calls out.

"You alright in there, ma'am?"

"I'm fine. Just having a shower and getting dressed. I'll be out in a few, Spider." The mode of address, which I'm going to have to put a stop to, has identified the unlucky prospect left to guard me today. Not that it's necessary now that Ethan St John-Davies is dead—and boy does that take some getting used to that I've no further need to worry that anyone's coming after me—but Wraith's still being cautious. Spider will probably think he's unlucky to be missing out on the action, but he might be one of the lucky ones if my fears are correct.

I get myself ready and then walk to the door. Every day I'm getting better at walking, and each time I walk unaided I feel a little bit prouder of myself. I don't even need to concentrate on every step I take, only when there are stairs involved—and luckily there's not many of those around the clubhouse—or I'm going over rough ground, which is more common as club's neglected to maintain some of the many paths linking the buildings together.

Opening the door, I find, as expected, Spider standing outside. He's a tall, lanky man, his frame giving rise to his name—his limbs seeming too long for his body. I've seen him in the gym, and he's trying hard, but there's obviously some way for him to go until he muscles up to be a match for the other men. In his early twenties, he still has the bearing of a boy rather than a man, emphasised by his impish good looks and the manners the club hasn't yet quite managed to knock out of him.

"You want to go down to the clubhouse, ma'am?"

"Oh for goodness sake, Spider, called me Soph. Or Wheels if you have to, but don't call me ma'am again, please. It makes me feel ancient."

An easy grin comes to his face. "Okay, ma'... Wheels." Although some of the brothers have copied Wraith in calling me Sophie, most still stick to the now redundant handle of Wheels.

I answer his original question. "Yes, I'm going to the clubhouse."

He looks around me into my room and points to the wheelchair. "Let's get you seated in that."

My eyes widen. "What?"

"Your chair."

As my brow creases, he continues, "Wraith told me I wouldn't get my patch if you so much as broke the nail on your little finger when he got back. I ain't takin' no risks. It's the chair or you stay here. Your choice."

I see a touch of the iron he'll need to develop as a fully-patched member of the club, but I still protest. "Spider, I've been out of that fucking chair for weeks. I don't need it anymore."

He shakes his head, turns his back and stands resolutely in the doorway. He might be a skinny lad, but I doubt I'd be able to push my way around him.

"For goodness sake, I can walk goddammit, hold my arm if you're worried."

Turning back, he frowns. "Don't think Wraith would want my hands on his ol' lady."

I can feel blood rushing to my cheeks as I inhale sharply. "Well I won't bloody well tell him if you don't."

Another dismissive shake of his head. "Not riskin' my patch," he proclaims adamantly and turns his head away.

I glance at the chair and then at his back. Oh, hell. If I want to go to the clubhouse it seems I'm going to have to give in. Unless he straps me to it, once I'm down there I won't be tied to it. "Okay, I give in. I'll use the bloody chair. I don't know why you're so hung up on it."

Now he's looking at me with a cheeky grin. "Perhaps I just like pushin' women around."

He's made me laugh. Still shaking my head and chuckling, I go behind the darn chair, grab the handles and push it myself to the door. After his pointed look, I give a sigh and sit in it. I let him wheel me along, and soon we're out in the bright sunshine and going down to the club, the beauty of the day, the endless blue sky above at odds with my black mood.

There's always something going on in the clubroom, generally brothers drinking or being serviced by the sweet butts at any time of the day. Sounds of pots banging and cooking smells generally fill the air, coming through from the kitchen. So to find the place completely deserted and quiet is disconcerting. I wasn't sure what I expected, the old ladies are around at least. The sweet butts are probably languishing the day away in their beds, Mouse is probably behind his computer screen, and God knows where Adam is.

"Looks like you're it for my company for today, Spider."

"Shush," he admonishes me fiercely.

It's at that point the unnatural still and quiet make me realise there's something wrong. I feel Spider's hands on the chair give a slight pull backwards, but before he can get me moving, a man steps out into the clubroom from the direction of the offices.

He has a gun in his hand and a face that I recognise. My hand goes to my mouth partly in disbelief, and partly to suppress an agonised howl of distress. I'd thought I was free, had thought I no longer had a threat hanging over me. I was wrong.

Hargreaves, Ethan's sidekick, is standing flanked by two men. Two men holding weapons as if they know exactly how to use them.

"Stop." Hargreaves gun points above my head, aimed towards Spider. "Take out your weapon and drop it now."

"Ain't carryin'." Spider's controlled reply comes from behind my head.

"I think you are. Take it out now. It will be easy enough to find *after* I shoot you in the head."

At the chilling words, I tremble violently. I can't have another prospect's death on my conscience. In a shaking voice I advise, "Do as he says, Spider."

He doesn't react immediately, but as Hargreaves brings his gun up and cocks it, I let out the breath I didn't know I was holding, as from the corner of my eye I see a weapon dangling from the prospect's hand.

"Now, very gently put it on the floor and kick it over to me."

Spider does so.

Hargreaves stares at the prospect for a moment. "Now the knife you've got on you."

Another slight delay, and then his blade joins the gun on the floor. Hargreaves picks it up, then sneers. "They let some wimps join motorcycle gangs nowadays, don't they?" He jerks his head at his two men, who dutifully laugh, but who don't lose focus and keep their guns trained on us. Now he's removed any threat, turns his attention to me. "Well, if it isn't the cripple. Ethan's been trying to find you. Thought the Rock Demons were going to bring you in, but never trust a motorcycle gang to do things right." A sneer accompanies his last comment. "The little cunts were frightened of going up against the Satan's Devils, so I had to come myself. My lucky day when I saw all the bikes going out this morning."

Deciding I've had enough of listening to his poison, I try to reason with him. "Your employer is dead. I don't understand why you're here."

A twinge of regret crosses his face. If I thought the man capable of any emotion, I'd say sadness was there too. "It's a pity," he says, his voice suddenly angry. "The world's lost an amazing man there. Shot down like a fucking dog. It's all that bitch Zoe's fault, and I'll deal with her too after I've finished with you."

Zoe? The realisation hits me that he's here to tie up loose ends. There's no point taking me, there's no longer anyone to deliver me too. He's going to kill me. All of a sudden, all the reasons I want to live come into my mind, and on the top of that list is Wraith. My phone starts ringing in my pocket.

"Don't answer that," he instructs.

It rings again, and again I'm forced to ignore it. I can't even surreptitiously use the keys to leave the line open—he's watching me so closely and he'd see my hands move.

"What do you want from me?" When whoever's trying to call me gives up, I try to keep him talking. It was probably Wraith, and hopefully he'll grasp something's wrong. *Or he'll think I'm in the shower.* A text pings, which I have to ignore as he answers my question.

"For you to stop breathing," he tells me, nonchalantly.

Spider moves in front of me. "You'll have to *take* me *out* with your *gun* first. Soph, I've got your *back covered*." There isn't much inflection on the particular words, but staring death in the face seems to sharpen my mind, and in a flash, I recall Wraith storing his extra gun in the back of his waistband. *Could Spider have one there too?*

He's hiding me from Hargreaves. Knowing if we live he'll forgive me if I start to grope him only to find I've interpreted him wrong, I move my fingers slowly, making sure I'm making no movement that Hargreaves can see. *He doesn't know I'm not wheelchair bound anymore.*

I was right, my fingers touch the cold hard metal of a gun. I've watched the men cleaning them often enough, and after my request to have one for myself, Wraith got as far as showing me how to check if one's loaded and how to take off the safety. I can only assume Spider put bullets in his today, but as I slide it free, I make sure it's ready to fire. Deciding there won't be another dead prospect today, I stand, pushing Spider to one side. With faster reactions he grabs at me, pulling me with him behind the couch. The back of my wheelchair explodes as bullets hit it almost as quickly as the gun is taken from my hand, and standing, Spider fires three shots of his own.

He might be a lanky son of a bitch, but what he lacks in muscle he makes up for with his accuracy, as there's no more returning fire. But as soon as the men are down, he leaps up over the couch and fires six more shots to make sure.

Hearing no sound except the ringing in my ears, I pull myself up. There's no doubt about it, all three are dead. Each has a bullet in the middle of his forehead and two more either side of each of their chests.

We exchange glances, my heart is beating like it's about to jump out of my chest and my lungs are heaving as though I've run a marathon.

"They're dead, Sophie." His hand might have been steady when he was shooting, but he's shaking now. I suddenly doubt he's shot at a live target before. Taking ammunition out of his cut, he reloads his gun.

I can't speak. The close brush with death, the tangy smell of blood and death turns my stomach, and I rush to the nearest sink to be sick. It's in the kitchen. I hear Spider calling out for me to wait and be careful, but I'm too intent on getting to my destination.

But reaching it I scream, "Spider!" Carmen and Sandy, along with the new girl, Ella, are tied up and gagged on the floor—they're not moving, they look dead.

The prospect rushes in and starts to feel for their pulses, grimacing when he sees the marks indicating they must have all put up a struggle. "They're breathin'. They might have been knocked out or drugged, I don't know which. We'll untie them, but be careful not to move them. We need Doc here."

Taking his phone out, he places a call to the medic. I do likewise, but my call is to Wraith. It goes unanswered.

He looks up, shaking his head, his eyes going so wide they're almost entirely white, and I grasp this is too much for one prospect to cope with, as he says in a grim and unsteady voice, "Where are Mouse and Adam? The shots should have brought them running!"

At that moment the kitchen door opens, and Crystal rushes in, Amy in her arms. "I heard shots. What's…" Her voice breaks off when she sees the other women on the floor. She hides Amy's face against her.

"Crystal, can you untie them, but don't disturb them. We don't know how badly they've been hurt. Doc should be on his way." I flick my eyes towards Spider and get his nod of confirmation. "But don't let Amy go into the clubroom," I continue, my eyes trying to relay she really wouldn't want to see the sights in there. As Crystal's eyes widen, showing she understands, I add, "Where are the sweet butts?

Crystal answers for him. "I heard the shots as I was on my way down, the whores sleep during the day, and their rooms are up at the back of the compound. They probably haven't heard."

At least that's something. Although I haven't taken to the other women, I didn't want to see anyone else hurt.

I nod to Spider. "We're going to try to find Mouse and Adam."

"Not you. You're stayin' here." Spider sounds firm.

"No, I'm coming with you. The threat's gone now, Spider." Without waiting for him to answer, I turn, and moving as quickly as I can, making my way across the clubroom and past the meeting room to Mouse's office, the most likely place where he'll be.

I open the door gingerly, dreading what I might find, fully expecting to find him dead. What I find is a tightly bound and gagged man rolling on the floor, struggling to get free despite the injuries that have been inflicted on him. His eyes flicker madly as the prospect and I rush in. Spider gets out his knife that he'd retrieved with his gun and undoes the ropes. As soon as his hands are free Mouse spits out the rag from his mouth.

"What's happened?"

"Three men were here for Wheels. I took them out." Mouse stares at him, then nods once, lifting his chin, his gesture showing his admiration.

"Mouse, are you alright?" I gasp out, eyeing the blood pouring from his scalp. "Doc's been called, Carmen, Sandy, and Ella—they're unconscious in the kitchen."

Mouse drags himself to his feet, staggering as he does so. "Bastards jumped me, overpowered me. Tried to get me to tell them where you were, Wheels. Thought they were gonna kill me, but they clobbered me instead." He lifts his hand to his head, grimacing when it comes away covered in blood. "Where the fuck is Adam?"

"We haven't seen him," Spider spits out.

Mouse goes to his laptop and calls up a program, squinting as he tries to get his eyes to focus. "His phone is by the gates."

Spider turns and runs, I follow more slowly—Mouse can only just keep up with me. He has to balance himself against the wall. When we get outside, Spider forgets his promise to Wraith and turns, pulling me into his arms and shielding me from the sight.

"Fuck!" Mouse shouts and stumbles over to his brother.

"Is, is he?"

"They fuckin' killed him!" Mouse confirms the bad news in a howl full of agony.

Seeing tears in Spider's eyes, I push him away, looking past him to see Mouse cradling his dead brother in his arms. That Adam is gone there can be no doubt, half his head is missing.

I'm shaking so much it's hard to keep my balance. Adam was such a fixture in the clubhouse—there hadn't been a time I could remember when he hadn't been glued to the games machines. Now he'll never play them again. I swallow back a sob, realising there's nothing I or anyone can do for Adam, and feeling a bit like an intruder. Wanting to give the bikers some privacy to grieve, I start to turn to go back to the women.

Suddenly Mouse rasps out, "Gates are wide open, Prospect."

Swinging back, I see Spider run to close them. As he's pulling them shut I hear the distinctive roar of a Harley coming up the roadway. Spider runs back, pushing past me, his gun already in his hand. "Wheels, get out of sight."

"It has to be Doc, hasn't it?" I'm hopeful, I can't take much more today.

"Fuckin' hope so, but I gotta make sure."

I get myself out of the way, hiding behind the wall of the garage, but as I hear a voice I recognise, I come out again to see the ex-Army medic is getting off his bike.

He's staring at me, assessing me. I know I must look a mess, pale and shaking, but I'm not the one who needs help. So forcing my voice to be calm, I bring him up to speed. "Adam's dead, Mouse has a head injury, and, Carmen, Sandy, and Ella are unconscious in the kitchen."

Doc's face is grim; he turns to Mouse.

The computer geek waves him off. "Take care of them first."

"Wheels, come with me. I might need your help." Not knowing how useful I can be, I follow him to the clubhouse and into the kitchen where he kneels next to each of the women, in turn lifting their eyelids to look at their pupils and taking their pulses. "I think they've just been drugged," he pronounces at last. "Crystal, can you go get some blankets so we can make them more comfortable. I don't want to move them until they come around in case they've got any head injuries."

By the time we've seen to the comfort of the unconscious women as best we can, Mouse has joined us. Doc makes him take a seat and starts to examine him.

"Why didn't they shoot you?" I ask, grateful that they hadn't, but also surprised.

"My lucky day?" Mouse suggests dourly. "Or they wanted to keep someone alive to interrogate in case they couldn't find you."

Doc nods. "Whatever the reason, I'm glad of it. Any news of the others, Mouse?"

That gets my attention. "Not when I last checked. But that would be," he consults the clock on the wall, "over an hour ago. Fuck. I'll go check."

"Not until I've finished examinin' you." Doc sounds stern and it's enough to make Mouse sit still.

"I tried to ring Wraith, there wasn't an answer."

Mouse glares at me. "Don't do that again, Wheels. Let them concentrate on what they're doing."

"But shouldn't they know?"

He heaves a sigh. "Sweetheart, I can't tell you what their plan is, but they need to follow it through. You call your man and he'll get distracted. Fuck, all of them will when they hear what's happened here and about Adam. And Viper, Slick, and Bullet will have a fit about the girls."

Reluctantly, I concede—he must know what he's talking about.

I feel faint and put my hand out to the table. Doc moves fast for such a big man, and soon has me sitting with my head between my knees. "You're in shock, darlin'," he tells me softly.

"Doc, you finished with me yet?"

"Yeah, son. You're good to go. Concussion watch though—you shouldn't be alone. Keep the prospect with you."

"I'll go with him," I offer, looking up. It would give me something useful to do rather than just hanging around worrying. And I'll be at the hub of information and hopefully learn Wraith's safe as soon as possible.

And he's got to come back to me.

CHAPTER 30
Wraith

Watching the Rock Demons clubhouse blow sky high is both exhilarating and horrifying at the same time. Seeing the flames shooting high into the air, knowing we'd be having no more trouble from that direction causes smiles and cheers from all around me, albeit tempered with a few 'fucks' and 'shits' as we all realise that could be our clubhouse burning and our members dying.

From the info Mouse had been feeding us, we know their prez and VP had been inside, together with their other officers, so we've definitely cut the head off the snake. When a couple of the non-ranking members flee the inferno, we decide enough is enough and let them go. We don't like killing men unnecessarily, and taking out the ones in command had achieved our primary objective. If we hadn't hit first, they'd have done the same to us. Now, hopefully, we won't have to watch our backs. Well, not unless they regroup and come for us again, but at the moment that seems unlikely, as we haven't left enough of them alive for that.

The plan had worked smoothly—Viper, Dart, and I had managed to get up close, planting the explosives at their points of weakness. Utilising the skills that got me my name, I'd gotten the most difficult target, their main entrance, but chose the moment they'd left it unguarded. Viper reported back that one of their sheds was being used as a meth lab, backing right onto their clubhouse. What idiots would do that? Of course, he took the time to rig that too. Sloppy motherfuckers hadn't seen us coming.

Even knowing about the lab, the size of the explosion took us by surprise, and the resulting pops and bangs from their obviously sizeable armoury, together with a few louder booms that made us query each other as to what the fuck they had stored in there. But hopefully, whatever it was would be sufficient that any investigation by the authorities would put the blame there and not look for outsider involvement. Any such scrutiny would probably be half-hearted in any event, as no one would shed many tears about the loss of a group of outlaw bikers.

We've retreated to a safe distance now, watching from afar as the increasingly growing sounds of sirens reach us. The smoke rising in the air would easily be visible from Phoenix.

I glance at my phone. Mouse has been out of contact for half-an-hour. Luckily he was online and keeping us all connected until we were ready to press the button, but after that he'd gone quiet. At first I put it down to a faulty signal, but now a sense of unease comes over me.

"Can't get hold of Mouse." I nudge Drummer. "The line's gone dead. I've tried ringin' him several times, but no answer."

Drum pulls his eyes away from the conflagration and gives his attention to me. "What the fuck? Are you tryin' his burner?"

"And his personal phone."

"Damn, he's the one brother who never goes incommunicado."

Taking out my phone, I try another number. It rings out.

Drummer's watching me carefully. "Tryin' Adam?"

I shake my head. "Yeah, but no joy there either." Next I try Sophie, but it just rings out. I send her a quick text. As Drum tilts his head towards me, I give a shake of mine. "Tried Spider too. No one's answerin'."

He runs his hand down his beard as I try to stifle the fear rapidly rising inside me. "Fuck. Trouble at home, VP. Think we need to get ourselves on the road." As he stands and waves the brothers with us together, I send a quick text to the other groups to let them know we're heading back, and to be prepared for anything when we get there.

Walking beside him to the bikes, he gets a text. He reads it, then tells me, "Red took out the drug runners. From what Mouse had got from the cameras earlier, there weren't many of the Demons that weren't inside their clubhouse. Don't see how it could be them making an attack on our compound."

"Who the fuck else could it be, Prez?"

He places his hand on my arm. "We don't know anythin's wrong yet."

I don't contradict him out loud, but I fucking know there is. Someone should have answered. *What the hell is going on?*

I pull on my brain bucket and put on my sunglasses. Drum wastes no time getting out on the road. I ride behind him, and shortly after Peg pulls up alongside, having joined us. We hadn't planned to meet up and ride back together; we were going back in small groups and not flying our colours as we didn't want to advertise that Satan's Devils were in Phoenix today. But Peg's throwing me a grim look, and I know he's worried too. I'm glad he'll be with us when we arrive.

Drummer signals to indicate we should pull over to the side. As he does so, I see he's talking on the phone.

"What...?" I can't hide my impatience, but he gesticulates showing he wants me to hold off for a moment.

Impatiently, I rise up and down on my heels, my hands tightening into fists as I grow more and more anxious about Wheels. Especially when I hear his side of the conversation.

"You okay man?"

"Fuck."

"FUCK!"

"Good lad!"

"The fuckin' women?"

I can barely hold myself back from snatching the phone from his hand. Looking at Peg, I see he's as impatient as I am to find out what's going on. My breathing becomes laboured as I remember Sophie this morning and her concerns about me leaving her alone. She'd been worried about me; I never thought I'd be the one ending up scared out of my mind for her.

At last Drum ends the call and turns to us with as grave a look on his face as I've ever seen.

"Sophie?" I ask, unable to be patient.

The shake of his head causes my heart to stop, but his dismissal wasn't for her. "She's fine," he reassures me. "But Adam's dead, Mouse has a concussion, and three of the women are unconscious, but Doc thinks they've been drugged and are probably going to be alright."

Heart, Viper, and Bullet are with another group so won't be finding out about their old ladies until they get back. For their sakes, I hope their women will have woken up by then.

"What the fuck did we miss?" Peg growls. "Was it the Demons?"

Drum looks at us steadily. "No, it was somethin' to do with that bastard after Wheels."

"But he's dead!" I'm incredulous, we thought the risk was gone.

"Seems like his sidekick wasn't. He had two men with him." Again Drum gives a shake of his head, but this time in disbelief. "Young Spider took out all three. He's an incredible shot it seems."

Peg gapes, then huffs a laugh. "Kid always aced it at the range practicin'. Fuck, but I'm proud of him." Then his face falls. "But Adam, fuck." He kicks at a rock on the ground. "FUCK!"

I'm itching to get back on the bike and home to Soph. Raising my eyebrow at Drum, he nods, understands my impatience, and wastes no time getting us back on our way.

We're the first group to return to the compound. Sophie's waiting for me and starts towards me as fast as she can. I'm off, and my arms are around her, holding her so tight. She's sobbing and tears come to my own eyes, understanding now the fear she had for me earlier today. I feel like holding her forever and never letting her go, but I'm the VP, others are waiting on me. Reluctantly, at last, I let her go, but keep a tight hold on her hand.

"Are you okay?"

"Yes, I'm alright. Spider was brilliant, Wraith, he shot them all." Her words are brave, but her hand is shaking in mine, letting me know three men gunned down in front of her probably took its toll.

"They would have taken you, darlin'"

She knows that. "They would have killed me."

Drum's slapping Spider on the back, and I've no doubt we'll be patching him in. Probably very soon—he'll certainly get my vote.

When the prez has finished with him, I beckon him over and grasp his shoulder with my free hand, squeezing it to show my heartfelt appreciation. "Thank you."

He looks at the ground. "Couldn't have done it without your ol' lady's help, VP. You've got a smart one there."

Now, this story I have to hear, but it will have to be later. Still holding her hand, I go into the clubhouse, my eyes widening at the carnage inside, but I've got admiration for the expert way in which the men were taken out. The attire and equipment of two of the bodies suggest to me they were professionals, and Spider again goes up in my estimation. Silencers are attached to the weapons, explaining how they got to Adam with no one else being aware.

Sophie's hiding her face in my side, so I don't linger, but go on through to the kitchen. There are three women sitting around the table, all looking worse for wear, Sandy with her head in her hands. Crystal's walking around with a tray, giving out bottles of water. The mood is sombre. There's been a death here today.

Doc comes over, Drum's followed us in. Glancing up at our retained medic, he indicates the old ladies.

Doc nods. "They were given some sort of sedative, all seem to have put up a bit of a fight, but they've got bumps and scrapes, nothing major. Mouse has a concussion." He closes his eyes for a second then opens them, his face crestfallen. "Adam was gone when I got here. He didn't have a chance."

"Stay here with Crystal for a minute?" I ask Sophie. She obviously wants to stay by my side, but I need to talk to Peg. I'm proud when she only has a second's hesitation before nodding and moving away.

I touch Doc's arm and jerk my head towards my woman, he follows me into the club room, his eyes narrowing as they fall on the bodies lying sprawled in the middle of the floor. He answers my question without me having to voice it. "She's a strong woman, your Wheels," he starts, "but what's gone down here today would be tough on anyone. Keep your eye on her, and don't be surprised if she lets it all out later on. She's in shock, but I don't think I have to treat her. Get some food into her, hell, give her a drink. But most of all, just be here for her. She's going to come down with a bang once the adrenaline wears off. Fuck, we all are. Don't normally have this trouble on our fuckin' doorstep."

"Thanks, Doc." As he goes back to treat his patients I go over to Peg.

"Spider took care of this better than I would have expected." He kicks at one of the prone figures. "I'll grab Marsh when he's back, and Blade, and we'll get these fuckers out of our damn clubhouse."

At that moment, a loud roar of engines signals the brothers are returning, and for the next hour or so it's all bringing them up to speed as they come back in, their staggered departure from Phoenix meaning we have to go over it a number of times. A red-faced Spider gets more and more overwhelmed by all the attention he's getting. I doubt anyone will be voting against him when the time comes.

A week later and again we gather along with our other charters at another funeral, and I for one hope it will be the last for quite some time.

Adam's final farewell marks the end of this period in the club's history. There's been no approach from any of the remaining Demons or their associates, and Sophie's last threat is rotting in the ground, high up in the forest.

As I watch my woman organise the sweet butts and assist the other old ladies, making sure all the visiting members are adequately catered to, it hits me how she's started to fit into our environment. Trouble's come too close to our door, but instead of rolling over she's stepped up to the mark, being quick to offer comfort and support to the other women who should have been able to feel protected in the safety of their own club. Unfortunately we've lost one, Ella having made the decision that biker cock was not worth everything that came along with it, and to Slick's great disappointment, is back living a civilian life in town. I know it's hurt him, but it takes a special woman to adapt to this life. One just like mine.

We've learned our lesson, never to leave the compound so unguarded again, and resolved to increase the number of members in the mother charter but, as I've found today, despite our recent issues, a few brothers from other chapters would be more than happy to patch over. We'll also need more prospects now.

Of course, as I expected, Spider was voted in and gained a new road name, Shooter. The way he protected my woman and killed the intruders made him a man we're all happy to call brother. Poor Marsh, now our only prospect, is being run ragged trying to keep all the members happy. Of course we're all being understanding. Not. *Uh uh.*

Deep in contemplation, the hefty slap on my back startles me. "How ya doin', Brother?"

I shrug. "It's been a shock to all of us, Red."

"Well, I helped where I could." I know his ambush on the drug runners was successful, and I thank him for taking some of the Demons off our back.

"How's Sophie copin'? She gonna be hangin' around?"

Now that's what I've been wondering, worrying about. Now that it's safe for her to go back to England, after everything that's gone down, will she still want to stay? I'm not a man who allows himself to have doubts, but about her? Nothing much frightens me in this life, but I've been too afraid to broach this particular subject.

So I shrug and tell him the other thing on my mind. "Not sharin' her again, Red."

He eyes me astutely. "Didn't expect you to, Brother. If I had someone like her I wouldn't want any fucker to touch her either. Even you."

I don't want him to feel bad. "But it helped mend her." And that's the other problem, she is mended. She'll never get her leg back, but mentally she's in a good place. And physically? Well, she's independent enough and now that she's no longer in danger she can go where she likes and do what she wants.

And then she passes us, giving a warm smile to Red, which I notice doesn't quite reach her eyes, and pauses to place a kiss on my cheek. She's got a plate of food in her arms and is managing to get through the jostling throng without too many problems. Just that brief touch of her lips has me hardening.

Red notices me adjusting myself and chuckles. "She's somethin', your woman. You want my opinion? If she hasn't already run for the hills, I doubt she'll be doin' so. Takes a lot for someone to stay after goin' through somethin' like that."

"I'm not so sure, Red. She's full of guilt over what happened. First Hank, then Adam."

"Shit happens in our world."

He's not wrong there.

As night falls, the clubhouse begins to get rowdier, and after excusing myself to Drum, I take Sophie back to our room, for once feeling nervous as I lead her inside. Tonight I'll be asking her the question, but if she's going to give me the answer I dread, I'm going to be inside her first.

As soon as we're inside the door, I undo the zip on the black top she's worn today, a mark of respect for the dead. She makes no protest as I slide the material down her arms, leaving it to pool on the floor. Reaching my hands around I undo the front fastening on her bra, letting her breasts fall free.

CHAPTER 31

Sophie

Wraith seems to be at odds with himself tonight, devastated at burying another of his brothers, I expect. He's holding me to him, teasing my nipples, but there's desperation there. He takes on the blame for leaving me alone that day; I blame myself for bringing yet more trouble to their door. We're a screwed-up couple, and I don't know where we go from here.

His hands are clutching at me as though he never wants to let me go, his hard cock is pressing into my arse, and though I know we should talk, right now a conversation is the last thing on my mind. His fingers are trailing down my stomach now, leaving a path of tingling skin in their wake as he makes every part of me feel alive.

As he undoes the button and takes down the zip, he puts his hands inside my underwear.

"You're wet for me, darlin'."

I groan in response and, putting my arm up, rest my fingers against the back of his head and try to pull him down to me. I want his mouth, and he doesn't disappoint. Turning me to face him, he brings his lips to mine and our mouths press together. Running his tongue along the seam, he demands entry. The day's been difficult—another funeral, another goodbye, and the way we kiss seems a celebration we're alive. Our tongues meet and swirl together, our tastes mingling until it's hard to tell them apart. I put all of me into that kiss, reaffirming my love for him. When he pulls away, a moan of protest escapes my lips. He smiles an enigmatic smile, then lowers his head to lave attention on my peaking nipples, his touch one of worship, making me feel special.

In no hurry, he uses his teeth, giving a little bite then soothing with a slide of his tongue, first one erect tip, and then the other. My clit is throbbing with need, my muscles spasming as he continues his exquisite torture.

"I need you," I gasp.

He pushes his hips into me. "I need you too."

Now he's lifting me, placing me on the bed. With an economy of movement, he removes my black trousers and then makes quick work freeing me from the prosthesis. He places a kiss to my stump, proving once again that he couldn't care less about my disability. He stands back, admiring the view, stroking himself through his jeans. As if a switch has been thrown, in one move he pulls off his cut and T-shirt, toes off his boots and removes his jeans. My eyes widen as he stands there in his boxers, and seeing my reaction, he hooks his fingers in the waistband and slides them down his legs, taking his socks off with them as he reaches his ankles.

Standing naked before me, he affords me a moment to admire the view, and a smirk comes to his face as my tongue comes out to lick my lips.

I sit up, reaching out my hands, wanting to touch him. He considers my unspoken offer, decides to accept, coming forward so I can take his cock in my hands. It's not new to me, but will never grow old—his dick twitches when I touch it, almost as though it's got a life of its own. I suck in my bottom lip, my teeth biting down on it, and swallow as I salivate at the thought of his taste in my mouth.

Coming closer, he puts his hand around the back of my head. "Suck me, darlin'."

He doesn't need to ask twice. Opening my mouth, I take him inside, first just the tip, licking the pre-cum that's oozing out, relishing the flavour that's uniquely him. My actions are making me even wetter than I was before.

As he presses my head forward, gently fisting his hands in my hair, I open wider, taking him in further, allowing him to control the pace. He begins to thrust in and out, gently, not forcing me, and I fondle his balls, which themselves seem to swell in my hands. As he pulls out, I massage his shaft before he pushes back in again. The rhythm we've adopted soon has him warning me he's about to come. I don't stop, and soon rivers of cum shoot down my throat. I lick him clean before pulling away.

"Fuck, darlin'. That felt so good." He leans down and kisses me, ravishing my mouth.

Pushing me back onto the bed, he skates down and pulls my legs apart, and I whimper in expectation. He breathes a warm breath, and I arch off the bed, already so sensitive and aroused he doesn't even need to touch me to tighten that bundle of nerves. Gently placing a first, then a second finger inside me, he curls them around, expertly finding that spot he's learned so well. Massaging me gently, I feel a slow build of tension tightening my muscles.

Next, he lowers his mouth, his tongue swirling, teasing, flicking lightly over my clit. My back bows as I try to push up, a desperate hint I need more pressure, but instead he pulls away.

"Want to feel you come around me."

"But I'm so close," I complain with a whine.

"Patience," he whispers.

He pulls his fingers out, and I feel the bed dip as he reaches over me to the drawer, which is now always fully stocked with condoms. There's a gleam in his eyes as he tears open the packet, and I can't tear my gaze away as he expertly smooths the latex over his cock, which has risen to the occasion once again. He pumps it slowly, noticing me watching him carefully, smirking, content in the knowledge of exactly what he's doing to me.

Lifting my hips, he positions himself and then starts pushing inside, my arousal, which hadn't diminished while he'd been preparing himself, increases rapidly to new highs. As he presses inside, an involuntary whimper escapes my lips as he stretches me, a delicious burn that makes me feel alive.

Then he thrusts home, touching my cervix, and as my muscles clench at his shaft, he rolls his head back at the sensation, for a moment keeping still. The scent of our joined sex reaches my nostrils, and I inhale deeply, the heavy breathing and soft moans—sounds of our lovemaking—reach my ears. I can still taste him in my mouth; there's not one of my senses that isn't full of him.

As he starts to move, sliding in and out, long, deep, slow strokes, I lose myself, unable to think of anything but the pleasure he brings. My womb's contracting, my legs feel weak—it's a slow build that's taking me higher than I've ever been before. I don't know how long he sensually tortures me, but just when I feel I can take no more he picks up the pace, thrusting into me. My head thrashes on the pillow in frustration as I need, I need...

And he knows, his fingers begin to strum my clit, flicking over it again and again and then, at last, giving me that pinch that takes me over the top.

I scream. My muscles grasp at his length, trying to keep him inside. He jerks, once, twice, and then again as he empties himself inside me.

Every fucking time it gets better.

My eyes have closed. I open them and look into his to see there's a shadow there.

Worry causes a reciprocal flash of doubt in mine. *Was he saying goodbye?*

His hands come to cup my face. "Sophie, are you alright?"

We're still joined, his softening cock not yet slid out of me.

I hardly want to speak, hardly dare ask, but I'd rather know now, while we're still so intimately entwined.

My heart's beating fast, not only from the exertion but from dread of the answer to the question I'm about to ask. "Where do we go from here, Wraith?" I hardly dare breathe, waiting for his reply.

My question doesn't seem to take him by surprise. He lowers his head until his forehead is touching mine.

CHAPTER 32
Wraith

I knew it. I had felt she was pulling away. All day at the funeral it was as if Sophie had been standing right beside me, but wasn't really there. As if she was withdrawing, saying goodbye. As we lie, skin to skin, my flaccid cock slipping out of her, regretting I'm not able to keep our bodies so intimately joined for a longer time, I know I've got one shot at this to make it right. Does she want this to be the end? Or is that what she expects now the reason for her being here is no longer valid?

Where do we go from here? That's what she asked. I inhale a deep breath and lift my head, staring down into her lovely blue eyes. "Well," I start to answer, but already pause, not wanting to rush this, "I thought we'd buy a house off the compound. Like the other brothers with the ol' ladies." Her eyes widen. "We'll get you a car—you'll have no problem drivin' an automatic." Her mouth falls open. "If you want, you can get a job."

"Wraith." She says my name slowly.

I put my finger to her lips. "If you don't want to work, that's fine too. Wouldn't have a problem pumpin' this belly full of babies."

She's blushing a deep red, but then a laugh bursts out of her. "Barefoot and pregnant in the kitchen, eh?"

"Works for me."

She slaps me on the shoulder, but she's grinning. She's fucking grinning. "You want me to stay?"

"Always have, darlin'. Anythin' else was all in your head."

"But after everything that's happened, after the trouble I've caused for the club?"

"You caused no trouble, shit happens, babe." I repeat the words Red had spoken earlier—they sum everything up. "Ain't no one here wantin' you to go. As you're my ol' lady, you're part of the club."

While she digests what I've told her, I decide to reveal my own insecurity. "Thought you wanted to leave me, darlin'. Thought you'd want to go back to England."

Now it's her hand caressing my cheek. "There's nothing for me there, nothing I'd want to go back to. I love you. I love Arizona, and I even love the club." She turns her head away, and then brings it back. "I just hate what I've done to it. I thought you'd tell me I had to go."

"Never!" As I smile my forceful denial, I think of everything we can do now. Those road trips I'd planned, the home we can make together. Fuck, I'm a lucky man.

My fingers idly rub over the back of her hand, her left hand. It's not the first time this past week that the idea's come to me, but the thought of tying her to me in every way I can is very attractive. I breathe in deeply, and then take the plunge,

"Sophie, darlin', what do you say to bein' my wife."

Her hand covers mine, her blue eyes are shining, her mouth parts slightly, then she closes it and opens it again before getting out the words. "Wraith, are you asking me to marry you?"

I grin. "Yeah, sorry it's not a more fancy proposal…"

And then I can't speak anymore as her lips are covering mine. After a moment I pull away. "Is that a yes?"

She laughs and lightly fists her hand to punch me in the arm. "Maybe I should have made you work harder for it, but life's too short, isn't it?" She sobers for a moment, and then that perfect smile lights up her face once again. "Yes, Wraith. Yes, I'll marry you."

It's a week later, Sophie's out with the old ladies, and the members are sitting in church. The usual shit being thrown around and Drummer trying to keep order, and it's back to business as normal. We're discussing patching-in three members from other charters, and remembering Buster, I give a caution about vetting them carefully.

Drum subjects me to his steely gaze. "Good point you're making there, VP. I'll give their presidents the third degree, don't want them dumpin' their misfits here."

Beef raises his hand. "One of the bouncers at the strip club has expressed an interest in prospectin'."

"He seem likely?"

"He's got to get himself a proper bike. Rides a rice rocket at the moment."

Cries of derision go swiftly around, and Drummer bangs his meaty fist hard on the table. "Shut the fuck up and let the man speak!"

"He competes in off-road events, so doubt he'll get rid of it, but as long as he doesn't bring it around here," Beef continues. "He's a good man, not too handsy with the dancers and gets on with his shit without needin' to be told."

"Well, when he's got a decent ride bring him around, we'll see what we make of him. Right, anythin' else?"

As is becoming typical at what we assume to be the end of the meeting, there's an interruption. And again it's Mouse who leans forward. "I've been contacted via the dark web," he starts.

What's this going to be? Guns, drugs? I sit back and fold my arms. As far as I'm concerned, the dark web, recently, hasn't held good news for us.

"Yeah, a woman made contact. She's got a rep for being an ace hacker."

"You findin' it hard getting' women in the real world, Mouse?" Dart laughs at his own joke.

Mouse flips him the finger. "She's trying to get a trace on Sophie."

Yes, since I've told them she's staying, I'm educating them on the use of her real name. They still slip up at times, though. Sometimes just to get a rise out of her. But what he's said is worrying, and I sit forward again. He's certainly got my attention.

"Is the name of her friend, the one she was coverin' for, a Zoe Baker?" He directs this question at me.

I think. Zoe definitely, but I don't think she ever gave me a family name. "Could be." It's the only answer I'll commit to.

"Well this hacker, who won't identify herself, says that a Zoe Baker is tryin' to find her."

"Why contact you, Mouse?" It's caught Drum's interest.

Mouse shrugs. "She's probably found out the same information that I did. I tracked the contract to the Demons, and she might have picked my connection up from there."

We all swear as he mentions their name.

Drum's eyes crease. "How she link it to you?"

"I can't tell you exactly. This hacker might be talented enough to follow my footprint. Though naturally, I tried to hide it. But she's got a rep, this woman. A good one—she's fuckin' genius. She knows Sophie's being protected by an MC, and I think she's narrowin' down which it might be. And she's not asking for much, only that this Zoe wants her to phone her. Given me the number to call."

Drum glances at me and I stare back at him, trying to work it through in my head. With St John-Davies and his sidekick dead, there shouldn't be anyone nefarious attempting to find her, and if it is her friend, then I know my woman would be over the moon.

Our prez is waiting for me to give my opinion, so I let him in on my thoughts. "Lettin' Soph ring the number isn't admittin' she's here. Just that we know where she is."

Rock groans. "And could invite shit down on us again."

"You're right to be cautious, Brother." Drum strokes his beard. I wait for him to offer his view. It's a few moments before he does, and I suspect he's been running through possible implications before he speaks. "Mouse, get back to this hacker and ask her to tell you somethin' only Zoe would know about Soph. Check it out that way. If it comes out it's kosher, we'll get Sophie to make the call. But on loudspeaker so we can all hear and judge what they're sayin'. We don't need more trouble. Now's the time to move forward and heal."

And if it is Sophie's friend, the healing would be good for her too.

Mouse has been tapping on his keyboard; he looks up. "She's online right now. Wraith, can you think of anythin' to ask?"

It comes into my mind at once, and with a laugh, I say. "What was Sophie doing when she ticked somethin' off on her bucket list with an electrician."

We wait. This is going to be interesting.

It only takes a few seconds before Mouse laughs out loud and reads the response. "Well, Zoe's hopin' she's got the right electrician, there could have been more than one she says, but she thinks you're referrin' to fuckin' him in a broom cupboard at her place of work."

The laughter rings out from all directions, and I scowl, suddenly realising perhaps that wasn't the best question to ask in front of my brothers.

"How you gonna top that, Wraith?" Slick waggles his tongue after throwing out his question.

"Shut the fuck up!" I swear back at him, and now it's my finger jerking up in the air.

"Oh, and Zoe says to tell Soph that she gets the sex thing now."

Blade snorts. "Hey, glad you said we could listen in on the call now, Drum. I can't fuckin' wait for this!"

Drum's laughing along with the rest of us. "Neither can I, Brother. Wraith, get her down here now."

Not quite sure whether to chuckle along with the rest of them or to dread what the phone call might reveal, I leave the meeting room and make my way to the kitchen, where I'm sure I'll find my woman. And that's where I do indeed find her, up to her elbows mixing something in a bowl. Sneaking up behind in the silent way I'm known for, I lift her hair to reveal her neck and give her a kiss.

"That better be you, Wraith, else my man will have something to say to you."

"If it was anybody else they'd be dead by now," I tell her directly into her ear.

Now she turns to face me. "Is the meeting finished?"

"Almost, but can you come and join us for a moment?"

Her face falls. "What? Why? Oh God." She covers her mouth with her hand and her eyes widen. "What's happened?"

Shit, I forgot the last time Drum called her in was to tell her about that fucking contract on her head, so I rush to reassure her, "Nothin' bad, darlin', the boys just want you to do somethin' for them."

Wiping flour off her hands with a cloth, she excuses herself with the other women who are looking at her with various expressions of concern to envy. Women, as a rule, don't get invited to church. Although I've tried to put her mind at ease, she's paled, and she's breathing fast.

As we approach the door there's laughter coming from behind it, and she sends me a quizzical look which only deepens when I take her inside, drawing her around to my customary seat at the table and pulling her onto my lap. As Drum wastes no time handing her a burner phone and a piece of paper, her eyebrows are almost up to her hairline.

I open my mouth to explain, but with a mischievous expression making his eyes sparkle, Drum stops me. "Just let her make the call, VP."

Grinning, anticipating her reaction when she hears who I hope is on the other end, I state, "We want you to make a call for us, darlin'."

Her brow furrows and she glances around at the rest of the members, who are all looking at me with varying expressions of amusement and expectation. "What, why? What do you want me to say?"

I wonder what's going through her head, but Drum just gives her a prod. "Just ring the number, sweetheart."

She shakes her head and looks down at the phone in bemusement, and then at the number on the piece of paper in case the answer lies there. It doesn't of course. My grin widens as I wonder whether she thinks she's going to be ringing a sex line or something and will end up the butt of the joke. But after throwing me a sharp look, letting me know in no uncertain terms if something like that's the case I'll suffer for it later, she picks up the phone and carefully taps the numbers in the keypad. Then I take it from her, put it on speaker, and put it in the middle of the table. It rings a couple of times.

"Hi." A female voice answers.

"Er… hi?" Sophie responds.

"Shit, she doesn't recognise her," Dart whispers.

"Shush," Drum admonishes him.

But then the other voice says, "Soph? Oh my God! Is that you, Sophie?"

Her hand covers her lips, and for a moment I don't think she's capable of responding, but then the words come spilling out. "Fuck, *Zoe*? Is that really you, bitch? What the fuck have you been up to? And who are you fucking?"

"Soph! Sophie! Are you alright? Where the fuck are you?" Zoe's speaking through her tears and Sophie's having a hard time fighting her own.

"Fuck, Zoe, you won't believe what's been happening to me... But you? Are you safe? Where are you?" her voice is so breathy and eager.

"Yeah, I'm good Soph. Really good. Hey, you're not going to believe this, babe, I'm getting married. You gotta come to my wedding."

"What? Who? You're getting fucking married, bitch? What the hell have you been up to? You're not rushing into anything again, are you?" Sophie's eyes narrow, and presumably she remembers what happened the last time Zoe got herself at a man.

"My man, Kadar, is nothing like Ethan. Oh, and I've been finding out what this sex thing is all about, Soph. That's what."

"You're fucking kidding me. You found someone with a big dick at last?"

"I've told you before, Soph, I'm not discussing the size of my man's cock with you. But let's just say he doesn't disappoint." There's a short burst of masculine laughter in the background.

Next to me, Drum laughs, and from behind his hand says in a stage whisper, "Dirty mouths on these bitches."

"Hey, who's that, is there someone else there?"

"Oh, sorry," Sophie explains, "you're on speaker. Got some news of my own. I'm with my man here, Zoe. And you're not going to believe this, he's the fucking vice president of a bloody motorcycle club in Arizona."

"*What?* Hang on a minute, got my man here too. He's a sheikh. Fucking topped you there, bitch! Hey, Kadar, come over here a sec. I'll put mine on speaker too. Soph, I just cannot freaking believe I'm speaking to you at last babe. I have missed you so frigging much!"

There's a moment's quiet, and then, "Hello? My name's Kadar, Emir of Amahad, to whom am I speaking?" He talks in a cultured voice with only a hint of an accent.

There're some snorts and other brothers are falling about the table in laughter. I wave at them to hush.

"I'm Drummer, President of the Satan's Devils motorcycle club here in Arizona. With me are my brothers and Wraith, Sophie's ol' man."

A chuckle from the emir's end. "Somehow I'm thinking you're not talking about her father."

"No, I'm her fiancé," I cut in.

"Fiancé? Bloody hell, Soph, you move as fast as I do. The two of us engaged to be married! Who'd have thought it?"

"So when's the wedding?" they both ask together and have to take a moment to stop giggling.

"You first," Sophie offers.

"In two weeks—it has to be fast. I'm preggers, babe."

"Fuck. Zoe! You taking the piss or what?" Sophie's wide eyes glance around the room as though we should be as shocked as she is.

"No, it's the truth, I'm pregnant! It wasn't planned. But we're so happy about it. So, Soph. So, can you come?"

Now the male voice again, "If you could you'd put the fucking icing on our wedding cake, Sophie. Zoe's been wishing she knew where you were so she could send you an invite."

Again the table falls about at the swear word falling from the lips of such an eminent man. Once more I shush them, particularly when they start imitating his accent.

Drum's glare has more success and our end quiets again.

"I'd love to come, if I can." She casts me a slightly nervous look and questions me with her eyes. "But where the fuck is it?"

"It's in Amahad. Soph, I need you. You'll be a bridesmaid, along with Sheikha Aiza, that's Kadar's sister, and Sheikha Cara will be my matron of honour. Oh, it will be fantastic."

"Where the fuck's Amahad?" I ask, my eyes creasing with concern, and not a little disturbed at the fancy titles she's dropping in there.

"Just off the Persian Gulf," Mouse replies to me as if that's going to help any. My knowledge of geography obviously needs brushing up.

"Oh, you must come, Sophie. I'm petrified of a state wedding, and you'll have to hold my hand."

State wedding?

"Oh, and don't worry, babe. We'll sort it out so you'll be okay in the wheelchair."

Sophie beams, even though her friend can't see her. "I don't use one anymore. I walk on a prosthesis. And that's thanks to this club."

Zoe gasps in obvious delight but doesn't get the chance to say anything.

"Drummer." It's Kadar taking over the call from their end again. "Am I right in thinking it's your club that has been keeping Sophie safe and protected?"

"Tryin' to, yes." Drum gives an honest response.

There's whispering on the other end. "I'm sorry, but I need to tell you that while we've dealt with the greater danger, Hargreaves, St John-Davies' sidekick has disappeared into the wind. It's just possible he's deranged enough to see Sophie as unfinished business."

Drum glances at me, I nod. "And I think we need to tell you that there's no reason to worry on that score anymore." He gives a chin lift to Shooter, who is sitting at the end of the table.

There's silence, then Zoe breaths almost inaudibly. "Thank God."

"If I understand you correctly, I hope it was with extreme prejudice, but I won't ask for details." That's from Kadar. Drum's eyebrows rise, and I wonder about the character we're talking to. Apart from the polite manner of speaking, we could be having a conversion with a president of another motorcycle club.

The emir continues speaking, "We'd like to thank you for protecting my woman's girl, so I extend the invitation to our wedding to all the members of your club."

"Why, thank you, Kadar. Er, am I breaking protocol by addressin' you without a title?"

"Fuck no," the emir responds with a laugh, "I don't count this as an official call. And for your information, my sister-in-law, Cara, assures me this is a clean line."

"That's the hacker," Mouse whispers.

Drum continues with a nod that the man on the other end of the line obviously can't see. "It might not be easy for us to travel so far, but we thank you kindly for the invitation."

Whispering on the other end, then an abrupt, 'Of course', then to us, "Don't worry about getting here. I'll send the private jet for you."

Dart's literally on the floor, his chair having fallen over backwards and his hand clutching his belly with laughter. Dollar's mouth's drops open, Beef is nudging Slick, and Heart's simply beaming. The others have reactions somewhere in between. Mouse is tapping on his laptop and then turns it around to show us the Amahadian Royal Jet. I might know bikes a whole lot better than planes, but it certainly isn't a small two seater affair. More like a jumbo jet.

Drum's leg is bouncing, and he's strumming his fingers on the table. "Tell you what, Kadar, you give us the dates and that and we'll have words this end and get back to you. Appreciate the mighty fine offer you're makin' there." Then after a pause he adds, "Look, I don't want to blow smoke up your ass, so I'll give it to you straight. I ain't thinkin' my boys will fit into the whole royal weddin' thing you've got going."

The two at the other end of the line laugh loudly, and it's Zoe who replies, "Oh there'll be a fine mix of people here, and I can't think your boys can be any of a rougher lot than the desert sheikhs."

Again we hear male laughter. "She's not wrong there. Oh, we'll have the standard, less tolerable formal stuff, but the celebrations will include showing off fighting and riding skills."

"Bikes?" Beef has been quiet up to now but that wakes him up.

"I'm afraid not." You can almost hear the smile in the emir's voice. "Horses or camels."

"I'm up for that!" Mouse, who was partly brought up on the reservation, obviously has some prowess in that area.

Suddenly there's a buzz around the table. This wedding is starting to sound quite appealing.

"What about wives or ol' ladies?" Heart asks. "And kids?"

Drum raises his eyebrow. "You've only got the one, haven't you? Unless you're a fuckin' fast worker."

Heart shrugs as Kadar replies, "Just get back to me with the numbers. We'll sort it out."

"Oh, Soph, I can't wait to see you. And I want to show you what I've done with the harem…"

"Your bloke's got a fucking harem? You have to share him?"

"Way to go, man!" Viper's nodding in approval. He fuckin' would be.

"No, it's not used like that anymore." Zoe's laughing loudly at my girl's question. "I'd cut his cock off if he looked at anyone else."

Drum looks around at his men, they're all looking like they haven't had so much fun in ages. "Kadar, man, it's been good speakin' to you, but maybe Soph and Zoe would like to get together for a private chat now that they've connected again. But I'd like to thank you. We've had a fuckin' tryin' time of it lately, and a trip to Amahad—at least for some of us, obviously we can't all make it—sounds mighty fine." His pointed gaze rounding the assembled group reminds us we couldn't all go and leave the compound unprotected or the businesses unmanned. "So I'd like to thank you for that."

"No problem, Drummer. It was nice speaking to you." Then, quietly, obviously to the woman with him, "Okay to say your goodbyes now, habiti?"

"Yes. Hey, Soph, got to go and keep my man happy now. You ring again soon, okay?"

"You try bloody stopping me!"

A few muttered 'goodbyes', 'I love you babes' and promises to give each other a bell—whatever the fuck that means—in the manner of all women who can't seem to simply put the phone down. Then Drum loses his patience and ends the call by pressing the key, which gets him a glare from Sophie. He ignores her and leans right back in his chair, propping one foot up against the edge of the table and running a hand over his beard.

"Well, fuck me," he says after a moment, shaking his head in disbelief. We've plotted murders and takedowns in this very room, and almost everything in between, but that must be the most bizarre phone call we've ever had. Then he starts to laugh. "Looks like the Satan's Devils motorcycle club gonna be in attendance at a fuckin' royal weddin'!"

As he bangs the gavel, we all hammer our fists on the table in approval.

Sophie throws her arms around my neck and leans back so she can look straight into my face. "Best fucking day ever!" she whispers to me.

IDENTITY CRISIS

Sean

When a 'package' is left for me at Grade A's reception, I hardly expect it to be a baby, nor to discover after DNA testing that she is mine. Fuck, me with a daughter? And I've no idea who the mother is – I've always been so careful! But the wording of the note left with the baby suggests whoever she is she's in trouble, so now I've got to discover her identity and then find and help her. All I know is that I was working in Amahad when the baby must have been conceived, so I return to that Arab country to call on the help of my old friends, members of the Kassis royal family.

Ben teams me up with Vanessa – I've no idea why. She hates me. It will be her first time investigating in the field and I know she isn't prepared to be thrown into something like this. Together we start our search not realising it will end up with lives at stake, including our own.

Vanessa

I've always fancied Sean, well, who wouldn't? But when I discover he's fathered a child and has no idea who the mother is it brings home to me his manwhoring ways. He's never going to change, is he?

And then there's the baby. It's not that I have an aversion to children, but any young child reminds me of a past I'm ashamed off and brings back many painful memories I'd much rather forget.

So when Ben offers me my first job out of the office, I protest going anywhere with Sean, but my boss is insistent. Then in Amahad I grow to see the man underneath the shallow exterior and it gets harder to resist my attraction to him. Gradually he learns my darkest secrets and the key to my heart.

But our search for Mollie's missing mother leads us into danger. Will we be able to stay alive long enough to explore what could be between us?

Blood Brothers #4: Identity Crisis

OTHER WORKS BY MANDA MELLETT

Blood Brothers

- *Stolen Lives* (#1 – Nijad & Cara)

- *Close Protection* (#2 – Jon & Mia)

- *Second Chances* (#3 – Kadar & Zoe)

- *Identity Crisis* (# 4 – Sean & Vanessa)

Coming 2017:

- *Dark Horses* (#5 – Jasim & Janna)

SATAN'S DEVILS MC

- *Turning Wheels* (Blood Brothers #3.5, Satan's Devils #1 – Wraith & Sophie)

- *Drummer's Beat* (# 2 – Drummer & Sam)

Coming 2017:

- *Slick Running* (#3 – Slick & Ella)

Sign up for my newsletter to hear about new releases in the Blood Brothers and Satan's Devils series:
http://eepurl.com/b1PXO5

ACKNOWLEDGEMENTS

A massive 'Thank You' to my beta readers, Alex Clark, Colleen, Foua, and of course, Steve who helped make sure any reference to motorcycles was correct. Your encouraging feedback and suggestions for improving the book were invaluable.

Cover design and formatting by Freeyourwords. Lia, you excelled yourself this time! I absolutely love the cover design you came up with!

Editing by Phil Henderson – thanks for knocking this book into shape, Phil. Enjoyed working with you.

I can't thank my husband enough for his support and encouragement, even taking the step nowadays to be a beta reader. For *Turning Wheels* this was invaluable as he's a biker and came up with some interesting tips and information for me to use. And my son must get a mention, even if it's only because he tells me he's proud of his mum.

And of course, I'm grateful to everyone who's taken the time to read *Turning Wheels*. If you enjoyed it, please leave a review – writers write in a vacuum, locked away in their lonely towers. We love to know what you think of our efforts and appreciate all feedback we receive.

STAY IN TOUCH

Email: manda@mandamellett.com
Website: www.mandamellett.com

Connect with me on Facebook:
https://www.facebook.com/mandamellett

Sign up for my newsletter to hear about new releases in the Blood Brothers and Satan's Devils series:

http://eepurl.com/b1PXO5

ABOUT THE AUTHOR

After commuting for too many years to London working in various senior management roles, Manda Mellett left the rat race and now fulfils her dream and writes full time. She draws on her background in psychology, the experience of working in different disciplines and personal life experiences in her books.

Manda lives in the beautiful countryside of North Essex with her husband and two slightly nutty Irish Setters. Walking her dogs gives her the thinking time to come up with plots for her novels, and she often dictates ideas onto her phone on the move, while looking over her shoulder hoping no one is around to listen to her. Manda's other main hobby is reading, and she devours as many books as she can.

Her biggest fan is her gay son (every mother should have one!). Her favourite pastime when he is home is the late night chatting sessions they enjoy, where no topic is taboo, and usually accompanied by a bottle of wine or two.

Photo by Carmel Jane Photography

Made in the
USA
Monee, IL